THE TRUE DARCY SPIRIT

Elizabeth Aston is a passionate Jane Austen devotee who studied English at Oxford. She lives in Oxford and Italy with her family.

Visit the official website www.elizabeth-aston.com for more information on Elizabeth Aston. For exclusive updates visit www.AuthorTracker.co.uk. For a reading guide to *The True Darcy Spirit* please visit www.ReadingGroups.co.uk.

Also by Elizabeth Aston

Mr Darcy's Daughters
The Exploits & Adventures of Miss Alethea Darcy

ELIZABETH ASTON

The True Darcy Spirit

HARPER

This novel is entirely a work of fiction.
The names, characters and incidents portrayed in it are
the work of the author's imagination. Any resemblance to
actual persons, living or dead, events or localities is
entirely coincidental.

Harper
An imprint of HarperCollins*Publishers*
77–85 Fulham Palace Road,
Hammersmith, London W6 8JB

www.harpercollins.co.uk

A Paperback Original 2007
1

A catalogue record for this book
is available from the British Library

ISBN 9780007808380

Set in Simoncini Garamond by Palimpsest Book Production Limited,
Grangemouth, Stirlingshire

Printed and bound in Great Britain by
Clays Ltd, St Ives plc

For Paul, with love

Chapter One

On the forenoon of a hot May day in 1819, two persons were on their way to the Inner Temple. They were almost strangers, but bound by ties of blood and kinship, and in very different situations of life.

Cassandra Darcy was on foot, walking to save the expense of the hackney-coach; the fee of a shilling was more than she could at present afford to spend. Nor, although young and gently bred, was she accompanied by a maid or a footman. Possessed of more than her fair share of good looks, she attracted a good deal of unwelcome attention, yet there was that about her direct look and her straight brows that carried her past even the most loutish of the Londoners going about their business. She was in good time, would, in fact, be early for her appointment.

It wasn't an encounter she was looking forward to. Not that she had anything to say for or against Mr. Horatio Darcy, but he was her stepfather's lawyer, and there was no doubt about her feelings toward Mr. Partington. Even though, in all fairness, she couldn't blame him for the predicament she found herself in. She had been rash, remarkably rash, and must take the blame and endure the consequences of her actions, and, she reflected, any consequences in which her disagreeable stepfather had a hand were likely to be of a most unpleasant nature.

She quickened her pace, as though to escape from the thoughts that crowded into her head. She had to think clearly, this was a time for rational thought and action, and yet feeling would intrude, driving out the clear thoughts that might help her to state her case and come to a reasonable solution of her problems.

Would that reason had played a larger part in her actions these last few weeks, but reason flew out of the window in such cases. She had often heard it said that it was so, but never dreamed that it might one day apply to her. And she, who prided herself on her self-control, had been the one to fling all restraint and sense aside. Her self-control had been her defence against the constant pricks and irritations of life at Rosings, but when she most needed it, it had deserted her.

Well—with an inner sigh—what was done was done. Now she must see how she could make the best of things. She cast a quick glance down at the map in the guidebook that Mrs. Dodd had lent her. It wasn't clear, and she wasn't used to maps, but an enquiry of a burly but amiable-looking hackney coachman gave her the right direction, and she turned off the Strand in the direction of the river. The narrow lane led through a noble gateway into the sanctum of the Inner Temple, one of London's four Inns of Court, where the lawyers belonging to the Inn had their chambers. It was a tranquil and charming place, its grounds stretching to the banks of the Thames and the bustle and hubbub of London no more than a distant murmur.

Cassandra hesitated, looking across the grassy central area to the surrounding buildings. Men in black gowns walked briskly by; clerks, documents tied with ribbon under their arms, hurried past; errand boys, whistling as errand boys always whistled, scurried on their way with messages and parcels.

Here was the staircase where Mr. Darcy had his chambers, here was his name on a wooden panel. Here was a suspicious clerk, demanding to know her name and business, looking behind her for a father, a brother, a footman, a maid.

The clerk had a long, thin nose, red at the tip, the kind of nose that would always have a drip on it come the chills and fogs of autumn. Cassandra didn't take to him, but then she wasn't interested in Josiah Henty, clerk; she had come to see Horatio Darcy, lawyer.

And cousin. Distant cousin, she reminded herself. They hardly had more than the name in common, the connection was not at all close. Still, it was a link, and a link she suspected might not please Horatio Darcy just at present.

They had first met when she was a small girl in a smock with her hair tumbling about her shoulders and a smudge on her cheek. He was a great boy in comparison to her, just started at his public school, lanky and self-contained, eight years older than she was. The third son of a younger brother, he was treated with a certain degree of contempt by Cassandra's grandmother, the formidable Lady Catherine de Bourgh, although with an eye too observant for her years, Cassandra noticed a spark in Horatio's eye, and she sensed that he wasn't a whit bothered by Lady Catherine.

She had seen him once more since then, had pelted him with crab apples, in fact. That was when she was twelve, and a tomboy climbing trees during a visit to her cousins at Pemberley, where he was also a visitor. He had looked up, and said what a hoyden she was and gone on his way, tall and still self-contained, with almost as much pride as his cousin Fitzwilliam Darcy, Mama had said, although with much less reason.

"Horatio Darcy does not have an income of ten thousand a year, indeed he has an income of nothing a year, except what his father gives him and what he may earn by his own efforts, nor does he own so much as a cottage, let alone a great estate like Pemberley. They say he is clever; he will need to be to make his way in the world, for even though his father was a Darcy, he was a younger son, and younger sons, you know . . ." This last with an affected sigh. "As was your dear father, of course."

Cassandra was less than happy to have her affairs brought under the scrutiny of Horatio Darcy, or indeed any of the Darcy clan. It was her misfortune, she thought, that she was related to the Darcys both through her mother and father. If she had taken her stepfather's name, as her mother had wanted her to, the Darcys would have had no concern for her present situation, and she might not be sitting here, waiting for her cousin, who was, she noticed with a glance at the clock that hung above the bookshelf opposite, late.

An unpunctual man.

In that case, the Darcys might have been content to shrug shoulders and wash their hands of her: "She always was a headstrong girl, Anne should have brought her up more strictly."

The thought brought a wry smile to her lips; in many ways it would be difficult to imagine any stricter upbringing than hers, with her stepfather a clergyman with very strict morals indeed, and a naturally overbearing disposition, and her mother always willing to agree with him on the raising of all her children; Cassandra as well as the two daughters and son by her second marriage.

Horatio Darcy was not on foot, but was travelling in an elegant carriage, seated beside the beautiful Lady Usborne. Not that the vehicle moved at much more than a walking pace in the crowded London thoroughfares, and walking fast and purposefully, as was his way, he could have covered the distance from Mount Street, where the Usbornes had their town house, to his chambers at the Inner Temple in much less time than the carriage was taking. He was an active, vigorous man, a young man in a hurry, his enemies said, and certainly not one to idle and linger his way through the day.

Yet here he was, with half the morning spent in a very idle, not to say, dissolute way, that made him no money and brought him no business. Time passed in the arms of the luscious Lady Usborne, although the connection might, at some point, bring him advancement—for the Usbornes were people of wealth and influence—was time wasted as far as his professional life was concerned.

A very pleasant amorous interlude on the chaise longue in her private sitting room, with the door locked against intrusive servants, who were supposed to believe that their mistress had need of yet another lengthy consultation with her handsome young lawyer, had led to a light nuncheon, and then, Lady Usborne declaring that she was driving out, to visit a milliner, it would have been churlish not to accept her request that he might accompany her at least part of the way.

There had been a slightly uncomfortable encounter with Lord Usborne in the hall of his lordship's town house. The older man was taller and better dressed than Darcy, and a raised eyebrow, a cynical twitch of his lordship's lip left Darcy feeling ruffled, so that he was anxious to part from Lady Usborne and return to the calmer waters of his chambers.

"Stop here," he called out to the coachman. A last, swift kiss, and then he jumped down on to the pavement, conscious of the fact that he carried with him the faint aroma of Lady Usborne's clinging scent, but with a sense of liberation.

He was late for his appointment with Miss Darcy, and he didn't like to be late. However, it might do this particular client good to kick her heels for a while, waiting could often put an awkward client into an anxious and more amenable frame of mind. Not that she was, strictly speaking, a client. It was a tiresome affair, and one that he had much rather not be mixed up in, but it was right to keep family matters, especially ones of this kind, within the family, where they might be dealt with swiftly and discreetly.

There she was, sitting in the clerk's room; why the devil hadn't Henty shown her in? Did he think she was going to snoop among his boxes and papers? Damn it, she was a Darcy, wasn't she? Although her behaviour might indicate . . .

He was taken aback as she rose and held out a hand. This assured, poised young woman with her direct look and considerable degree of beauty was not at all what he had been expecting. A fluttering young woman, overcome with guilt, would be more appropriate, or a pale-faced, wretched creature, needing masculine support and advice. She certainly didn't take after her mother, not in appearance. No, he would have known her anywhere for a Darcy, and that irked him. How dare she behave in such a very discreditable way and then appear to be so much in command of herself and of the situation?

When had he last seen her? Nine, ten years ago? At Pemberley, if his memory served him rightly. She had been sitting astride the bow of a tree above his head, hurling crab apples down on him, in a very unfeminine way. He'd been at Westminster School then, not inclined to take any notice of his hoydenish and fortunately distant young cousin.

Horatio Darcy ushered Cassandra into a big, handsome room, with windows overlooking the river. She looked around her, her attention diverted from her problems by the novelty of her surroundings. Shelves lined the walls, crammed with dusty tomes and stacks of papers tied up with faded ribbons. Dozens of boxes were lodged on the topmost shelves, each with a name written on the front in a spidery copperplate too small to decipher. A large desk stood in the centre of the room, and Mr. Darcy placed a chair for her, before retreating to his side of the desk and sitting down with his hands steepled together.

Her cousin had grown into a remarkably handsome man, with a fine, tall figure, but he didn't look to have become any more amiable in the years that had passed since their last encounter.

"You have come alone?" he asked. "Mr. Eyre is not with you?"

He spoke the name in an icy tone, which made Cassandra wince inwardly. As if the very mention of James Eyre didn't make her heart turn over. She took a deep breath to make sure none of her emotion showed in her voice or expression. "Mr. Eyre is presently out of the country," she said. "And this has nothing to do with him."

Mr. Darcy's eyebrows shot up. "No? I would have thought his presence was of the first importance in such a matter."

"If you have summoned me here to talk about Mr. Eyre, then I may tell you at once, that I shall not listen to you." She began to rise from her seat.

"Sit down," he said. "To be perfectly correct, I haven't summoned you, I merely sent you an appointment. It was Mr. Partington, your father—"

"Stepfather."

"Very well, your stepfather, who asked me to have this interview with you. I question the wisdom of your coming here alone, that is, without Mr. Eyre, because he must surely have a say in what is to be agreed."

"Nothing is to be agreed that need concern Mr. Eyre." It caused her a pang to say it, even though it was the simple truth.

"Your marriage to Mr. Eyre is only one of the matters that has to be discussed, but since it is the key to everything else, let us discuss that first."

"There is nothing to discuss with regard to any marriage between Mr. Eyre and me. I told Mr. Partington how matters stood. If he chooses to disbelieve me, then that is his own affair." She took another deep breath, she must not show how fragile was her self-possession. "I received a message from you asking me to wait upon you on a matter of business. I did not expect to have my private affairs raked over by you."

"I am a lawyer, acting for your father."

"Stepfather."

"I also have the honour to be a member of the family to which you yourself belong. You bear an ancient and an honourable name, and since you seem determined to drag it in the dust, it is the duty of all the male members of your family to point out to you how wrong is your wilful decision not to marry Mr. Eyre."

"It is odd," Cassandra remarked in a conversational tone, "how everyone now is wild for me to marry Mr. Eyre, whereas only a few weeks ago, it was the last outcome that my family wished."

"That was before you ran away with the gentleman in question," said Mr. Darcy coldly.

"Eloped," Cassandra said.

"Elopements end in marriage, not in cohabitation in London lodgings."

Cassandra flushed, hating to have her connection with James spoken of in those terms, although God knew, Mr. Darcy was right. She felt she must defend herself. "When I left Bath in the company of Mr. Eyre, it was on the assumption that we were heading for Gretna Green, where we would be married under Scottish law."

"That was not, however, the case, and you were perhaps naïve to assume any such thing. By putting yourself in the power of a man such as Mr. Eyre, you surely must have been aware that you were laying yourself open to all kinds of dangers."

"You do not know Mr. Eyre, I believe? So pray do not speak of him in those terms. I and Mr. Eyre have . . ." Despite herself, her voice faltered. "We have parted, but even so . . ." She paused, and frowned, her eyes fastened on the floor. Then she raised them to look directly at her cousin. "Have you ever been in love, Mr. Darcy?"

Horatio Darcy was thunderstruck. "What did you say?"

"I asked if you had ever been in love. If not, you may be unable to understand how things were between Mr. Eyre and me. I believed then that he was a man I could trust in every way."

"If your relationship was as amiable and trusting as your words imply, then it came to a very unfortunate outcome."

"When one is in love—"

"Love, Cassandra, has no place in a lawyer's office."

"There, I felt sure that you had never fallen head over heels in love, or you would be less disapproving of my behaviour."

"My personal life has no bearing on this whatsoever. The case is simple. You ran away from the protection of your family, you were under the care of your aunt—"

"Of my stepfather's sister, in fact."

"Very well, of Mrs."—he glanced down at the paper in front of him—"Cathcart, who stood in loco parentis to you, I believe, your mother and stepfather having placed you in her care. As I say, you ran away from her house in Bath, and put yourself under the protection of an unmarried man. With whom you lived on terms of intimacy—"

"As man and wife, in fact."

"—terms of intimacy, with, apparently, no concern as to the irregularity of your union."

The words were beginning to anger Cassandra, chasing away the surge of unhappiness that swept over her when she thought and spoke of James, of what he had meant to her, of how it had ended. *Irregularity of their union;* what cold, unfeeling words! True, it was a union unsanctified by church or state, but they had fallen in love, had chosen one another as their life's companion—or so she had thought—and did a few days or weeks make so very much difference, even in the eyes of God?

She should have known how it would end, of course; from the moment the coach bowling out of Bath took the London road instead of the road to the north, she should have known that Mr. Eyre had quite a different scheme in mind from what was planned.

Never for a moment had she doubted his love for her, any more than she doubted her own affections. But prudence had appeared from nowhere, a prudence and a caution she would never have expected in the gallant officer who had swept her off her feet.

"It will be better to tie the knot when the arrangements have been made with your family," James had said, leaning forward in the carriage, so that she could not see his face.

Arrangements. Money, of course, it was money that lay at the heart of his stepping back from an immediate marriage, although prudence hadn't kept him out of her bed.

"I dare say," he had said, succumbing to his passions just as she did, "that this will make it harder for your family to send me packing."

He didn't know her stepfather, and so it had ended, not at the altar, but in this lawyer's room, with her cousin's words recalling her to the present.

"I would be grateful for your attention," Horatio said drily. "Under the terms of your late grandmother's will—"

"I know the terms of the will. Rosings and the land and property naturally go to my brother. I, and my two sisters, are to be provided, upon our marriages, with such fortunes as Mama and my stepfather see fit. One hundred and fifty thousand pounds was set aside for our dowries."

"Of which—"

"Of which, my stepfather was prepared to give me not a penny, and on that basis, Mr. Eyre declared he would not marry me. Now he says he will take me with twenty thousand pounds, and the family, to which you have the honour to belong, has put a great deal of pressure on my stepfather to agree to this. The settlements are drawn, the bridals may take place as soon as possible."

Horatio looked at Cassandra with cold distaste. "I see you like to come to the heart of the issue."

"I do."

"Yet, having thrown yourself into the arms of this man, whom you claim to love, you now refuse to marry him."

"There are other conditions, I believe."

Horatio Darcy looked down at his papers, flicked through them, and took one up. "There are. First, the marriage is to take place discreetly, in London. Second, Mr. Eyre is to leave the navy. Third, immediately you have exchanged your vows, you are to leave the country and spend at least the next twelve months abroad, in Switzerland, where a house will be provided for you. On return to this country, you will live out of London, and at some distance from both Kent and Derbyshire."

From Derbyshire? "Is the great Mr. Darcy of Pemberley really afraid that my residing there would pollute his neighbourhood?"

"This condition comes from your mother. She does not wish you to associate in any way with any member of your family after your marriage. You will not be allowed to visit Rosings, nor to communicate with your brother and sisters."

"Half brother and half sisters."

"I can see you might find these conditions onerous—"

"Outrageous, I would say, but it does not matter how they are to be described. Since I will not marry Mr. Eyre, the rest has no relevance."

"Let me continue. If you persist in your stubborn refusal to marry Mr. Eyre, then you have two choices. I tell you this, since I have been instructed to do so; however, I feel sure that your good sense and your duty to your family will lead you to make the only proper decision, of agreeing that the marriage will take place. If not, then your mother and f—stepfather have decided that you must live out of the world. You are ruined, you have lost your good name, and for your own protection and for the sake of those connected with you, you need to live quietly, out of the public eye, and a long way from your immediate family, so that this fatal step you have taken may, in time, be forgotten."

"Where is this place of retirement to be? Ireland? Some remote part of the Scottish Highlands? Or perhaps abroad? I believe English people who are ruined often go to live in Calais."

"Those are people who face financial ruin."

"You mean I won't?"

Horatio Darcy's voice was growing colder by the minute, and it gave Cassandra some satisfaction to see that she was needling him.

"I may say that your levity, at such a time, is ill-assumed, Miss Darcy. Perhaps you could restrain yourself and allow me to finish what I have to say. The accommodation your parents have in mind is to live under the care of one Mrs. Norris—ah, I see you recognize the name—who presently resides in Cheltenham, in the company of the disgraced Mrs. Rushworth, Maria Bertram as was, who, like you, took a step that removed her irrevocably from the company and society that her birth and upbringing entitled her to."

Nothing this man had said so far had sent such a chill with her. That would be a punishment indeed; she had heard much about Mrs. Norris from her stepfather, and knew her for a cold-hearted woman with a mean temper and narrow outlook. She could scarcely imagine a worse fate. "Live with Mrs. Norris! You cannot be serious."

"I am perfectly serious."

"Well, whatever happens, I will not do so. You said I had two choices; pray, what is the second?"

"If you will neither marry nor go to live with Mrs. Norris, then your family, your mother, and stepfather wash their hands of you. You have, I understand, a small income from your late aunt of some ninety pounds per annum. This will be paid to you quarterly, and your parents will never see nor speak to you again."

Cassandra couldn't help it; tears were welling in her eyes. She dug in her reticule, took out a small lace handkerchief, and blew her nose.

"Allow me," Horatio said, getting up and handing her a clean and much larger handkerchief. She waved it away, unable to bring herself to speak.

"Don't be foolish. Take it. I am not surprised you are upset, for this is a very harsh treatment. However, I would point out that there are parents who would choose such a rejection of a daughter who has behaved as you have done, without offering what I think are very generous alternative arrangements."

The desolation in Cassandra's heart almost overwhelmed her, and she strove to compose herself, with the result that her words sounded, even to her ears, cold and uncaring. "I cannot marry Mr. Eyre. I will not marry a man who doesn't love me enough to marry me without a fortune or my family's approval. And I cannot consent to a life of misery such as would be mine were I to live under the same roof as Mrs. Norris."

"Then you must resign yourself to a single life, knowing every day that you have incurred the wholehearted disapproval of every single member of your family, close and distant, and that you are cast off from everything you have known up until now: a home, the affection and concern of those nearest to you, and the life of a young girl of good family and fortune. There are places where you can live on ninety pounds a year, but it would not permit your residence in London, for example."

"I shall have to earn my living, I can see, just as you do."

He looked affronted. "I hardly think that any duties you may undertake to augment your income are on a par with my profession. Besides, with a tarnished reputation and no references, you will find it very hard to secure employment of any kind. To be brutally frank, the future that awaits you is far more likely to be that you will come upon the town."

"You do indeed have a low opinion of my morals if you assume that I would ever become one of those women."

"I am a realist. I know what London is, that is all, and what is the fate of most women in your situation. My recommendation to you, should you commit yourself to an independent life, is that you move to a provincial town where you may live quietly and inexpensively."

"Could not you give me a reference, so that I might find respectable employment?"

"Certainly not."

"I thought, the very first time I met you, that you had a kindness about you. I remember you picking me up when I fell off my pony, and defending me against my governess's wrath. I see that I was mistaken." Cassandra got up.

"I do not expect you to give me an answer now. I am instructed to allow you a week to—"

"Come to my senses, is that what my stepfather says? Believe me, Mr. Darcy, I do not need three minutes to make my decision."

Horatio hesitated. "Speaking, not as a lawyer, but as your cousin, Cassandra, and as a man who has lived in London long enough to know what a terrifying place it can be to those cast adrift upon it, I beseech you to think most carefully what you are about."

"You are worried lest a Miss Darcy be known to have joined the impures, is that it?"

"Really, I do think . . . Cassandra, you have no idea what it means to come upon the town!"

"You may set your mind at rest. I shall not use the name of Darcy from now on. My family casts me off; very well, I do the same to them."

Cassandra went slowly down the staircase from Mr. Darcy's chambers, blinking as she came out of the shadows into the bright sunlight. She felt numb, as though all power of sensation had drained away from her. Her mind, though, was far from numb, and indeed she saw the outside world with an extra clarity; grass, pathways, trees, figures all as though they had been outlined with a sharp pen.

In that brief half hour within Mr. Darcy's chambers, her life had changed. A door had shut behind her and she was excluded from every part of her life that she had formerly known. Why should she feel this now, and not think that her old life had ended some other critical moment? Why not when she had left Rosings; now, as she knew, for the last time? Why not when she had arrived in Bath, or left it, with James? Why not when she had reached London, and had spent a night in his arms?

It was, her mind told her, because, in those chambers, she had made the decision. It was not circumstances or chance or the authority or advice of a parent or a lover—or, indeed, of a lawyer—that had, inside that room, laid down the pattern of her future life. It owed nothing to any other being, only to herself.

She walked away across the green towards the broad gravel walk that ran alongside the river. On such a fine day, there were several people promenading up and down beside the river; it was a favourite spot for Londoners, the clerk had grudgingly informed her. She watched a middle-aged couple strolling along, the man in a brown hat and his wife holding a parasol at an elegant angle to shield her complexion from the sun. A pair of young women walked arm in arm, laughing and talking together, the feathers on their hats fluttering in the slight breeze, their muslin skirts playing around their ankles as they walked. One of them was leading a little dog that pranced along on its short legs, excited to be out and snuffing the smells of the river bank.

Not being a Londoner, and having spent no more than a few hours in her whole life in the capital before she came there with James Eyre, Cassandra had never seen the Thames. James, learning this, and laughing at her for being a mere country girl, had taken her to see the river on their first morning in London, and she had been entranced by the teeming waterway.

"It is never twice the same," he told her, and she had seen it dark under grey skies with him, and now, gleaming and glinting under a blue sky, with the sun shining upon it. She stood and watched strings of barges under sail going up and down, and the watermen plying their trade and calling to one another across the water. These moving craft made their way among a forest of masts, more than three thousand, James had said, amused at her amazement, promising that they would take a day out on the river, travel up to Kew to visit the botanic gardens, or ride to Richmond.

Excursions they would never take, she thought despairingly. But she wasn't going to give in to despair, nor let regrets cloud her mind, she told herself as she walked up and down, the gravel scrunching lightly under her feet. She could not allow herself the indulgence of reflections and memories.

Horatio stood at the window. A tap on the door and Thomas Bailey, a colleague of Horatio's, came into the room and went across to the window, his eyes following Horatio's as they dwelt on the slim, upright figure walking to and fro upon the gravel.

"Damned fine woman," said Bailey.

Horatio turned on him. "That happens to be my cousin, Miss Darcy."

Bailey took a step backwards. "She's still a very good-looking young lady. Isn't she the one who ran away with a naval officer, causing all your family no end of trouble? An heiress, no doubt, all you Darcys are as rich as Croesus, and to throw herself away on a mere lieutenant! It doesn't bear thinking of."

"You have a vulgar mind, Thomas," Darcy said coldly. "And as for rich, you know very well I have a younger son's portion." He was silent for a moment. "She is a very distant cousin," he added in a harsher voice.

"What is she doing here, in the Inner Temple?" said Bailey. "Oh, I suppose she has come to see you. Has her father asked you to crack the whip? And who's the lucky fellow, I wouldn't mind—" He saw the fury on Horatio's face and stopped himself in time, turning the rest of his sentence into a half cough.

Normally, Horatio found Bailey a very good kind of fellow, but today he was filled with irritation at the sight of him. "Haven't you any work to do?"

"I can take a hint," said Bailey, amiably enough. He went out with Henty, telling him to look out the papers on Lady Ludlow's estate.

Horatio, still standing at the window, saw Cassandra check her pace and then straighten her shoulders, as though taking up a burden, before she made her way to the gate that led out of the Inner Temple.

He was filled with a sudden rage, at her obstinacy, her refusal to see sense, to conform to the rules and proprieties of that order of society into which she had been born. Would her stepfather really cast her off? Would her mother, who was after all her own flesh and blood, allow him to do so? He was not closely acquainted with Mrs. Partington, but what little he had seen of her he hadn't admired. She seemed to be completely ruled by her second husband, a poor fellow, in comparison to the clever, amiable man that the late Thaddeus Darcy had apparently been.

Well, there was nothing he could do about it. He could merely wait and hope that during the next few days his cousin would come to her senses. Perhaps Eyre would return from Ireland and her affection for him, which must be considerable in order for such a girl to cast herself under his protection, would be sufficient to persuade her that marriage to her naval lieutenant was the best hope of a reasonable future that she had.

At the same time he felt a sudden loathing for Eyre. Had he meant to ruin Cassandra? No, that wasn't likely. By all accounts he had left Bath in a hurry because of his indebtedness. And he wasn't the kind of man not to seize the chance of a pretty companion, especially one who he knew might well be possessed of a large fortune.

How could Cassandra be guilty of such folly as not to see that Eyre was only interested in her fortune? Although he supposed that he might have had some feeling for her as a person as well. She was well-looking enough, although he himself would never choose to live with a girl who had a look as direct and alarming as Cassandra's—or so pigheaded a character. She reminded him, uncomfortably, of Mr. Fitzwilliam Darcy, also his cousin, and a formidable man.

Damn it, where was Henty? Here was the day half-gone and no work done, nothing achieved. He flung open the door into the outer office and curtly told his clerk to come in, that there was much to be done.

He started to dictate a letter, to go to Mr. Partington, in Kent.

Then he thought better of it. This was a family affair. He would write to Partington himself that evening, and give him a brief account of the meeting that he had had with Cassandra, saying that he had duly passed on Mr. Partington's message and the conditions that he laid down for his stepdaughter. When he had an answer from Cassandra, which he was sure would be in favour of marriage, he would again be in communication with him.

He said no more about Miss Darcy to Henty, and indeed made every effort as the day went on not to think of his cousin. If he was going to think of any woman, he would prefer to think of Lady Usborne, with her pretty, flattering ways, and no grey eyes sparkling with anger, or—and this irked him even more—amusement, when she looked at him.

Cassandra found that the flowing river, the people walking at their leisure taking in the air, enjoying the sunshine and the warmth of the day, jarred with her mood. It was too leisurely, too comfortable here. She wanted to be in motion, she needed to take action, not to muse or brood.

So she left the Inner Temple, with its calmness of centuries of learning and law, and went out through the handsome Inigo Jones gate into the Strand. There the traffic was as busy as ever and the clamour of London rang in her ears: horses' hooves ringing on the cobbled way, the screeching sound of wagon wheels, the rattle and clatter of carriages, and all around her, voices raised in laughter or argument, peddlers and street men selling their wares, a woman shrieking loudly at a disobedient child, small boys squealing amongst themselves as they played with the stone that they sent skittering across the cobbles trying to bring down a passing horse.

There were shops all along the Strand, their bay windows full of enticing goods. None of these caught Cassandra's attention. In fact, after the first impact of the scene with all its movement and life, she hardly noticed what was going on around her nor where her steps were leading to. She was considering Mr. Darcy's parting words to her, his warning that even a young lady such as herself, well-born and carefully raised, could, by setting her will against the wishes of her family, easily find herself come upon the town.

And Cassandra knew precisely what the phrase meant. Despite the apparent strictness of her upbringing under her stepfather's rigid control—and Mr. Partington was a man very strong on morality—she was no prude. An innocent abroad she might be; ignorant, she was not. Many years of friendship with Emily Croscombe, a lively young woman of just Cassandra's age, had made sure of that, for Emily had an unusual mother, an educated woman, positively a blue-stocking, who believed modern girls should not be kept in a state of passive ignorance, and what Emily knew, so did her friend and confidante, Cassandra.

There had been a case in the village, when the attorney's daughter had, at the age of fifteen, run off with a member of the militia; Emily had told Cassandra that the girl, abandoned by her lover, had come upon the town to make her living and she also told her that Sarah was enjoying her new life, much to the outrage of the village.

Mrs. Croscombe pointed out to the girls, in a matter-of-fact rather than a moralising way, that while Sarah was young and pretty and had her health, she might find her life in London not disagreeable. But those years soon passed, and a girl lost her bloom, and then with no family, no means of support and nothing of youth and beauty left, the prospects for a single woman in that situation were nothing if not bleak.

Cassandra came out of her reverie to find herself outside a shop which did catch her attention, for as the door opened to let out a customer, a poignantly familiar smell wafted out. This was a colourist's shop, and the smell was an unmistakable mixture of linseed oil and pigment that carried her at once back to her attic studio at Rosings, where so many hours of her girlhood and early womanhood had been spent in the absorbed happiness of working at her easel or her drawing table.

Rosings! An image of her home came before her eyes, an artist's image of the façade painted in early spring, with green flecking the trees and the family posed for the picture. Rosings wasn't one of the great houses of England, it was not a house to compare with a Chatsworth or a Wilton, but it was still a fine, imposing house—and, for Cassandra, the place where she had spent the previous nineteen years of her life, until she had driven away from it, with scarcely a backward glance, only a few weeks since.

What a difference those few short weeks had made, what a complete change in her circumstances had been wrought in that time. She looked with unseeing eyes at the little piles of colour set out in trays behind the tiny panes of the shop window, wondering if there were a time or place she could pinpoint that marked the turning point; a day, an incident, which had propelled her on the course that had so changed her life?

Chapter Two

It had been a morning at the beginning of April when Cassandra rode over to Croscombe House from Rosings with some exciting news. Croscombe House was two miles distant from the village of Hunsford, where Rosings was situated, and Cassandra could have found her way there blindfold, so much time had she spent there over the years in Emily's company.

It was the fashion for owners of large and elegant houses to have them painted: house, park and, generally, the family lined up in front of the building. Mr. Partington, never one to be outdone by his neighbours, had, through the good offices of Herr Winter, a painter who lived in Hunsford, engaged an up-and-coming young artist to come down to Rosings and paint the house and family.

"Imagine," Cassandra told Emily. "He is only four-and-twenty, but already, Herr Winter says, he is making a reputation for himself in London as an artist."

"Is he English?"

"No, he is a fellow countryman of Herr Winter, who knew his father when he lived in Germany. But he speaks excellent English, Mr. Partington was insistent on that point, of course, he would be, for otherwise how could he tell him what to do, and how to paint the picture? Oh, I can't wait for him to arrive, it is a great opportunity for me, to see such an artist at work."

"You won't be able to see much," Emily observed. "Not when you're sitting still, looking like a well-bred young lady for hours on end, under the portico."

"That is what I feared, but all is well, it is to be a portrait of the Partington family, and of course I am a Darcy."

Mrs. Croscombe was so shocked she could hardly speak. "Do you mean that you are not to be painted with your mother and sisters and brother?"

"Half sisters and half brother, as Mr. Partington is always so quick to point out. No, and don't look so horrified, for I don't give a button for being painted. I should very much prefer to be on the other side of the process, I do assure you."

Emily could see that her mother had a great deal more to say on the subject, so she intervened: "What is this painter's name? When is he to come?"

"He is called Henry Lisser, and he will arrive on Thursday se'ennight. By which time we will have another visitor, I forgot to mention that, because Mr. Lisser is so much more exciting."

"Not another clergyman?" said Emily.

"No, not at all. It is my cousin Belle, Isabel Darcy. I have no recollection of her, although I know we met as children, when I visited Pemberley."

"So she is one of your cousin Mr. Darcy's daughters," said Mrs. Croscombe. "He has five, has he not? Isabel will be one of the younger ones, I think, for I am sure the older two are married."

"Yes, and her twin sister Georgina is lately married and gone to live in Paris. And, in the strictest confidence, although Mama won't say anything, and Mr. Partington just tut-tuts and looks grave, I have a notion that she has been in some kind of a scrape, and that she is coming to Rosings to be out of the way and kept out of mischief."

"I would have thought Pemberley would keep her out of mischief."

"Oh, I believe her parents are abroad or some such thing, but do not want her to stay in London for the summer."

"She will be company for you, is she about your age?"

"She is eighteen."

"What is she like?" Emily asked. "Is she pretty?"

"I have no idea, but you may see for yourself, for she arrives tomorrow, so unless she is to be kept strictly within bounds, or cannot ride a horse, I shall bring her over to make your acquaintance."

Belle was no horsewoman, but the visit was paid nonetheless, Cassandra being allowed to take her cousin with her in the carriage. "Which," she said to Emily as she jumped down outside the steps of Croscombe House, "shows you how rich and important Belle's papa is, for you know how Mr. Partington hates to have the horses put to the carriage on my behalf."

Belle, angelically fair, with striking violet eyes, had a discontented expression on her pretty face as she stepped down from the carriage. She made no bones about telling Emily and Cassandra why she had been posted off to Rosings. "It is because I am in love with the most handsome, dashing man, my dearest Ferdie, only my family consider I am too young and too volatile in my affections to enter into an engagement."

Mrs. Croscombe had, through an intricate network of friends and acquaintances, found out more than this. When Emily told her at breakfast the next morning what Belle had said, and expressed her indignation at any family being so gothic as to stand between a girl and the object of her affections—"For he is a perfectly respectable parti, an eldest son, and very well-connected"—her mother thought it only right to say that this was the third young man within a year that Belle, "who is but eighteen, my dear," had fallen in love with and wished to marry.

Emily was much struck with this, and passed the information on to Cassandra, warning her not to reveal to Belle how much Mrs. Croscombe, who had a wide correspondence, and kept up with all the gossip of town, knew about her. Cassandra thought it a very good joke. "Perhaps she will next fall in love with one of Mr. Partington's clerical protégés, or with one of your rejected beaux."

"I do not mind whom she falls in love with, so long as it is not my Charles," said Emily.

There was no danger of that. Charles Egerton, while appreciating Belle's undoubted prettiness—although he was wise enough not to comment on that to Emily—had no time for such a flighty piece of perfection. "She is very silly," he said disapprovingly. "She would drive any man of sense to distraction. Her father and mother are very right to remove her from London, for it will be much better for her to grow up and become more sensible before she marries any of her lovers."

Nor did any other of the young men of the district seem to take her fancy. "In fact," Belle confided to Cassandra, with a prodigious yawn, "I do wish they had let me visit my sister in Paris. I have never been so bored in all my life. This is even worse than Pemberley, how do you stand it?"

"I have plenty to occupy myself. You could do some sketching, if you choose, or there is the pianoforte, in tune, and very willing to be used."

"Oh, I never play the piano if I can help it. I leave all that to my younger sister, Alethea, who is a prodigiously fine musician. I play the harp, and my sister Georgina was used to sing with me, but now she is in Paris, and I have not brought my harp with me, and besides, what is the point of playing, if there are no young men to listen and applaud? And as for sketching, I have no talent in that direction, none at all."

"You could read. The library here is very good."

"I've looked, and it's all fusty stuff. Nothing modern, does not your mama buy any novels?"

"My stepfather does not approve of novels."

Belle stared. "You mean you do not read novels?"

"I do, only without his permission. Emily lends me what I want, she and her mother are both great readers."

"Mrs. Croscombe is very learned, is not she? The books she reads must be very dull."

"Some of them are, but she enjoys novels as much as Emily does. When we next go over there, ask to borrow one."

Another yawn from Belle. "Why don't you take my portrait?" she suggested, brightening up at the thought. "I would like to have my portrait painted, of me on my own, because whenever anyone has drawn or painted me, it has always been with my sister. If you take my likeness, I can smuggle it out to send to my dearest Ferdie, would not that be a very good plan?"

Cassandra was always happy to have a new model, and Belle went off to change into her prettiest dress and a smart new bonnet, while Cassandra rang for Petifer and went up to her studio, which she had set up in one of the attics, as far away as possible from both the public rooms and the family rooms.

Petifer had been detailed to look after Miss Darcy, once she reached an age to have her own maid, and she was kind, fierce, and devoted to Cassandra. Taking her side against Mr. Partington, whom she despised, Petifer aided and abetted Cassandra in her painting, even though she thought it a strange occupation for a lady, and she had become very handy with the paints and canvases. She also did Cassandra a further service, which her mistress knew nothing about, by keeping the servants from gossiping too much about the hours Miss Darcy spent up in her attic with all those odorous paints.

Cassandra had never had a more chatty subject, for Belle wouldn't stop talking.

"My sister Camilla is lately married, to a very agreeable man, and he had her portrait painted, it is considered a very good likeness. She is wearing yellow, which is her favourite colour, and it makes her look almost pretty. She is the least handsome of us, but Wytton, that is her husband, does not seem to mind. Or perhaps he has not noticed, his mind is taken up with antiquities and ancient Egypt and that kind of thing. Did not you say that Mr. Partington has engaged an artist to paint you all? Perhaps he might draw me as well. When does he arrive? At least it will be more company, or will he be consigned to the servants' quarters?"

"He is to stay with Herr Winter, who is an old friend of his family. But I believe the habit of treating artists as tradesmen has quite gone out. Mr. Lawrence dines with the king, you know, and a fashionable painter, such as I believe this Mr. Lisser to be, is received in all the best houses." Cassandra didn't add, as she might have done, that it had taken considerable persuasion and an extremely large fee to entice Mr. Lisser away from London and down to Rosings. Anyone who could command so much money was unlikely to find himself dining among the servants.

Henry Lisser posted down from London, and word of his arrival at Herr Winter's house flew around Hunsford. The next day he came to Rosings, and stepped out of the carriage sent for him by Mr. Partington, followed by his servant, a thin, undernourished young man, who unloaded a surprising number of boxes and cases and several canvases under Mr. Lisser's directions.

Mr. Partington sailed out to greet the young artist with more than his usual condescension. He was taken aback, Cassandra saw, to find Henry Lisser seemingly quite unimpressed by his surroundings and company; here was no bowing and scraping young man, over-whelmed by the grandeur of Rosings. The young artist cast a quick glance around, looked Mr. Partington up and down, and, Cassandra felt sure, took his measure in those few seconds, and held out his hand.

Belle was watching from an upstairs window. "Do not you think him a remarkably handsome young man?" she said as soon as Cassandra joined her.

"I didn't notice," Cassandra said. "He seems pleasant enough. I shall know more about him if I am allowed to watch him while he works. Some artists won't allow it, you know, but Herr Winter promised to put in a word for me."

"Oh, you will be more interested in his palette and paintbrushes and how he mixes his paints than in his countenance," Belle said with a toss of her head. "I shall ask if I may watch, too."

That rather alarmed Cassandra; while she knew she could tuck herself in a corner and not be noticed, Belle was never happy unless she was conspicuous.

"It will be very tedious to watch, you know, unless you happened to be interested in technique as I am. Besides, you will catch Sally's eye and give her the giggles, you know you will, and that will put Mr. Partington into a temper, and get Sally a scolding."

"He is not so very tall, and I like a man to be tall, but he has a good figure. And those eyes, they are very fine, his eyes. Do you not think he would look well upon a horse?"

"I think you had much better return to your novel, you said it was most exciting; I dare say much more exciting than any painter."

Chapter Three

The previous evening, dining with his old friend Joachim Winter, Henry Lisser had questioned him about the family at Rosings.

Herr Winter was a retired artist of some distinction, who had been obliged to lay down his brushes on account of rheumatism in his fingers. However, he had taken on a new career, as master to the many young ladies who lived in the neighbourhood, and who wished to improve their drawing and painting skills beyond the instruction that their governesses could provide. It became quite the thing among the families to employ Herr Winter; kind, tolerant and conciliatory, he was a great favourite with his young pupils.

It was fortunate for Cassandra that her grandmother, the formidable Lady Catherine de Bourgh, had agreed that she might learn with Herr Winter. Lady Catherine, who had been thwarted in her attempts to make her own sickly daughter, Anne, as accomplished as she would have wished, was determined that Cassandra was going to turn out the most accomplished young lady in the country. So when the governess, Miss Wilson, came to her ladyship with the suggestion that a master might be engaged to instruct Cassandra in drawing and water-colours, she was listened to.

"Pray, why cannot you instruct the girl?" was Lady Catherine's immediate reaction.

This was rough ground, and must be got over as lightly as

possible—Miss Wilson's brother was in the army, and she often thought of her life at Rosings in military terms. "Indeed, I can, and she has made good progress. However, there is a notable master come to live in Hunsford, a Herr Winter. He is retired, but is taking pupils: He goes to Croscombe House to teach the Croscombe girls, and Miss Emily is doing remarkably well under his tuition. The Tremaynes think so highly of him that they send a carriage over, twice a week, for him to attend at Hunsford Lodge, where he instructs Mr. Ralph, who has considerable talent in that direction, and all the Miss Tremaynes."

"Croscombe House, you say, and Hunsford Lodge?"

"And several other pupils besides. He is so much in demand, that I fear he may be unable to take on any more at present."

No master was going to refuse to teach Lady Catherine's granddaughter. The amiable Herr Winter was summoned, subjected to an impolite interrogation as to his background and abilities, and informed that he was to have the honour of teaching Miss Darcy.

Fortunately, Herr Winter was possessed of a sense of humour, and he had taken a liking to this Cassandra, with her wide grey eyes and ill-contained energy. At first, he had expected no more of her than of his other female pupils, who needed to sketch and draw and do water-colours as an accomplishment and as an agreeable way to pass the empty hours of leisure, and he had been astonished to find in Cassandra a talent far beyond that of the usual run of young ladies.

Very soon discovering that there were few of his male pupils, in Germany or in London, who had ever shown more promise, he forgot about her sex and simply enjoyed unfolding to her the mysteries of his craft. "Art, I cannot teach," he would always say. "That comes from the soul and cannot be taught."

Water-colours and pastels weren't enough for her, and by the time she was fourteen, she was already an accomplished painter in oils, a skill she took care to keep hidden from her mother. He would have liked her to tackle some bigger themes, but Cassandra was firm about where her tastes and skills lay: She could paint from nature well enough, for her early training with her father had made her observant, and the liveliness of her flowers and trees and landscapes made them delightful, but her real love, and gift, was for portraiture.

Herr Winter showed some of her work to young Henry Lisser, who was duly impressed. "Were she not a young lady, and born into an English gentleman's household, she could make a living from her brush," he said.

"Look at the upstairs parlour at Rosings, if you are able," Herr Winter said. "She painted the panels in there; they thought I did it, but she wanted to learn fresco techniques, and so I showed her, and let her do the work. It was irksome for me to take the credit and the fee, but the pleasure and pride she took in the work were their own reward for her, and the main reward for me. It is much admired, I could not have produced anything so charming myself, and I was besieged with requests from other houses to do a similar thing. I had to say that my fingers were giving me considerable pain, since otherwise it might be noticed that those exquisite pastoral scenes did not come from my brush."

Henry Lisser shrugged. "It is a waste of a talent," he said, almost to himself. "However, she will marry a country squire and settle down to be a wife or mother, as is her destiny."

Herr Winter put Cassandra's work back in its portfolio. There was a tiny frown on his amiable countenance. "Part of me hopes that this will be the case. But, with this particular young lady, I do wonder about her future. I think it may not be as you describe. Her life at Rosings is not altogether a happy one; I only hope that she does not break out some day, tired of the smallness of her life, and perhaps take some disastrous step that she will come to regret."

Once Mr. Lisser began work at Rosings, he saw for himself what Herr Winter meant. However, he kept his thoughts to himself, and, in truth, he was not much interested in a set of persons whom, he imagined, he would never see again, once the painting was finished. He had a good deal of reserve, and liked to keep a professional distance between himself and his clients.

Mr. Partington tried to draw him out—what was his background, what were his antecedents?—but he gave little away. He had studied in Leipzig and Vienna and Paris, before coming to London, he said, and no more could be got out of him.

Mr. Lisser had been surprised to find that the family arranged in front of the view of Rosings that he was to paint was to consist of only five members of the family. Mr. Partington chose the grouping, with him standing protectively behind his wife, who was seated with her baby son in her arms. Their youngest daughter sat cross-legged at her feet, in a foaming muslin dress with a pink sash, and her older sister, similarly attired, sat on a nearby swing.

It was a charming composition, very much in the modern taste, showing a paterfamilias enjoying the pleasures of family life, and the dutiful and fecund wife serene and contented, under his care.

"You have another daughter," Henry Lisser said abruptly. "Is she not to be in the painting?"

She was not, Mr. Partington said snappishly, since she was a Darcy, a mere stepdaughter, not a Partington. However, Mr. Partington would be very much obliged if Mr. Lisser would include one or two of his prized Shorthorn cattle in the picture.

Chapter Four

Cassandra was exasperated. Belle had been introduced, thanks to Mrs. Croscombe, to several agreeable and handsome young men; why did her volatile fancy have to alight on Mr. Lisser? And while she might tell her stepfather that such an artist would be a welcome addition to the dinner table at many a lofty home, it didn't mean that he would in any way be considered a suitable lover for a Miss Isabel Darcy, with a fortune of some thirty thousand pounds or more.

Belle was a flirt, a determined and accomplished flirt, and now her attention was fixed on Mr. Lisser, there was nothing Cassandra could do to prevent her cousin from playing off her tricks. And it seemed that Henry Lisser was not displeased by the pleasure Belle took in his company. When he was at work, his attention was focussed entirely upon his subject. He was grave and uncommunicative, saying little to his subjects, and those few words merely a request to move this way or that, or to place a hand or reposition an arm. He gave instructions to his assistant, as necessary, and sometimes spoke to Cassandra, as to a pupil, but in a low, indifferent voice.

To her admiration, he banished Belle from his presence while he painted, in a kind enough way, but with sufficient authority that she accepted his rejection with no more than a toss of her head. The children, of course, could not hold their poses for very long, so he had filled in their small shapes and then dismissed them, bidding them to run along and play with their cousin Miss Belle. They skipped off, and he was left to do some more work on the patient Partingtons.

Cassandra was fascinated to see how he worked, it was so very different from her own style of painting. He took numerous sketches, charcoal or graphite, and had always a sketchbook in his hand, drawing the house from numerous angles: "You must see the whole in your mind, even while you only paint one view."

Cassandra was full of admiration and questions. He asked to see her notebooks, making few direct comments, but suggesting a shading here, another grouping of a composition there, and gave her some valuable advice as to portraiture, although, as he said, his own genius did not lie in that direction. Oh, yes, he could paint figures in a landscape, but head and shoulders or full-length portraits were not for him.

"You should travel, Miss Darcy, it would be of great benefit to you to go to Italy, to study the works of the masters and also to see for yourself the landscapes of that country."

"Italy! Why, Mr. Lisser, Bath would be an adventure for me, and as for London, I long to go there, but"—with a sigh—"it is not at present possible."

Mr. Lisser remembered what Herr Winter had said about his talented pupil, and said no more about her painting or travel. Instead he wanted to talk about Belle.

"She is your cousin, I believe?"

"The relationship is not such a close one. We share great-grandparents through her father and my mother, and there is also a connection through my father, who was the younger son of a younger son. Belle's father is the eldest son of an eldest son. Do you have brothers and sisters, Mr. Lisser?"

"I have a younger brother, and two sisters."

"Are they artistic?"

"My brother is destined for the military. One of my sisters is a good musician, the other has no artistic bent that we are aware of."

"And they live in Germany?"

"Yes."

"Yet you chose to come to London to work."

"There are reasons . . ." His face took on a reserved look. Then he smiled, a smile that transformed his features. "London is a good place for those who wish to make their way as a painter, and I have to earn my bread like this. In the future perhaps—"

"You will prefer different subjects, a different style?"

"I hope so. But meanwhile I can benefit from the English love of landscape, especially when a painting portrays their own handsome property set in the midst of it. I have noticed that these kinds of paintings and family portraits are what hang on the walls of most houses that I visit."

Cassandra thought of the dozens of portraits that hung in the public rooms at Rosings and also in corridors and passages where they were never noticed. And on the top floor, a picture gallery ran the length of the central part of the house, where the finest portraits hung, from stiff Tudor faces, all very much alike, through the long, big-eyed, livelier Stuarts, a riot of lace and silk and satin, for the de Bourghs had always held to the royalist cause, to the wide-skirted and gold-laced men and women of the last century.

Belle came dancing into the room, a vision in a figured muslin, with a wide sash about her slim waist, and a fetching hat in her hand. Now, as he rose to his feet, Mr. Lisser had no eyes or thoughts for anyone but Belle; she was a minx, to lead him on like that. Cassandra stood up, too.

"I am going to show Mr. Lisser the gallery of family portraits," she said.

"Oh, let me do that, you are wanted in your mama's room, she asked me to look for you."

Belle went off with Mr. Lisser, and Cassandra dutifully went to her mother's chamber, where her mother was surprised to see her; no, she hadn't summoned her, she had merely remarked to Belle that she might find her cousin downstairs with Mr. Lisser.

"And I wish, my love, that you will not spend so much time with Mr. Lisser. He is here to work, you know, not to talk."

"He is giving me some very helpful advice, Mama."

Mrs. Partington gave a faint smile. "He is very kind, but you must not presume upon his kindness. He is no Herr Winter, not a drawing master, but an accomplished artist, he is not to be wasting his time on your little drawings and sketches."

"Thank you, Mama," said Cassandra, whisking herself away before she should say something she would regret.

Mr. Partington also disapproved of the time Cassandra spent with Mr. Lisser, and told his wife so. "She is putting herself forward, it is always so. She talks to him as though she were an equal, another artist; very unbecoming behaviour in a young girl. And she is too often alone with him. While he has too much sense to take advantage, word will get around, tongues will wag. It is not appropriate for a Miss Darcy to be closeted for hours on end with a young man, however much their talk is of grounds and colours and form."

"I have already mentioned the matter to her, my dear," said Mrs. Partington in soothing tones.

So Cassandra had to snatch moments with Henry Lisser at such times as her mother was out visiting, and Mr. Partington was out inspecting a pig or giving instructions for his early wheat.

"I should like to paint Mr. Partington in his farmer's smock," said Mr. Lisser, showing Cassandra a sketch he had made without Mr. Partington's knowledge. "He seems more at home out on the land than he does in the drawing room in his fine clothes. No, don't frown, I am not speaking ill of your stepfather, I admire him for it. My father, also, is a keen farmer." Again, that reserved look. Did he feel that his origins were low, that it was a disgrace to be the son of a farmer? Certainly, there was no hint of the clodpole about Mr. Lisser, his manners were polished and he was a man at ease in his company.

Although less so in Belle's company; as the days passed, Cassandra noticed that he was stiff and uncomfortable when Belle was with them, and that there was a warmth in his eyes when he looked at her frivolous cousin that suggested his feelings for her might be deepening beyond mere flirtation.

There was nothing she could say, she could not advise a man several years her senior, a guest, a virtual stranger. But she did drop a hint as to the reason why Belle was at Rosings. He laughed, genuinely amused. "Miss Belle is of a type, but she is good-hearted beneath the frippery, I believe."

Cassandra couldn't agree with him, she thought Belle entirely heartless, and especially so to lead on a man in Henry Lisser's position; it could bring nothing but unhappiness to him, and even trouble in his professional life. Why could not Belle be more careful what she was about?

It irked her slightly that the eyes and suspicions of her parents and even her governess were directed at her. She liked and admired Mr. Lisser, she was anxious to learn all she could from him, but as a man, he did not interest her. She had not yet met a man who did.

She remonstrated with Belle, who gave a familiar toss of her head, and pouted, and said that Cassandra knew nothing about it, and she was not flirting with Mr. Lisser, nor had he captured her heart, the idea was absurd.

"I am very sure that is the case," Cassandra said. "For I know how attached you are to your Ferdie."

"Ferdie?" said Belle. "Oh, him. Yes, of course."

"I do believe she has forgotten him," Cassandra said to Emily on her next visit to Croscombe House. "She is the most cold-hearted, thoughtless girl I ever met."

"I do not think she is heartless, exactly," said Emily. "I think she likes to flirt, and men take it more seriously than she intends, and then she likes the excitement and drama of a supposed attachment that she knows will not meet with her family's approval, however worthy the man, because she is so young. One day, she will find a man she can give her heart to, and then she will change, you will see, it will all be different."

Cassandra supposed that on matters of the heart, Emily knew much better than she, but she still wished that Belle were not at Rosings just now.

The picture was going on excellently, Mr. and Mrs. Partington were very pleased, and busy discussing where it might hang. Not in the gallery, that was too out of the way, no one ever went there, except the children in wet weather, when they slid up and down on the polished floor and played skittles. The great drawing room would be the best place, so fresh hangings and new wallpaper would be required. Samples of fabric and wall coverings were ordered down from London, and Cassandra's mama became almost animated as she occupied herself with choosing and matching and planning.

Mr. Partington was out of doors most of the day, as the weather continued fine, and almost grudged the time required for his sittings. However, the picture was nearly done, it would soon be finished, would be taken to London for varnishing and framing, and then Mr. Lisser would be gone.

Belle grew melancholy at the prospect, and Cassandra began to suspect that Mr. Lisser was taking longer than necessary to finish his work. Poor deluded man; now, although she had rejoiced in his being in the house for so many hours each day, she longed for him to be gone, before Belle forgot herself, and found herself once again in disgrace.

It was not to be. It was Cassandra who found herself in disgrace, in deep and unjustified disgrace.

"Mrs. Lawton saw you, do not deny it," her mother said, her voice tearful.

Mr. Partington was red with anger. "To be embracing a man, a guest in the house, and, I may point out, a man very much your social inferior, what were you about? If you had no thought for your own reputation, could you not consider in how difficult a situation you placed Mr. Lisser?"

"Shame on you for that," cried her mother. "You have led him on."

"Indeed you must have, for he is too sensible a man to behave in this way otherwise. I am outraged that such a thing should happen in my house," announced Mr. Partington. "You will go to your room and stay there until I consider what is to be done with you."

Why, Cassandra asked herself, had she not protested, defended herself, said at once that she had not lingered in the shrubbery with Mr. Lisser, no, nor any man?

Partly because she was so shocked at her parents' at once jumping to the conclusion that if any young lady were dallying with a young man, then it must be Cassandra. They had immediately blamed her, without seeking any further for the truth, or even considering that Belle, who, after all, had a history of such a kind of behaviour, might be the young lady in Mr. Lisser's arms.

Nor did they seem inclined to hold Mr. Lisser himself at fault: They assumed he had been led on, had taken Cassandra's free and easy ways for something quite else, and had supposed that it must arise from careless parents, who were not troubled to restrain and guide their daughter into a proper way of behaving.

She also felt a sisterly solidarity that meant she was reluctant to accuse Belle, who was, after all, already in trouble with her family. And she had an inkling that if she were the guilty party, Mr. Lisser would not be held so much at fault, whereas if he had been embracing Belle, then the guilt would be entirely his.

She wasn't quite sure why this should be, but it was. So she held her chin high and said nothing as the tide of Mr. Partington's wrath flowed over her. Once out of his presence, though, she went upstairs to her own chamber so swiftly that at the end she was positively running, anxious to reach the privacy of her room before giving way to the rage that threatened to overcome her.

She taxed Belle with it that evening, after a miserable dinner of bread and water; did her stepfather think he was living between the covers of one of those despised novels?

"It was you with Mr. Lisser, was it not?"

Belle pouted and hung her head.

"I am sure it was, so you need not trouble yourself to lie. Why do you not say so?"

A jumbled, mumbled speech came out, of her parents' dismay, of not wishing to bring any harm to Henry—

Henry, forsooth? Cassandra said to herself.

—of her fear that he might be sent away, that she might be sent away, that they might be parted; the words flowed disjointedly from Belle's pretty lips, and her violet eyes brimmed with tears.

"And what if they send me away?" said Cassandra.

Belle brightened. "Why, it would be the best thing in the world for you to be away from Rosings."

"What, under a cloud?"

"Oh, as to that, talk of clouds is all nonsense. What is a stolen kiss, after all? It is nothing so very much."

"Kisses exchanged with a person of our own order might not matter so very much, as you say, but Mr. Lisser is not in that position. Besides, to my mother and stepfather it does matter. Mr. Partington is old-fashioned in his views."

Belle cast Cassandra a long, thoughtful look. "He dislikes you, so I dare say he is building it all up, just so that he may send you away."

Cassandra was astonished that Belle should have so much insight, for she didn't care to admit to Mr. Partington's dislike of her even to herself. She and her stepfather had never got on very well, it was true, but then a man of his type and age would expect to have nothing in common with a young lady, any young lady, let alone one with a mind of her own.

"I am surprised your mother will allow him to ride roughshod over you," Belle was saying, "but it is often so in marriages. I shall make very sure that I do not marry a man who has anything of the tyrant in him. Henry has a very sweet disposition, and—"

"You need not talk of Mr. Lisser in that way, for you know that is all a hum about marriage; you would not be permitted to marry Mr. Lisser."

A mulish look came over Belle's face. "I am very tired, and I want to blow out my candle and go to sleep, so I would be obliged if you would leave me. Besides, you are supposed to stay in your own chamber, there will be more trouble for you if you are found creeping around, you will be locked in."

At any other time, Cassandra might have laughed at Belle's effrontery. Only the situation was too serious for that, and she found herself wishing with all her heart that Belle had never come to Rosings. She sat down to pen a note to Emily, to tell her what had happened, and early the next morning she had a reply.

Mrs. Partington had driven over to Mrs. Croscombe first thing, supposedly to bring her neighbour a basket of fruit from Rosings' succession houses, but in fact to bemoan the wickedness of her elder daughter, and complain how ill-natured her husband was at present.

"She will sacrifice you to have peace at home," Emily wrote, "and I believe both your parents are anxious lest this means the portrait will not be finished. Mama has said that it is all nonsense to make so much fuss, that she does not believe you at all attached to Mr. Lisser—no mention of Belle was made—and that your mama had much better take up the old plan of your going to London to stay with your cousins the Fitzwilliams."

Mr. Partington would not hear of it. What, let loose in London a girl who had shown so clearly that she had such scant respect for the conventions or what was due from a girl of her breeding? It was not to be thought of. And, while he would not speak ill of his dear wife's family, he had no very good opinion of Lady Fanny, whose life was given over to pleasure and frivolity.

Mrs. Partington roused herself to protest, "My dear, she is a very good mother to her children."

"That is as may be, but I notice that she was unable to control Mr. Darcy's daughters when they were in London last year."

"Three of the girls have made very good matches."

"Indeed, you think so? There is Miss Camilla married to a rackety man, never content to stay in England and attend to his estates, while Miss Georgina ran off with Sir Joshua, yes, I know they were married and it was all hushed up and covered over, but that does not excuse the sin. And they are obliged to live in Paris, which is a less censorious, in fact a lax city, but I would not wish for any such fate to befall any daughter of mine, nor even a stepdaughter."

"Letty married a clergyman," said his wife in placatory tones.

"That is true, but he is not sound on doctrine, he has a very liberal, free-thinking way about him, which I cannot approve. No, it will not do. London is a sink of corruption, a den of iniquity, she cannot go there."

Mrs. Partington much disliked it when her husband remembered that he was still an ordained clergyman; fortunately, except when a fit of morality came upon him, he thought more about mangel-wurzels and spring corn than about God these days.

It seemed, though, when his mind did turn to spiritual matters, that he was much more strict and rigid in his principles than he had ever been when inhabiting the parsonage at Hunsford. Then he had reproved the village girls who got into trouble, but married them just the same, large bellies and all. Now, when he heard of those who had fallen from the narrow path of virtue, he was wont to recommend hellfire and a good whipping as a suitable remedy for the sin.

"I'm sure you know best," Mrs. Partington said. "Perhaps Bath, I believe it is a very quiet, genteel place these days."

"I was on the very point of suggesting it, had you not interrupted me," he said. "She shall go to my sister Cathcart, that will be best. And I shall tell her to look around at once for a husband, it is the only thing for Cassandra, then she will pass into another's hands, and there will be no opportunity for her lax ways to be passed on to our daughters."

"No, heaven forbid," said Mrs. Partington, who hadn't considered this alarming possibility. Secretly, she thought that Mr. Partington was making too much of it all, as Mrs. Croscombe had forcefully pointed out. Yet at the same time she felt that life at Rosings might go on more agreeably without her older daughter's presence.

Mr. Partington was delighted by the opportunity to be rid of Cassandra—for once and for all, if his sister did her duty. And there was no reason why she should not. She had raised three daughters on the strictest principles, and sent three meek and dutiful young ladies off into the arms of highly respectable husbands. Well, she could do the same for the troublesome Miss Darcy. And he would no longer have to put up with that quizzical look she had, as though seeing straight through you, nor with all that haughty Darcy pride and her strong-willed ways.

"In some ways, she is very like my dear mama," murmured his wife.

"Not at all," said Mr. Partington. "Lady Catherine filled her high position with grace and a strong sense of duty. Cassandra is simply a spoilt young miss. You have indulged her too much, with all this painting and so forth, and now see what has come of it. I told you it would be so."

Chapter Five

The journey to Bath was one of more than an hundred and fifty miles, a considerable distance, and not one to be covered in a single day. Cassandra and her cousin were to change horses at the Bell in Bromley, on the first part of their journey from Hunsford, and to spend the night with their cousin Lady Fanny Fitzwilliam, in her house in Aubrey Square in London.

From London, Cassandra might very well travel on the mail, her mother had said peevishly, but Mr. Partington pursed his lips. While always keen to save his pocket, he knew it would not do, a Miss Darcy, the granddaughter of a Lady Catherine, could not travel on the mail, even accompanied by a maid. Besides, what would his sister Mrs. Cathcart say when Cassandra arrived at the posting inn instead of driving up to her front door in Laura Place, as befitted her rank in life?

Their send-off was no very merry affair. There were pleasant enough farewells for Belle, but nothing more than a few moralising words from Mr. Partington and a sad look and mournful expression on her mother's part for Cassandra, which her daughter knew had nothing to do with her missing her and everything to do with her supposedly shocking behaviour.

"I have sent an express to my sister giving her full details of this shameful affair," Mr. Partington said repressively. "So she knows what has led us to send you to Bath, do not imagine that she will receive you in any spirit of holiday."

Thank you, Cassandra said inwardly, as the groom let go the horses' heads and the carriage moved forward, to bowl down the drive, through the great gates, and along the road by the parsonage. The parson was in his garden, sweeping off his broad-brimmed, black hat and bowing as the carriage went by, and further along, as they swept through the village, Cassandra saw Emily standing in front of Mrs. Humble's shop, waving furiously as she went past. At least there was one smiling face to see her off.

Belle sat back against the squabs, looking thoroughly discontented. "It's too bad that I have to be packed off to London, just because they think you've been misbehaving and might have been a bad influence on me. I don't see the reason in that."

"They feel you would find it dull, with no one of your own age to keep you company."

"Much they know, how could it be dull with Henry there?" For a moment, Belle glowed. Then the dissatisfied look came back to her face. "Besides, I'm supposed to find it dull, I was only sent to Rosings because of the fuss everybody made about my marrying Ferdie."

"Do you still want to marry him?"

Belle cast her cousin a dark look. "Of course I do not. It does not matter whom I wish to marry, they will always say no, I am too young, I do not know what I want, on and on and on. Were they never young, were they never in love? It is too bad, and I hate them all."

The rest of the journey to London was accomplished with no mishap beyond Belle throwing a tantrum when she remembered she had left a favourite novel behind on the sofa in her room.

"I had not finished it, and it was so exciting, what am I to read now?"

"I dare say you may find a copy of it in one of the libraries, or Lady Fanny may have it, if it is a new book."

"Oh, yes, well, perhaps you are right, everyone is reading it, to be sure, and I dare say Fanny will have subscribed for it."

The carriage turned into Aubrey Square as the shadows were

lengthening across the garden in the centre of the square. Lady Fanny's children came running to the gate to greet their cousins, pursued by a harassed nursemaid, bidding them to "Give over, do, and remember your manners."

"I do not know how it is, but there is always a bustle and noise when any of the Darcy girls arrive, they are all the same," said Mr. Fitzwilliam to his wife. But he greeted his cousins affectionately enough, observing that Cassandra had grown a good deal since he'd last seen her. Belle, who knew to perfection how to please any man, be he boy or lover or staid older cousin, dimpled at him, and swept a pretty curtsy and won herself a pinched cheek and a "Well, here you are again, Cousin, and in mighty fine looks; country life suits you."

That earned him a pout and a toss of her fair hair. "It does not, not at all, it is so dull in the country I can't tell you, nothing but green and no paths that aren't muddy and hardly anyone to talk to or call on, unless you make a great trek to some other house."

He laughed, thinking how pretty and agreeable she was; while Cassandra, whom he didn't know at all well, had that Darcy look, which he never liked to see in a young woman. Pride and intelligence sat ill on feminine shoulders, he considered, look at Alethea Darcy, the image of her imperious father and a rare handful. Now thankfully married off. "They'll have trouble finding a husband for Cassandra," he said to his wife, as they made ready for bed. "She will put the men off and find she has but few suitors to choose from. Unlike Belle, who grows prettier every day."

"Who has all too much choice, with the men all wild for her as they are," said Fanny, with a yawn. She passed her earrings to her hovering maid. "Belle needs an older man, someone who will be a steadying influence."

"Cassandra will have to change her ways or she will get no husband at all, not if she makes a habit of slipping away to the shrubbery with unsuitable men. A foreign painter, I never heard of such a thing!"

"Oh, as to that, I don't believe a word of it. Very likely Anne made a mistake, you know how often she gets hold of the wrong end of a story. Cassandra has grown into a very handsome young woman; I wish she may find a husband soon, for I do not think life at Rosings can be easy for her."

Neither Lady Fanny nor Mr. Fitzwilliam cared for Anne's second husband, Mr. Fitzwilliam stigmatising him as a prosy bore and Lady Fanny of the opinion that his deep-set eyes were far too close together.

The next day, Cassandra set off for Bath, slightly wistful at not being able to spend any time in London, but consoled by Fanny's assurances that London was hot and too full of company at that time of year, and she would find Bath a delightful place for shopping and amusements. "And we shall be setting off ourselves, tomorrow," she said, giving Cassandra a soft, affectionate hug. "We are going with Belle to Pemberley, you know, for a stay of several weeks."

"Pemberley!" said Belle without enthusiasm. "More country; Lord, how bored I shall be."

Cassandra was heartily bored herself by the time she and Petifer reached Bath the next day, after a tedious if uneventful journey. There were delightful things to be seen from the carriage, but the motion was too great and their speed too fast for her to be able to make any more than the roughest sketches. She had brought a book with her, but it made her feel queasy to read, and so she sat back and let the passing landscape slip by.

She was heartily glad when they reached the final stage of their journey. As they made their way down the hill into Bath, the air thickened, the coachman was obliged to slow his horses to a walking pace, and Cassandra sat up to take in the to-ing and fro-ing of coaches and carriages and carts and riders and pedestrians. Her spirits rose. She had parted from her family in disgrace, it was true, and Mrs. Cathcart was the least amiable of her relations, but Bath must have compensations to offer to a young woman who had spent so much of her life hitherto in the quiet seclusion of the Kent countryside.

Chapter Six

Mr. Partington's sister Cathcart was a widow who had been left comfortably off, and whose life in Bath was largely taken up with gossip and religion. Life in Bath suited her exactly; genteel society, but not so grand that it would despise the relict of a successful merchant, and its daily round of meeting friends at the Pump Room, with perhaps a visit to the theatre or a ball in the evenings, for Mrs. Cathcart, although a religious woman, was no puritan.

She did, however, have stern views on the behaviour and upbringing of girls. On her visits to Rosings, she had been shocked to see how much licence was permitted to Cassandra, and had spoken to her sister-in-law about it. "If she is allowed to run wild in this way, and indulge her fancies, you will pay for it later on, for she will never find herself a husband."

She had learned with satisfaction of Cassandra's disgraceful behaviour, for she loved to be proved right in her judgements. It was a good thing they had sent the girl to Bath, before it was too late, she thought, as she devoured the shocking tale written to her in her brother's neat, small hand. Under her strict and careful guidance, the hoydenish and wilful side of her nature might be suppressed, at least enough for her to be found a suitable husband, for it was, her brother informed her, his and his wife's dearest wish that Cassandra might be married off as quickly as possible. Before she got herself into worse trouble, and, he added bluntly, so that he might be relieved of her presence at Rosings. She was a bad influence on the younger children, he feared, and would no doubt be happier in an establishment of her own, preferably at the other side of the country and under the care of a watchful and no doubt stern husband.

As soon as she received her brother's letter, Mrs. Cathcart put on her newest bonnet and sailed round to her near neighbour in Henrietta Street, a Mrs. Quail, to talk the matter over. Mrs. Quail had but one daughter, a plain girl somewhat older than Cassandra, who had recently become engaged to a worthy gentleman who had a good estate and a seat in Parliament.

Together, over several cups of tea, made by Mrs. Quail herself, for she was not inclined to hand over the key to her tea chest to any of the servants, with it the best China, and costing an amazing number of shillings the pound, the two women discussed the marriageable talent presently in Bath.

"Mr. Bedford might do. A civil, agreeable young man, but they say he is of a consumptive constitution, and while it is no bad thing to be a widow, it is best postponed for a few years in the case of such a young woman as Miss Darcy." There was always Sir Gilbert Jesperson, but somehow he did not seem to be the marrying kind, no end of keen mamas had dangled their daughters in front of him, but to no avail.

"They say," Mrs. Quail said, lowering her voice, although there were no others present in her handsome drawing room, "that he has a mistress in keeping, and that it suits him very well to remain single."

Mrs. Cathcart professed herself shocked, although the mistress came as no news to her. "In these immoral times, men do marry and keep the mistress as well, but I could not condone such behaviour. We will leave Sir Gilbert to one side."

"There is Mr. Makepiece—only he is rather old, is he not past forty?"

"An older man might do very well for my niece. She is a headstrong girl, not at all well brought up, although it pains me to say so, and an older man might suit her very well, an older man has more authority over a young wife, you know."

"I did hear, it was only a rumour, to be sure, that Mr. Makepiece has offered for Miss Carteret."

Mrs. Cathcart's eyebrows shot up. "That I had not heard." She gave a sniff. "I would have thought a mere Honourable not high enough for Lady Dalrymple's daughter, such airs as that woman gives herself, for you cannot say that a viscountcy is the same thing as an earldom."

Mr. Frankson was considered, and rejected, too much of the shop about him, although of course he was very wealthy. "I do not think my dear brother would approve the connection," Mrs. Cathcart said. "Tobacco is profitable, but low."

A pause, while both ladies took small sips of the fragrantly scented tea, and then Mrs. Quail put down her cup and gave a little cry of triumph. "I have it! Why did I not think of him at once? Mr. Wexford is come to Bath, to take the waters. He would be the very man for your niece."

"Mr. Wexford? I do not know the name, and why does he take the waters? An invalid is not a good prospect as a husband, even for my niece, for there is the question of children to be considered. Is Mr. Wexford an elderly gentleman—I assume he is a gentleman?"

"No, no, he is in his thirties, and not at all an invalid. He had a bad fall from his horse a while back, and the doctors have recommended the hot baths for his knee, which has not perfectly healed. Otherwise, he is of a sound constitution. He has a good estate not far from Bath, at Combe Magna, and is of an excellent sound family. He was engaged to be married some years ago, but the young lady, she was a Gregson, if I remember rightly, was killed in a carriage accident, a tragic affair. It was before you came to Bath, otherwise you would know all about it, and about Mr. Wexford."

Mrs. Cathcart didn't care to admit to any gaps in her knowledge. "I have heard his name and of his misfortune, of course, now you remind me. I believe he has not recently been in Bath?"

"No, but here he is now, just at this very time when we need him, what could be more fortunate?"

"You are acquainted with him, I take it?"

"Indeed, I am, for his late father and my dear husband were at Cambridge together."

"A man of some fortune, you say?"

"What my husband would call a very tidy fortune, no great wealth, but sufficient to keep a wife in comfort. Pray"—coming to the heart of the matter with feigned indifference—"what may Miss Darcy's portion be?"

"As to that, there is a son, you know, and two more daughters to be provided for."

Mrs. Cathcart was striking a delicate balance here. Whilst she knew that her brother wanted her to find a husband for Cassandra that would take her with the smallest possible share of the fortune that was to be divided among the girls by their mother, which meant in practice by Mr. Partington, she liked the consequence of having a niece, even a stepniece, who was in possession of a handsome fortune. "All these Darcys are as rich as may be," she added carelessly.

And although Mrs. Cathcart was eager to find a match for Cassandra, she would prefer that her niece didn't marry a richer man than her own daughters had. Mr. Wexford sounded as though he might do very well.

"I do not know why I did not think of him sooner," said Mrs. Quail. "And you say that your niece is a high-spirited girl—"

"I shall soon put her in a better way of behaving."

"Miss Gregson, you see, was a lively girl. So another such might well take his fancy. If you wish, I will write to him directly, my servant can very quickly find out where he lodges, and then we may arrange for a meeting. When does Miss Darcy arrive?"

Chapter Seven

Cassandra went to bed on the night of her arrival in Bath tired after the journey, and no longer in good spirits. Mrs. Cathcart was worse than she remembered her: officious, disapproving, and moralising. Cassandra had had to endure a lecture over supper on her folly, how grave could be the consequences of any straying from the true path of virtue, and how her aunt, if she might call herself so, expected conduct of the most correct kind while she was in Bath.

"For bad news travels fast, you know, and we cannot count on word of your shocking behaviour in Rosings not having already reached Bath."

Cassandra, endeavouring not to yawn, felt quite sure it had, Mrs. Cathcart would have seen to that, if she were any judge. And it was all so absurd, over an embrace in the garden that had never in fact taken place. You would think she had attempted to run off with a groom; almost she wished she had, if it had spared her the prospect of several weeks in Mrs. Cathcart's company.

"And there is to be none of that drawing and sketching and painting while you are here. My brother is strongly of the opinion that you have been allowed too much freedom in that direction, and what should be one of many accomplishments has taken on too much importance in your life."

Cassandra, before she went to bed, asked Petifer to hide the sketchbooks and crayons and water-colours and brushes she had brought with her; she wouldn't put it past her aunt to remove them if she knew about them.

The next morning, with the natural ebullience of youth, Cassandra awoke feeling that things weren't so very bad. True, there was the oppressive Mrs. Cathcart, but then there was also Bath: new sights and scenes, shops and people, and the sun was shining, and who knew what the day might bring?

The first thing the day brought was the sturdy, thin-lipped Miss Quail, come at her mother's bidding, to take Miss Darcy out for a walk, and show her something of Bath.

"Of course," said her mother, "Mrs. Cathcart will go with her to write her name in the visitors' book and all that kind of thing, but first she may learn her way around with you, for it is to be understood that she may never go out unless under supervision."

Mrs. Cathcart had, the previous evening, relieved Cassandra of the sum of money which Mr. Partington had bestowed upon her when she'd left Rosings. Since she knew to the penny how much this was, it was clear that it had been arranged beforehand. "It is not suitable for a young girl to have so much money"—it was, Cassandra thought, a miserly sum, to last her for a long stay—"so I will take care of it, and you may ask me for such small sums as you may need to disburse while you are here. There cannot be many expenses, you know, while you are my guest."

Now she gave Cassandra exactly enough to pay for a subscription at the circulating library. "I do not approve of novels, and you are not to bring any into the house"—how like her brother, Cassandra thought—"but you may borrow works of an improving nature. It is quite the thing to go to the library to exchange your books, it would be thought odd if you did not do so."

Along with her sketchbooks and paints, Cassandra had carefully hidden some money that her aunt knew nothing about. Her mother had given her ten pounds—guilt money, Cassandra thought bitterly—with an injunction not to tell her stepfather about it, it was for those little fripperies that a girl might need, which Mr. Partington didn't precisely understand.

In addition, Mrs. Croscombe had pressed a note on her, via Emily. "Mama says she is sure that Mr. P. will send you off with very little money—no, it is a present, she will be offended if you do not accept it."

And then she had some money of her own put by; although she spent most of her allowance on her materials, she had some money left to her by her godmother, paid quarterly; not a large sum, and one that Mr. Partington insisted on seeing accounts for, but accounts need not be strictly accurate.

How odd it was that strict morality led to deception and less than openness, Cassandra said to herself as she put on a straw bonnet trimmed with cherries.

The cherries did not meet with Mrs. Cathcart's approval. "Cherries? This fashion for fruit on hats is most unsuitable. Still, if you have nothing else to wear, I suppose it is not possible to remove them just now."

"Not without tearing the straw away," said Cassandra, determined at all costs to keep her cherries.

Cassandra did not take to Miss Quail, who had a solemn way about her, and a great deal of satisfaction at being an engaged woman. She brought the phrase into her conversation at every opportunity, as they walked across Pulteney Bridge and into the main part of town. "As an engaged woman, I'm sure you will allow me to tell you how one should go on in Bath. I understand you have led a very retired life until now."

"I live in the country, but I suppose I shall go on in Bath much as I would anywhere else."

"No, indeed, for within the privacy of a country estate, behaviour passes without comment, whereas in Bath, let me assure you, as an engaged woman with some knowledge of life, this is not the case at all; one cannot be too careful about one's reputation."

She lowered her voice, as if Cassandra's reputation were in danger from the mere mention of the word.

"A young girl, a young single girl, cannot be too careful," she reiterated.

They walked up Milsom Street, Miss Quail prosing on, while Cassandra's eyes were everywhere, delighting in the busy streets and shops. Somehow, she must contrive to slip out on her own, and make some purchases, which she knew her hostess would not permit.

"There are a remarkable number of people in chairs and on crutches," she observed. "That must be depressing after a while, to live in a place with so many people in poor health."

Miss Quail bristled. "It is only a small number, I assure you, there is nowhere in the whole kingdom less depressing to the spirits than Bath. At this time of day, you know, the invalids come out to go to drink the waters, or take the hot bath."

"Where will you live when you are married?" said Cassandra, not wishing to goad Miss Quail any further.

"In Bristol, my dearest Mr. Northcott lives in Bristol. Well, not in Bristol itself, not in the city, of course, he has an estate at Clifton, a house with a park around it. And we are to have two carriages," she added with pride. "I suppose you keep a carriage at your home in Kent? Mrs. Kingston tells us that Rosings is a considerable property."

Cassandra stared at her; what was this talk about carriages? "We keep a carriage, yes," she said.

"And I dare say a great many horses? Mr. Northcott has a pair of carriage horses, in addition to his own horse. Some people merely hire them, you know, but we are to have our own pair."

"Is there always such a glare from the buildings? I think Bath is very hot in summer, I wonder that people choose to come."

"Indeed, it can be rather warm, but that is partly the hot waters, you know. People say there is positively a miasma hanging over the city on some days, but I have never noticed it, I find it a very good climate. Not as good as the air of Clifton, of course, we shall be in a very good air in Clifton. Now, here we are at the library. If you put your name down, I will show you where the books are that you will want to borrow."

As she led the way to a shelf full of very dull-looking essays and sermons, she felt that here was another reason for slipping out on her own, so that she might borrow the kind of books she wanted to read.

"Why, you have chosen nothing," said Miss Quail, clutching a fat volume. From the way her hand hid the title, and she sidled away from Cassandra to have the book written down for her, Cassandra had a strong suspicion that the chosen book was a far cry from being a worthy tome such as had been recommended to her. So Miss Quail was hypocritical as well as tiresome; it didn't surprise her.

They walked to the Pump Room, where they joined Mrs. Quail and Mrs. Cathcart, and Cassandra was introduced to their numerous acquaintance, a tribe of women all very much the same as themselves, all holding themselves quite stiff in the presence of a Miss Darcy, for however much Mrs. Cathcart might talk about her brother Partington as though he were the master of Rosings, they knew that he had been a mere clergyman, whereas Cassandra was the granddaughter of a Lady Catherine, and related to an earl and other members of the nobility.

Altogether, Cassandra reflected, as she stood, head bowed, at the dinner table, while Mrs. Cathcart intoned an interminable grace, an interesting day. Not interesting in itself, but in the information it provided as to the likely course of her stay in Bath. The first, and most important, thing was to find some time to herself. Were she always to find herself in the company of Mrs. Cathcart and the Quails, she would go mad.

Cassandra, although she had learned to be careful about keeping some of her artistic pursuits out of sight of her stepfather, was not, by nature, a dissembler. Her frank and open manners were one of the characteristics that Mr. Partington disliked, and she was not entirely sure how she might go about achieving any degree of independence for herself. She felt uncomfortable being under scrutiny all the time; there must be a way to be alone.

The next day was Sunday, and here she saw an opportunity. Although Mrs. Carthcart's brother was a clergyman of the Established Church, she had married a Methodist, and she herself chose to worship among the small group who gathered at the chapel of the

Countess of Huntington, feeling that the aristocratic foundations of the Methodist sect gave it extra lustre. She rather hoped that she could require Cassandra to go with her, but here Cassandra felt on sure ground. She was a member of the Church of England, her mama would be upset to learn that she had not attended divine service at a suitable church.

"Such as the Abbey," she suggested. "I shall go to the Abbey."

And, she thought, sit at the back, and slip out while no one is looking, and have at least a chance of a walk by myself.

Mrs. Cathcart had to agree. She could not foist either of the Quails on to Cassandra, for they were also Methodists. "You must take your maid, it will not do for you to be out unaccompanied."

Nothing could suit Cassandra's purposes better, and she sallied forth to attend the service, with Petifer beside her, both of them pleased to be out of the house. "For a more witless set of servants I never saw," she told Cassandra.

They duly slipped out of the Abbey, Petifer shaking her head when she realised what Cassandra was about. They walked swiftly away from the Abbey, into one of the smaller, quieter streets on the other side of Union Street. There, after a short tussle, they parted, Petifer agreeing to spend an hour looking around the town, while Cassandra spent some time on her own.

"Don't look so put out, Petifer; you have seen for yourself how many young ladies go about alone. There won't be so very many people about at this time, they will be at home or in church until after twelve."

"Where are you going?"

"Only up Milsom Street and from there up into the Broad Walk, the air will be pleasant up there." Cassandra went briskly off, very pleased of the opportunity to stretch her legs and have the pleasure of her own company for a while. She had a small sketchbook tucked in her reticule, and after a stroll along the Broad Walk, she sat herself on a bench and became absorbed in drawing the details of the scene around her.

She felt, rather than saw, a hovering presence, and looked up. A young man was standing a few feet away, watching her intently. As she saw him, he bowed, and apologised for disturbing her.

"You do not do so, and you will not do so if you walk on," she said. He was a gentleman, by his voices and clothes. A good-looking man, with dark red hair and a pale complexion that spoke of Celtic ancestry. She wondered if he were going to make a nuisance of himself, try to scrape her acquaintance, but he took off his hat, bowed once more, and apologised again for disturbing her, then strode away.

Her work interrupted, she made an impromptu sketch of the red-headed man she had just encountered, for there was a liveliness about him that she liked. Then she returned to her earlier sketch, working diligently and, as so often when absorbed in a picture, losing all sense of time.

She was jolted out of her work by Petifer's indignant voice sounding in her ears: "I knew how it would be, once you sat down and took out that sketchbook. The service finished a good while ago, everyone is out of church now."

"We were to meet in the lower part of town," said Cassandra, as she tucked away her sketchbook and pencil.

"I knew I would still be there waiting for you an hour hence, so I came to find you."

"What time does Mrs. Cathcart return from church, do you suppose?" Cassandra asked as they set off down the hill and back towards Laura Place.

"It's a long service at that chapel she goes to, from what the servants say, and I think they talk together afterwards."

"If we hurry, we shall be home before her," Cassandra said, and quickened her pace.

Which they were, by a few moments, but that was enough for Petifer to vanish into the basement, and for Cassandra to run upstairs and whisk off her hat. As they ate a nuncheon of cold meats, Mrs. Cathcart interrogated Cassandra on the sermon she had heard, which questions Cassandra was hard put to answer, falling back in the end on memories of one of the Hunsford parson's less dull sermons. However, Mrs. Cathcart wasn't really interested in what passed for a sermon in the Church of England, and instead bored Cassandra with a detailed account of the excellent sermon that the Reverend Snook had preached.

Cassandra was startled by Mrs. Cathcart's enthusiasm for fire and brimstone and the tortures of the damned, and she wondered whether her aunt felt that she was numbered among the sinners and likely to pay for those sins in the world to come.

"Tomorrow," Mrs. Cathcart informed her, "I have arranged a treat for you."

Cassandra's heart sank.

"We are to go for a picnic, on Lansdowne. Bath is very stuffy just now, and it will do us good to breathe a fresher air for a few hours. Mrs. Quail and her daughter will accompany us, and some others. We shall be quite a little party."

Chapter Eight

Mr. Northcott, who was engaged to Miss Quail, was a stolid young man with a large nose and an air of self-consequence. Miss Quail hung upon his arm and simpered and smirked, while Mrs. Quail beamed her approval: "Such a handsome young couple, don't you think? And"—in a whisper—"an income of at least two thousand a year."

They went in an open carriage, with the young ladies sitting forward, and Mr. Northcott trotting alongside on horseback. It was a slow haul up the steep hills, but the air became noticeably better as they made the ascent, and Cassandra was, after all, glad that she had come.

Mrs. Quail had arranged a meeting place, a shady spot beneath some trees, and they were the first to arrive. "We are waiting for Mrs. Lawson and her daughter, a most amiable creature, very young, only just out of the schoolroom," Mrs. Quail told Cassandra. "And my dear friend Mr. Wexford, and a guest of his, a Mr. Eyre, I believe, make up our party. Now, here, even as I speak, is Mrs. Lawson's carriage arriving, and close on their heels Mr. Wexford and his friend."

When Cassandra had met the redheaded man on the Broad Walk, she had had no idea who he was, had supposed that she might meet him again while she was in Bath, although it seemed unlikely that he would move in Mrs. Cathcart's circle. Yet there was a kind of inevitability to this, their second meeting.

Cassandra was introduced, first to Mrs. Lawson, then to Mr. Wexford, by Mrs. Quail, and finally the man with the red hair, who had been standing back, was ushered forward with something like pride by Mr. Wexford. Mr. Wexford was very tall, very thin, and had a bland but agreeable enough countenance. Had Cassandra been asked five minutes after they were introduced to describe him, she could not have done so.

"This is Lieutenant Eyre, of the Royal Navy, who is presently staying with me, while waiting for a ship," said Mr. Wexford.

Mr. Eyre's manners were excellent, even if his mouth twitched when Mrs. Cathcart, disapproval written all over her, began to question him about his antecedents. Mrs. Quail discovered more by drawing Mr. Wexford to one side and plying him with questions about his guest.

"He seems a pleasant young man, is he cast ashore on half pay?" This was the fate of many naval officers, with the war over, and chances of promotion hard to come by.

"He is, but he has many good friends, and hopes to have another ship soon." Lowering his voice, Mr. Wexford went on, "He is the Earl of Littleton's son, you know. A younger son, he has four older brothers, and it is an Irish title, of course, but coming of a good family, being a gentleman, as it were, still carries weight in the Royal Navy, I am glad to say."

"And I am glad to hear it," cried Mrs. Quail. She was longing to ask if the young man had means of his own, or whether he had to live on the hundred or so pounds a year that the government paid a serving lieutenant when he was ashore.

"He is not a rich man," Mr. Wexford said, "but he is very good at his profession and will make his mark in the world, I am sure. He fought in some notable actions, he was on board the *Shannon,* when the *Chesapeake* was taken in the American war, were you not, James?"

Mr. Eyre took his eyes from Cassandra and laughed. "I was a midshipman you know, the lowest of the low, but, yes, I was there, it was a notable engagement, and a very bloody one."

Miss Lawson rolled her eyes in his direction, it was clear that she had taken a liking to the red-haired young man. "Were you wounded?"

"A mere scratch, nothing in comparison to some of the officers and men. But it was worth it," he added, a fine fervour showing in his face.

Mrs. Cathcart decided that she didn't care for this young man with his Irish ancestry and hair and fine manners. She almost pushed Cassandra forward, towards Mr. Wexford. "My dear, this is an historic place, as Mr. Wexford can tell you. Was not there a great battle fought here, Mr. Wexford, during the English war?"

"There was indeed," said Mr. Wexford, his face brightening. "Is Miss Darcy interested in history?"

"Indeed she is," said Mrs. Cathcart, before Cassandra had a chance to answer. Cassandra had not the slightest interest in history, was, in fact, woefully ignorant upon the subject, although she had heard tell of the Civil War in the century before last, when the king fought Parliament and lost his head as a consequence.

Mr. Wexford was not at all ignorant of the war. In fact he was appallingly well-informed, and a stream of information, from the death of Strafford to the defeat of Charles II at Worcester—"with his famous flight and hiding up an oak tree, you will know the story, Miss Darcy." He also knew every detail of the battle that had been fought on that very spot, and he expounded with enthusiasm about the positioning of the Roundhead forces, the charge that Prince Rupert had made, and the exact regiments that were involved.

Cassandra was too polite not to listen, but her eyes slid round to where Eyre was talking to Miss Lawson, what could he find to talk about in that animated way to her? She wished she might be talking to him, instead of being obliged to endure a history lesson from Mr. Wexford. Fortunately, their lunch was now spread out beneath the trees, and she could be spared any more facts and figures about what seemed to have been an interminable war.

Mrs. Cathcart took pains to make sure that Mr. Eyre was not

seated anywhere near Cassandra; her sharp eyes had noticed the effect he was having upon Miss Lawson, and even Miss Quail, while apparently listening to Mr. Northcott imparting some tedious anecdotes of the Civil War, had been giving the young man some covert glances.

Cassandra found herself sitting next to Miss Lawson, who was shy, and who turned big, anxious eyes towards Cassandra when she was addressed by her. But she grew more at ease, finding that Miss Darcy wasn't as toplofty and disagreeable as Miss Quail had said, and confided to her, as they ate a delicate honey ham pasty, that her mama had said that Miss Darcy was to make a match of it with Mr. Wexford, and was that indeed so?

Cassandra nearly choked on her food. "Why," she said in a much louder voice than she had intended, then, more quietly, "that is all nonsense, I have only met the man today, and I have no intention of marrying anyone just at present."

Colour flared into Miss Lawson's cheeks. "Oh, I am sorry, then, to have spoken as I did. I must have misunderstood. So many girls come to Bath looking for husbands, you know, and they say Mr. Wexford is a very good catch, for he is quite rich. Only, he's rather old, don't you think?"

"In his thirties, I would imagine," Cassandra said, having recovered her calm. "Too old for one of your years, perhaps, or indeed for me, but he will do very well for some young woman of six- or seven-and-twenty who may be looking out for a husband."

"La, would he marry such an old maid?" said Miss Lawson, looking shocked. "My mama says I'm too young to be thinking of a husband, for I am but seventeen, but my best friend from school was married at seventeen, indeed on her seventeenth birthday, do not you think that odd?"

Lunch was over, and a walk was agreed upon, a gentle walk of a mile or two along the ridge would offer them a most astonishing view. "And I can show you where the Royalist army camped the night before the battle," Mr. Wexford said to Cassandra.

Quite how it happened, Cassandra was never sure, but as the

group walked along the lane, Mr. Wexford fell into deep conversation with Mrs. Cathcart, Mrs. Quail kept up with them, wanting to hear what they were saying, Mrs. Lawson, no great walker, fell behind, and then said she would rest on the bank, and await their return; that her daughter would stay with her—at which what was almost a pout might be seen on Miss Lawson's pretty face—and so it was that Cassandra found herself walking beside the gallant lieutenant.

How different his conversation was from that of any man she had known. He was witty and droll, and told stories about naval life that were about other men, not about himself. He drew her out, but in a courteous way, that could give no offence, asked her about her drawing—"For when I saw you on Sunday, you were sketching, were not you?"—and said that he had met a Miss Darcy, a Miss Isabel Darcy, in London; was she a relation? An entrancing creature," he said, "and I am sure I heard that she was engaged to a Mr. Roper."

"Nothing came of that," Cassandra said. "There never was anything in it. She has lately been staying with us. Are you making a long stay in Bath, Mr. Eyre?"

"I wasn't," he said at once, "but I find that there are one or two things that may keep me in the area for a little while yet."

Chapter Nine

Cassandra was in love. It had come to her as a bolt from the blue, but by the end of the picnic, she was aware that she had never taken such pleasure in any man's company as she did in Mr. Eyre's. For her, it was a new world, as though the sun had suddenly come out from behind dark clouds, illuminating everything; her life was at once full of joy, combined with a heightened awareness of the world about her. Bird-song sounded sweeter than it ever had, the green of the trees was more intense than she had ever seen it, and people around her looked to be as glad to be alive as she was.

"Is it not a wonderful day?" she said to Petifer when her maid drew back the curtains around her bed and opened the shutters.

Petifer took a sceptical glance out of the window at a blustery Bath day, and sniffed. She knew quite well what was up with her mistress, and she was much alarmed—only what could she do about it? Caution Miss Darcy? As well caution the wind or the waves as try to bring someone down to earth who felt the way Cassandra did. Drat that man for being in Bath, and for being so handsome and charming and so obviously delighted by her mistress.

It was a strange, secretive courtship. Cassandra quickly learned to be inventive and, she thought ruefully, two-faced. Her former self would have deplored such behaviour in anyone else, and, looking back to her days at Rosings, she would have told anyone who suggested that she might ever behave in such a way, that it was impossible, preposterous.

And to do it all for a man, she, who had thought it possible, nay, likely that she would never marry, who scorned her friends as they laid aside their childish habits of girlhood, their Amazon ways, to pretty themselves and simper, and regard every single man as a potential husband.

At least that she had never done. If she'd been on the lookout for a husband, Mr. Wexford, who was clearly very taken with her, would have been the better choice, in any worldly sense.

That was how she'd been able to deceive the wily, watchful Mrs. Cathcart. Mr. Wexford liked Cassandra, sought out her company, suggested to Mrs. Cathcart that her niece might attend a ball or a supper party, or an outing of pleasure or a picnic, or a walk among ruins, or along shady paths or up hills to gaze out at the surrounding countryside. All good schemes for dalliance, only, where Mr. Wexford went, there, too, went his good friend Mr. Eyre. Mr. Wexford was uncommonly proud of James Eyre, openly envious of his naval career, looking up to him as a much cleverer man than he was, and admiring his ready wit and savoir faire.

Mrs. Quail uttered words of warning; she heard from Miss Quail how often Cassandra and Eyre wandered off, while Mr. Wexford happily stayed with the rest of the party, talking about his everlasting battles and campaigns. So much so that Miss Quail was moved to protest: Why did he not become a soldier himself? Then he could fight battles and skirmishes and engagements on his own account, and spare them the details of all that long-ago warfare.

This rebellious outburst astonished her mother, who said reprovingly that she was picking up Miss Darcy's outspoken ways, and she wanted to hear no more such comments about Mr. Wexford, who was as civil, agreeable a man as ever lived. But if what her daughter said was true, that Mr. Eyre was intent on cutting out his friend with Cassandra, then Mrs. Cathcart must be told.

"I would not do so," said Miss Quail, smarting under her mother's reproof. "Mrs. Cathcart will see what she wants to see, and

Mr. Wexford is monstrous taken with Miss Darcy, although I cannot see what there is about her to make the gentlemen admire her. She flirts with Mr. Eyre, but she will marry Mr. Wexford."

Her words gave her mama pause for thought, and she held her tongue, watched Cassandra with a hawkish eye, and, thanks to Cassandra's well-bred manners and natural reserve, concluded that it was no more than flirtation. Not that she would care to see any daughter of hers carrying on in such a way.

She would have been shaken if she had seen Mr. Eyre and Miss Darcy slip away while on an outing to the Sydney Gardens, on a summer evening when scent of the flowers hung heavy in the air, and fireworks distracted everyone's attention; only Miss Quail noticed the brightness of Cassandra's eyes as she looked about her and then removed herself unobtrusively from their company.

How almost delirious with happiness Cassandra had been, when she found herself in James's arms, to meet his lips with hers, to lose herself in a passionate embrace and give herself up to those sensations which were so wholly new to her. And the happiness lasted when they parted, and she arrived back to join the others, a little breathless, her eyes aglow, her heart pounding. That night she hardly slept, as the intense joy of knowing that she loved and was loved was beyond anything she had ever known.

And two nights later, Mrs. Cathcart had found her locked in a passionate embrace in the best parlour. Wrapped up in one another, whispering words of love and ardour when their lips reluctantly parted, they had not heard the approaching footsteps, the door handle turning. By the time they sprang apart, it was too late, a furious Mrs. Cathcart was in the room, a torrent of abuse pouring out of her; Cassandra was no better than a whore, fit to be whipped at the cart's end, a drab, fie on her for bringing her sluttish ways into a respectable household, while James, horrified, sidled to the door and escaped.

Mrs. Cathcart's remedy for such wickedness was simple. She locked Cassandra in her room, forbade all the servants to speak to her, and took her a tray of bread and water morning and evening. She had written to her brother Partington, how angry he and Mrs. Partington would be to hear of this further disgrace, Cassandra was beyond redemption, if she were her stepfather, she would whip her and then have her shut up in an asylum, for she must be mad to behave in such a way.

Cassandra, hungry, defiant, and contemptuous of Mrs. Cathcart's melodramatic outbursts, dropped a note out of the window into Petifer's hands. Mrs. Cathcart had plans to send her off the next day by coach to Rosings, she wrote. James's reply, bringing the offer of his hand and a dash to Gretna Green, was slipped under her door after her hostess had retired to bed.

Marriage! Did she want to be married? To be in love was intoxicating, but could it last a lifetime? a voice of caution in her head asked her. How right Emily had been, when she'd predicted that Cassandra would one day meet a man who would mean more to her than her art or anything else in her life; surely that man was James?

Chapter Ten

Now here she was in London, alone, with little money and no friends or acquaintances to ask for help. She must stop dwelling on what was past, even though her heart still ached from her betrayal by James Eyre, from the knowledge that her lover's affection for her was not equal to hers for him, that prudence had ruled his emotions as it had not hers.

It was time to take stock of her situation and start planning her future. Life must go on. First, she decided, she should return to her lodgings, and collect her few belongings before moving elsewhere. That in itself seemed an insuperable problem, she had not the least idea how to go about finding respectable new lodgings.

She looked at the window on the other side of the doorway into the shop. There were prints and two paintings on display; looking at a water-colour of a collection of flowers, she told herself that she could do very much better than that, and if such paintings might be sold, then why not hers?

Cheered up by this, she opened the shop door and went inside, a bell proclaiming her arrival to the wrinkle-faced man who came bustling into the shop from an inner room. The air smelt of linseed oil and varnish, and gave Cassandra comfort. This was a familiar world, and one where she might find a truer base for happiness—if not survival.

She bid the shopkeeper good day, in her pleasant, well-bred

voice. He glanced behind her, expecting, Cassandra knew, to see an accompanying maid or a companion of some kind.

She would begin with a purchase.

Mr. Rudge had the new blocks of water-colour, and she had to restrain her impulse to buy a boxful; she must take care of her money now. Then a chance mention of Herr Winter brought a smile and a gleam to the faded blue eyes of the shopkeeper. Herr Winter had long been a customer, a friend, he would venture to say, such a shame that he had had to leave London.

Of course, for any acquaintance of his, a pupil, did she say . . . ? Indeed, then it was a privilege to help, and Cassandra found that the prices were suddenly less than had originally been quoted.

"Is there anything more I can do for you?" he asked, as he made a neat brown paper parcel of her small purchases.

She hesitated. "Perhaps. I am to make a little stay in London, and my friends, with whom I was to stay, are longer out of town than they had planned," she said, improvising rapidly. Did he know of some respectable woman who let out rooms?

He pursed his lips, and shook his head from side to side. "Not that would be suitable for a lady of quality," he said regretfully.

It was an impasse, for she could hardly claim not to be what she so obviously was.

The bell tinkled, and a middle-aged woman, of smart appearance, dressed in bombazine, came into the shop. Cassandra stood to one side, hoping to have a further word with the proprietor when he had finished with this new arrival, who seemed to be an honoured customer. The design for a screen was ready, she would wish to see it and approve before any more work was done on the panels. He hurried into the back, and reappeared with several sheets of paper intricately worked with a pattern of peacocks and urns.

An unbalanced design, Cassandra said to herself, but she said nothing.

Mrs. Nettleton—for that was how Mr. Rudge addressed her—studied and questioned and approved. Then she turned and smiled at Cassandra.

"I am sorry to have interrupted your business here; I had thought you were finished."

Her voice was ladylike, and her smile was pleasant but not over-familiar.

"No, pray do not worry. I have made my purchases, I was linger-ing to ask Mr. Rudge about another matter."

"A pupil of Herr Winter's," Mr. Rudge told Mrs. Nettleton. "I mention it, for you bought one of his paintings some years ago, a fine work, on a mythological theme, if I remember correctly. Miss"—he looked enquiringly at Cassandra—

"Kent," she said quickly.

"—is but recently come to town, but finds herself at a stand for lodgings, her friends not having returned as soon as they were expected. Your best course," he said, addressing Cassandra, "will be to put up at one of the hotels."

Mrs. Nettleton nodded her approval, but the look she gave Cas-sandra was shrewd and appraising.

"Do you live far from London?"

More invention came into Cassandra's head. "I have come from Bath, where I resided until recently. I am a widow, my husband was wounded at Waterloo, and was never well again, and he died last year. From his wounds. My friends, Mr. and Mrs. Fortescue, dwell in Wimpole Street." Cassandra had little idea of where Wimpole Street was, but had heard Emily describe it as the kind of place where maiden aunts with no great social position or money often chose to live.

Mrs. Nettleton looked faintly surprised. "Wimpole Street? Indeed. I would have thought . . . but that is no matter. Are there no servants at home?"

"The knocker is off the door. They have been away in Scotland, but were due to return last week; I can only conclude they have been delayed. I hope no mishap can have befallen them."

"Is your stay in London to be of some while?" Mrs. Nettleton asked.

Cassandra blushed. "I intend to establish myself here, I am well-taught as an artist, and I hope that I may find employment instructing young ladies"—she turned with a smile to Mr. Rudge—"as Herr Winter did me."

"Have you no family in London, no other acquaintance?" Mrs. Nettleton said.

"I fear not. My parents are dead, I have no brothers or sisters." Cassandra felt a momentary qualm, consigning her mama to the grave, but she didn't want Mr. Rudge to pursue the subject of her family; it was best to keep away from the county of Kent.

Mrs. Nettleton searched in her reticule and produced a card, which she handed to Cassandra. It was engraved in an elegant copperplate, and gave her address as 7 St. James's Square.

"It so happens that I have a room which I let out from time to time, only to ladies of good family, and generally to persons I know. My house is large, and I am glad of the company that a lodger provides. It is a comfortable apartment, on the second floor."

Cassandra stared at the card and then looked up at Mrs. Nettleton. Could her problem be solved in this fortuitous way?

"You know nothing about me," she said.

"Mr. Rudge vouches for your master, at least, and I am sure Herr Winter would instruct none but those who came from the best houses, is that not so, Mr. Rudge?"

"Indeed, a man of Herr Winter's standing and reputation might pick and choose where he chose to teach, and I did hear that he has pupils at several great houses in his neighbourhood. . . ." Mr. Rudge looked questioningly at Cassandra.

"That is so," said Cassandra. "But he also instructs young people from more modest establishments, such as myself. My late papa was a clergyman."

Why had she not thought to say that sooner? It was not so far from the truth as some of her wicked lies, for was not her stepfather, although still alive, an ordained clergyman?

The clerical touch worked magic. Mrs. Nettleton and Mr. Rudge beamed approval. She was placed, she was respectable.

"Pray step round at any time to suit you," said Mrs. Nettleton. "You have my direction. Where are you staying at present?"

"With my old nurse, in Parker Street, but it is not precisely convenient for her. . . ."

"And not suitable for a young lady such as yourself," said Mrs. Nettleton firmly. "I have a numerous acquaintance; perhaps it will be possible for me to find some houses with daughters in need of a drawing teacher."

"I will keep my ears open, also," promised Mr. Rudge, "although it is an overcrowded profession, especially here in London. However, a pupil of Herr Winter's would come highly recommended, I feel sure."

The two women left the shop together, shaking hands as they stood outside on the pavement.

"I hope to see you soon, my dear Mrs. Kent," said Mrs. Nettleton. "Shall we say tomorrow morning?"

Cassandra walked back to Covent Garden with a lighter heart than she had had for many days. Even the hostility of Mrs. Dodd, who was not her old nurse at all, but James Eyre's, could not upset her that evening. Mrs. Dodd thoroughly disapproved of her, for she had a great fondness for James, as was only natural, and knew that he and Cassandra had had a violent quarrel. Cassandra suspected that only the knowledge that Mr. Eyre would expect to find Cassandra there when he came back prevented Mrs. Dodd from tossing her and her possessions out into the street. She was grateful for that small mercy, but nonetheless, she must be gone before James did return. He was in Ireland, to visit a sick godfather, from whom he had expectations; he had said he would be away less than a week, and that time was nearly up.

She had arrived at Parker Street in Covent Garden in quite a different mood to that of the present. Their departure from Bath had been sudden and thrilling, slipping out from Laura Place at midnight, the door left on the latch for her by a reluctant Petifer, with the few things she could bring with her hastily made into a bundle.

She had left a note for Mrs. Cathcart, saying that she was bound for Gretna Green; this she had laid on her own pillow, knowing that by the time it was discovered in the morning, she and James would be many miles on their way northwards.

It was not until the first raptures of their journey had abated, that Cassandra had discovered they were not heading for the border.

"On reflection, my love," James had said, "I came to the conclusion that we are better off in London. It will be harder for them to trace or follow us, you know, and after all we do not wish to be hauled back like a pair of school runaways. In London, we may make our plans without any fear of interference."

Cassandra would willingly have accepted a suggestion that they set off for the steppes or the wilds of Turkestan, if that had been what James wanted. He was older than she was, and much more experienced in the ways of the world. And the last thing she wanted was to find Mrs. Cathcart banging on an inn door on the road to Scotland, summoning her for retribution and separating her from James.

She asked whether they could be married so easily in London, since she was underage, but he smiled at her tenderly, and said that anything could be arranged in London, she was to leave it all to him. It might take a little time to arrange, but as long as they were together, what did a few days matter?

"We had best tell Mrs. Dodd that we are married, however," he said. "I do not suppose you have a ring you could wear, no, of course not. We must stop and purchase one, only I am very short of funds just at present. It's a dashed nuisance."

"I have my mother's wedding ring," Cassandra said. "Will Mrs. Dodd believe that you are married, with no announcement of an engagement or a wedding?"

"She is used to my impulsive ways, and when she meets you, she will love you as much as I do, and not ask any awkward questions, you need have no fears on that score."

Mrs. Dodd did not seem exactly enthusiastic over their arrival, but she was obviously fond of James, if suspicious of Cassandra. "You're in a scrape, James, and too old for me to get you out of it as I used to when you were a little boy. You may have the best bedchamber, you and the new Mrs. Eyre."

Even if there was a hint of sarcasm in Mrs. Dodd's voice, it warmed Cassandra's heart to be called Mrs. Eyre. And an idyllic night of love with her beloved James made her care even less when and how their marriage was to take place. She was living for the moment, and these moments were filled with rapture and happiness. In the daytime, they strolled arm in arm about London, exploring and laughing together. He told her tales of his nautical life, and she hung on his every word. She gave him all her money, although it seemed sadly depleted; she must have spent more in Bath than she had thought.

"It's only a temporary difficulty," James said. "I shall come back from Ireland with full pockets, and this will last us meanwhile."

Cassandra could not bear to be parted from him. "Must you go to Ireland?"

"I wouldn't leave you dear heart, not for an hour, if it were not necessary. My godfather has not been well for some years, and he looks forward to my visits, I cannot disappoint him. And you know, he has named me in his will, I do not want to incur his displeasure. I shall leave on Tuesday, and be back by that day se'ennight, if I travel fast."

What a fool she had been, how wrapped up in her love and in James! Cassandra looked about the best bedchamber with an aching sadness; how could she imagine that her dream could shatter in such a way?

"Shall we be married when you return from Ireland?" she had asked him.

"I have it all in hand, do not concern yourself about it." He gave her a hearty kiss. "I am going to leave you in here for an hour, no more, for I have some business to conduct, and Mrs. Dodd has given me the use of her parlour. I beg you will not stir from here, do not come downstairs, for I would not have you seen."

"Is this business with someone I know?" she asked in a teasing voice.

"No, why should it be? Of course not. What put such an idea in your head?"

"Do not snap at me, it was a remark, I do not mean to meddle in your private affairs."

"My affairs are your affairs, but in matters of business, you know, one deals face-to-face, and does better with no distractions." Another kiss, and he was gone, shutting the door firmly behind him.

The room overlooked a small yard, in which grew a mulberry tree. Cassandra opened the casement as wide as it would go and sat herself down on the wide window seat with her sketching book, happy to spend an hour catching the exact shape of a leaf, and, more difficult, the movement of the leaves in the slight breeze.

It was a hot day. The sun shone down on the garden, and the sounds of London, the city that was never still, never quiet, were all around her. She could hear voices, someone singing a popular catch, someone bawling out the details of sweetmeats he had to sell, a groom talking to a horse. Closer now, that was James's voice, coming up from the room below; the window downstairs must be open, too. She smiled, just the timbre of his voice made her feel warm inside.

She stiffened, as another voice reached her ears. An all too familiar voice. No, it couldn't be, it was impossible, it was another man who sounded the same, that was all. She kneeled on the window seat and leant out as far as she could. James and whoever he was with had moved closer to the window downstairs, now she could hear them more clearly.

Good God, she was not mistaken. Mr. Partington was there, downstairs, talking to James. He had traced her, how was it possible? Her heart was thumping, and she bit her lip, should she run downstairs, be at James's side?

Her reason, striking with cold clarity, told her that this was no unforeseen encounter. James had known that Mr. Partington was coming. There had been an appointment, her stepfather was expected, this was no sudden discovery.

No, she cried to herself, inside her head, no, that wasn't right. James had gone down to see someone else, and then, out of the blue, in had walked Mr. Partington.

Nonsense, said her reason, and now her ears confirmed it. She could hear what they were saying; Mr. Partington had raised his voice, was almost shouting at James. Who seemed to be keeping his temper admirably, but what was he saying?

She sat and listened numbly, unable to take in James's betrayal. Yes, he would marry her, but if, and only if . . . and not until he had assurances, written settlements, lawyers' letters, stating that Cassandra came to him with a fortune. With, in fact, twenty thousand pounds. Yes, they were living together as man and wife; no, he would not be stigmatised as a rogue, for he would let it be known that Miss Darcy had made all the running, had fallen so desperately in love with him that she would live with him upon any terms. Her name would be dragged through the mud, not his, for that was the way of the world.

Horror crept over Cassandra. This could not be James speaking, her merry, open-hearted, kind James.

Only it was. There it was. He didn't mind whether he married her or not, but he could not marry a woman without money, so, if she had no fortune, then she would have no wedding ring put upon her finger by James Eyre. No, Mr. Partington need not bluster and talk of prosecution for abduction of a minor, that would simply ensure that the tale spread more quickly. "The broadsheets, you know, sir," James said. "They love a scandal of this nature."

More furious words from Mr. Partington, which she could not quite catch, and then the sound of James's laughter, the laughter that had so enchanted her. And he seemed genuinely amused. No, Mr. Partington might try to break him, but it would not wash. He had no ship, was a half-pay lieutenant, but he still had friends and his family had influence enough to make sure his career would not suffer.

Then the two men below moved away from the window, and Cassandra heard no more.

She had heard quite enough, and although it was half an hour before James came bounding up the stairs and burst into the room in the best of spirits, it seemed to her as though only minutes had passed.

"Well, my dearest," he began, "there is my business concluded, and most successfully, too."

The words echoed in her ears as she began to sort out her possessions, her few possessions. The row that ensued had been so passionate, so vehement, that it brought Mrs. Dodd to the door, banging and shouting out to be heard, fearful that they were killing one another. Then James had thrown some clothes into a portmanteau and stormed out, he was leaving for Ireland directly, anything to get away from such a shrew; when he returned, all would be settled and they would marry directly. "Only you will enact me no such scenes when we are wed, by God you will not."

No, indeed, she wouldn't, for they wouldn't be wed.

She had sat down, his angry words ringing in her head, to write a note to Mr. Partington. He would be staying at Aubrey Square, she had heard a mention of Mr. Fitzwilliam's name. She asked him to wait on her, she had something of the first importance to say.

Back came a curt, impersonal note. Mr. Partington had no wish to see or speak to Miss Darcy, now or ever again. Any communications would henceforth be through a lawyer, and any letter to her mother would be torn up, burnt, destroyed, unread.

She wasn't going to dwell on it. These memories were bitter, she must lock them away, she had enough to do in the present, there was no time to let what was past take up her thoughts and energies. Her immediate need was money; were she to take the room offered by Mrs. Nettleton, she might be expected to pay in advance. All the money she had in the world was the few coins in her purse.

She could go back to Mr. Horatio Darcy and ask for an advance on her income, but she would much rather not. She had had enough of her cousin with his supercilious ways and scorn, thank you.

As she shook out a pelisse, something fluttered to the floor. A note! It was the money that Emily had given her, from Mrs.

Croscombe. She had been right in her calculations, she had not spent so much in Bath. Thank God she had not found it sooner, thank God it had been caught up in the pelisse which was too warm to wear in this hot weather, and not in a muslin scarf or dress, where she would have discovered it at once, and handed it over to James.

Chapter Eleven

⁓⁓❦⁓⁓

St. James's Square was situated between Piccadilly and the Thames, a big square with a railed garden in the centre; Cassandra was impressed by its size and elegance. Many of the fine houses, built in the last century, and with the characteristic handsome sash-windowed façades of that time, were let out as lodgings, since the more aristocratic and richer families now preferred to have their London houses in the fashionable squares and streets of Mayfair, further to the north.

Number seven was on the south side. Cassandra lifted the big brass knocker, shaped in the form of a dolphin, and was admitted by a tidily dressed maid, who bobbed a curtsy and said that her mistress was expecting her. Cassandra followed the maid up the wide staircase and through double doors into the drawing room to be greeted by Mrs. Nettleton, dressed in a morning gown, who came forward to greet her in the kindest way.

"I am so glad you are come, now sit down, and Betsy will bring us a pot of coffee directly. Do you like coffee? Yes, I was sure you were a coffee drinker, I can always tell."

The room was furnished with green covers and hangings, and done up with some style. Cassandra's eyes went first to the pictures, none of which she found particularly interesting; most were on mythological themes, with a preponderance of scantily clad nymphs and some saucy-looking cupids. However, there was a landscape above the fireplace that she could admire: a pastoral scene, done in the rococo manner, with shepherds and shepherdesses dallying beside a gently flowing river while their woolly charges frolicked in a grassy meadow behind them. She would not herself have had the simpering figures, but the natural part of the scene was exquisitely done.

Mrs. Nettleton was as pleasant as she had seemed the day before. She drew Cassandra out, asking about her drawing and painting, and said that as soon as she were settled, were she to decide that the accommodation met with her approval, then she must, positively must, show Mrs. Nettleton some of her efforts.

Coffee came, and was drunk, and then Mrs. Nettleton took Cassandra upstairs to view the room. It was a large room on the second floor, and overlooked the garden to the rear of the house.

"It is quieter, you see, on this side, for although St. James's Square is not half as busy as some in London, there is always some noise, of carriages and people coming and going, and then at night, there are the night carts, you know. So it will be more peaceful for you here, and young people need their sleep, and you are young, for all that you are a widow. It is sad to see such a young widow, for you can hardly be more than one-and-twenty."

Cassandra smiled, and said, yes, she was but one-and-twenty. She had an idea that it would be better for Mrs. Nettleton to think she was of age. She preferred, she added truthfully, not to speak of her late, dear husband, as she found it upset her too much.

That should put a stop to any awkward questions. The trouble with lies was that once started, the fiction had to be continued, and it was hard always to be remembering details that you had made up upon the spur of the moment.

She was delighted with the room, and couldn't believe her good fortune. With a little money in hand, and a comfortable roof over her head, she could begin to make her way in London. With some diffidence she enquired about terms, and was surprised at how reasonable the rent was.

"I do not wish to make money, you know; as I say, I like to have a lodger because it livens up the house, so big as it is, and only me and the servants, and from time to time my young nieces who come to stay, I have a vast number of relations, and their mamas are very keen to have their daughters come to London and be under my care. However, just now, I have no guests, and if you will dine with me on some evenings, then you will be obliging me, and you may meet some interesting people, for my little dinner parties are quite famous. I also hold card parties from time to time, but I will understand if you do not wish to join me for those, since the stakes are often quite high, and if you are at present living on slender means . . ."

Cassandra assured her that her means were indeed slender, quite sufficient to pay the rent, but not to gamble with. "I must take care of what I have."

"Why, as to that, I have no doubt that I shall very soon fix you up with the best imaginable position—as a drawing instructor, I mean. Such an one as yourself, with your ladylike ways and good looks, for I assure you those count in any employment; who would choose to have ugly people about them, while they might look on beauty?"

Cassandra's private opinion was that anyone who employed her to teach their children would not care how plain she looked; in fact, she had a very good idea that mothers, at least, might prefer to have their governesses and people of that kind as unprepossessing as possible. She would dress simply and keep a severe expression on her face when she went for interviews.

Without knowing it, a severe look came over her face as she was thinking this, and it caused Mrs. Nettleton to give her a sharp look. "It is quite extraordinary, I do not know if you are related to anyone of the name of Darcy, for upon my word, you do have a look of Mr. Darcy of Pemberley! Not that I have ever met the gentleman, although I have many aristocratic friends, he is not one of those . . . we do not move in the same circle. However, there was recently a portrait of him that I saw exhibited at Somerset House. A very fine likeness, everyone said, and for a moment the similarity was striking. As to expression, of course, rather than feature."

Cassandra was filled with alarm. If she were to be recognised wherever she went as a Darcy, then it would be hard to keep up the pretence of being Mrs. Kent, of Bath. Best to tell something of the truth. "I have a distant cousin, much older than I am, of quite a different generation, whose mother was a Darcy, and I am said to be very like her. Her relationship to the Mr. Darcy of whom you speak must be slight, for she comes of a younger branch of the family; they live in Westmoreland.

"That accounts for it," said Mrs. Nettleton, seemingly satisfied, but she was not yet finished with the Darcys. "Mr. Darcy is famous for his daughters, five of them, only imagine, with barely a few years between them, they were all in London last year, taking the town quite by storm. He has younger boys, a relief for him after such a troop of daughters, I dare say. He married beneath him, quite a nobody the present Mrs. Darcy, she was a Miss Bennet, I think, before her marriage."

Cassandra smiled politely, trying to look as people did when listening to gossip about a set of persons that they neither knew nor cared about.

"Three of the girls married last season. One to Wytton, that was a fine catch, even for a Darcy, although he has a reputation for being an eccentric, his father was just the same. The eldest girl married a clergyman, that was no very great match, when you consider her name and fortune. And a younger sister ran off with Sir Joshua Mordaunt, whom I am very well-acquainted with. It was all hushed up, of course, and they are married and living in Paris, no one minds what you do in Paris."

Cassandra was somewhat alarmed to learn of Mrs. Nettleton's friendship with Sir Joshua; anything that was associated with her family spelt danger for her, she felt. So she was relieved when Mrs. Nettleton went on to say that it was some years now since she had seen Sir Joshua, and then it had merely been to pass the time of day. "For, before he ran off with the Darcy girl, which was quite shocking in itself, he being so much older than her, he had in keeping a French lady, who lived in the country where he has an estate. Indeed, she was still there, under his protection, even while he was whisking Miss Georgina off to France!"

Why this fact should have meant that Mrs. Nettleton only passed the time of day with Sir Joshua, Cassandra wasn't quite sure. Perhaps Mrs. Nettleton was a woman with a strong moral sense, in which case, she must make doubly sure that she never found out about Cassandra's own disastrous elopement.

"You have brought some of your things, I see," Mrs. Nettleton went on. Her eyes swept around the room, which was prettily furnished. "You will need another table in here, for your drawing and painting, I will see to it directly. Then you can arrange for the rest of your boxes to be sent here."

That might be awkward, since Cassandra had only what she had carried away with her from Bath. She could hardly ask Mrs. Cathcart to send the rest of her clothes on, nor send a request to Rosings, not judging by the way any communication from her would be consigned to the fire, she had Mr. Partington's word for that. Well, she would write to Emily, she was sure that Emily, while she would be deeply shocked at what Cassandra had done, would stand her friend on this. She could ask her mother, Mrs. Croscombe, to intercede at Rosings; what use would her things be to anyone there?

She had better do that at once, before the week was out, and Horatio Darcy, not hearing from her, would write to Mr. Partington to tell him of Cassandra's refusal to accept her stepfather's terms. While there was still hope of her marriage, her possessions, and especially all her work, stored in the studio in the East Wing at Rosings, might be safe from Mr. Partington's fury.

She asked Mrs. Nettleton if she might have a sheet of paper and a pen, so that she could write for her boxes to be sent up to London.

"Of course, there is paper and ink in this little writing table here. When it is ready, leave it on the hall table downstairs, and I will get it franked for you, I have many friends who can frank letters from me."

Cassandra smiled politely and sat herself down at the desk. Leave an addressed letter downstairs for Mrs. Nettleton to see the direction? No, she would write small, and pay for the postage for herself, even if she had to watch every penny, that would be sixpence well spent.

An hour later, she was on her way out into the square, relishing the warmth, and feeling in better spirits than she had for many days. The pain at the loss of her love for James, and the anger at herself for allowing herself to be so taken in—she, who prized herself on her sense and reason!—was a lurking unhappiness, but she had no time to indulge in feelings of regret or sorrow. That was the past, she must now look to her future.

Chapter Twelve

Mrs. Nettleton was eager for Cassandra to dine with her and some friends that very evening, but Cassandra politely refused the invitation. "For I have nothing suitable to wear," she explained.

Mrs. Nettleton put her head on one side. "That not need bother you, for my nieces leave clothes here, and something may fit you."

How odd, Cassandra thought. What kind of a niece left gowns behind? Besides, she did not wish to wear some stranger's garments. Mrs. Nettleton was insistent, however. "Lord Usborne comes to dine, he can frank your letter, then you will soon have your own clothes and necessities. But meanwhile, you must allow me to provide what you need."

Cassandra would not have it. "I am tired, and not fit for company," she said.

Mrs. Nettleton gave her a searching glance, and this reason appeared to satisfy her. "Indeed, you are not in your best looks, there is a weariness about your eyes. You shall dine off a tray in your room, I will send up a supper for you on a tray."

Cassandra was touched by this kindness, and there was a slight catch in her voice as she thanked Mrs. Nettleton.

"I dare say London is very strange to you just now, but you will grow used to it very soon. Give me your letter—oh, you posted it while you were out?" She laughed. "It will seem strange to you to ask for a frank, but I assure you, my friends are very willing to do this small favour for me, and will do so for any guest of mine."

She noticed the parcel that Cassandra was carrying, and looked a question.

"Some paints that I needed; Mr. Rudge is an expert colourist, I find."

"And I see you took your sketchbook with you, how I admire such industry. May I see?"

With a little reluctance, but how could she refuse when Mrs. Nettleton was being so very kind? Cassandra handed her the sketchbook. She had spent part of the afternoon in St. James's Park, admiring the walks and the views, and had done some charming drawings of a man asleep on a bench, with details of water lilies and birds upon the water in front of him.

Mrs. Nettleton's eyes narrowed. "Upon my word, Mrs. Kent, I can see that you were indeed taught by a master! Pray tell me, how do you like my pastoral scene there, above the fireplace?"

"I like it extremely."

"Have you ever done such a work?"

"Not in precisely that style. But I have done frescoes, I painted a series of panels around a parlour at . . . at a great house near to where I lived."

"Fresco? That is where you paint on to plaster, is it not?"

"Yes."

Another searching look. "It is not usual, I believe, for young ladies to take their artistic skills beyond drawing and water-colours. Do you also paint in oils?"

"I have done so. I have some talent, and it was encouraged, and Herr Winter was perfectly willing to teach me all he knew. I never imagined how grateful I would be to him, but now that I am obliged to earn my living, I will need more than a mere accomplishment."

Mrs. Nettleton appeared lost in thought. "I have a morning room," she said. "It would be monstrous pretty to have it decorated with scenes from nature, trees and flowers and birds and so on, with some nymphs and swains as well. Pray, come and see the room, and tell me what you think."

Cassandra looked around the small room, which was on the ground floor, looking over the garden. "The light is good, and one could give the impression that it is an ante-room to the garden itself," she said, prowling round the room. "It could be done in the Italianate style, with an impression of stonework, a balustrade, for example, leading the eye towards the garden."

Mrs. Nettleton looked pleased. "Then you have your first commission. I shall wish to see your designs, first, and then, if I like what you propose, which I am sure I shall, then you may set to work. It might suit you to pay your rent in this manner, I should much prefer it to the guineas."

Cassandra didn't hesitate. She knew that Mrs. Nettleton would be getting a bargain, but the joy of working on this scale, and the knowledge that she could thus stretch her meagre resources a little further clinched the matter.

"You will obtain what you need from Mr. Rudge, we will discuss all that when I have seen the design for the whole. I will like it if you include some roses, I am excessively fond of roses, and you see there are some in the garden, but they do not flourish as they ought, the soil is not quite right for them."

"You shall have a veritable rose garden," Cassandra promised, not sure that roses were a true setting for nymphs and swains, but she felt she had a good idea of what her landlady's taste was, and now she must please her client, her patron, not herself.

As she sat in her room that evening, drawing and drawing, with only a short pause to eat the excellent dinner brought up to her as Mrs. Nettleton had promised, she heard the sounds of company below.

"It seems your mistress has a large party, tonight," she said to the maidservant who came to take the tray away. She was a tall, ungainly girl, with a slight limp and a sharp eye.

"Mrs. Nettleton likes to entertain," she said, and Cassandra caught the scorn in the girl's voice. She looked up, not used to being addressed by servants in quite that tone.

"Is there anything else, miss?" the servant went on.

"I am Mrs. Kent," Cassandra said, and although she spoke in a friendly voice, a natural hauteur came through, and the maidservant gave her an even sharper look. "What is your name?"

"Betsy, miss, I mean, ma'am."

"Thank you, Betsy. That will be all."

She went back to her outline of intertwined leaves and flowers, slightly puzzled by Betsy. Mrs. Nettleton was a fashionable woman, and her house was done up in a fine style. She would have expected her to have more comely servants. The one who had let her in when she first arrived had been a plain creature, neatly dressed, but no one's idea of a smart servant. Well, Mrs. Nettleton seemed to have a kind heart indeed, for it must be kindness that led her to employ girls who would otherwise find it hard to get a position in a house such as this.

The next days passed in a whirl of activity. Sooner than she could have believed possible, a letter came from Emily, sent to the Receiving House as she had requested, telling her that a trunk was being sent up by the carrier to await collection. Would it not be better to send it to her address in London? Or perhaps she was in temporary accommodation, and would no longer be there by the time it arrived.

Her letter was overflowing with warmth, a warmth that brought tears to Cassandra's eyes. Emily assumed that she was to be married, and she found it romantic and exciting that Cassandra should have eloped; she always knew that her dearest Cassandra would one day fall very much in love. Mrs. Croscombe was full of dismay of the dangerous step that Cassandra had taken.

"I was supposed to know nothing about it," Emily wrote, "but I told Mama of the lines I had had from you. Mama at once decided to beard the lion in his den, and drove over to Rosings. Your mama is prostrate, positively glued to her vinaigrette, and drooping on sofas, my mother says it is very wrong of you to have caused her such distress, but I think Mrs. P. likes to lie about in a state of interesting woe. Mr. P. is beside himself with rage and disapproval, you are a child of

Satan as far as he is concerned, although he tried to keep up a good front, muttering about settlements and so forth and you staying with friends in London. He hopes that the news of your elopement and marriage will not get abroad until the knot is tied. He says that you will not be received at Rosings, is this true? It seems very harsh, but then men say this and that when in a rage, and he will see, when he is in a calmer frame of mind, that it will reflect badly upon him and your mama if you do not come to Rosings when you are Mrs. Eyre.

"I am to go over and pack up such clothes as you need. Where are you to live? Mr. P. told Mama that you will be living abroad. This means that I will not see you soon, shall you be back in England at any time during the autumn or winter?"

The letter finished with affectionate greetings; would Emily stand her friend when she and Mrs. Croscombe learned that Cassandra had no intention of marrying the man she had run off with?

She had contemplated sending a message at once to Mr. Horatio Darcy, informing him of her decision, but, no, she would wait until her week was up.

Meanwhile, she lost herself in work, finding consolation in the hours she spent working out her plan for Mrs. Nettleton's morning room, hours when she forgot James and her stepfather and everything except what her skilful hand was creating on the paper in front of her. She was drawing from memory, re-creating on the sheets of paper the rose garden at Rosings, with its pergolas of trailing roses and blooms of every type. It had been created by her grandmother, who considered that a house called Rosings should have a magnificent rose garden. Lady Catherine had prided herself on the taste and charm of the scheme, which she was persuaded had come entirely from her.

Cassandra knew the truth of this, which she had from the old gardener who had worked for Lady Catherine. She often visited him in his cottage, where he led a happy retirement, looking after his own tiny plot with as much enthusiasm as he had once presided over the acres of garden and parkland, with a small army of underlings to do his bidding.

"Her ladyship, she had a lot of cranky ideas, and not much of an eye for a garden, if you'll excuse me saying so, Miss Cassandra. So I'd touch my forehead, in the way she liked, and say, 'Yes, my lady, and just as your ladyship wishes,' and then make sure it was planted out as it should be. I'd flatter her, do you see, tell her what a fine idea such an arch or a type of rose was, and she'd end up believing it was all her idea."

Cassandra remembered him with affection; would her mother visit him, now that she was no longer there to carry out that particular duty? Mrs. Partington was inclined to neglect her duties towards old servants and dependents. Would he welcome a visit from Mrs. Partington? He was an independent-minded old man, who had looked over her drawings of flowers and plants, and marvelled how she could capture them on the page. "I grow them and you paint them, and I don't know which is more lifelike," he'd say with a wheezy chuckle. "Only maybe yours are better, Miss Cassandra, for they flower all year round!"

She knew the prospect through the rose garden to the formal garden beyond by heart, and now, in faraway London, its image was re-created by her busy fingers. There was no more talk from Mrs. Nettleton about her borrowing a gown; she must have sensed Cassandra's dislike of the idea.

"As soon as your trunk arrives, my dear, I shall invite several of my most interesting friends to dine, and we shall have a merry party."

Cassandra was not at all sure that Mrs. Nettleton's notion of a merry party exactly fitted her own, but she owed her the courtesy of accepting the invitation in due course. For Cassandra had a good idea that—despite the trappings and the genteel manner of Mrs. Nettleton's speech, and her airy references to her numerous acquaintance among the nobility—her landlady was not, as the saying went, quite the thing.

Her morning visitors were women very much of her own sort; no Lady this or Viscountess that came at the obligatory calling hour, although gentlemen did call, and from the glimpses Cassandra had of them and their horses or carriages, they did look as though they were men of rank. It was odd, but she gave it little thought; Mrs. Nettleton's circle was her own affair, and need not trouble Cassandra.

Cassandra was also somewhat surprised to find how late into the night Mrs. Nettleton's parties continued. It was true, fashionable people in London dined late, but her guests were wont to arrive well after midnight—"They come on to meet friends and have a bite of supper after the play or the opera," Mrs. Nettleton told her, when she apologised for the knocker sounding in the early hours of the morning. "I trust it does not disturb you, I trust you are a sound sleeper."

The trunk arrived at the collecting office, and was duly delivered, under Cassandra's instructions, to St. James's Square, once she had removed the labels addressed to Miss Darcy. And, that very day, she took up her pen once more, and wrote to Mr. Darcy at his chambers, a few lines to tell him that she had not changed her mind, and would send him in due course directions as to where her quarterly allowance might be paid.

Mrs. Nettleton was there when the trunk was brought home, and at once said that Cassandra must put aside her charcoal and colours for a few hours, and join her and her friends for dinner; this time she would brook no refusal.

Cassandra was used to dinner parties in Kent, for although she had not had a London season, she had been regarded as being out for the past two years, and often dined at neighbouring houses in the summer months and when the weather and the moon permitted during the winter. So her party manners were assured, she was used to meeting strangers, although not so many as she would face here in London, and she did not approach the party with any particular trepidation. She felt no need to impress, cared little what anyone who might be there would think of her, and simply hoped that none of those present would be acquainted with her family.

She dressed in the best of her gowns, although she knew that to those used to London fashions, she would appear countrified and dowdy. Mrs. Nettleton frowned when she saw her.

"I see that you are behind the times in Bath, your gown is cut very high across the bosom for evening wear, and it is very plain. Let me see if we can give you a more modish appearance."

Before Cassandra could protest, Mrs. Nettleton and the grim, middle-aged woman who was her maid, and who certainly turned her mistress out in some style, were busy at her dress, tucking and pinning it here, tightening it there, until she wanted to push them away, or snap at them to take their hands off her. But she submitted, it would be discourteous to Mrs. Nettleton to do otherwise, and she allowed a spangled shawl to be draped across her shoulders.

"Have you no jewellery other than this pearl necklace?"

"I have what I had as a girl, my husband was not in such circumstances that he could be buying me jewels."

"What a pity, with your looks you pay for dressing. I shall lend you some pieces. No, no, do not refuse, they are mere trinkets, but I can assure you, you need a sparkle around your neck and at your ears for any evening party in London. I will fetch you a diamond cross, you may wear it about your neck on a velvet ribbon."

Cassandra was not inclined to wear Mrs. Nettleton's diamonds about her neck. She smiled her thanks, shook her head, and put on her string of pearls.

"They are mighty fine ones," Mrs. Nettleton said.

Too fine for a clergyman's daughter, Cassandra realised. "My godmother gave them to me, upon the occasion of my marriage. I value them highly."

At eight o'clock, Cassandra was in the drawing room with Mrs. Nettleton. "Here we are, *rayonnant,*" Mrs. Nettleton said with a laugh, "and no other guests are come. Hark, there is a knock on the door."

Cassandra was presented to a Lord Usborne, a tall, clever-looking man with a saturnine face, who looked her up and down as though she were a racehorse, she thought indignantly. He was joined by a Colonel Palmer and a young and beautifully dressed Mrs. Palmer, who lacked refinement in her vowels, but made up for it in her jewels. Close on their heels came a Mr. Harry Fanshawe, a goggle-eyed young man in the elegant evening uniform of the Tenth, who had a lopsided smile and very blue eyes. He slid an arm around Mrs. Palmer's waist and gave her a kiss upon her cheek, then greeted Mrs. Nettleton with a most affectionate hug and a merry quip about his lateness. Cassandra, startled by this familiarity, was even more startled when he took and held her hand, gazed into her eyes, and murmured, "Enchanting, utterly enchanting."

They went in to dinner, Mrs. Nettleton telling Lord Usborne to take Mrs. Kent in. He sat beside her, through the excellent dinner, and plied her with wine, of which she drank very little, and questions, which she tried not to answer. Was she but lately come to London? Where was she from? Her husband was an ex-soldier? What regiment? Who were her family, a daughter of a clergyman, Mrs. Nettleton had said, where had he had his parish?

Cassandra grew more and more uncomfortable, and was finally provoked into telling his lordship that she considered a stream of questions to be no sort of conversation. He laughed, and said he liked a woman who could hold her ground, and then turned to talk to Mrs. Nettleton. This left her with Colonel Palmer, who was on her other side, and who was, Cassandra felt sure, fondling his wife's leg beneath the table.

Cassandra might not have been out in the world, but she had a strong notion that this was not the kind of dinner party that, for instance, her cousin Camilla would attend, married woman or no. There was a looseness about the talk, which she much disliked; however, as though sensing this, Lord Usborne, showing himself to be better bred than either of the other two gentlemen, toned down his remarks, and began to talk about painters of the day in a sensible and well-informed manner, "for Mrs. Nettleton has told me that you are an accomplished artist yourself, and take a great interest in the subject. Tell me, are you also a musician? Might we have the honour of hearing you play this evening?"

Mrs. Palmer pouted and looked not best pleased at this suggestion; she for one didn't want to listen to some long, dull sonata, she informed the company.

"Do not concern yourself," Cassandra said. "For although I was well-taught and indeed can play a number of long and dull sonatas, I have no real talent upon the pianoforte, nor upon any musical instrument, and have no wish to inflict my very moderate playing upon any company."

Lord Usborne began now to talk about music to Cassandra; it was almost as though he did not believe that she ever had learnt to play. "So much accomplishment for a clergyman's daughter," he said mockingly. "Do you play Clementi, or Cramer, or perhaps the compositions of that admirable young composer Mr. Field?"

Cassandra did not choose to be patronised. "I have learned several Clementi pieces, but Cramer is too difficult for me to do justice to, since a high degree of execution is necessary to be able to play his compositions, and I have it not."

Cassandra longed for the dinner to come to an end, so that she might escape from Lord Usborne's questions and civilities. At last, Mrs. Nettleton rose, told the gentlemen not to linger over their wine, and took Cassandra and Mrs. Palmer up to the drawing room. There Mrs. Palmer flung herself upon a sofa, and yawned prodigiously. "I swear, Mrs. N., I have never spent a more tedious time in your house, with this talk of painting and music. All on account of this genteel Mrs. Kent"—here she shot a look of dislike at Cassandra—"I wonder you consider it worth the effort."

A footman came in with the tea tray, and, to her astonishment, Cassandra saw Mrs. Palmer give him a broad wink. Mrs. Nettleton's mouth lost its cheerful curve and she frowned at Mrs. Palmer before abruptly dismissing the footman.

"Mrs. N.'s footmen always have the finest calves of any servants in London," said Mrs. Palmer, sitting up to take her tea. "I do hope the gentlemen are not much longer, for we are very dull here."

Cassandra agreed with her as to the dullness, but not with her desire to have the gentlemen appear. However, they came in soon after, in good spirits. Mrs. Nettleton at once desired the Palmers and Mr. Fanshawe to join her at the card table, and told Lord Usborne that he might entertain Mrs. Kent while they played a hand or two.

"You do not care for cards, Mrs. Kent?" he asked, sitting down beside her.

"No."

"Ah, that is a London habit we shall have to accustom you to; I assure you, everyone in London is a gamester these days."

She smiled politely. "I am not in a position to gamble, even for low stakes."

Lord Usborne began to speak in a more confidential tone. "You are in a difficult situation, how fortunate for you that you met Mrs. Nettleton, who can show you how to go on in London, for it can be a hazardous city for those unfamiliar with its ways. And you have no family or acquaintance in London, I believe?"

"Not at present, no." And she was beginning to wonder just how fortunate she was in her meeting with Mrs. Nettleton, if it obliged her to spend many evenings like this.

"Tell me, have you seen much of the neighbourhood? Or of the rest of London? You must allow me to show you some of the sights, I am acknowledged by my friends to be a notable guide to the city. Let me call for you tomorrow, in the afternoon, in my curricle. Should you care to look at pictures, I can gain admittance to many of the best private collections."

Cassandra thanked him, and declined, but he would not take no for an answer. He raised his voice. "Mrs. Nettleton, here is Mrs. Kent declaring she will not drive with me, I rely upon you to change her mind. She may command me to go wherever she chooses; now, is that not a reasonable offer?"

At last the evening was at an end. Two of the gentlemen were going on to their club, and Mrs. Palmer was twining herself affectionately around the colonel, telling him that he must call his carriage, that she longed to go home, and, with a languishing look, to bed.

Mr. Fanshawe seized Cassandra's hand again, and carried it to his lips. Lord Usborne bowed gracefully, and said that he would be outside the house the next afternoon, at five o'clock. "You will persuade her to come, will you not, Mrs. Nettleton?"

Before Cassandra could utter another protest, the gentlemen were gone, and Cassandra was finally able to escape upstairs after bidding Mrs. Nettleton a rapid and polite good-night, saying that she was much too tired to think about what she might do upon the morrow.

Chapter Thirteen

The morrow brought her landlady into her room behind Betsy, who was carrying Cassandra's morning dish of hot chocolate. Mrs. Nettleton had a purpose to this untimely visitation, she was there to tell Cassandra she must not be a goose and turn down Lord Usborne's civil offer.

"For he is a man of considerable influence, you must know; related to quite half the House of Lords." If anyone could find her teaching positions in the households of the haut ton, then it was he.

"Indeed?" said Cassandra drily. "I cannot believe that any mama would expect to employ a drawing teacher recommended by a man, however well-connected."

"It may be so in the country for all I know, but allow me to know better than you how we go on in London. Let Lord Usborne but mention your name to a few ladies of quality, and you will find a host of enquiries come your way. Now, we must decide what you are to wear this afternoon, for if you are to drive out with a gentleman of fashion, you must be seen to look your best."

The trouble was, Cassandra reflected, as she searched for the words to resist Mrs. Nettleton, that somehow the energy needed to be resolute had left her. She was not sleeping well, tossing and turning and reliving the events of the last few weeks in a distorted, unhappy fashion. In her dreams, James became a monster, which he was not, and the journeys she had made, from Rosings to London and Bath, and then from Bath to London, became nightmarish excursions, fanciful versions of the more prosaic reality.

It was as though her betrayal by James, her double betrayal, she supposed, had left her drained of feeling and therefore without the strength of character that she so desperately needed if she were to make her way in the world.

It was, in the end, easier to acquiesce. Mrs. Nettleton gave up her demand that Cassandra go for a drive alone with Lord Usborne; she would accompany them, she declared. She had her own carriage, of course, but a drive out with a gentleman, and such a handsome one as Lord Usborne—did not Cassandra find him a very handsome man?—must always be a greater pleasure.

The day was bright and sunny, but without the heat of the last few days. Mrs. Nettleton pressed a shawl on Cassandra. "Cashmere, you know, but feel how soft and warm! For your pelisse is sadly out of fashion, and it is not quite the thing for you to be wearing muslins all the time, like a miss. Did not you have wedding clothes made upon your marriage? I did not like to mention it, but it is certainly not quite the thing for you to dress quite so young and maidenly."

That had not occurred to Cassandra. Secure with her mother's band around her finger, she hadn't given her clothes a second thought, and had dressed just as she had always done, in the light colours and fabrics of her girlhood. Now she cast her mind back to Emily's preparations for her wedding to Charles Egerton; it gave her a pang, to think that she would not stand at the church door to wish her oldest friend well on the threshold of her new life as a married woman. The pretty muslins were to be replaced by the richer silks and patterns of the young married woman; Emily had delighted in her new clothes as they were sent home.

It was a change marked in so many ways, the passage from girlhood to womanhood symbolised by the vows and the separation from the childhood home. How different had been her own transition from one state to the other, leaving Rosings a girl, setting up in London as a woman, but with none of the rituals that should have accompanied such a step. She ran her mind over her meagre wardrobe. There was no question of her buying new clothes, yet somehow, she must contrive. She could not, she now saw, present herself at a house, seeking employment, dressed like a well-bred miss from the country. She had told herself that it would be well to dress plainly, but there was plain and plain.

How complicated it all was. How agreeable to be a savage and not to have to spend a moment thinking of what to wear.

Now Mrs. Nettleton, seeing Cassandra's hesitation, saw her opportunity. Dresses were brought out from the clothes-press: "This will fit you very well, is it not smart? Indeed, my niece will not mind at all, she left it here because she felt it never suited her so very well. She has not your colouring, she is very fair, and this bronze stuff did her no favours."

Could there be any harm in borrowing a dress? Again, she could not summon up her powers of resistance, it was much easier to say yes. And how well she looked in the gown, with its small tucks and ruffles and a waist lower than she was used to. Mrs. Nettleton exclaimed, as did Betsy; they exchanged looks of complicity, but Cassandra, whose senses were not as keen as they should be, did not notice.

She did notice, observing herself in the long glass, that she appeared older. It was remarkable the change that an item of clothing made. And it would do well for her to look older, both for maintaining the fiction of her widowhood and for obtaining work.

She thanked Mrs. Nettleton, and was in the drawing room dressed in the bronze gown, and in a dashing bonnet that went with it, when his lordship arrived on the dot of five o'clock. He bowed when Mrs. Nettleton said that, with his permission, she would drive out with them, handed them both into the open carriage, and told the coachman to drive on.

"We are going to the park," Mrs. Nettleton whispered in Cassandra's ear. "This is the fashionable hour to drive out, and to see and be seen."

This brought Cassandra no joy. There was no one she wished to see, and she most certainly did not want to be seen by anyone who knew her, but who was there to recognise her?

She was unlucky. As the carriage turned into the park and began to bowl along at a steady pace, amid a stream of other carriages, men and women on horseback, and pedestrians, all dressed in what Cassandra could see were fashionable outfits, a carriage came the other way, driven by a man in the same livery as Lord Usborne's coachman. She heard him say, very low, "The devil take it," then he took off his hat to the occupants of the other carriage, a lovely woman, with dark hair and a beautiful complexion, her extravagant hat dancing with feathers. And, beside her, Mr. Horatio Darcy.

Colour flared into Cassandra's cheeks, and as the carriages passed, she put up a hand to shield her face from sight. Thank God, Mr. Darcy seemed as anxious not to look into their carriage as she was to avoid his gaze. Thank goodness she had been wearing Mrs. Nettleton's clothes; there was a good chance that Mr. Darcy might, had he looked that way at all, have noticed nothing but a woman with her head turned away.

The carriages were past each other. Lord Usborne frowned; Mrs. Nettleton raised her eyebrows at him, but said nothing.

If her cousin were driving with a lady clearly known to Lord Usborne, and he had noticed Cassandra, then might he be able to trace her through this connection?

She pulled herself together. He had not seen her, and if he had, why should he want to trace her? He had done what he had been asked to do, had carried out what he clearly felt was a disagreeable task, and that was an end of it; he would take no more interest in her or her affairs than if she had been a stranger.

A letter that came the very next day, however, caused a renewed sense of alarm. She had gone to the Receiving House in St. Martin's Lane with no expectation of there being any correspondence for her, but it gave a purpose to her walk, and she needed to get out of the house.

To her annoyance, Mrs. Nettleton, who seemed to have wide

views as to the duties of a landlady, insisted that she take Betsy with her. "It will not do for you to be walking around London unaccompanied, not a beautiful young woman like yourself. And you are not yet familiar with London, you do not know where you can go safely and the places you should avoid, for fear of unpleasantness or molestation. London is awash with thieves and other hazards, and Betsy, who is born and bred a Londoner, will be of the greatest use to you. And she will be pleased to go with you, is that not so, Betsy?"

Betsy bobbed a curtsy, and she did look pleased, for, as she told Cassandra once they had set out, she would much rather be out walking in the streets than slaving away at number seven. And, to Cassandra's chagrin, she at once proved her worth and Mrs. Nettleton's words of warning.

"No, miss, I mean, ma'am, you cannot go that way."

Cassandra consulted her map. "Look, it is much the most direct route."

"I can't read no map, but I do know that Mrs. Nettleton would skin me alive if I let you walk up St. James's Street, for it is a thing ladies had best not do."

"Why ever not?"

"It is where all the gentlemen's clubs are situated, and they sit in the windows and ogle the ladies with their eyes and glasses. And besides, there are, well, houses there, that aren't quite respectable."

"What kind of houses?"

Betsy's face took on a cunning look. "Perhaps you wouldn't know about them, coming from Bath, so Mrs. Nettleton told me. Betsy lowered her voice and looked around, lest anyone going past might hear her. "Bagnios. Seraglios, they call them sometimes. Where the nuns live."

"Nuns?" Now Cassandra was utterly confused. How had nuns crept into the conversation? "Are they religious houses, then?" How could a religious house be called a seraglio, it made no sense.

That brought a peal of laughter from Betsy. "Houses of love, that's what they are, and the women in them, those are the nuns, not at all respectable." A wistful tone came into her voice. "But very fine looking, and they have everything they want, in the way of clothes and jewels, and some of them end up rich and living in Belgrave Square, so they say. I wish I had the looks to be one of them," she added with a sigh.

Naïve, Cassandra might be, but she was not a fool, and her acquaintance with Mrs. Croscombe had taught her things that many a well-brought-up young lady would have no knowledge of. Betsy was talking about houses of ill repute, where women sold themselves for gain.

A chill came over her, and she began to walk away from the forbidden territory. Suddenly, she yearned for the familiar park and lanes and fields of her native Kent. It was odd, that in London, there were clearly boundaries far more defined than those in the country, where it was a matter of who owned the land. Here, such a street belonged to no one, but to walk along it was to commit a trespass of another kind.

At the post office, she told Betsy to wait outside. Betsy at first looked stubborn, but Cassandra was firm. "I merely go in to make an enquiry, no one will approach me or trouble me in there, and I shall not be long."

And there was the letter, from Emily, she recognized the writing at once. She tucked it into her reticule; she longed to read it at once, but did not want Betsy to know that she had a letter, she would wait until she could be alone. If Betsy knew there was a letter, then Mrs. Nettleton would find out about it, also, and then she would question Cassandra, in the most friendly way, and yet it was an intrusion into her private life that Cassandra was not at all happy with. She would have the luxury of reading the letter that evening, in her bedchamber.

My dearest Cassandra

I have heard some news of you that I can hardly believe, that you are not to be married, and that you have been cut off from your family? Can this be true? Mama will say nothing, although I am sure she is in Mrs. Partington's confidence. She has not forbidden me to write to you, and I am glad of it, for I

would certainly disobey. What, not communicate with my
dearest friend—and if you are, indeed, in trouble, then you
will have need of a true friend. I will tell you what I know,
and then please write to me, by return, to tell me the truth of
the matter.

This is what I know: Yesterday, while I was out walking
with Charles, a horseman came past. He was a tall, fine-
looking young man, and he stopped briefly to exchange
greetings with Charles, with whom he is slightly acquainted, it
turned out, and he bowed to me, before going on his way.

"Who is that?" I enquired, when he had ridden on.

"It is Mr. Horatio Darcy. I know him from my schooldays.
He is a lawyer now, in London, a mighty clever fellow who
will doubtless make a name for himself. I wonder what brings
him to these parts."

I said that perhaps he was going to Rosings about a legal
matter—I at once thought of you, and settlements and so on.

My dear Charles said, yes, he might well be there upon
some legal matter, some family business, because of the family
connection. Well, I was quite correct in this, for I learned from
John, our groom, who is courting Mary, the parlourmaid at
Rosings, you remember, that the horseman, this Mr. Darcy,
did indeed arrive at Rosings, and was closeted with Mr.
Partington for quite half an hour, and I gather that voices
were raised—Mr. Partington's was, in any event.

And then this young man, who appears to have a very
forceful character—I can believe he is indeed a relation of
yours—waited upon your mother, although it seems that Mr.
Partington was not at all desirous that he should do so.

One should not eavesdrop, but servants always do, and
one should not listen to servants' gossip, so Mama is always
telling me, but one always does. The story they are all telling
is that Mr. Eyre will not marry you without a fortune, and
that Mr. Partington agreed to a dowry, and that now you say
you will not marry him after all. Can this be true? And that

*you are going to live with one Mrs. Norris, and that you will
never be permitted again to cross the threshold of Rosings, for
"as long as you live," were Mr. Partington's harsh words.*

*I do so hope that all this is a mistake and there is some
confusion here. I am concerned lest you are gone out of
London to this Mrs. Norris, and my letter will not reach you.
If it does, pray write to me at once, to tell me how things are
with you, if there is anything you need, if there is anything I
may do to assist you, in as far as I am able.*

*I am sure that if you are not to marry Mr. Eyre, you have a
very good reason for it, but, oh, Cassandra, are you sure what
you are about? To elope with a man is a rash step, but not to
marry him will carry consequences far more awful—but you
don't need me to tell you this.*

Cassandra folded the letter, and sat with it in her hands, staring at
the wall and seeing only an image of Emily's merry face, of Mrs.
Croscombe's kind one, of the skipping, capering figures of her little
sisters. Tears sprang to her eyes, she brushed them away with a furious hand, but it would not do, they would come, and she threw herself on the bed, racked with sobs, desolate beyond anything she had
ever known.

Chapter Fourteen

Cassandra was angry with herself for her weakness. What difference did it make, that Horatio Darcy had been told that she was now residing with Mrs. Norris? Nothing had changed; she was no more truly cut off from her family and from Rosings than when she sat in Mr. Darcy's chambers and said that she would not marry Mr. Eyre. That was the moment when—no, it was not. The moment when she turned her back on her family, on Rosings, on her natural place in the world, had been the moment she stepped into the carriage with Mr. Eyre in Bath. Or was it later, when she discovered they were not bound for Scotland, but were on the London road? Then, she might still have said she would have gone no further and insisted that James turn back. Petifer would have let her into the house somehow, and no one, but herself and James and Petifer, would have been any the wiser.

Petifer, who had stood outside the house in Laura Place, her face white and worried. She knew she could not dissuade her mistress from taking this rash plunge into disaster; she had known, Cassandra suspected, that James Eyre was not a man to be trusted, but was Cassandra at that time capable of listening to anyone who spoke sense or reason to her?

Where was Petifer? Back in Kent, no doubt, with new duties. She must write to her in due course, when she had established herself, and could say that she was well and happy.

What did it matter, she asked herself, what Mr. Darcy, or anyone, thought of her? She went over to the jug of water in the corner of her room and splashed some on her face and wrists. But the thoughts still went round and round in her mind. Mr. Darcy had cared enough to go all the way to Rosings, a fair way from London, to remonstrate with her stepfather. She liked him the better for that, but why had he done it? For the sake of the good name of the family, she supposed; he was strong on the family name.

Summoned to take tea with Mrs. Nettleton, she found herself almost glad of the distraction from these painful thoughts. To take her mind off Mr. Darcy and Rosings, she asked Mrs. Nettleton who the man and woman in the other carriage were, when they were out in the park with Lord Usborne.

"Which carriage? We passed so many, as one does at that time of day, when anyone who is anyone is in the park."

"The first one we encountered, when we were just inside the gates. A dark-haired woman, with a young man. The woman had a hat with several plumes, dark red and pink, very smart."

Mrs. Nettleton looked, for the first time since Cassandra had known her, slightly lost for words. "I am not sure who . . . oh, I suppose you mean Lady Usborne."

"Lady Usborne?" Cassandra had a moment of wild conjecture. A stepmother, a dowager Lady Usborne? Of course not! "Lord Usborne's wife? He has a wife?"

"My dear, of course he does, a man of his fortune and background and his years, for he is eight-and-thirty, is bound to have a wife."

"Good heavens, what must she have thought of him, driving with other women in the park."

Mrs. Nettleton broke into a peal of laughter. "Lord, one can see you have lived a retired life! She is quite used to it, it would be very unfashionable to be seen out driving with your husband, let me assure you. They are not on good terms, in any case. There are no children in that marriage, and they grew bored with one another very soon after they were married. People said at the time that it was a love match, but that was all nonsense. She could have had her pick of the eligible men, for she is very well-born, related to the Melbournes, if that is anything to boast about these days. And she brought a considerable fortune with her. He was a good catch, too, with a reputation for being a gallant soldier when he fought in Spain, and with an ancient name. However, they found they were not quite as fond of one another after all, once the knot was tied, as is so often the case, and the marriage dwindled into indifference. Men like variety, let me tell you, they don't care to fall into a pattern of domesticity and faithfulness."

"Then shame on them," cried Cassandra.

"My dear, you speak as one who is still very young, and, I was forgetting, who lost a husband after only a short time of being married; your experience of matrimony is limited, is it not? How long did you say you were wed before your poor husband breathed his last— eighteen months before he fell into a consumption, I think you said."

Cassandra had said no such thing. "He died of a wound he received at Waterloo, that never quite healed, and then grew worse, there was some metal that was inside the wound, some shrapnel, which later festered."

"Of course, how foolish of me," said Mrs. Nettleton, with what Cassandra considered a knowing look.

"But before you take up cudgels on behalf of Lady Usborne," Mrs. Nettleton went on, "only think who was in the carriage with her. That is her lawyer, it is a new name for a lover, but then the likes of Lady Usborne must try to protect themselves from the clack of vulgar tongues. Reputation is all, in London, as I am sure you are aware, dear Mrs. Kent."

Mrs. Nettleton's words were barbs. How much of Cassandra's story did this woman, who might not be nearly as kind as she had at first seemed, believe? Cassandra went hot and cold at the thought of discovery; she had been so careful, and her story of widowhood was not such an uncommon one; why should it not be true? She must take great care, however, not to over-egg the cake, as Emily would say.

She assumed a nonchalance she did not feel. "So Lady Usborne has found consolation in the arms of another; well, one cannot blame her, I dare say. But with a lawyer, why does she not choose a man of her own sort?"

"Oh, as to that, he is a Darcy, we have spoken of them, and there is no older family in England, I dare say, they may go anywhere. He has no money, of course, but he is not a cit or at all low. He is a younger son with his way to make in the world; she is influential and no doubt he thinks she will help him in his career."

"You do not think he cares for her?"

Mrs. Nettleton shrugged. "She is a pretty enough armful, but some seven or eight years his senior. It is a fair exchange; she has a handsome young lover, and he has a valuable patroness."

And this was the man who had preached morality to her, Cassandra thought indignantly. To dally with a married woman, to commit adultery, in fact, was no slur on a man's reputation, it seemed, whereas . . . Well, that was the way of the world. What was allowed to one-half of creation was not permitted for an instant to the other.

"I suppose, then, that Lord Usborne has a mistress," Cassandra said. "Why was he not out driving with her?"

"Oh, do not be jealous," Mrs. Nettleton cried.

"I? Jealous? Whatever can you mean? I have only the slightest acquaintance with Lord Usborne, as you very well know, and if I never saw him again, I should be very happy."

"Do not you like him? Do not you find him a very fine gentleman?"

"I do not like him, no."

"Ah"—this with a broad wink—"but you said yourself, you barely know him. As you get to know him better, you will come to appreciate what he has to offer."

"What can he have to offer me, pray?"

"I mean, as to—he is very good company, and a clever man. I myself can't abide a stupid man, and I feel sure you are the same."

She sounded flustered. Cassandra had no desire to talk any more about Lord Usborne, but Mrs. Nettleton was not inclined to let the subject drop.

"As to a mistress, he had a very fine young lady under his protection, a Harriet Foxley. But she was a foolish girl, and she left him for a penniless artist, or some such person."

Cassandra was finding this whole conversation distasteful, and it confirmed what she had begun to suspect, that Mrs. Nettleton had not a right way of thinking about such matters. She was a kind woman, that was true, but not one with whom Cassandra had much in common.

Mrs. Nettleton seemed to sense the unease on Cassandra's part, and she adroitly turned the conversation to the painting of the downstairs parlour.

"I have drawn the designs and coloured them on large sheets of paper," Cassandra said, "so that they may be pinned to the wall and you can see how they look and whether the whole meets with your approval."

"I am certain it will, such a clever creature as you are with your charcoal and paint, I am all admiration. Tomorrow you shall show me, and then we may discuss what else you need from Mr. Rudge. You are to buy whatever you please, put it all down in my name, I will settle his bills myself."

Chapter Fifteen

Camilla Wytton and her husband had taken a house in Harte Street. Wytton owned a large house in Grosvenor Square, which he had inherited from his father, but he had never cared for it.

On his return from Egypt with Camilla, his bride of only a few months, he had wanted to sell the house, in order to be rid of it altogether, "for I am quite sure we shall never want to live there," but his man of business had made tut-tutting noises at the suggestion.

"London is expanding, and the demand for property, now that the war is behind us, will increase. I do not say that the recent unrest, the very distressing incident in Manchester, has not depressed the market, but it will recover, mark my words. Let me find you an acceptable tenant, and then you and Mrs. Wytton may rent a smaller house, more to your liking."

He was as good as his word, and the house in Grosvenor Square was let for a handsome rent to the ambassador from the Court of Hanover, who had come to London with a cheerful wife, numerous offspring, and a large entourage of attendants and servants. Meanwhile, Wytton and Camilla viewed several houses, and took a long lease on one in Harte Street, with a pleasant prospect over the park, and not too many stuffy neighbours. It was convenient for Wytton to visit the Royal Society, and Camilla, too, felt that she was only a step away from the many delights London had to offer to a rich young married woman.

They gave frequent dinner parties, for they enjoyed company, and Camilla was going through the menu for one that evening when Wytton came into the breakfast parlour. He took a seat, picked up the *Morning Post* that lay on the table, glanced at some of the notices, and put it down. "We shall be one more at dinner tonight, with your agreement, my love," he said.

"Why, whom have you invited? Someone new?"

"He is but a very recent acquaintance of mine, but you know him, indeed, you are related to him. It is Mr. Horatio Darcy."

Camilla wrinkled her brow. "He is a cousin, I know, although I am not sure exactly how we are related. He is in his twenties, is he not? And a younger son. He came sometimes to Pemberley, but I confess I don't remember much about him. He thought himself superior to all us young ladies, that I do remember, and he had a good deal of reserve about him, although he may just have been shy."

"He is not shy at all now. A rising man in his profession; it turns out that we are both members of Pink's, and falling into conversation there, and realising that he was your cousin, I invited him to dine with us. I think you will be pleased with him."

Camilla was. She found him a good-looking man, with excellent address and lively, unaffected manners, not at all like some of the stuffy lawyers she had met in London. He enquired after her parents, and her sisters.

"Not that I knew any of you well, for you were but children when last I saw you. I had the honour of meeting Lady Mordaunt while I was in Paris recently. She has a twin sister, does she not?"

"Isabel, you would remember her as Belle."

Mr. Darcy put his head on one side. Camilla liked the good-humoured quirk of his mouth as he recalled the uppity little miss that Belle had been.

"Golden hair and very pretty, but bidding fair to be a handful."

"You have her to a T," Camilla said. "And, since we are cousins, I may tell you that she is even prettier now, but still very much inclined to have things her own way. She is in London, staying with our cousin Fitzwilliam and Lady Fanny, I dare say you will meet her by and by. She was not here earlier in the season, for she was sent down to Rosings."

She was surprised to see his face darken at the mention of Rosings. He must know the house, must have been acquainted with Lady Catherine, did he have unfortunate memories of Rosings?

He spoke in a low voice, after a quick glance to make sure the person sitting on his other side was engaged in another conversation, and would not hear what he said.

"It is a coincidence that you mention Rosings, for I was there only yesterday." He hesitated. "I dare say you have heard of Cassandra Darcy's folly? It must be known to all the family."

Camilla drew in her breath. "No, she is in Bath, is not she? Belle travelled to London in her company, but Cassandra only spent a single night in Aubrey Square, it appears that her stepfather, a most odious man, did not want her to stay in London, although Cassandra very much wanted to. She is a most talented artist you know, and longs to visit the collections and study the works of the masters, and that you can only do in London."

"Unfortunately, she is no longer in Bath, and I doubt if she will ever come to London again. While in Bath, she met a man, a half-pay naval officer, and eloped with him."

"She is married? I had no idea! How come we were not told?"

"Because she is not married, nor will she be."

"What?" Camilla's exclamation came out louder than she had intended, and the talk around her stopped, as her husband and the other guests looked at her.

"What is it?" Wytton asked. "Is something amiss?"

"No, no," she said. "I have just heard some news, about a member of the family, which surprised me, no, do not look concerned, no one has fallen out of the carriage and broke their leg, nor been carried off by an apoplexy."

She turned back to Horatio. "Tell me everything. Does my father know of this? He always felt that Cassandra did not have an easy life at Rosings, with such a mother and with the younger ones taking all her mother's affection."

"That is all over, now, for Mr. Partington declares, like some character in the play, that she is an ungrateful, unnatural wretch, who shall never darken his door again. I forbore from pointing out that it is not exactly his door, but never mind that. However, Cassandra has thrown her bonnet over the windmill, as the saying goes, and now she must suffer the consequences."

"How like a man to say that," Camilla said with some indignation. "As though men didn't do such things every day of the week, and nobody takes any notice of it. But tell me, this officer abandoned her, you say? This is quite dreadful! Where is she now?"

"He did nothing of the sort," said Horatio, a trifle stiffly. "She refused to marry him when it came to the point. It was all arranged. He was after her fortune, of course, he would not consent to marry her unless she had a dowry. Mr. Partington fretted and fumed, although it is not his money, and in the end he agreed, with certain conditions as to their living abroad and so forth."

"So what went wrong?"

"Why, Cassandra, who is as obstinate a young lady as I have ever met, flatly refused to marry the man! She said that if he did not care enough to marry her without a fortune, then she wanted none of him."

"I applaud her for her feelings, which I can understand, but, Lord, what a dreadful position this must leave her in. Surely she can be persuaded, somehow? She must have a great liking for the man, to run away with him. Or did she," she added shrewdly, "run away from home for other reasons as well? Was she in Bath, or did this take place at Rosings?"

"She met the man in Bath, although I gather there had been some contretemps at Rosings not long before. She was sent to stay with a Mrs. Cathcart, a sister of Mr. Partington's."

"And probably a narrow-minded, unpleasant woman, just the sort to make a creature like Cassandra feel wretched. If I am not mistaken, there is more to this than meets the eye, and she has been ill-treated in some way."

Horatio Darcy drew himself away from the table to allow the footman to remove his plate and pour him more wine. "Do not have any romantic notions about this, Mrs. Wytton. Whatever the provocation, or the reason for her flight, and I myself am sure it was no more than an unwise passion which drove her to do what she did, it has deprived her of her family, of her position in society, and of any hope of establishing herself in a suitable marriage."

"But where is she?"

"Apparently, she has gone to live with one Mrs. Norris, who resides in Cheltenham, with a young lady whom I believe also suffered some kind of disgrace, a Mrs. Rushworth."

Now his other neighbour was paying attention. "Do you speak of that terrible Mrs. Norris? I would not let my pet dog live with her. Poor Mrs. Rushworth, what she did was very wrong, but such a punishment; not even purgatory, but a veritable hell, living with Mrs. Norris. Mrs. Rushworth was Maria Bertram, you know, before her marriage. It is an old scandal now, but it was one of the Crim. Cons. of its time."

"What is Mr. Partington's connection with this Mrs. Norris?" Camilla said to Horatio when the rest of the table were talking of other matters.

"She is the widow of a clergyman, and Mr. Partington, who is in holy orders, although no longer in a living, was at one time curate to the late Mr. Norris."

"So he has decided to punish his stepdaughter by packing her off to live with this unpleasant woman and repent her sins."

Horatio Darcy shrugged. "She should have considered what the consequences of so rash an action might be."

"I dare say when you are eloping with the man you love, the prospect of a Mrs. Norris does not enter your mind."

"Perhaps it should."

"You are cold-hearted, I find, Cousin."

Chapter Sixteen

Later that night, long after Cassandra was in bed, restlessly asleep, Lord Usborne paid a visit to Mrs. Nettleton. She gave him a glass of champagne, and he sat on her sofa in a negligent pose, one hand fondling the silky ears of her spaniel, the other holding the sparkling wine up to the light thrown by the candles which gave out their soft glow from the chandelier in the centre of the room.

"You are quite right, this Cassandra of yours is indeed a beauty," he said. "A charming name to match her charming person."

"Just to your taste," said Mrs. Nettleton.

"Yes, young, but no virgin, I can't do with virgins, simpering misses who know nothing of the amorous arts. Yet there is nothing of the slut about her, she will have sufficient experience to please me, and sufficient innocence to make a charming pupil of Venus. Yes, I congratulate you. But what is she, Polly, where is she from? For she is a lady, unquestionably, and I want no impertinent brothers or uncles springing up out of the woodwork and accusing me of seduction or rape."

"Now, as to that, I was somewhat perplexed, but I have been making enquiries. Of course, she is not at all what she says, there is no husband dead of wounds, that is a touching story, but quite untrue. No, no, I knew that was all a hum. What gave me a clue was her likeness to Mr. Darcy of Pemberley."

"A by-blow of Darcy's? I would not have thought it of him, the most devoted of husbands by all accounts. How old is the soi-disant Mrs. Kent? Not above one-and-twenty, I am sure. Mr. Darcy unfaithful so soon after his marriage! I doubt it."

"I know nothing of Mr. Darcy, beyond his name and the fact that he is exceedingly rich, I have never had to do with him, and I dare say he is completely faithful to his wife, it is becoming quite the fashion, I regret to say. No, Mrs. Kent is not his daughter, and the connection is not so very close. They are cousins. Mrs. Kent is Miss Darcy, daughter of the late Thaddeus Darcy, he died some dozen or more years since. A younger son, but he married the daughter of Lady Catherine de Bourgh . . ."

"Of Rosings, in Kent. Hence her name!"

"It seems that Miss Darcy was sent to Bath, in disgrace, some incident in the shrubbery with a man, a servant or some such unsuitable person. She went to a Mrs. Cathcart, sister to her stepfather. I know nothing of her, but I am acquainted with a friend and neighbour of hers, Amelia Quail, and I had the whole story from her in a letter this morning. Miss Darcy ran off, eloped at the dead of night, with a half-pay officer, one James Eyre. A naval man. It was supposed at first that they were going to Gretna Green, for a Scottish marriage, but it was not so, they came to London and lived together without marrying."

"Go on," said Usborne, his voice lazy, but his eyes alert. "This is most interesting."

"I do not know whether it was their intention to wed, or whether Mr. Eyre merely took a pleasant companion to amuse him when he left Bath, with debts unsettled, all that kind of thing."

"It is an old story."

"However, they were traced by her stepfather, the worthy Mr. Partington, and everything was arranged, there was to be a wedding, and settlements, all in a hope of it being hushed up and to prevent it being generally known about their living together as man and wife before the ceremony."

"So what happened to prevent this happy outcome?"

Mrs. Nettleton looked peeved. "That I cannot tell you. The fortune must not have been sufficient, or the terms were too onerous, who can say? But it did not come off, Mr. Eyre took himself off to Ireland, and whether he is returned or no, I do not know. Certainly, Miss Darcy found herself alone in the world, cast off by her family, only by the greatest good fortune she chanced to encounter myself."

"Who out of charity and the goodness of her heart, provided her with a bed and a roof over her head."

Mrs. Nettleton's company laugh was a ladylike one, but in the company of an old friend like Usborne, she allowed herself the natural, rollicking version. As Polly Scriggins, she had come to London to look for work, been taken up by the proprietor of one of the most exclusive houses in St. James's Street, had found favour with several rich gentlemen, had been careful with her earnings, unlike most of her kind, had made shrewd investments on the advice of the more astute of her admirers, had never fallen prey to wine or gin, and had put together enough money to buy the lease of this house on the less fashionable side of St. James's Square, and face the loss of her youthful beauty with equanimity.

"I have had enough of men between the sheets to last any woman a lifetime," she had told her then protector, the Marquis of Dorne. "So good-bye to you, and your place will be taken with cards and gossip and doing just as I please."

"Well, Polly," the marquis had said, taking this in good part, "if you are to leave me in the lurch, you may look about for another to take your place. None of your very young girls, they are too demanding and too expensive. Find me an amiable woman, with some flesh on her, I dearly love a plump bosom, and I will set her up in style, as I did you, and I will make it worth your while."

Being an *entremetteuse* exactly suited Mrs. Nettleton's temperament. It allowed her to keep her hand in, as she put it, and to enjoy the company of gentlemen while keeping her independence. "For once you have been used to being with the highest and most powerful men in the land, you miss their conversation and style," she told her good friend Mrs. Dubois.

Having a keen sense of business, she kept her ear to the ground, and thus heard of Lord Usborne's contretemps with Harriet. She had at once determined that she should find him a replacement. None but the best for him, he liked them ladylike and intelligent, able to converse and grace a table as well as a bed. Such an one as Amy de Courcy, as she called herself, born Amy Wood, as Mrs. Nettleton very well knew, might do for a Colonel Palmer, but was much too vulgar for his lordship.

"Tell me then, Mrs. Nettleton, is she willing?"

"As to that, given her family and upbringing, and the fact that she is probably still pining for the worthless fellow who abandoned her, we must go carefully. However, she will see sense when she finds that her purse has not enough in it to pay the rent, and that I am not quite so generous as she thought. What choice has she?"

"What relation is she to Horatio Darcy, that tiresome young man who dangles after my wife? Is he not some kind of a Darcy? Lady Usborne tells me he is a lawyer."

"That is his profession, and he acted for Cassandra's stepfather over the negotiations for her marriage, money and settlements and so on."

"He doesn't seem to have made a very good job of it, I am glad my affairs are not in his hands."

And they both laughed heartily.

"But, can you assure me that he won't kick up a fuss, that he has no interest in her? Proud as Lucifer all these Darcys, and trouble of that kind is so boring and detrimental to a relationship."

"He will have washed his hands of her, I am sure. As long as she is not come upon the town under her own name, I do not suppose any of them cares what becomes of her. They should be very pleased if she is taken under your protection, it is far better than anything she can have hoped for."

"What is this painting and drawing she does?"

"That's all fancy, she has a little accomplishment and thinks she can turn it to good measure and earn herself a living. It is all impossible, of course."

"For I do not want a woman who has paint on the tip of her nose when I want to go out to the opera, or who imagines she has taste and wants to bore me with her uninteresting views on art."

"You will set her in a right way of thinking. Tell me what you will offer her, and then I shall begin to work on her. But visit frequently. Let her get to know you, charm her, woo her. She won't be won over easily, nor by mercenary promises alone, she will need to believe she is valued as a person."

"I like a challenge, but I will not wait for ever, Polly. Delightful though she is, there are many others of character and beauty who would not need to be asked twice, I do not have to beg for favours from any woman!"

Chapter Seventeen

Mrs. Nettleton would brook no refusal. "Here is such a beautiful summer's day, with just the hint of a breeze to make the weather pleasant, I never saw a more perfect day. And, since it is a Wednesday, I'm planning a little outing to the pleasure gardens at Vauxhall. You shall be my guest, I insist upon it, I will not take no for an answer. I do value your company, my dear Mrs. Kent, so pretty and lively as you are, and Mrs. Palmer, who is also to be of our party, will be so pleased to see you. You must make the most of summer evenings, 'One's youth is the time exactly fitted for such frivolity,' she said to me, 'and if Mrs. Kent has never been to Vauxhall, then we must go.' No . . ." seeing that Cassandra was still hesitating, "do not let considerations of cost deter you, for it is to be my treat, you must allow me this little indulgence. When I let you the room, we agreed, did we not? that you were sometimes to act as a companion to me, and this is one of those occasions when you may do so."

Was there a slight note of warning in Mrs. Nettleton's words? Cassandra wondered. Her rent was unusually low, she had discovered upon studying the advertisements for rooms in the daily newspapers, and the sum Mrs. Nettleton had mentioned to her did seem very little for the apartment she occupied.

Besides, she had long wanted to visit Vauxhall Gardens; they did sound such great fun, and it was such a lovely day.

"It will be worth the three and sixpence just to watch your face when you see the cascade," Mrs. Nettleton went on. "Among all the other delights and wonders to be seen. Now, you should wear the green dress—no, no, say nothing about it, my niece will never wear it again, and as for jewellery, here is a little trinket that I found, which I beg you will accept, a mere trifle; it sets off your neck in such a dress to perfection."

This was not the first gift Mrs. Nettleton had pressed upon Cassandra, and she wished that her landlady would not do so. And she had insisted on presenting Cassandra with the length of material for a morning dress, "for it is a shame to see a young lady such as yourself, wearing so many unfashionable clothes. In London, one must never be behind the times, it is fatal to any woman's prospects."

What clothes had to do with Cassandra's prospects, she could not have said.

"We shall arrive in time for the concert at eight, for I am dotingly fond of that kind of music, they never play anything that jars the ear; nothing in advance of the times, none of that rowdy music by Mr. Beethoven from Germany that some forward thinkers go into ecstasies about. No, you will hear nothing but good tunes and pleasing melodies at Vauxhall."

Their party was to be a small one, consisting of the Palmers, a young man whom Cassandra had not met before, one Mr. Gimpel, and an older man, a Mr. Josbert, who seemed on easy terms with Mrs. Nettleton, and who, so she informed Cassandra, was her man of business; very up to everything to do with money and the city, who liked to come out for an evening's entertainment in good company.

"At Vauxhall, where all sorts of people mingle, there is no harm in his coming along. I would not invite him to one of my more elegant card parties, nor to dine with others, but for Vauxhall, one may relax the rules a little. Do not let him disturb you, he is a good-hearted enough fellow, and no fear of his sliding an arm round your waist, as some of these older men are inclined to do, not that there is anything wrong with older men, and they must have their affections the same as anyone else; indeed, an older man may be so much richer and so much more established—however, that is nothing to the point. The heart of the matter is, that Mr. Josbert is not an admirer of the fairer sex, and so you may be quite easy on that score."

Since it hadn't occurred to Cassandra to be concerned in the first place, she merely spent a moment puzzling as to why Mrs. Nettleton should take the trouble to reassure her on this point, then sensibly put it out of her mind.

Mr. Josbert was escorting them to the grounds, where they would meet up with the rest of their little group. And from the moment Cassandra went through the west entrance, she was enchanted. She exclaimed that she had never seen anything like the orchestra, where the concerts were held, "with marble pillars and such statues!"

"They are not marble," Mr. Josbert said, laughing at her astonishment. "Nor plaster of Paris, neither, which is too fragile, and would not withstand the weather, let alone the daily wear and tear. No, they are made of a new material, which is a more robust and stronger kind of plaster of Paris. I've been into it in quite some detail, for I'm thinking of investing in the company that produces it, there is a future for such a substance, do not you agree?"

Cassandra was paying him scant attention, for her eyes were riveted by the extraordinary display of lights which lined the broad paths and hung shimmering in the trees, twinkling and glowing as far as the eye could see.

"More than fifteen thousand lights," Mr. Josbert informed her. "One for every person who comes to the gardens, for on a busy night, such as tonight, there will be upward of fifteen thousand souls here. Fifteen thousand! Only imagine it. At three shillings and sixpence the head, that's . . ." He muttered under his breath as he did the calculation. "That's two thousand, six hundred and twenty-five pounds. And the gardens are open presently for three evenings a week, so the weekly takings amount to a sum of seven thousand, eight hundred and seventy-five pounds. You may understand now, how they are able to expend so very much money on the displays, and also on the musicians, for they only employ the best singers and performers."

It was the most extraordinary place that Cassandra had ever been to. The size of it alone amazed her; it was astonishing to think that there could be gardens as big as these so near to the centre of London, for it had not taken them long, in Mr. Josbert's comfortable chaise, to travel the distance from St. James's Square to Lambeth, where the gardens were situated.

"Only four miles from the centre of London, it is nothing by carriage, a mere four miles," Mr. Josbert informed her.

The restless, brilliant throng were an attraction in themselves, and Cassandra's observant eye saw the truth of what Mrs. Nettleton had said, for the gardens certainly seemed to attract every class of person. There was a woman she recognized from an engraving she had seen of a portrait done by Mr. Lawrence, Lady Digby, and over there were a merry bunch of what Mr. Josbert jovially dismissed as mere cits.

"Which is amusing," Mrs. Nettleton whispered in her ear, "since that is what he is himself. At least, his mother was the daughter of a well-to-do squire, so perhaps he has a right to think of himself as belonging to a different rank from them."

The colours and the movement fascinated Cassandra, and she hardly heard the music, until the concert was suddenly at an end, and Mrs. Nettleton was saying they must make their way to the box she had taken.

"When I proposed the outing, Mr. Josbert said he would treat us, if I would but arrange it, so there you are, it is not costing us a single penny. Although the food will cost us more than a few pennies, unless he means to treat us to that also, for although very good, it is not cheap; no one can call the food they serve at Vauxhall cheap. Now, here we are, that painting on the front of the box will interest you, with your artistic eye, for it was painted in the last century by a painter called Mr. Hogarth, I dare say you may have heard of him. He caught London life to the perfection, things were really very wild and licentious in those days, we are all so much better behaved in these enlightened times, is that not so, Mr. Josbert?"

Mr. Josbert had not been listening; he had his eyeglass up and was openly ogling a slender youth in tight, striped pantaloons.

"What?" he said, reluctantly withdrawing his gaze and responding to Mrs. Nettleton.

"Never mind, Mr. Josbert, you have to find your pleasure where you can," she said, giving him an inelegant dig in the ribs. "Now, here come the Palmers, how well Mrs. Palmer looks this evening, all in white, although that shape of hat is not right for her."

"Sukie, my dear, what a ravishing hat," she exclaimed, as the Palmers reached the box. "Now, you all know each other, but here is Mr. Gimpel. Mrs. Kent, may I present Mr. Gimpel, a young man of fashion, as you see, and also of an artistic temperament, I know that you will get along famously."

Cassandra didn't quite like the way that Colonel Palmer's eye rested on her exposed bosom, and was glad of Mr. Josbert's apparent indifference to such things; she could have wished it were an indifference shared by Mr. Gimpel.

When he first came to the box, he had rather a bored and world-weary expression on his face, almost bordering on petulance, but as soon as he was introduced to Cassandra, he became more alert. A tongue slipped over his rather large mouth, and his eyes travelled with evident satisfaction, first over her face, and then over her figure.

"Charming, charming," he said, seating himself beside her with alacrity. "Mrs. Nettleton tells me you are but newly come to London, Mrs. Kent."

Eager to get away from his intent gaze, Cassandra jumped to her feet when Mrs. Nettleton proposed a stroll around the gardens, "So that Mrs. Kent may have an idea of just how vast they are, and how many delights are on offer."

Mr. Josbert hooked his arm for Mrs. Nettleton, who swept out of the box, leaving Cassandra to follow with Mr. Gimpel. The Palmers, who were more than familiar with what Vauxhall had to offer, preferred to remain behind and watch the singer just coming on to the performing area.

Cassandra could have wished that Mr. Gimpel had been of a musical disposition, and she tried to keep her distance from him, which was not easy, when he took every opportunity to press himself to her side. She ostentatiously ruffled her skirt out, trying to give herself more room, but he took no notice, and remained too close to her, breathing information in a husky whisper into her ear. He wore a perfume she could not identify, but did not like; altogether, she thought him a most objectionable young man.

At one point, Mr. Josbert called to him to watch a particularly neat trick by a tightrope walker, and Mrs. Nettleton gave Cassandra a knowing smile and a wink. "How do you like Mr. Gimpel? Is he not a fine young man?"

"I do not like him at all," said Cassandra directly, and with a coldness in her voice that brought a frown to Mrs. Nettleton's brow.

"You are too quick to judge, my dear; that is all very well for the schoolroom, where you may say, 'I like this, I don't like that,' but it will not do out in the world. Mr. Gimpel is a very rich gentleman. He owns thousands of acres in Cheshire, beside coal mines and all kinds of profitable ventures in the north. He is not to be scorned, he could be a very good friend to you."

"To me? I hardly think so. I prefer to choose my own friends, as I'm sure you do, and I do not think one could ever be friends with such a man."

"*Friend* is not perhaps the right word," Mrs. Nettleton conceded with a somewhat foxy smile. "But then, relations between men and women are rarely ones of friendship."

The men rejoined them before Cassandra could say any more, and once again, Mr. Gimpel was glued to her side.

They walked along the Broad Walk, Cassandra always edging away from Mr. Gimpel, and finding that his closeness was bidding fair to spoil her enjoyment of the lights, the clothes of the fashionable merrymakers, the statues, the little temples, the novelties that met their eyes at every turn of the path.

"Over there," said Mrs. Nettleton, "is a pretty little wilderness, with winding paths and groves among the trees, quite different from here and so attractive. Take her there, Mr. Gimpel, we will catch up with you and rejoin you in a minute or two, for I see an old acquaintance that I must speak to."

Before Cassandra could utter a word of protest, Mr. Gimpel had seized her arm and was hustling her far deeper into the groves than she cared for.

"Thank you," she said, endeavouring to detach herself from his surprisingly firm grasp, "but I would prefer to stay on the main walks. I do not care for the scenery here."

"Scenery," he cried. He forced her round, so that she was facing him, and as she tried to pull away, he ran his hands up her arm, to cup first her chin, and then, as his hand wandered further, to slide it, clammy and disagreeable, into the front of her dress and down over her breast.

She was furious, and summoning all her strength managed to pull herself free.

He devoured her with his hot eyes and, to her fury, was laughing at her. "My dear Mrs. Kent," he said in mocking tones. "Why this false modesty? You are a woman of experience, you know what I am about, now admit that it pleases you as much as it does me. Here we are in a hunt of pleasure, under a balmy moon, it is the time and the place to yield to the sense and let yourself enjoy the embraces of a man who—"

"It is no such thing," said Cassandra, delivering a hearty slap to his face before springing away from him and plunging wildly and blindly towards the path that seemed to offer the best chance of escape.

She heard his peal of laughter behind her as he followed her. "Ah, you like to play games, you enjoy the chase, well, my Diana, I am coming to get you, and I am no Adonis to be slain by any goddess, the goddess of love is my tutelary spirit, and she will waft you to my arms. . . ."

His legs were longer than hers, and Cassandra had a horrible feeling that he, unlike herself, knew exactly where this twisting path led. Pray God it would take her back to one of the principal walkways.

It didn't. After a few more curves, it opened out into a small grove, festooned with lights, quite empty. At its centre was a tiny temple, with a domed roof and two shallow steps leading into its interior.

He was at her side again. "Perfect," he said. "I was sure you knew where you were going, to the temple of love, for that figure there"—he pointed to a one-armed statue—"is Venus herself. Now, let us—"

"I think," said a cold voice, "that the lady is not so inclined to the pleasures of Venus as you think, Mr. Gimpel."

Cassandra stood frozen to the spot. Relief at there being another person in the grove mingled with growing recognition; she knew that voice.

The figure stepped out of the shadows, and walked up to them. "Your servant," he said, bowing to Cassandra. And to Mr. Gimpel: "Unhand the lady, if you please, before I make you do so in a way that you will regret."

It was Mr. Darcy.

One glance told Mr. Gimpel that it would be an unequal contest, and he reluctantly dropped his hold on Cassandra, who stepped quickly away from him.

"It's none of your business, Darcy," said Gimpel. "I don't know what you think you're doing, barging in like that, it's a gross intrusion on a private moment."

Mr. Darcy gave Gimpel a look so full of haughty scorn, that Cassandra felt like applauding. However, something told her that her cousin, who looked exceedingly angry, would not appreciate the gesture.

"Come," he said to her, hooking his arm. "I think we shall leave Gimpel to contemplate his goddess on his own."

It took only a few moments for Cassandra to realize that the anger was directed at her, even more than at Mr. Gimpel.

"Boorish young puppy," said Darcy contemptuously. "What are you thinking of, to be wandering about the gardens in his company?"

What answer could she make to that? "We were with others, and then, somehow, became separated. I had no idea . . ."

"Then it is time you began to have some idea, at least of how to behave. And what are you doing here? This is not living in seclusion, as your stepfather stipulated."

Cassandra was puzzled for a moment, and then it came to her that

Mr. Darcy was talking about her banishment to Cheltenham. Of course, he had believed Mr. Partington's lies, and supposed her to be living there in the company of Mrs. Norris.

"I do not think that my actions are any business of yours," she said.

"They are indeed, for your stepfather has made them so. Please believe me when I say that I have not the slightest interest in your whereabouts, provided that you are in respectable company and living in a proper way. I assumed that was the case, that this Mrs. Norris was well able to take care of a young lady in your circumstances, and then I find you locked in an embrace with Mr. Gimpel. Do you not know that despite his youth, he is as dissipated a young man as has ever been let loose in London? He is lecherous, and feckless, and associates with a set of fellows whom I wouldn't give house room to. He may be immensely wealthy, but as to his morals and manners, that is another matter. How came you to be with him? You say you are with others, where are they, pray? And how came Mr. Gimpel to be among them?"

"I never met the wretched man before this evening, and he forced his attentions on me. I will be more careful in future."

"I think you must be given no opportunity to be anything else," he said with a lofty air that infuriated her.

Horatio Darcy was himself furious, furious with Gimpel for behaving in that loutish fashion, although it was nothing unexpected in his case. He was furious with this Mrs. Norris for not taking better care of her charge, and most of all, he was furious with Cassandra. He had disliked her from the moment he had set eyes on her, as he had told himself frequently since that first meeting—a meeting that replayed over and over in his mind, which annoyed him even more.

He had found himself dwelling on the iniquities of James Eyre, and half-inclined to seek him out and give him a lesson he wouldn't forget. Yet who could blame him? Cassandra was a beauty, if you cared for those kind of looks, which he himself didn't, not at all, and came with the prospect of a fine fortune, it would be a rare man in Eyre's circumstances who wouldn't make a pitch for such a prize. But she, she must be of a naturally bad disposition; she must have encouraged Eyre and led him on.

Such a picture of alarm and innocence as she presented, protesting that she had not intended to wander off the path with Gimpel, apparently frightened and alarmed by his ardour. All show, no doubt, he should have left them to it, he had misjudged the situation, when he glimpsed the couple from the path and saw what Gimpel was about, he should merely have shrugged his shoulders at the impropriety of it and gone on his way.

"I am so grateful to you for rescuing me," she was saying.

She has a golden voice, he thought. One could listen to such a voice all day, and never tire of it.

He pulled himself up, frowning. What was he thinking of? A voice didn't come on its own, and in her case, it came with what he suspected was a considerable intelligence and probably a witty tongue—he couldn't abide a woman with any pretensions to wit. And innocent she was not; her recent and damaging escapade was proof of that. And what a way for a woman to behave, how fickle, hardly to have cast off one lover before she was entangled with another.

He knew this to be unfair; his reasonable self told him that she had not shown the least inclination to respond to Gimpel's advances. But he wanted to feed his anger, so he told himself that she had probably had a stream of lovers, that tale of the painter, what was his name, Lisser, and the mishap in the shrubbery that Mr. Partington had spoken of, that was probably quite her usual behaviour.

Well, he'd write to Mr. Partington, and express in the strongest terms his disapproval of Mrs. Norris bringing her charge to London; letting Cassandra be out anywhere in London was ill-advised, and as for Vauxhall! She should be repenting of her errors, not enjoying the music and lights of a pleasure garden.

Even as these thoughts flitted through his head, he felt the injustice of them. He almost spoke them aloud; he wanted to lash out at Cassandra, to wound her.

Against his will, against all his instincts, he had been impressed by her when she came to his chambers. While knowing that she was making a mistake, and wholly disapproving of any woman taking such a rash step, and then refusing the offer and security of marriage, he had to admire the steadfastness of character which made her insist that she would only marry a man who cared for her as she was, and not for her fortune.

In normal circumstances, such a stand would be praiseworthy, but of course, once a young woman had cast caution and propriety to the wind as she had done, there was no choice left to her. Yet she had decided that there was, going against reason and custom. Well, she was paying for it now, perhaps after this incident, she would discover just how very ill-equipped she was to look after herself, even for the space of half an hour on a summer's evening.

They had reached the Broad Walk once more, even more crowded with people than it had been before. Cassandra took her arm out of his. "Thank you for your escort, but I need trouble you no further, I can easily find my way back to my supper box from here."

Mr. Darcy took no notice, and stayed at her side as she increased her pace, walking noticeably faster than the more leisurely pleasure-seekers around them.

"Don't worry," he said drily. "I have no wish to inflict my company on your party." Although he would like to get a look at this Mrs. Norris . . . No, he wouldn't. It really was absolutely nothing to do with him, he must keep reminding himself of it, and there was Cassandra very much of the same way of thinking; she clearly wanted to have her own way in that, as in so much else. How had Mr. Partington brought up such a headstrong stepdaughter? Her mother must have been very much at fault to let her grow up so independent-minded.

"Now I really must beg you to leave me," Cassandra said, as they came near to the main arena, where an orchestra was busy tuning up for the next performance. "I can come to no harm here."

"I think you could come to harm anywhere, Miss Darcy," he said coldly. He bowed, and watched her walk quickly away towards the boxes. He turned, bumping as he did so into a tall, languorous-looking man who was sauntering alone with a jaunty air. "Why, Jack, good evening to you."

"Horatio! What brings a hardworking lawyer to this site of frivolity and wickedness? Ah, accompanying the dazzling Lady Usborne, of course, why didn't I think of it? You're out of your league there, dear fellow, definitely walking in a dangerous place there. Oh, I dare say there's no harm in her ladyship, beyond her not being too strong on the moral side, but Lord Usborne is an ugly customer if crossed."

"Do leave my private affairs out of the conversation, Jack, there's a good fellow. Lord Usborne and his wife ceased to care for one another years ago, it is a hollow marriage, as most of them are."

"Is that why you haven't married? Well, things are not always what they seem within a marriage, that's one thing that an ill-spent life has taught me."

"I don't marry because I can't afford to keep a wife, and if I could, I've never met a woman I should wish to set up house with."

As Darcy spoke, his eyes were on Cassandra, just going into a box on the first level. Jack followed his gaze.

"What a pretty creature," he exclaimed. "Horatio, you dog, Lady Usborne on one arm, and chasing after a dazzler with the other."

"You're mixing your metaphors, and I don't know what you're talking about."

"Tell you what, she puts me in mind of Mrs. Wytton, now there's a happy bride, and a devilish contented husband, too; Wytton's quite lost all his quick-tempered and bearish ways since he settled down with her. She's a cousin of yours, ain't she? Is this girl a relation? Don't I know that woman she's talking to?" His eyes narrowed.

Damn Jack and his impertinence. "That's one Mrs. Norris, who's supposed to be her chaperone, although she isn't much good at it, if you ask me."

"Mrs. Norris, eh? Funny, I could have sworn . . ."

But his attention, never very constant, was distracted by the sight of another old friend in the crowd, and he made an abrupt departure, calling out to Horatio that he'd seen Urquhart over there. "He owes me a pony, let's see if I can't get him to buy me supper."

Supper! Horatio had never felt less like eating the chicken and ham that Vauxhall was famous for. Nor did he much care to return to his mistress, who would be waiting for him in another of the groves; she had come with several friends, but made an assignation with him at a favourite spot. She loved these elements of intrigue; Darcy was beginning to feel that there might be something to be said for the calm of a domestic life, such as the Wyttons enjoyed. Only for a moment, though, there was no question of that for him for many years, if at all. Wytton was an eldest son, with a considerable estate and no financial worries, he was well able to afford a wife.

Jack had often suggested Darcy try his hand at an heiress: "You're a good-looking fellow, with pleasing manners when you're not on your high horse about something. Why waste your time and talents on a Lady U., when you might collar a thirty- or forty-thousand pounder?"

Because he didn't choose to. In a world where no one bothered about money, except as to how to spend it, Horatio had very different views from the norm. He had no wish to live on a wife's fortune. Naturally, upon marriage, his wife's money would become his, for married women could own neither property nor wealth of any kind, everything they had was deemed to belong to their husband, but still, the inequality of such a match would always leave a sensitive man at a moral disadvantage.

No, he would prefer to make a name and fortune of his own, like an honest man. Like some lowly cit, he said to himself with dissatisfaction, wishing for a moment that he could share some of Jack's insouciance. Jack would marry an heiress tomorrow, if he could find any father fool enough to permit it, for although Jack was the eldest son of Lord Frinton, he would inherit all his father's debts, which were even bigger than his own. He would find some wealthy merchant or banker, though, in the end, a cit out in the market for a title for his daughter. That was the way of the world, no point railing against it. He wasn't going to give that dratted woman another thought, he told himself, as he glanced again at the box where she was sitting with her friends. If Mrs. Norris wasn't going to look after her properly, that was her lookout, and shame on Mr. Partington for not taking better care of her in the first place.

Cassandra was still feeling shaken, and also angry at letting herself be so unwary as to end up in a compromising situation with that dreadful Mr. Gimpel, and even more angry at being discovered by Mr. Darcy. Hateful man, with his superior ways; yes, she was glad to have been helped out of a fix, but why had it had to be that man, of all the men in London who was there at that moment?

Fate, she thought bitterly. Wasn't that what the legends that her papa had loved to tell her were all about? Mortals struggling in vain against the devices of the gods?

That brought her sense of humour back. Whatever Mr. Darcy was, he wasn't any kind of Olympian god, just a prejudiced man, as one from his background would be. She would put him and the whole incident out of her mind. So when Mrs. Nettleton questioned her as to the whereabouts of Mr. Gimpel, she replied in a tolerably even voice that he had gone off to find some other acquaintance.

"I dare say he will be back shortly," said Mrs. Nettleton comfortably. "I am pleased to see the two of you getting along so well together," she added, with an arch look.

"We do not get on at all," Cassandra said; best not to leave any doubt in Mrs. Nettleton's mind on that score. "He is an ill-behaved man; I do not care for his company in the least."

"Fie, so high and mighty," cried Mrs. Nettleton. "Let me tell you, that for a girl in your circumstances . . ." She stopped abruptly, her face suddenly wreathed in smiles.

Cassandra turned to see who had wrought this transformation in her, and found herself face-to-face with Lord Usborne.

Mrs. Nettleton greeted him with effusiveness, begging him to sit down and join them, the famous wafer-thin ham would be arriving shortly, and Mr. Josbert had been so good as to order several of the tiny chickens, besides a quart of arrack. But perhaps he was in another box, with other company?

Lord Usborne said that was so, and it looked for a moment as though he were about to take his leave, but something decided him against it, and he drew out the chair beside Cassandra, and began to talk to her, about the spectacles on offer. "Wait until you see the cascade, they will ring a bell shortly, it is nearly ten o'clock, and then you will see a remarkable sight."

The cascade was indeed quite unlike anything that Cassandra had ever seen, but although she was entertained by the image of the water mill, its wheel turning, and an apparent stream of water tumbling down to the bottom, her heart was no longer in the mood for that kind of amusement. She felt bruised, and was longing for solitude. How often her evenings with Mrs. Nettleton seemed to end with her wishing for them to be over, so that she might retire to the tranquillity of her chamber.

Lord Usborne was behaving in a most gentlemanlike fashion, although when he suggested a postprandial stroll along one of the walkways, she declined his invitation, despite urgent nods and becks of encouragement from Mrs. Nettleton. Afterwards, as they left their box, she heard her landlady whispering to Lord Usborne about an unfortunate chance that had left Mrs. Kent alone in a deserted place with Mr. Gimpel, at least that was what she concluded must have happened, and it was not to Mrs. Kent's taste.

"I shouldn't think Gimpel was to any woman of sense's taste," she heard Lord Usborne reply in a testy voice.

Chapter Eighteen

Cassandra awoke early, after a dark, oppressive dream. She had slept with the curtains around her bed drawn back, since she never liked the feeling of being hemmed in while she slept. But in her dream, she had had the sense of being confined to an uncomfortable degree. She had dreamt she was in the drawing room downstairs in St. James's Square, a room which in her dream was entirely green, a shadowy, ominous colour that spread over floors and windows and walls and ceiling. All the furniture was green, as well, upholstered in thick velvet, a velvet that seemed to come out and smother her so that she found it difficult to breathe.

The walls appeared to close in on her, stifling her further. She wanted to reach the window, to throw up a sash and let in the outside world, but when she struggled to one, the panes were also green and blank and let in no light; the windows were in fact mere painted shapes, as was the door when she tried to escape from the room that way. She was in a closed box that was shrinking towards her, drawing the life out of her, silencing her attempt to call out.

She woke with a scream sounding in her ears. Her own scream, she realized as she lay blinking in the early light of dawn. Had she really cried out, had she woken the household, would servants, Mrs. Nettleton, come hammering on her door to enquire what was amiss?

Silence reigned, the scream must have been lost in the dream;

nightmare, rather, that had left her shaken and not at all inclined to sink back into slumber. It had been so vivid, it made her look anxiously around the bedchamber, as though the images of her mind were more real than what she saw before her, with her eyes.

Yet she knew there was truth in the dream, for the house in St. James's Square, which had seemed a refuge, a place of comfort, and one furnished with some elegance, was becoming uncomfortable. She felt uneasy when she was there, and could not imagine why this should be so. Perhaps she was simply spending too long indoors. Country bred and raised, she was a vigorous walker at home, and there were few days when she did not go out riding. If bad weather kept her within doors for any length of time, then she would be almost desperate to escape outside, to work off the fidgets that came over her if she did not exercise.

Home! She no longer had a home. No park to ride in, no elm walk to stroll along with Emily or her little sisters, no more impromptu dances at neighbouring houses or the delights of private or assembly balls. All that lay beyond a door that had slammed behind her as firmly as the door of the carriage that she and Eyre had travelled in on that fateful night.

Now she dwelt in a town house, a good size for London, but less than a cottage in comparison to Rosings. Outside, were streets and people and noise, and only parks or river walks for Londoners to take the air and exercise their limbs.

Well, today she would not stay indoors with her paints and brushes. She would go to Rudge's. Then she would walk back via the Receiving House. There might be a letter from Emily, although it seemed unlikely; her friend would be deep in wedding plans, which would take up all her time and thoughts. Still, it made an object for a walk, and would keep her out of the house for a little while longer.

By the time Betsy came in to bring her dish of chocolate and draw the curtains back, Cassandra was up. Mrs. Nettleton, she was informed, was still abed and likely to be so for at least another hour, she had been up very late the night before, not retiring until gone three in the morning, Betsy said, unable to hide a yawn.

It was a bright day, but there was a brisk wind, which made Cassandra glad of her pelisse. She had managed to come out alone, assuring Betsy that she was only going to walk for a little while in the park to get some air, she found it stuffy indoors and needed to clear her head.

Was Mrs. Nettleton really concerned for her safety in the big, bad city, as she claimed, or was Betsy's job to keep a watch on her, as though Mrs. Nettleton was afraid she might run off? It could merely be concern for the rent, or maybe the whole thing was just a ridiculous fancy, and Mrs. Nettleton, who appeared to be all consideration, was in fact chary of her lodger venturing out alone.

Cassandra had found a copy of *The Picture of London* in her bedchamber, a fat volume, only a year or two out-of-date, and surely London could not have changed so very much in that time? It was packed with useful advice, apart from the many worthy pages about the history of the Great Metropolis, and as to crime and the safety of walking abroad, it pooh-poohed the notion that the city was a dangerous place.

Travellers arriving in London, she read, might be held up by footpads on Blackfriars or Hampstead Heath, or, apparently, have any luggage that was strapped to a coach cut off and stolen; well, she had escaped that inconvenience. Other than that, the author of the guide merely warned tourists to be wary of the nimbleness and address of pickpockets, avoid hawkers, and take care to note the number of any hackney-coach before getting into it, and, most comfortingly, asserted that no city was more free from danger to those who passed the streets at all hours.

She knew that none of this sound advice applied to ladies of quality; such women, especially young and pretty ones, did not venture abroad unaccompanied. Well, she might have been born one of these privileged persons, but she must now number herself among the less fortunate of London's citizens, and fend for herself.

Provided she did not dawdle, she told herself, but looked as though she were a native of the town rather than a lamb for fleecing, then she did not believe she would be offered any insult or suffer any assault; how could she be, in such a bustling, populous place, where a call for help would bring a dozen stout citizens to her aid and probably the watch besides?

She tucked the little volume into her reticule—it contained several useful maps apart from such valuable information as the quantity of milk drunk in London each year and an account of London's various prisons; which pages made grim reading. At the thought of debtors' prisons, a coldness came over Cassandra, aware as she was of how slender were her resources and how precarious her existence must be until she could find some kind of employment.

And not the kind of employment Betsy hankered after, either. What had she said? "They may call them by fancy names, but it is one, they are but whorehouses, however fine the women dress."

Cassandra had caught the resentment and envy in Betsy's voice, the regret of a plain woman for her lack of looks. Yet she had employment, and Mrs. Nettleton seemed a good enough mistress, would she rather work in one of those establishments? Cassandra thought it better not to ask the question. It was an old profession, she knew, if not an honourable one, and most of those women would do the work not out of pleasure but from chance or necessity, a pretty, fresh country girl cozened into the trade by a woman pretending to be looking for a servant. Or a young woman seduced and betrayed.

Like her. No, not like her. She hadn't been seduced, she had fallen willingly into Eyre's arms and into his bed. Her passion for James and her longing to escape from the more respectable life that beckoned if she married Mr. Wexford had been the cause of her present condition.

Would Mr. Partington and Mrs. Cathcart, and her mother, even, have forced her to marry Mr. Wexford? Of course not. And Mr. Wexford would not have wanted an unwilling bride; the days of weeping brides dragged to the altar by an enraged father or a brutal brother were long past, and even in the last century, Cassandra doubted if there had actually been many such matches.

Her spirits, dampened by these lowering thoughts, rose as she left behind the streets around St. James's and came to the less fashionable streets where Mr. Rudge had his establishment.

Mr. Rudge himself was busy with a customer, a big man with bushy eyebrows, dressed in a snuff-coloured coat. Mr. Rudge's assistant, a Mr. Fingal, a gangly, intense young man with copper-coloured hair and intelligent eyes, attended to Cassandra, and he whispered to her that Mr. Rudge's customer was Mr. Haydon, the history painter, she must have heard of him?

She had, and was intrigued to see him, and to listen surreptitiously to his conversation with Mr. Rudge, as much about his fellow painters as about the sable brushes he was buying. Henry Lisser's name was mentioned, and she tried hard to hear what was being said about him, but just then Mr. Fingal brought out a sample of a yellow newly come from Germany, where they were, he told her, experimenting with several chrome paints, and began to tell her why it was superior to the Naples yellow she normally used. She was obliged to listen, and, indeed, found his enthusiasm and knowledge of the new paints being developed fascinating; by the time he had finished, Mr. Rudge and Mr. Haydon had concluded their business, and the painter left the shop with a courteous bow to Cassandra and a bluff "Good morning" to Mr. Rudge and Mr. Fingal.

The paints were ordered, yes, Mr. Rudge would send the bill to Mrs. Nettleton, and, yes, he would place her notice offering lessons at reasonable rates among other such announcements pinned on his wall. Many of them had a faded appearance, with curled edges; Cassandra could not hold great hopes of any success through this means of advertisement.

Mr. Rudge seemed to read her thoughts, and he shook his head in a regretful way. "It is the same as with everything, it is connections that count, it is whom you know and who knows you that matters. However, do not despair, I shall mention your name whenever it seems appropriate, you may depend on it."

Mrs. Nettleton had promised the same, so perhaps, in spite of her doubts, something would come of her or Mr. Rudge's efforts.

Not wanting to return to St. James's Square quite yet, Cassandra set off for the Receiving House. To her surprise, there was a letter from Emily after all, or rather a note, a few brief lines, begging Cassandra to write again, not to disappear as she seemed to have done, she would write further when she was more at leisure, but remained always, her most affectionate friend . . .

Cassandra read it through swiftly as she left the office, then tucked it into her reticule. She didn't notice the figure that slipped out behind her and followed her as she walked slowly down St. Martin's Lane. She wouldn't have noticed if someone far more noticeable had been dogging her footsteps, no, nor if her shadow had jumped in front of her and called her by name.

For Cassandra was far away from London, back in Kent, in her attic room at Rosings, five years before, painting Emily, who was dressed in her favourite blue dress with a yellow sash, holding a kitten in her lap. Cassandra's painting was full of faults, but it had a life and a freshness to it that made Mrs. Croscombe open her eyes when a triumphant Emily carried it home.

Now Emily was a woman, not a girl, and about to become a bride; the kitten had grown into a sleek kitchen cat, famous for her mousing ability, and Cassandra . . . well, Cassandra had grown into an artist and an outcast from her family, from her attic, and from her home. Even from her oldest friend, from Emily.

Cassandra walked into St. James's Square, hesitated, then went into the garden, not wanting to go back yet into the house. She spied a bench, went over, and sat down upon it. A nursemaid was standing by the railings on the other side, flirting with a young man wearing the leather jerkin and gaiters of a groom. She was pretty and happy, and not too wrapped up in her companion to forget her charges, casting them a glance from time to time to make sure the little boys were still scampering up and down, one inexpertly bowling a metal hoop, the other pretending to ride a horse.

Cassandra drew out her sketchbook and was instantly absorbed in catching the pert tilt of the nursemaid's head, and her sparkling eyes. So absorbed, that at first she did not catch the voice whispering her name.

"Miss Darcy. Miss Darcy!"

Horror-stricken, she dropped her pencil and half stood up, looking to see who was there, who it was who knew her as Miss Darcy. Although she knew who it was, even before her eyes found her, lurking behind a large shrub.

"Petifer! For God's sake, what are you doing here! What a fright you gave me!"

"I'm sorry for that," said Petifer, emerging from her hiding place. Then she froze, and vanished out of sight again, as a tall, elegant figure came along the path towards where Cassandra was sitting.

"My dear Mrs. Kent," said Lord Usborne, as he made a leg. "They told me you were not at home, and then by the merest chance I spotted you here, in the square."

Cassandra hastily picked up her sketchbook and stuffed it into her reticule.

Lord Usborne raised his eyebrows. "Running away from me, Mrs. Kent?"

She reddened. "No, I have finished what I was doing here."

"Which was?"

Up went her chin. What right had he to question her movements or activities. "I think that is my business, my lord."

He laughed. "Oh, I stand rebuked. If you are finished here, allow me to escort you back to your house."

"I thank you, it is but a step as you know."

He walked alongside her, and she wished he would not. He was too close to her, observing her more closely than she cared for. Eyre's looks of admiration had given her pleasure, Lord Usborne's made her wary. And she was eager to find out what Petifer was doing here, Petifer, of all people! Thank goodness she had withdrawn so swiftly; she just hoped that Lord Usborne had not been passing on the other side of the railings at that point when Petifer called out to her as Miss Darcy. Had she come from Kent? Could she have a message from Rosings for her? Oh, why did the tiresome man have to appear just at that moment?

He clearly meant to accompany her into the house, but she forestalled him, holding out her hand in a firm way.

"It was my intention to wait upon you—and Mrs. Nettleton, of course," he said, mounting the steps beside her.

"As to Mrs. Nettleton, I cannot say, but I find I have the headache, and so you will excuse me." As soon as the door was opened to his knock, she was inside and making good her escape. She knew his eyes were following her up the stairs, so she moved swiftly to the next floor. Let him go and chat to Mrs. Nettleton if he felt so inclined; yes, as she paused outside her room, she heard him being admitted into the morning parlour below. She opened her door, went in, walked across the wooden floor with deliberately heavy feet, then tiptoed back, and was out, flying down the stairs and letting herself out of the front door.

Then she was at the gate to the garden in the square again, and once inside the railings, she looked around for Petifer. There she was, sitting on the very bench where Cassandra had sat and sketched. The nursemaid and her charges had gone, and the groom was eyeing Petifer up and down; he clearly had a roving eye.

"Saucebox!" said Petifer indignantly, getting up as she saw Cassandra. "Very free in their ways they are in London, miss, and no mistake. Asked me if I grew up in a garden on account of the roses blooming in my cheeks!"

"Petifer, I can't linger here, for—" Cassandra was going to say "for we may be overlooked from number seven," but instead she led the way out of the garden, and into Charles Street on the east side of the square. "Now, I must know at once why you are come to London?"

Chapter Nineteen

It was not a happy story, and one that made Cassandra ashamed. How could she have been so heartless, so careless, so thoughtless? Why had it not occurred to her that Mrs. Cathcart might vent some of her fury at Cassandra's elopement on her maid, the maid who had come from Kent with her, her own, dear Petifer, who had looked after her and been a painter's assistant, and protected her on numerous occasions from getting into scrapes with her mother and stepfather?

"She turned me off directly, the very morning you were gone. She said I knew what you had planned, and that I should have gone straightway to her, so that she could put a stop to such wickedness."

"Petifer, you didn't know I was running away with Mr. Eyre. I made sure not to breathe a word of it, for that very reason, that Mrs. Cathcart would be so angry with you."

"I guessed you were up to something, Miss Darcy, what with you so lovey-dovey with that Mr. Eyre, and creeping out of the house. I can tell when a man is up to no good."

"Can you? Then it's more than I can, I wish I had had such foresight. But then"—with a sigh—"I was doomed to believe what he said, and to trust him. I was a fool, that's all there is to it. Never mind that, why did you not go back to Kent when Mrs. Cathcart treated you so badly? My mother would have listened to you, she always had a kindness for you."

"Mrs. Cathcart was writing directly to Mr. Partington, to say that I was a poor servant and not to be trusted; I know I would have been turned away if I went back to Rosings, and that would mean the extra fare to pay and other expenses besides."

"Surely Mrs. Cathcart was obliged to pay you your wages before she turned you off?"

Petifer shook her head. "Not she, the old cat, nor would she give me a character, although I hoped that Mrs. Partington might, if it blew over, if that is you became Mrs. Eyre. Or, that, if you were indeed a married woman, as I hoped and thought you would be, then you'd need a maid and perhaps be willing to take me on."

Cassandra's heart sank. "I would, I would indeed, but I am not married, nor likely to become a wife to any man. I can hardly afford to keep myself. We are in the same boat, you and I, Petifer, both turned off, as it were."

Except that her lack of funds was her own fault, and the situation Petifer found herself in was none of her own making, but entirely that of Cassandra's.

"How come you in London? Have you found employment?"

"Not without a reference, and . . ."

"But I can write you a reference. That at least I can do."

"No, thank you all the same. I don't want to work for anyone else except you."

"Oh, Petifer, don't you see that it is impossible?"

"I've got my savings. I've put something by ever since I began work. My nan told me to do that: 'Don't spend it all on a ribbon or other fripperies, for the day will come when you'll thank the Lord you've got a bit of money of your own,' she would say to me, and she was right, and that day is now. Soon as I knew what you'd done, soon as that old bat threw me out, I thought, I'll follow her to London—"

"We had planned to go to Gretna Green, not London."

"Pardon me, you might have thought you was going to Scotland, but Mr. Eyre's groom knew it was London from the start. I struck up a friendship with one of the maidservants, who works at nineteen Laura Place. Her brother's an ostler at the Christopher, and he overheard Mr. Eyre talking about it. You don't plan to change horses at Hungerford if you're heading north, even I know that."

It was nothing more than Cassandra had suspected, but it was lowering to have to accept that James Eyre had lied to her about his original intention to head for Gretna Green. For the only conclusion she could draw from his lie was that he had always had an eye to her fortune.

"How did you get to London?"

"With Jemmy's help, he's the ostler I spoke of. He's friends with all the mail coach drivers, and one of them took me up as a favour."

"Not on the waybill? Without paying?"

"I paid all right, having to listen to his wisecracks and jokes all the way from Bath to the Saracen's Head. He had a free and easy way of looking and speaking, you might say, and he wasn't restrained with his hands, neither."

Petifer's disapproving face made Cassandra laugh. "What courage and resolution. Where are you putting up? London is a dangerous place."

"As you're discovering, Miss Darcy," Petifer retorted. "My sister Margaret married a man who keeps a market garden out Camberwell way. They have a stall in Covent Garden and bring stuff in every morning. I've been coming in with them, and giving them a hand, which they're glad of, business being quite brisk, and then I have the rest of my time, once the market closes, to look for you."

"How came you to find me?"

"I wrote to Miss Emily and asked her if she had your address, she wrote back at once and said she wrote to you at the Receiving House in St. Martin's Lane, so I've been going there nearly every day. Today you were there, so when you came out I followed you."

"Why didn't you call out, there at the post office, if you saw me?"

"Because I wanted to find out where you were lodging. Otherwise you would most likely have given me the slip again."

Cassandra gestured across to the square.

"This is where I'm staying at present. All very respectable, as you see. I have a room and a pleasant landlady."

Petifer sniffed. "A room! That's a come-down from Rosings, to be sure. My sister says this area is far from respectable, that there are a lot of ladies who live here who are no better than they ought to be."

"Yes, but that might be said of almost anywhere in town."

"If this landlady of yours is so respectable, what does she think of a young woman of quality such as you are tipping up on her doorstep without a maid or anyone in attendance?"

Cassandra reddened. "She thinks I am a widow."

"Widow! You look like a widow, I dare say. How can she swallow such a tale?"

"Well, she did. Petifer, I can't say how glad I am to see you, it does me good just to see you smile and hear your voice. I wish I could do something for you, and I can, as far as that reference goes. There is no hope of my being able to take you on again, now or in the future. I have to earn my living somehow, you know, and there will be no money to spare."

"Go on! How do you hope to earn a living? I never heard of such a thing, and besides, your family wouldn't permit it."

"My family won't have anything to do with me, I've been cast off, just like you."

"That's that mean-fisted, tight-arsed old fart! Forgive my language, miss, but it makes me see red, to think of that Mr. Partington having the right to turn you out of Rosings, where you were born. Lady Catherine's granddaughter earning her living? I never heard of such a thing. Let word of that get back to Mrs. Partington and even she'll come to her senses, and make Mr. Partington do what's right by you. You're her daughter, and nothing he says can change that. She won't let him behave in such a way."

"Do you think so? I do not. Besides, I don't want to go back. Not now." Cassandra stood up. "No, you must be sensible, Petifer, and find another position. For my sake as much as for your own; how do you think I shall feel, knowing you are using up your savings, while waiting to work for me again, which can't happen?"

"I've as much right to do what I want with my money as you've got to go round calling yourself a widow and saying you're going to earn a living. Which you won't, given that there's nothing any lady of your sort can do, bar become a governess."

"I trust it won't come to that, for I fear I should make a poor show of it. I plan to teach drawing and painting. To young ladies. There is always a demand for that, in London."

Petifer looked unconvinced, and she made a clicking noise with her tongue. "It isn't right, but you always were one to do what you wanted, and now see where being headstrong has got you, into as bad a scrape as anyone could think of. You're not fit to be out and that's the truth of it. Now, your landlady will likely have an attic where I can sleep, so you just tell her your maid's here, and I'll be back with my bundle, ready to take up my duty, which is to take care of you, since you can't do it for yourself."

"She knows I can barely pay the rent, and to have a maid arrive— no, it's impossible, Petifer. I am truly sorry, but even though I might wish for your company, I can't accept your services."

Petifer did not have the look of a person who was going to do as she was told. But she got up from the bench and gave a tight-lipped little nod. "As you say, miss, I can see it might be awkward for you, but I tell you plain, you need me. So I'll be back, discreet like, every day. So as soon as you find you need me, which you will, as soon as I can do anything for you, why, there I'll be."

Before Cassandra could remonstrate with her, Petifer was off, hurrying out of the garden and round the corner, oblivious to her name being called after her by her erstwhile employer.

Her departure left Cassandra torn between tears and laughter. How could she have been so thoughtless? Was there to be no end to the consequences of her action? Petifer's loyalty was touching, and her reward for years of faithful service was to be turned off by that dreadful woman, who had no doubt had a lot more unpleasant things to say than Petifer had reported.

Well, at least she had a home with her sister, and maybe she would make Petifer see sense, where Cassandra couldn't.

*   *   *

It was as well she weren't a fly on the wall that evening, when Petifer was at home with her sister, being cross-examined on her day's activities. Margaret, who was the older by several years, had noticed the satisfied look on her sister's face, and she soon had the truth out of her.

"So you've found her, and in St. James's Square. Well, I told you how it would be, she's come on the town, for sure."

"She has not. Miss Darcy would never do that. She's lodging with a respectable woman, and passing herself off as a widow, so that she doesn't get asked any questions."

"We all know the kind of woman who passes herself off as a widow."

"Do we?"

"You may not, because you've lived in the country all your life, and you've no idea what life in a big city such as London is like. She's lost her reputation, has that young lady; since the gent she ran off with didn't make an honest woman of her, she's no chance of keeping her good name. She'll end up with a protector, that's all she can do, go into some man's keeping, and then she's on a slippery slope to the devil's home, I can tell you. You leave well alone, my girl. You say you can't go back to Kent, very well, we'll find you a position in London, where I can keep an eye on you."

"No, thank you. Miss Darcy's who I work for, I don't need any other mistress or master."

"It's not what you want in this life, it's what you get that you have to do with. You'll run out of money soon enough, then you'll see sense. Now, give me a hand with these sacks, and let's hear no more about Miss Darcy." She went to the door. "Rob! Rob! Where is that dratted man? Men are never about when you want them, like your young lady's finding out the hard way."

Had Cassandra been privy to this conversation, she might have responded that unfortunately men were all too often there when you didn't want them. Lord Usborne was a visitor at the house in St. James's Square again that evening, in a high good humour, talkative and lively; did the man spend no time at all at home with his wife, was it his habit to haunt the house in St. James's Square?

Cassandra could deceive herself no longer. Lord Usborne was growing particular in his attentions, and there was something disagreeable in his easy manners, as though he was certain that where his fancy fell he would meet with success.

He takes me for a woman of no virtue or morals, Cassandra said inwardly, as she moved from the sofa where he had sat himself beside her, to another chair. Well, that might be so in the eyes of the world, but she had better morals than his lordship; he had a wife to make what he was doing adultery, a greater lapse, in her view than eloping with a man you loved. Or thought you loved, she corrected herself.

A visit to the theatre was being planned. *Hamlet* was showing at the Haymarket. Mrs. Kent would honour them with her company?

As it happened, Cassandra had never been to a play. She would like to see *Hamlet,* the play that her father had loved above all others, that he used to read out loud to her when she was a child, taking all the parts in turn, so that although she only understood the half of it, she knew many of the speeches by heart.

Could there be any harm in it? Would not a visit to the theatre be preferable to the intimacy of the rooms at St. James's Square? Mrs. Nettleton was going, and some others, it was not as though she would be obliged to spend the evening alone with Lord Usborne.

The moment she stepped into the carriage, Cassandra knew she had made a mistake. Lord Usborne was there to hand her in, very fine in his evening clothes. Mrs. Nettleton wore a gown of pink silk that made Cassandra blink; the others in their party turned out to be Mrs. Palmer, but a Mrs. Palmer escorted not by Colonel Palmer, but by a leggy young man called Rolandson, who came from the north of England and who was, so the quondam Mrs. Palmer whispered to Cassandra, amazingly rich.

What of Colonel Palmer? Cassandra was forced to conclude that the relationship between the Palmers had never been sanctified in church, that the *Mrs.* was no more than a convenience. Any more than her own *Mrs.* was, she reminded herself somewhat ruefully; who was she to cast stones?

Chapter Twenty

The two men met in the hall, both in evening clothes, one arriving as the other left. It was ironic that it was Lord Usborne, whose house it was, who was on his way out, and Mr. Horatio Darcy, the visitor, who was coming in.

Horatio glanced up to the galleried landing at the top of the first flight of stairs, where stood Lady Usborne, dressed most elegantly in a gown of black and white crape, with black velvet Vandykes on the body and on the flounce. For a moment, he was taken aback by her remoteness; she looked beautiful, detached, and unhappy as she watched the encounter between her husband and her lover at the foot of the staircase.

"Good evening, Mr. Darcy," said Lord Usborne, with a bow.

Horatio returned the bow, as the butler took his hat from him.

"You are taking Lady Usborne to the theatre, I believe?"

Another bow from Horatio.

"I trust you enjoy the performance." Lord Usborne glanced up at his wife. "And you, my dear. Going to the theatre is often so much more than the play, is that not so?"

"You refer to the farce. I do not often stay for the farce."

"I am aware of that. I, however, enjoy the entire performance." He made a leg to the half-seen figure, and went through the door, his eyes, with something of malice in them, resting on Horatio for the briefest of moments before the door closed behind him.

Horatio felt strangely discomfited by this chance meeting. It was not as though it were not perfectly correct for a friend to take a married woman out to the theatre; indeed, Lady Usborne called those who went out with their husbands quite gothic. "It is fine in the first flush of married bliss, if there is such a thing," she declared, "but when you have been married as long as Usborne and I have—it is several years, you know—then you hardly wish to be seen everywhere together like an old Darby and Joan, or who are those tiresome Greeks that people go on about?"

"I believe you refer to Philemon and Baucis."

"Just so." Her eyes were glinting, and for a moment, Horatio Darcy suspected tears. No, Lady Usborne never cried, at least not in his presence, and why should she want to weep now? He went up the stairs, two steps at a time, took her hand, drew it to his lips, and led her into the drawing room. He complimented her on her gown, a new one, he noticed.

"That is a difference between you and Lord Usborne," she said, with a tight smile. "You notice what I wear, he never does. It is unusual in a man, I find. Men take no heed of clothes, and then, when one is wearing some gown that has seen the light of day a dozen times, will remark, 'Is that new? I have not seen it before.' One day you will make some woman a good husband, I dare say."

Horatio could hear anguish in her voice, and for a moment it alarmed him. He did not care for this talk of husbands and wives. He certainly had no intention of marrying at present, or at any time in the foreseeable future. What could a wife give him that would compare with the delights offered by Lady Usborne's company?

The frisson of adultery added a spice to their connection; he was half in love with her, and that was enough. With such an enchanting creature, for she had the reputation of being a veritable Circe, there might be some danger of a younger man, such as himself, tumbling desperately in love with her, becoming her slave, making wild entreaties to her to risk all and run away with him, but there was nothing so dramatic in their relationship. She was too experienced and he was too wary and too ambitious in his profession for that to be a danger.

Lady Usborne made a tiny correction to a ruffle in his neckcloth, a proprietary gesture that pleased him, although it would have annoyed his valet, who liked to send him out in a state of perfection, and was primly peeved when his master returned somewhat more dishevelled than when he had set out. The neckcloth rearranged in the darkness of a lady's chamber, even with her nimble fingers in assistance, was never quite the same.

"Lord Usborne seems in a hurry this evening," he observed, taking the glass of wine that the flat-faced footman had poured for him. They were in good time; the theatre would not begin until seven o'clock, and for a fleeting second, the harmony of a moment of quiet domesticity, of companionship rather than immediate desire, struck Horatio as being peculiarly pleasant. He dismissed the thought and the feeling instantly; good Lord, was he getting old to have such an idea?

"My husband has a new interest in his life," Lady Usborne said drily.

"Interest?"

"I mean a woman. A mistress. A dazzler, a chestnut-haired dazzler."

"I am sure her hair is not so dazzling as yours," Darcy said at once. Lady Usborne was rightly proud of her chestnut hair; he was not to know that that very evening, she had found a thread of silver among her glossy locks and had frowned as she tugged it out and looked at it coiled in her hand.

"She is a young woman, newly come upon the town, I expect. You saw her the other day, when we were driving in the park. She was in a carriage with Lord Usborne and that wretched Mrs. Nettleton woman."

"I did not notice her," Horatio said. Lord Usborne's latest bird of paradise didn't interest him in the least.

"She is but nineteen," Lady Usborne went on, a trace of bitterness sounding in her voice. "The last one was young as well."

"Last one?"

"Harriet Foxley was the slut's name, only she left him. My word, what a temper that put him in," she said, with considerable satisfaction. "He is not used to that, he is accustomed to give his women their congé, not the other way around. She was unwise; it does not do to arouse his ire. He savours revenge, and will wait to achieve it."

"Very melodramatic. I trust he will not extend this courtesy to me."

"Oh, I am just a possession, not the object of his affections."

This time the bitterness in her words was unmistakable, and Horatio looked at her closely from under hooded lids, while he seemed to be admiring the colour of his wine. She was not looking at him, however, and did not notice the glance.

"I suppose he will set her up in King Street, in Harriet's place, and he will give her diamonds and a carriage and let her redecorate the house as she wishes."

"An expensive business," Horatio said, keeping his voice deliberately light.

"He is rich enough not to notice it, and after all, he has no children, or no legitimate children to save his money for. His heir is his cousin, you know, that idiotic Lancelot Browne, and Usborne sees no need to preserve his fortune for his sake."

Lady Usborne rarely referred to the fact that they had no children. "No chance of that," she had said to Darcy early on in their acquaintance. "And I took care that it should not be so, nothing is so deleterious to a woman's looks as breeding."

"His new mistress is presently residing in St. James's Square," she went on, "with the odious Mrs. Nettleton. I believe she is newly come from the country. She is a widow, or purports to be one."

"How do you know so much about her?"

"I have a spy," said Lady Usborne. "Unbeknownst to Usborne, his groom is in my pay. He knows just where his master goes, and passes the information on to me."

Horatio found this slightly shocking, and even alarming. "It is a bad servant who spies on his master."

"And a good servant who obeys his mistress. I found him the

place, he is an efficient groom who does his work well, my husband is pleased with him, so we are all happy."

Horatio longed to ask why she wanted to know all her husband's movements, it seemed odd to him. Did she care greatly? All that she said gave him the impression—no, the certainty—that their marriage was a sham, that neither of them cared for each other. Wasn't her liaison with him the proof of that? Yet, here she was, keeping tabs on her husband in his outings and love affairs.

"Her name is Cassandra," Lady Usborne was saying. "Pretty enough, but not the one she was given at the font, I should suppose; no woman of that class would have such a name."

"Did you say Cassandra?" Horatio let his surprise show, and Lady Usborne noticed it at once.

"Do you know her?"

"It is an unusual name, that is all." Surely it was a coincidence. Of course it was. Cassandra Darcy was in Cheltenham, with Maria Rushworth and Mrs. Norris.

"Mrs. Kent, Mrs. Cassandra Kent." There was feeling in Lady Usborne's voice, something more than contempt. Horatio wasn't attending, and in any case would not have recognised the pain, not covered as it was by a particularly radiant smile.

Coincidence, that was all. "Usborne can never find a mistress as beautiful and attractive as you," he said, putting down his wineglass and, with a glance at the closed door, going over to join her on the little sofa. He stroked her cheek with the back of his hand, then drew her towards him.

Her kiss was passionate and arousing; that there might be desperation in it, did not occur to him.

Footsteps sounded outside the door. They drew apart, and Horatio was on his feet, and standing by the window when the footman came in to announce that the carriage was below.

Cassandra sat in the front of the box, her eyes stretched as she took in the glittering, shifting scene. The theatre seemed so big, and the din of three thousand people, all speaking at the top of their voices, made her ears ring. So many candles, so much red and gold, so many gorgeous gowns set off by the mostly sombre coats of the men. She was enthralled, and hardly listened to the conversation of the others as they noticed friends and acquaintances and enemies, and, in the case of Mrs. Nettleton and Mrs. Palmer, passed unfavourable comments on the gowns and jewels of various members of the audience.

Cassandra was wearing another of the dresses from Mrs. Nettleton's wardrobe, of dark red silk, much the most daring dress she had ever had on, a far cry from the maidenly muslins and pale colours she was accustomed to. Although very many of the women were wearing white, she noticed, not the simple white of a girl's dress, but dashing, frothy confections, cut with a line that her artist's eye noticed and admired. In a moment when Lord Usborne was speaking to Mrs. Palmer, she commented on this to Mrs. Nettleton.

"Oh, my dear, one forgets you are come from Bath and not familiar with the fashions of town. It is quite the thing among certain ladies to wear white, it shows off jewels and a fine skin to perfection, and it is so difficult and expensive to keep clean that it proclaims to the world that the wearer has the wherewithal to keep herself decked out in such a style."

Mrs. Nettleton turned back to share a joke with Lord Usborne, and Cassandra returned to surveying the restless crowd below. She became aware of a prickling sensation at the nape of her neck, that feeling of being watched, and, without being too obvious about it, she slowly turned her head to see if she was right, if someone was staring.

Dear God, it was Horatio Darcy. Sitting in a box on the other side of the house, in company with a finely dressed woman, heavens, with Lady Usborne. Well, there was no surprise there, not after what Mrs. Nettleton had told her, but she would very much rather that he hadn't seen her, not here, dressed like this, in Lord Usborne's company.

His initial, startled look turned to one of anger. He was not going to acknowledge her, that was clear; he was favouring her with nothing more than a rigid stare.

Furious with herself for caring, Cassandra felt a flush rising to her cheeks, and she put a hand up to touch her glowing face.

Lord Usborne leant forward. "You are feeling the heat, my dear. You should have brought a fan."

Smells of musky scent assailed her nostrils, the lights danced and broke into stars before her eyes, the red velvet was the colour of blood, then everything came together in a kaleidoscope of colour and sound, filling her head and making her want to cry out in distress.

"What is it?" hissed Mrs. Nettleton, as Cassandra rose, her hand pressed to her mouth.

"I will be back directly," said Cassandra, and brushed past Lord Usborne, who was rising to his feet. She whisked herself out of the box and walked quickly, nearly running, along the passage. Men and women and flunkeys stared at her, someone tittered. Where was the way out? She must breathe some air, she had to be out of this place, away from the red and gold and heat, away from painted Mrs. Nettleton, away from the affected laughter and voice of Mrs. Palmer, and, most of all, out of reach of Lord Usborne.

She found her way at last down the stairs to the entrance lobby, thronged with people, and plunged out into the street.

No one could have called the night London air fresh; it smelt of smoke and nearby hot-food stalls and horses, and a number of other odours that Cassandra could not have identified, but to her, it was nectar.

People jostled her as she stood, the polite company going into the theatre with a murmur of apology, others with an oath. A man stopped, eyed her up and down, and opened his mouth to address her, and then, miracle of miracles, Petifer was beside her. Cassandra, coming to her senses, stared at the man, with such a look of aloof disgust on her face that he moved hastily away. Petifer took her arm and dragged her away from the crush.

"Petifer! What are you doing here?"

"I followed you. I told you, Miss Cassandra, I was going to keep an eye on you, and it looks like you need it."

"It was only a visit to the theatre, you know," Cassandra said, with an attempt at a laugh.

"What, in the company of that man, his lordship, and Mrs. Nettleton. There's a word for women like her, and it isn't a nice one. Fine company for a Miss Darcy."

"Ssh," said Cassandra. "Petifer, you must not use that name."

"And why not? It's the name you were born with, and it's the name you'll have until you're married."

"Then it will always be my name, but for heaven's sake, Petifer, not here, not in public. Mrs. Kent, if you please."

They were walking away from St. James's Square now, up Haymarket. Cassandra was not really aware of the direction they were taking, but realised they were in Piccadilly Circus, with its bustle of traffic.

"I go the other way," she said to Petifer.

"If you mean to St. James's Square, you do not," Petifer said. "That's one reason why I followed you this evening, for there's a thing or two about that establishment you're staying in that you need to know."

"How can you know anything about where I lodge?"

Petifer stopped, her arms akimbo. "There may or may not be respectable houses in that square, but believe me, number seven isn't one of them."

Cassandra's head was beginning to throb in earnest now. "Petifer, do stop it," she said wearily. "You know nothing about it."

"Oh, yes, I do. One thing about being a servant is that it's easy enough to strike up a conversation with other servants. There's a girl called Betsy works for Mrs. Nettleton, and when she was out at market this morning, I got chatting with her. Gabby girl, I wouldn't keep her as a maid, and she's ill-favoured to look at. Which is all part of Mrs. Nettleton's schemes, for she doesn't care to have good-looking girls as servants in the house, doesn't want her gentlemen callers being distracted, that's why."

"What do you mean?"

"Mrs. Nettleton is in business, and her business is human flesh, female flesh. She knows a lot of rich men, like that Lord Usborne, who like to meet beautiful young women, sometimes just for a night or a week or so, sometimes—and this is where she makes her money—for a longer arrangement. Like when the gentleman sets a girl up in her own establishment, everything fine about it, under his protection. He pays Mrs. Nettleton for the introduction, and she takes a cut of everything the woman gets out of her protector."

Cassandra tried to make sense of what Petifer was saying. "You mean she's"—she searched her mind for the word—"an *entremetteuse*?"

"If that's the word for a high-class procuress, yes. That woman you were with this evening, she's one of Mrs. Nettleton's wares. Only she's picky, takes up with a man for a little while, then decides he isn't right for her, not rich and generous enough, most likely, and back she comes to Ma Nettleton for another go. She's an eye to Lord Usborne, but he only takes a fancy to the ladylike ones. Which she isn't. Which you are."

"Even if what you say is true—"

"It is."

"—it doesn't follow that I'm going to fall into the clutches of Lord Usborne, or Lord Anybody."

"That's what you say, and what you think, but what happens at the end of the month, when you can't pay your rent, and Mrs. N. threatens to have the law on you? Do you fancy a stint in the Clink, in the Marshalsea? Do you think, even if Mr. Partington got to hear of it, he would bail you out, or let your ma come to your rescue?"

They had drawn to the side of the street. Piccadilly was brightly illuminated with gas-lights, and Cassandra could see the curious glances of people sauntering or hurrying past them. They were speaking in loud, urgent whispers, hardly audible above the rumble of carriages and wagons and the cries of street hawkers, out to catch the evening theatre-goers and revellers.

"Petifer, you should be on the stage, I never heard such a wild flight of fancy."

"It isn't flight of anything. It's the sober truth, only you never did like to see what was in front of your nose, you're the one who lives in a world of fancy, that's what."

"Petifer!"

"It's time I spoke my mind. Go on, think of it. No money, the law going to be called in. What do you do? Decide you've lost your reputation in any case, and that Lord Usborne, who's a handsome man, I'll give him that, might not be the worst that can happen."

"It's all nonsense," Cassandra said firmly, although inwardly she had a cold fear that what Petifer was saying might be true. Could Mrs. Nettleton be capable of such double-dealing? She hardly knew her, a week or so's acquaintance, what was that?

"There is no problem with the rent. She asks a reasonable amount, and part of it I am paying in kind, I am painting her morning parlour."

Petifer made a disgusted sound. "And you have that in writing, I dare say."

"No, I do not, it is hardly necessary."

"That woman's as sly and slippery as an eel, and I wouldn't trust her as far as I can see her. And you're a born fool if you do."

A fool indeed, Cassandra said to herself. So grateful for the meeting, for the offer of the room. Yet Mr. Rudge knew Mrs. Nettleton, she seemed to be a woman of substance, of standing.

They were attracting too much attention, standing there, Petifer in her drab servant's gown, Cassandra in her finery. Despite the warmth of the evening, Cassandra gave a shiver. "Come, we must move on," she said. She hurried across the road, digging in her purse for a penny for the crossing sweeper, and turned into Jermyn Street, her head a whirl of uncomfortable thoughts.

Jermyn Street, with its tall, elegant houses on either side, was more dimly lit than the main thoroughfare. A solitary young woman was walking slowly along the street ahead of them. Petifer pursed her lips. "Another of them, this town is full of—" Before she could say the word, the woman lurched and stumbled. Cassandra leapt forward, but was too late to catch the woman, who fell to the ground and lay there in a crumpled heap, a smear of mud on her dark green gown.

Twilight was coming on, and candlelight was shimmering out from behind some of the windows, but the street itself was quiet, with no passers-by to come to their aid. The two of them lifted the unfortunate woman to a sitting position, and Cassandra was relieved to see her eyelids flutter as they drew her up. She was a young woman, perhaps a year or two older than Cassandra, and pale as a ghost.

Cassandra heard footsteps and twisted round to look up into a brightly painted face, and a very exposed bosom.

"Serve her right," said the new arrival. "Pushing in on our patch."

She was joined by another, taller woman, wearing a vivid purple gown, and with her hair piled up in a heap of improbable curls.

Ladies of the night, Cassandra said to herself.

"She's all white," said the taller whore. "Going to peg out, do you think?"

The blowsy one bent over to peer more closely at the woman in green. "Starving, I'd say."

At those words, the woman on the ground murmured something intelligible, and her eyes opened. She blinked up at Cassandra and the others, and drew her hand across her eyes.

"I fell," she said. "I was dizzy and I fell."

"Yes, well," said the first whore, "watch where you walk, otherwise you'll fall again. And for why? Because I'll have put out my foot and tripped you up, that's why." She gave a screech of laughter and sauntered off.

The tall woman hitched the front of her purple gown back into place. "Get her out of here before the watch finds you," she advised. "Nothing wrong with her that a bite of food won't put right." Then she, too, was gone.

"Is she right?" Cassandra said to Petifer. "About her being weak from hunger?"

"I'll ask her," said Petifer, sounding put out. "She'd better have a good reason for falling flat on her face like that. I think she's drunk."

The woman uttered a faint protest. The colour was still drained from her cheeks, and Cassandra had a strong idea that if she stood up, her legs wouldn't support her.

"You stay with her," she said, and darted away back towards Haymarket before Petifer could reply. A pie man was standing on the corner, calling his wares. Cassandra wrinkled her nose at the hot, greasy smells, and bought a cheese one. "Country cheese, best you'll ever taste, my lady," he said with a wink. "Set you up lovely for the night's work."

Cassandra took the pie, gave him a coin, and was back in Jermyn Street, her heart thumping, and her mind unsure whether to laugh or cry at being taken herself for one of the local whores.

She knelt down beside the woman, and broke the pie in half.

"Don't eat it too quickly, mind," warned Petifer. "Otherwise it'll come straight back up."

The girl was extremely pretty, Cassandra noticed, with huge blue eyes and hair much the colour of her own—or it would be, if it had been washed and brushed; as it was, it hung in a bedraggled fashion about her bony shoulders.

"She tells me her name's Harriet," Petifer said. "Harriet Morris, and she hasn't eaten for two days."

"The poor thing!"

"And, no, she isn't one of them types." This accompanied by a gesture towards the shadowy women standing in the doorway, still watching them.

The girl munched her way through the pie, despite her hunger eating it quite daintily. When she thanked Cassandra, it was in a pleasant voice, not a voice of the streets, nor indeed of London.

"I think we'd best get you out of here," Petifer said. "Those women there might get frisky again, and the Lord knows, we don't want any of their customers giving us the once-over."

"Which way?" said Cassandra, looking up and down the street.

"It's quieter that way, and there's a patch of grass at the end with a bench. Provided it's not being used for other purposes, which in this part of London you can't say it won't be, she can have a bit of a sit-down."

The bench was big enough for the three of them, and the area seemed quite deserted. It was, Cassandra thought, as good a place as any.

It was strange, for this last half hour she hadn't given a second's thought to her own predicament. Concern for someone else was a good remedy for taking the mind off one's own troubles, and she felt a spurt of gratitude to this unknown Harriet.

"You are in a sad way," she said. "How came you in this fix? What may we do to help you?"

"I saw you with Lord Usborne," Harriet said. "At the theatre."

Cassandra stiffened. "What has Lord Usborne to do with this?"

"That dreadful, dreadful man. He is the cause of all my misfortune."

Chapter Twenty-one

"She has been gone a good while," said Lord Usborne to Mrs. Nettleton, making as though to rise to his feet. "I think I had better go and look for her. She seemed in some distress."

Mrs. Nettleton laid a restraining hand on his lordship's arm. "It was only the heat," she said in soothing tones. "She will be back directly; indeed, I expect she is outside this box this very minute, for I hear someone lurking."

She was quite right, but the lurker was a flunkey, whom Cassandra had paused to give a message to on her way from the theatre. "Mrs. Kent desired me to tell you that she has the headache and has taken a hackney-coach home, she begs you not to be concerned."

Usborne's face darkened. "A pretty way to behave, leaving a message with that man."

"Indeed, do not concern yourself," said Mrs. Nettleton quickly. "She is very sensible, she suffers from the heat and is prone to the headache, it is often so, you know, with women come up to town from the country, they are not used to the noise and smoke and close air of the town, particularly not when the days are so warm and oppressive as they are just now. We may expect a thunderstorm, and then there will be no more headaches. Betsy will give her a powder, and she will sleep until morning. Call upon her then, at eleven, and you will see for yourself that she will have her pretty colour back once more."

Lord Usborne looked as though he was going to argue the matter, but then he shrugged and sat back in his seat, much to Mrs. Nettleton's relief. Drat the girl, running off like that. Had she seen someone she knew at the theatre? Some former lover, an acquaintance, a creditor? Any of those might cause her to decamp as she had done; well, she'd get the truth out of her in the morning. It was time she had a talk with the girl, put her right as to a thing or two, and make her see that it would do her no good to keep Lord Usborne at arm's length.

What an opportunity for the girl it was, if only she could be brought to see sense. What a triumph, to land a gentleman of Usborne's standing and wealth, and without making any effort to attract him. If she was not mistaken, and she seldom was in these matters, Lord Usborne was hot for her, he was drawn to her by more than her undoubted beauty, there was that in her disposition that appealed to him, and that, if she behaved and did nothing to cross him, augured well for a relationship more lasting than many of that kind.

In fact, she mused, Mrs. Kent was not unlike Lady Usborne in appearance, although she was many years the younger, of course. Mrs. Nettleton remembered when Lord Usborne had met Lady Usborne, Miss Minhampton, as she then was, a vivid newcomer to the ranks of the debutantes. Of good family, of course, and with a fine fortune to help her find a rich husband, her vivacity and beauty had enchanted Lord Usborne. She had fallen in love with him, and all had seemed set for a happy marriage. However, in matters of the heart, you could never predict how things would turn out, and now a more distant couple you would not find in the whole of London.

Which was all to her benefit, for contented husbands were no good clients of hers. Single men and old roués and men who took no pleasure in the marriage bed were what kept her in the style she liked. This Cassandra Kent could consider herself fortunate to have attracted a Lord Usborne, a handsome man, whatever his temper, instead of a hardened old buck with a stomach swelling over his breeches and a face coarsened and reddened by years of high living.

Headache, yes, no doubt, brought about by the smell of the paints in the morning parlour, what did Cassandra think she was about?

Mrs. Nettleton had had to check her hands and face for traces of paint before letting her put on that gown this evening. How could any woman take herself so seriously? It was not that she didn't have some talent. Mrs. Nettleton had enough of an eye to know that the room would look very well, very well indeed, but that did not mean the chit could set herself up as an artist. A well-bred girl such as she seemed to be, whoever heard of such a thing? It was an affront to her sex, more scandalous, in Mrs. Nettleton's opinion, than living as the mistress of a married man.

That was the custom and perfectly natural.

A woman painter—that went against all the laws of nature, and of society. Let women take their place in a man's world, and where would it end? No, no, it would never do. There were some women of the last century who had set themselves up as artists, but that was in another age, things were different then. And besides, they came from artists' families, and learned their trade at their father's knee, that was quite another thing, if still very inappropriate for any woman worthy of the name!

Horatio Darcy saw Cassandra rise and leave the box. He felt a mounting indignation as well as anger; they had hoodwinked him, Miss Darcy and her unappealing stepfather. Mr. Partington had told him nothing but lies, pretending that she was gone to Cheltenham, while all the time he knew she had done no such thing, but was continuing on her path of immorality, under Lord Usborne's protection.

A fine thing for a Miss Darcy, and a fine way to bring dishonour upon her family! Although Lady Usborne had not used the name of Darcy when she was describing her husband's new acquisition. What had she called her? Kent. Well, at least the girl must have some vestiges of shame, not to use her own name.

Lord Usborne. Of all the rakish, worthless fellows to end up with, had she no idea of what she was about? A house and all that went with it, and as much pin money as she could spend, no doubt, but what a price she would pay for it. For his lordship would weary of her soon enough, it was the way of such connections. Where there was no genuine attachment, and no prospect of stronger ties, then the couple would not stay long together. Soon, Cassandra Darcy would be out in the streets again, looking for another man to give her a roof over her head and the necessities—luxuries, then—of life, in return for favours granted.

Then, as her looks faded, or if she bore children—

Her fate would be the punishment of her rash actions, of her defiance of her stepfather's arrangements, her refusal to consent to marriage to the man who had been her ruin, her disdain for his own good advice.

He sat heedless through the interminable play; usually a devotee of the works of William Shakespeare, he found the drama a distant object, with no power to draw him in through words or action. The actors were strutting puppets, and he only paid proper attention when his ear caught Hamlet's brutal words to Ophelia: "Get thee to a nunnery."

The prince of Denmark had the right of it, with his disgust for the treachery and wiles of women. Elizabethan London was not so different from the modern city, that was one thing that hadn't changed over the years. Whores were still called nuns, and brothels, abbeys, and that was most likely where Cassandra would end up, under the care of some abbess, as they were known, selling her out for a few guineas a night.

Which was disgraceful, for a woman of her quality and breeding, all because of her obstinacy and inability to see what was sensible and right. And she a Darcy, his own kin. The thought brought a flush of rage to his face, not noticed by Lady Usborne, who was leaning forward, following the play with eager attention.

It irked him in a way that he did not care to examine to think of Cassandra languishing in Lord Usborne's practiced embraces. Why should it disturb him? It did not worry him to know that on occasion, his mistress shared a bed with her errant husband, so why did he mind about Cassandra Darcy caught up in voluptuous pleasures with his lordship?

Thoroughly out of sorts, he was short-tempered in the carriage as it made its slow way through the London streets, which were busy with revellers of the lower sort as well as gentlemen going to and from engagements and clubs, and the crowds coming out from the theatres and opera houses.

"You are in a bad mood, I find," Lady Usborne chided him. "You are growling like a veritable bear."

"Am I? I am sorry for it, I have something on my mind."

"As long as it only has this depressing effect on your mind, and not on other parts," she said with a sly smile. "May I know what is causing you such concern, such sudden concern?"

"It is a family matter, that is all."

"It came upon you very suddenly, this ill mood, for you were in the best of good humour when we started for the play."

"I caught sight of someone—in the pit," he added hastily. "Which reminded me of the problem, that is all."

They came to her house, and he stepped out first to hand her down. Then he escorted her to the door.

"You are not leaving me?" she said, in some surprise. And, in a whisper: "The night is young, and his lordship will not be home until the early hours of the morning, I promise you. I saw you did not quite like to meet him when you arrived this evening."

"It is nothing to do with his lordship, but I am afraid I would be but poor company tonight."

He had displeased her, he saw that, as she gave a shrug, held out her hand to shake his, and then disappeared into the house. Had he upset her? He doubted it. He had few illusions about the nature of their relationship. Should he fail to satisfy her, either between the sheets or in other ways, she would cast him off, and look about her for another handsome young man to ensnare and tempt into her willing arms.

She and her husband were a pair of tomcats, he told himself with some feeling. And then, for he preferred to be honest with himself when the consequences weren't too unsettling, he had to laugh and ask what else he was? By God, if Lady Usborne were his wife, she would not stray as she did. It came of moving in Prinny's circle, no doubt, where morality had no meaning, and it was every man and woman for him- and herself.

He walked back to his rooms in Half Moon Street. His valet came into the sitting room upon hearing his master's arrival, to enquire if he wanted anything.

"You may take that look of surprise off your face, Marston."

"I am merely surprised to see you home so early. I trust you enjoyed the play."

"No, I did not. Fetch me something to eat, and take this damned coat away, I never had one that was so ill-fitting."

Marston eased the coat off Horatio Darcy's wide shoulders, where it fitted without a wrinkle or the hint of a stretch.

"I have some papers I wish to deal with."

Work, and it was a nice legal point that he had to deal with, pleasing in its complexity, did not bring its usual calm to his ruffled spirits. He found he could not concentrate, that he did not care whether his client or the plaintiff had the right of it, or, more important, which of them was likely to win the case.

He poured himself a glass of wine and stood beside the window, lost in thought. He could not get that damned girl's image out of his mind. In the end, he took himself to bed at an unaccustomed early hour, much to Marston's ill-concealed astonishment, where he tossed and turned in an effort to find the sleep that eluded him. The watch had cried out, "Three o'clock on a fine morning, and all's well," before he fell into a troubled slumber, to find himself dreaming he was making love to a Lady Usborne whose chestnut locks had turned into a Gorgon's snakes, before dissolving into another figure altogether, so that he found himself gazing into the wide grey eyes of Cassandra Darcy.

Waking, he banged his head against his pillow, composed himself for sleep once more, and this time slept soundly until Marston wakened him with his customary cup of coffee and the prediction of a baking hot day, sir.

Chapter Twenty-two

Cassandra watched the pale grey of the sky turn to pink and gold and the outlines of smoke drifting up from numerous chimneys. The sounds of a new day came up from below, the creak of a bed, a woman calling out of the window to the driver of a passing wagon; she could hear its wheels squeaking as it rumbled over the cobbles.

Petifer, lying snugly on the truckle bed, was still fast asleep. Cassandra had wanted to take the truckle bed, but Petifer wouldn't hear of it. "I'm used to it, and you aren't," she said.

A truckle bed might be the least of what she had to get used to, Cassandra thought ruefully. Never in her life had she slept in a room like this, in a house like this, in a district like this. They were at 42 Bow Street, Covent Garden. On the ground floor was a shop, selling pots and pans. The first floor was rented out to a man who owned several market stalls, and he lived there with his wife and his five children and a large cat, a fine mouser, one of the children had told Cassandra with pride as he passed her on the stairs, the squirming feline clutched in his youthful arms.

On the next floor lived Mr. and Mrs. Mantel, who owned the house. They were a stout and amiable middle-aged pair, their children grown up and with families of their own, and it was in the attic where three of their children had formerly slept, that she and Petifer had spent the night. Cassandra sat up. She was wearing her shift, and she looked over to where Petifer had carefully hung her gown over a pole attached to the sloping ceiling.

Cassandra liked the room, and she liked the Mantels. Cousins of Petifer's brother-in-law, Margaret's husband, they had accepted their arrival the night before with a kind of phlegmatic pleasure, and a bob of a curtsy to Cassandra. They were always ready to welcome one of the family, they said to Petifer, and if Miss Cassandra was in need of a bed, why, there was the room upstairs, nothing fine—with a doubtful look at Cassandra—not what a lady might be used to, but clean and comfortable, the mattress stuffed with their own straw, no bedbugs in sight, and fresh linen, washed and aired by her herself, and laid by with lavender to keep it sweet.

Cassandra could smell the lavender now, its scent mingling with the smell of fresh baking which wafted through the tiny window. She slid out of bed and went to look out, over a sea of roofs; this was an unknown and fascinating London.

She went back to the bed, and sat down. She needed to do some serious thinking. Mrs. Mantel was kind and hospitable, but the truth was that Cassandra was homeless and penniless, and only her own wits and Petifer's indomitable spirit stood between her and despair.

She opened her purse, and counted out the meagre amount of money she had left. Petifer had not wanted her to give so much money to Harriet—but how could she not help her when what she needed was, in all honesty, so very little. And it was little enough to pay for the story that Harriet had told them, a story that might well have saved Cassandra from a similar or even sadder fate.

Harriet told them, as she sat on the bench, that she had nowhere to go. She owed rent to her landlady, and had no money to pay it. She had intended to slip out with her few possessions, "and indeed, I hated to do it, for she has been kind enough, and she has her living to earn, the same as everyone else."

What had happened to bring her to such a state of desperation? "For you are gently born, don't tell me no lies," Petifer had said with more directness than Cassandra would have employed.

It was odd, how her story echoed Cassandra's, only it contained fewer falsehoods.

"I was born Harriet Foxley, the daughter of a clergyman, in a poor parish in Devon." A fiery blush spread up her face. "When I was sixteen, which was a year after my mother died, I ran away from home. I shall not say why it was, but I was no longer welcome there. I had a little money, and I came to London, where I lodged with a woman from my village who had married a London man. I had to find employment, and since I am very fond of children, and was used to care for my little brothers and sisters, I obtained employment in a household with a large nursery. I was happy there. Until, one day, while out in the park with two of my charges, I had the ill luck to encounter Lord Usborne."

Another blush. "He was persuasive and handsome, and made me feel not at all like a servant."

"Nothing wrong with being a servant," said Petifer.

"Oh, nothing in the world, and how I wish I had remained in my position as nursery maid. However, I was foolish, and succumbed to temptation, and allowed myself to put aside all the moral teaching I had had from my mother—in short, I put myself under the protection of Lord Usborne, and consented to become his mistress and live with him on terms other than marriage. It was wrong of me, very wrong, but I did not then know that he was already married, I told myself that he was in love with me, and would marry me, but of course he had a wife."

"Of course," said Petifer. "A man of his years, and standing and wealth, and not one of the other kind, he would be bound to have a wife, as you must have known."

"Well, I did not care to think about it, and when I found out about the existence of Lady Usborne, I was already installed in a pretty little house in King Street, with servants of my own and a carriage and fine clothes and luxuries that I had never known. He took me out, to the play and to the opera and to masked balls and to parties, but never among any people except those who were of the demimonde, which was what I had become, one of the impures. I knew that I had no chance of a respectable life, of marriage, only of staying what I was, and then, when he tired of me, moving under the protection of another such man, as long as I kept my looks and charm. Only Lord Usborne is a difficult man, very clever and with a terrible temper, and he is jealous. If I so much as looked at another man, it would rile him. He treated me as a possession, not of as much value as his horse, perhaps, and a little higher in his esteem than his dog, but what he had, he held."

"So what happened?" said Cassandra.

"While I was a nursery maid I had became acquainted with a young man, Mr. Morris—well, not so very young, he is near thirty. He is an engraver, and we were on more than friendly terms; you might say we were courting. Only, then I went off with his lordship and had to put him out of my mind. You may imagine my surprise when one morning there was a ring on the door, and he was shown into my sitting room, come to deliver a set of engravings ordered by Usborne!"

Petifer gave her a shrewd look. "So who got you in the family way, his lordship or this engraver fellow?"

She was with child. That accounted for the fainting as much as the hunger; indeed, weren't women in her condition often much hungrier than usual? Cassandra cast Petifer an enquiring glance, how had she known?

"Pray do not speak of him with contempt," said Harriet, tears filling her blue eyes. "For indeed I love him, and he is my husband, and the child I carry is his."

"Husband?" said Petifer sharply. "If you are married, where is this husband?"

"He is in hiding. He was arrested for debt, on a trumped-up charge, when his lordship found out that I had been seeing him, that I was attached to him. He does not know we are married, he would not care. As far as he is concerned, another man dared to take what belonged to him, so he threw me out of the house, and used his influence, which is considerable, to have my dear Richard seized by the bailiffs and thrown into a sponging house."

"Your husband is in jail?"

"Not any more. I scraped together every penny I could, and bribed the turnkey to look the other way, and he escaped. Only Lord Usborne found out and is scouring London for him; I do not know what he will do if he finds him, indeed, he will not do so, for Richard has found a man who will let him work his passage to America. Richard was pressed in the late war, you see, and so he is of use on board a ship. It is arranged that I am to accompany him, as a passenger, only how can I go with not a stitch to my back but what I have on now? How can I even get to the ship in time? For it sails tomorrow evening, and will not miss its tide for any passenger!"

"To begin with, stop crying, which never did anyone any good, and use such wits as the good Lord gave you," said Petifer.

"You must join your husband," Cassandra said. "What will he do when you reach America, how will he support you?"

"He is a fine craftsman, a master of his trade. He has served his time and will find work, I am sure. He has relations over there, in Boston, and he plans to work and save and then set up his own business."

"Very creditable," said Cassandra. "Where are your lodgings, where is this landlady of yours?"

Harriet shrank back. "It is no use; she will not let me have my things. If she sees me, she will raise a hue and cry, and then I, in my turn, will be thrown into a sponging house."

"You won't," said Cassandra. "I shall give you the money to pay what you owe."

"You are very kind," said Harriet, shaking her head. "But I cannot accept it. You don't know me, and how can I ever repay you?"

"You have told me what kind of a man Lord Usborne is, and that information will be of great benefit to me. In return, I will settle your debts—at least, I will if they are not too great."

Petifer was up, in her usual brisk way, and was, Cassandra saw, putting on her bonnet, as though to go out.

"Where are you going?"

"To St. James's Square, Miss Darcy, to collect your things."

Cassandra sat down on the side of the iron bed. "They will not give them to you, not without you pay the rent, and even if Mrs. Nettleton were to accept the sum agreed, which, if what Betsy told you was the truth, is unlikely, I do not have that amount of money left." She gave Petifer a shrewd look. "And if you pay her out of your savings, Petifer, I shall never forgive you."

"I dare say that Betsy was truthful enough in what she said, although a poor misguided creature in most ways. It's of no account, and I wouldn't give a farthing to that woman, not after what she had planned for you. No, I'll find a way, don't you fret about it."

"It is for me to face Mrs. Nettleton, Petifer, not you. I can fight my own battles."

That earned her a snort from Petifer. "You may be a match for Mrs. Nettleton, and when your temper's up, I warrant you would be, but you can't go capering about London in your shift, can you now? Besides, it's best you keep away from St. James's Square, it isn't Mrs. Nettleton that should bother you as much as his lordship. For the way he was eyeing you, he's taken a great fancy to you, and such a man doesn't like to let his prey slip, I tell you that for nothing. Now, I shall take this horrid gown back, to think of you wearing such a thing. You wait here until I get back."

Cassandra had to consent, although she wasn't happy about it. What might Mrs. Nettleton say to Petifer? How could Petifer possibly come off the best from such an unequal encounter?

"No problem at all," said Petifer triumphantly, placing Cassandra's portmanteau on the bed beside her and unbuckling the straps, and requesting Mr. Mantel, who was clutching Cassandra's trunk, to place it on the floor. He did so, told Petifer that if she fancied a bite to eat, just to let Mrs. Mantel know, and left the room.

"All your things, every last stocking and pin," said Petifer, with great satisfaction.

"How did you manage it? And you are back so soon?"

"I took a hackney-coach both ways. It goes against the grain, to spend the shillings, although I suppose the cabmen, cheeky fellows they are, have got to earn a living, same as anyone else. I picked out a big fellow, with an amiable face, apart from the scar over his eye, I think he was once a prizefighter by the look of him. I told him to wait for me, and if I wasn't out within the fifteen minutes, then he was to knock on the door and ask for me."

"Gracious," said Cassandra, whose respect for Petifer was growing by the hour. She had always known her for an efficient manager, but it was becoming clear that she had had insufficient scope for her talents within the staid surroundings of a country house like Rosings.

"Mrs. Nettleton was in, and very haughty and high-and-mighty, but I soon put a stop to that, by putting my nose in the air and saying as how I was your maid, sent by your brother, now in town to collect your possessions."

"Brother! I have no brother!"

"I know that, and you know that, but how should Mrs. Nettleton have any idea that you don't have half a dozen of them, all ready to descend on her house and ask what she is about? Her cunning schemes only work when a girl is on her own and has no one to look out for her."

"But she knows I never mentioned a brother, surely she did not believe you?"

"Maybe she did, maybe she didn't, but she's not one to take a risk. I said that you and your brother had had a disagreement, because he hadn't got on with your late husband, but now it's all made up, and you'll be staying with him." Petifer paused, looking shrewish. "If you ask me, she doesn't believe in that husband you invented, but I think the mention of a brother alarmed her."

Petifer's voice held a note of triumph, which Cassandra felt was fully deserved.

"What about the rent?"

"I said to send an account of what was due to Crillon's hotel, care of Mr. Barnaby, and it would be attended to. As it will, by being thrown out with the rubbish after it's sat there a few weeks."

"I must and shall pay her, I owe her the money."

"Not so fast, for she was quick enough to give me this," and Petifer handed over a sheet of paper, closely written. "It is an account of some paints you bought, I am not sure what she was speaking of, but I said you would see to it. Time was running short, and I wanted to be out of there. So upstairs I went, with that Betsy, who isn't a bad creature, although not so good at dusting, judging by the stair treads, and had your things packed up in a trice. Then I summoned the cabman to help with the trunk, and I was out of the house, within the quarter hour, and back here as you see."

Cassandra was looking at the paper. "I do not know what to do about this. It is a bill for all the paints and brushes and so forth that I bought on Mrs. Nettleton's behalf. Everything is still there, I suppose, in the room where I was working."

"And, not being one to waste much, I know her sort, Mrs. Nettleton will find some other starving artist to finish the work for her. I couldn't carry away a lot of paints, or I'd have asked for them."

"I think that would have been impossible," Cassandra agreed, but with a sigh, for the little bladders of paint would have been appreciated. "But however am I to pay such an account? It is far more than the rent."

Petifer was practical. "Go to another paint shop, if you need one, that is all you can do. He will dun Mrs. N., first, and when she sends him after you, with no address, I dare say he will write it off as a bad debt."

Cassandra was frowning. "No, I must pay him, it would not be right, he has been so pleasant and helpful and friendly. But I cannot do so until next quarter day when I shall have some money, and that is five weeks away. And there is the matter of the card, I put a card in his shop, offering my services as a teacher, and directing enquirers to St. James's Square, I should remove it."

"Then I shall go and ask him to take it down, on your behalf, he will not be in the least concerned about the money owing yet, no one in London pays their bills on the dot, you may be sure."

"Petifer, it is a good thing that your mother or nan cannot hear you now."

Petifer grinned. "That it is, and my sister Margaret would have more than a few words to say if she knew what I was up to, but there you are, needs must when the devil drives, as the reverend himself used to say. I'm a grown woman, and answerable to no one, and it's for me to decide what's right and what's wrong."

Cassandra laughed. "That is true for both of us, and I am very sure that your judgements are a great deal sounder than mine, for I fear that I choose the wrong path every time."

"Now don't go falling into a fit of the glums," said Petifer. "I've got your clothes to get in order, for they're in a shocking state. I'm glad to see that Miss Emily saw to it that your pattern dress got put in, for you'll need new clothes if you're to stay in London, we need to give you a more modish appearance; your clothes are countrified, if I may say so."

Stay in London? Cassandra was lost in reflection as Petifer busied herself with the contents of trunk and portmanteau, shaking her head over a crumpled gown and searching tenaciously for the missing half of a pair of stockings.

How could she stay in London? She was more shaken than she would admit to Petifer by the whole Mrs. Nettleton business; it brought home to her just how insecure her existence now was. She had thought she could take care of herself, but look how easily she had been duped by Mrs. Nettleton. She was not used to people living as it were behind masks, that was a lesson she must learn, she supposed.

But for now, what a fix she was in. Her heart sank as she considered the alternatives. To go back to Rosings, with her tail between her legs, and to be bundled into a carriage, the thunderbolts of her stepfather's wrath raining about her as she was sent off in disgrace to live a miserable life in the company of the ferocious and unpleasant Mrs. Norris and Mrs. Rushworth, who had a reputation for being mighty disagreeable—well, would not any woman be, in her situation?

What had happened to the man Maria Rushworth had run off with? No virtual imprisonment for him, with Mrs. Norris as gaoler, no indeed. He had an estate in Norfolk, and was, so she remembered hearing, now married to a sweet and gentle girl, of large fortune, who doted upon him. Hardly an uncommon story.

Although if Lady Usborne were anything to go by, it was possible for a married woman with a complaisant husband to have her own amours. Maria Rushworth's mistake had been to marry a man she did not love, who was not in the least inclined to turn a blind eye to his wife's affairs.

She had run off with her lover, that was the difference, and Lady Usborne clearly had no intention of running off with any man. She would be too shrewd, she would value her position and the respectability of her marriage too much ever to do anything so rash.

None of this was any use to Cassandra. She had no husband, no home, no money, and there was nothing to be gained by allowing her mind to drift away from these facts to think of the lot of other women. What could she do?

Was there truly any possibility of her being able to earn a living for herself, here in a town thronged with eager artists, no doubt of far greater accomplishment and experience than she was? As Mr. Rudge had rightly said, it was whom you knew that brought you work—and whom did she know? Nobody.

No, she saw no alternative. She would have to do what she had sworn she would not do. She must go to James Eyre and throw herself on his mercy. It was not too late, Mr. Partington would doubtless come up with the money he demanded, and then they must rub along together as best they might. Could the flames of their affection be rekindled, after such a violent parting? Perhaps. They would live abroad, at least for a while, and that would bring new scenery, new acquaintances, new prospects, into her life, which might soften the penance of living with a man who did not care for her, but for her fortune.

"No, Petifer," she said, when she was dressed and Petifer had arranged her hair and twitched her skirts into proper order. "I am going out alone; there is something I have to do. It is broad daylight, my destination is not far from here, I shall come to no harm." She fastened the ribbons under the wide-brimmed straw hat—Lord, the last time she had worn that, it had been in Bath, when she had slipped out for an illicit meeting with James Eyre. "I shall return directly."

"And where are you going?" said Petifer, looking at her with suspicious eyes.

"That is a private matter, something I have to do." And Cassandra whisked herself out of the door before Petifer could say another word.

Chapter Twenty-three

The maid who answered the door at Cecil Court gave a start of recognition when she saw Cassandra. She was a slatternly girl, who had come to the door with a mop in her hand.

It seemed she was about to close the door in Cassandra's face, but Cassandra was too quick for her, and was inside the hall before she could be denied. "Is Mr. Eyre at home?" she asked.

"That he is not, and I'll thank you to leave directly, you hussy, we want none of the likes of you in this house!" Mrs. Dodd stood before her, red and angry, her hands on the hips, the picture of outraged womanhood. "I won't forgive you for what you've done to Mr. James; you had no right to treat him like that. So be off with you."

Cassandra had gone pale, but her voice was steady. "Is he not here at present? When may he return?"

"Don't you look down your nose at me, missy, I know you for what you are. Throw over an honest man, entrap him like you did and then just walk out. Well, he won't be back tonight, nor this week or month, or next year, neither."

Cassandra was beginning to feel alarmed. "Pray, tell me where he is. He has not met with an accident, surely?" Ridiculous visions of his challenging Mr. Partington to a duel and being struck down, or of him casting himself into the Thames in a morbid—and inebriated— fit of self-pity rose before her eyes. "He has not come to any harm?"

"Harm, is it? I tell you this, I'll be glad to see him home and well and in one piece, but there's not much chance of that, not where he's gone." She noticed that the slatternly girl was listening to every word, with her mouth hanging open. "Get back downstairs," she snapped. "And take that mop with you, what are you thinking of, to answer the door with it in your hand"—with an angry look at Cassandra—"even if what's standing on the doorstep is the likes of her!"

Cassandra wasn't leaving until she had the truth out of Mrs. Dodd, and she told her so. "I shall camp on your doorstep and ring the bell all day until you say what has become of Mr. Eyre."

Another glare from Mrs. Dodd. Then, with a glance down the staircase, for she knew as well as Cassandra did that the girl and the mop had retreated no further than the foot of the flight of stone stairs leading down into the basement, she opened the parlour door and held it for Cassandra to go through.

She did not invite Cassandra to sit down. "I'll tell you, Miss whatever your name is, where he's gone. He's gone to the other side of the world, that's where he's gone. And the only good thing about it is that he's out of your clutches, because there's no way you can reach him now."

Cassandra looked at her blankly for a moment. "The other side of the world?" Then she realised what Mrs. Dodd must mean. "He has a ship, that is what you are saying."

"He has gone to be first lieutenant to Lord Cochrane, who's away making mischief among the foreigners in South America, all natives and papists they are, from what Mr. James tells me."

"The famous Lord Cochrane?"

"There's only one I ever heard tell of."

"How is Mr. Eyre getting there?"

"He sailed on the *Nautilus* this very morning; he was up before dawn to catch the tide at Tilbury. He's been gone these five hours and more, he'll be out at sea and likely to be away for two or three years or more. 'I may settle and make a new life for myself out there,' he says to me. 'For there's nothing left in this country or Ireland for me.' "

Cassandra saw angry tears start into Mrs. Dodd's eyes. "So he has gone to Chile," she said slowly. "I am grieved to hear it."

"And so you should be, for if you'd had a heart inside your breast, you'd have let him make an honest woman of you, that you would, and he'd never have gone off where he'll be drowned or have his leg blown off!"

"He has not had that misfortune yet, although it is a hazard of his profession," Cassandra pointed out.

"Oh, much you care! Now, I've told you what you wanted, so be off with you, and I hope I never set eyes on you again."

Cassandra went towards the door, then, as a thought struck her, she turned back to Mrs. Dodd.

"How came he by the posting? I know he was hard put to find a position, it is very difficult to get a ship these days."

"He is not a nobody, his father is a lord, that's what you forgot, with your pride and stubbornness. He has influential relatives and friends, and one of those, Lord Usborne, who is a friend of the Prince of Wales, no less, arranged for him to get a ship. I can only be thankful he has some friends, he who deserves them, a sweet boy as he always was, and grown into a kind, good man, and far too good for the likes of you!"

"He's gone, hasn't he?" Petifer said, as Cassandra came into the room.

"He?"

"That Mr. Eyre, that's the *he* I'm speaking about." Petifer was on her hands and knees, smoothing out the pattern dress, and now she sat back on her heels, a large pair of scissors held in her right hand and a fierce expression on her face.

Cassandra had to laugh. "You look like one of the Fates, snipping life's thread with your scissors."

"I'd like to cut something else with these scissors, so I would."

"No, you wouldn't. Besides, he's left Mrs. Dodd's house, I didn't see him."

Petifer snorted. "So he's gone back to Ireland, has he? Good riddance is what I say."

"No, he has gone much further afield than that," Cassandra said, plumping herself down on the bed with a sigh. "How did you know I'd gone to see him?"

"It wasn't so hard to guess, you had that look on your face, like you were jumping off a cliff, which is what taking up with him again would be, if you ask me."

"It seemed as though it were the only solution to my problems. I was certain you would approve, for it would restore my good name to some degree, and with the income from my fortune, I dare say we could have lived well enough."

"That might be so, but a man who will run off with one woman may sooner or later run off with another. No, you're better off without him, and while there's life, there's hope, as my nan always said."

Cassandra could not feel that Petifer's nan's homespun philosophy was of any great use to her in her present predicament. And she felt a bleakness of spirits at James's departure, for although he had offended her, and she had been so shocked by his scheming to have both love and fortune—if he had indeed loved her at all—she had still abandoned home and respectability on his account, and had enjoyed rapturous hours in his arms.

"Don't sit slouching like that, Miss Cassandra, whatever would Miss Wilson say if she could see you now? I'd be sent directly for the backboard."

"Well," said Cassandra, with an attempt to look more cheerful, "I must put my thinking cap on and see what can be done."

Petifer put down her scissors, and stood up. "Isn't there somewhere in London where you can go and look at pictures? For no amount of brooding is going to help you, but I reckon spending a bit of time gazing at those paintings you're so fond of would do your spirits good."

"Oh, Petifer, it's a kind thought, and I should love to go to the Royal Academy, for the summer exhibition is on. But I believe it costs a shilling, and I must watch every penny."

"If you're planning to make a living by your brush, then it's money well spent to see what all the other artists are up to. There's fashion in art, same as in clothes and everything else, that's what that uppity youngster who was assistant to Mr. Lisser told me. And I've a fancy to see some paintings, perhaps there'll be one by Mr. Lisser himself."

There was a knock on the door, and Mrs. Mantel's amiable face looked round it. "Sorry to disturb you, miss, but a boy's come round with this, and he made me promise I'd put it straight into your hands, and no one else's."

"For me?" said Cassandra, puzzled, taking the battered-looking casket that was held out by Mrs. Mantel. "Do you know whom it's from?"

"He said there was a note inside, then he scarpered."

Her face was expectant, and Cassandra felt obliged to lift the curved lid and see what was inside. It seemed to be a bundle of letters, wrapped round several times in a faded blue ribbon. On top was a scrap of paper, with a few neatly written words: "Pray accept these, and keep them close to you, and indeed, hidden well. They are all I have of value, to repay you for your very great kindness to me." The note was signed "Harriet."

"Thank you, Mrs. Mantel," Petifer said. "It is nothing of any importance, just some bits and pieces Miss Cassandra left behind."

Cassandra took out the letters and turned them over in her hand. "I cannot imagine why Harriet has sent me her letters. I am sure they are precious to her, but how can they be of value to anyone else?"

"You could read them," said Petifer. "See what they say, maybe there's instructions telling you where some treasure is hid."

"Oh, very likely, don't you think?" said Cassandra, laughing. "No, these are private letters, and I will put them by and keep them safe. Perhaps, when she is arrived in America, I may send them back to her."

Petifer pursed her lips, but didn't press the point.

"Pray do not go looking at them when I am not present," said Cassandra, serious again.

"Would I ever do such a thing?"

"Yes, you would, if you thought it was to my advantage, but there is nothing to interest or concern us in some old letters. I think you are right as to the pictures," she went on. "We may walk from here to the Royal Academy."

The charge for entry was indeed a shilling, but Cassandra would not let Petifer spend another shilling on a catalogue. "We do not need it, it is likely that the paintings will be labelled. Besides," she said, catching sight of a painting suffused with yellow light, "I am sure we shall recognise the hand of the masters. From what Herr Winter has told and shown me, that painting there, for instance, must come from the brush of Mr. Turner."

She moved towards it, to inspect it more closely, and collided with a woman in a dark green dress who at that moment took a step back from the picture. An apology died on her lips as she stared at Cassandra; then her face broke into a smile. "Why, if it is not Cassandra! Do not you recognise me? I am Camilla, your cousin Camilla!"

Chapter Twenty-four

There was a great likeness between the two cousins, although the relationship was not a close one. Cassandra had inherited her chestnut hair from her father, whose glossy brown locks had not been the least of his attractions for the mousy Anne de Bourgh. Cassandra's hair was almost of the same shade as Camilla's; there was a liveliness in both the cousins' expressions, and a sparkle to their eyes that was also similar, although Camilla had her mother's dark eyes, while Cassandra's were an unusual shade of grey.

So, although Camilla had not seen her cousin for several years, not since they were girls, in fact, she recognised her at once. She was perceptive, and as she took in the similarity in their looks, she also noticed the signs of strain in Cassandra's face, the hint of a shadow about her eyes, an unhappy look to a mouth that was naturally smiling, the tension in her bearing.

She took her by the elbow. "Come, we are standing in the way of all these people, come over here, I so much want to talk to you."

"Do you think you should be seen with me?" Cassandra said, with some bitterness. "I may be your cousin, but I assure you, I am no longer considered a member of your family, or indeed of any other."

"Such nonsense. That is your absurd, no, not absurd, foolish and unchristian stepfather speaking. What has he to say about any Darcy? You are one of us, and always will be."

That made Cassandra smile. "You are generous, but the connection is distant, we are not such close cousins that you have to acknowledge me. And"—with a lift to her chin that Camilla admired—"I do not at present go under the name of Darcy."

"You did not marry that man, after all?" exclaimed Camilla.

Cassandra's mouth tightened. "Is my story so well-known?"

Camilla could see that this upset her. "It was bound to be so," she said quietly. "We had it from Mr. Horatio Darcy—ah, I see you know him; of course you do, for he acted for your stepfather. Much against his will, I may say, he told us that your stepfather was not a man he could admire or wish to have any dealings with. He felt obliged to do so in this case, however, as he felt he owed it to you."

"He owed it to the family name, he has no concern for me."

"There I think you wrong him, but let us not argue about it. Now, tell me everything. How are you situated? Where are you living? For we have been worried for you, we heard that you had gone to live shut away in Cheltenham, and yet here you are in London. She would never let you come to London, I feel sure. Is this your maid with you?"

"Yes, that is Petifer, who has looked after me since I was a girl, at Rosings."

"I am so glad she is come with you."

"It is not quite what it seems. But I am not living with Mrs. Norris, although it may yet come to that."

Camilla could see that her kindness was making it difficult for Cassandra not to break down, and here, in front of all these people, that would never do. "Have you yet seen the exhibition?"

"No," said Cassandra, glad for the chance to move on to a more neutral subject. "For we have only just arrived."

"Then let us go round together. I should so much appreciate it, for I have heard what a skilled artist you are yourself; I never had the least inclination in that direction, my drawing had my governess in despair. But I love to look at paintings, and you may tell me what I should think of them."

It was a shrewd move on Camilla's part, because by the time they had stood before two or three canvases and Cassandra had eagerly pointed out details of brushwork and the use of light and the arrangement of the subject and the balance of the composition, she had quite forgotten to think about herself.

Camilla was startled by the depth of Cassandra's knowledge, for she had expected no more than any of her artistically inclined friends could have provided in the way of explanation. And her cousin's concentration and observation were absolute, she looked at the paintings in a way that opened Camilla's eyes. She was, she reflected, as passionate about art as her younger sister Alethea was about music. Which boded ill for a young woman in a censorious world, where female enthusiasms were expected to be of a milder kind. Not that Camilla had ever been a great one for the stuffier conventions; she had married a clever, eccentric man, and was enjoying the freedom that marriage gave her to think for herself and express as well as form her own opinions.

She knew that an understanding of art did not necessarily go with any great degree of skill or genius, but had a good idea that Cassandra's own painting and drawing might be much beyond the usual run. Her sketches, when she came to Pemberley as a girl, had made her father lift his eyebrows, she remembered, and say, "Remarkable, quite remarkable."

Cassandra was entranced by the Turners in the exhibition. She turned to Camilla with shining eyes. "Look at the light, how does he do that? I never saw such a luminous quality to a painting!"

"Do you paint landscapes?" Camilla asked.

"I like to do so, but my true love is portraiture." She was looking through Camilla's catalogue. "There are some portraits by James Lonsdale, I should very much like to see those."

"I admire those who can capture a likeness," Camilla remarked, as they stood before a striking portrait of Mrs. Siddons. "There is a famous picture of her, painted when she was much younger, by Mr. Gainsborough."

"I have never seen it, although I have seen an engraving. He did better by her nose than this artist does, for in her case, such a notable feature brings out the whole strength of her character. That is the real art of taking a likeness, of course, to express the nature of the sitter as well as his or her appearance."

Cassandra lingered for a moment in front of a large canvas, a portrait of the Prince of Wales. "Is this the Prince Regent?"

"Yes," said Camilla. "Lower your voice before you pass judgement, for he is extremely touchy about his appearance. He had Leigh Hunt thrown into jail for calling him a fat Adonis."

"Well, if he does not think that is true, he must have turned all his mirrors to the wall, for I never saw a grosser man. The artist is clearly afraid that he might also be thrown into jail, for he has painted nothing more than a paper and straw person, draped in regal robes, there is no insight into the soul or nature of the man at all."

"I think I would prefer not to see inside Prinny's soul, if he has one," Camilla said in a whisper. "He is not popular, you know; and my husband, Wytton, whom you must meet, cannot abide him."

Camilla could have bitten her tongue; even as the words came out, she saw Cassandra stiffen, and the wary look come back into her eyes.

"You are very kind, but I do not think my circumstances will permit of my having any social engagements while I am in London."

"Oh, stuff!" said Camilla. "One may make judgements on a painting, or even on a prince, but Wytton is not about to pass any judgement on you, I assure you. He is not that kind of a man at all."

Although that was not strictly true, she reminded herself. Wytton, who knew and liked Eyre, had been quite harsh about Cassandra. "She has thrown over a good fellow, on a whim," he had said, frowning.

"She was right to do so, if his liking and willingness to marry her were dependent on her fortune."

"That is the case in most matches, and besides, she liked him well enough to run away with him. So why did she not swallow her pride and marry him? It makes no sense, she must be an idiot of a girl, this cousin of yours, not to consider what she was about. Eyre is very cut up about it, he cared for her, whatever you may say about only wanting her fortune."

Men, even the best of them, saw things from a very different viewpoint, Camilla told herself, and she did not want to get into an argument with Wytton about it, so she turned the subject, and kept her own, very different views to herself.

Once Wytton had a chance to meet Cassandra, he would be of a different opinion, Camilla felt quite sure of that. No one who spoke to her for five minutes would call her idiotic; foolish, maybe, but her folly was the action of a moment, not an innate part of her. He would recognise the Darcy pride and the Darcy spirit as soon as he got to know her, and that would change his mind, and give him a better understanding of why she had behaved as she had.

"That is enough of paintings," Camilla said briskly, after an hour of inspecting canvases. "My mind cannot at present take in any more, so let us call a halt to it, and I shall take you to drink tea and then you may tell me all about what you are doing in London and what your plans are. No, no, do not look at me in that way, if you please. I am an inquisitive creature, and you are family, whatever you say, and perhaps I may help you in some way."

Petifer, who had been unashamedly listening to their conversation, nodded her head at this. "Show some sense for once, miss. You go with Mrs. Wytton, as she says."

Camilla looked at Petifer with approval. "Thank you, Petifer, is that right? Don't worry for your mistress, for I shall see her home if you will give me your direction."

Cassandra opened her mouth to protest, but Petifer spoke before she could stop her. Well, it didn't matter so very much; it was only a temporary address, she could not stay there for much longer. This lowering thought brought all her problems, forgotten in the delight of being at the exhibition, flowing back into her mind, and it was with a heavy heart that she followed Camilla out of the Royal Academy.

"We could go to Gunter's," Camilla said, with a frown. "However, it is a hotbed of gossip—"

"No, you do not want anyone to know you have been keeping my company," Cassandra said quickly.

"What a goose you are! That is not what I mean at all, only that we are speaking of private matters, and there is no need to shout them to the whole of London, as is what happens at Gunter's. I know of a little tea room nearby, very quiet and respectable, that will be much more suitable."

They sat together in a corner, while a broad man in a long apron, who seemed to know Camilla quite well, came to attend to them. Camilla ordered tea, and some pastries.

"He is now set up in this business," Camilla told Cassandra, "because he has a game leg, did you notice the limp? Formerly, he was in my husband's employ, he accompanied him to Egypt, and was of the greatest use, so Mr. Wytton says."

It took skilful questioning, interspersed with refreshing cups of tea and deliciously light pastries, for Camilla to pry any useful information about Cassandra. Her cousin was cagey and cautious, but Camilla was quick of understanding, and had not grown up with four difficult and temperamental sisters without learning how to extract the truth from someone such as Cassandra.

"Your situation then, is this. Your stepfather and mother have cast you out, which is cruel and unfeeling, but I dare say your mama is under the thumb of Mr. Partington, and so dare not let her maternal feelings influence her. You do not wish to live with Mrs. Norris, which is wise, for that would truly be a fate worse than death, if anything can be. You have no money at present, and your quarterly allowance will not be sufficient to permit you to stay in London without you finding some other source of income. You have nowhere to live beyond perhaps the next few days."

None of this came as news to Cassandra, but stated in these plain words by Camilla, it seemed suddenly too much for her to bear. Petifer was matter-of-fact and bracing, everyone else was censorious. Camilla's voice, even with this clear, even ruthless, exposition of her predicament, was warm with sympathy; and sympathy, Cassandra found, quite undid her.

"No, do not cry," Camilla said.

"I am not going to cry," said Cassandra, dabbing fiercely at her eyes with her handkerchief. "It is only that I feel so powerless and helpless. How different it would all be if I were a man."

"That is what my sister Alethea often says, but you cannot change your sex. You can find employment, though, that is the first thing to be done."

"Then there is the bill at Rudge's," said Cassandra inconsequentially. "He will not be expecting it to be paid at once, but yet I shall have to meet it. The world of colourists is bound to be a close-knit one, and I cannot afford to be turned away as a customer by any of them."

"I see you have not yet told me everything," said Camilla. She poured more tea. She would drink pints of tea and consume far more pastries than was good for her, if that was what was necessary to get to the bottom of Cassandra's troubles. She had a feeling that she had not yet heard the half of it.

When, an hour later, she had wrung every last detail out of Cassandra, she sat back with satisfaction. "There, don't you feel better for sharing your troubles?"

"I have shared them, with Petifer, and despite the saying, it does no good to one's spirits."

"It may not, but Petifer has given you a great deal of practical help, and I can give you some more. No, do not start up with all that nonsense again. I shan't offer you money, but I think I may be able to provide you with a suitable place to live. My former governess is a writer, Eliza Griffin, you may have heard of her?"

Cassandra's face lit up. "Oh, yes, indeed I have, I am extremely fond of her books. Mama and Mr. Partington did not approve of novels, but I had some good friends who lent me all of theirs, and we were all so delighted to read Eliza Griffin's novels."

Camilla was pleased. "She will be pleased if you tell her so, for she has a very modest estimation of her talents. The point is, she has a house, not far from here, and I know that her lodger left at the end of the last quarter. I am almost sure she has not yet let the rooms. She is very particular as to whom she shares her house with, and would prefer to have the rooms empty than to have a lodger she does not feel comfortable with. I have an idea that you and she might get along very well together. Writers and artists often do, I find, since both live in a world of fancy."

Miss Griffin lived in Soho, which was a warren of streets on the eastern side of Nash's new Regent Street. It boasted some more modern houses among those in the old style, some of them still with the overhanging roofs that made the narrow streets below seem dark even on the brightest day. Miss Griffin's house was on the corner of Soho Square, which, although small, had a pleasant green space in its centre.

It was at an unfashionably early hour that Camilla stood on the doorstep of Miss Griffin's house. A boy admitted her, and showed her into the room on the ground floor where Miss Griffin was already seated at her desk.

She pursed her lips at being interrupted at her labours.

"I am sorry to come at this hour," Camilla said, casting off her hat and making herself comfortable. "I would not do so, except that I need your help."

"In some scrape, are you?" Miss Griffin rose and gave the bell-pull a tug. The boy appeared, and she ordered him to bring coffee.

"Not I, no, but another member of my family is."

Miss Griffin frowned. "Not Belle again? Or has Alethea come to her senses, and jilted that man?"

"Unfortunately not. No, this time it is none of us. It concerns a cousin, Cassandra Darcy. Do you remember her?"

"I do indeed. It always astonished me that her mother could ever have had such a daughter. I suppose she takes after her father."

"Tell me about him, he died some while ago, did he not?"

Miss Griffin had been with Camilla's family for most of her working life, looking after the five sisters as they grew up at Pemberley. A discreet, sensible woman, she was regarded by all the Darcy family as utterly trustworthy, and there was little she didn't know about them or their tribe of relations.

"He was a Thaddeus Darcy. His father was your grandfather's younger brother, so your father and Mr. Thaddeus were first cousins. I don't know if you ever heard that Lady Catherine de Bourgh had always intended that her daughter, your cousin Anne, should marry your father—"

Camilla burst out laughing. "Papa marry Cousin Anne? Oh, you cannot be serious. She is such a fading-away, wilting kind of person, she would never have done for Papa, even if he hadn't fallen in love with Mama!"

"That's as may be, but it came to nothing, and Lady Catherine was extremely annoyed. Her daughter, who was cross and sickly, I will agree, didn't take, and I suspect her ladyship was getting desperate to find her a husband. Word has it that Mr. Collins, as he was then, suggested that if one Mr. Darcy wasn't available, then another might do."

"Oh, that dreadful Mr. Collins! Only no longer plain Mr. Collins, now that they've made him a bishop. What had it to do with him?"

"He held the living at Hunsford, and was highly regarded by Lady Catherine, I believe. Mr. Thaddeus Darcy, who was a younger son and a poet, but by all accounts a very amiable man, was summoned, and Anne de Bourgh fell in love with him—he was very good-looking, I heard—and they were married. However, he was never strong, he had a weakness to his chest from a child, and was carried off after catching influenza one winter. Cassandra Darcy must have been about five, then; I remember your mother and father putting on their blacks for him."

"And so Cousin Anne married again, this time to the very disagreeable Mr. Partington, who has made Cassandra's life so difficult."

"He was a clergyman, who held the living at Hunsford after Mr. Collins. Lady Catherine was not best pleased, she considered him to be much beneath her daughter in rank. However, all that was forgiven when, after two more daughters, your cousin gave birth to a son."

"Thus putting Cassandra's nose quite out of joint."

"That is the usual way of it, especially when there is a stepfather in the case."

The coffee came, and was poured, and drunk. Miss Griffin sat very upright in her chair. "So your cousin Cassandra has been up to mischief, has she? I heard something about that from Belle. I'm not altogether surprised; she struck me as being a very lively, determined child, although I haven't seen her for a good many years."

Camilla had no scruples about laying bare Cassandra's sad story to her old governess. The story would go no further, and if she were to enlist her help, then Miss Griffin must know the whole.

"So that's your plan, is it?" said Miss Griffin at last. "A Miss Darcy earning her living as a painter. I never heard of such a thing."

"You earn your living by your pen."

"That is quite different, I come from quite another order in life."

"She no longer goes by the name of Darcy, as I told you. She has to earn her bread, I do not see that you can criticise her because she is well-bred."

"No, no, we women must stick together when we can. Send your carriage for her, Camilla, for I know I will have no peace unless I go along with what you want."

"I am sure your stepfather would disapprove of this part of London," Camilla said to Cassandra as she and Petifer alighted from the carriage, "for any number of painters and writers and artists live here. The great Mr. Lawrence has his studio not far away, in Greek Street."

Her first sight of Miss Griffin made Cassandra's heart sink. This severe-looking woman, clearly a person of the strictest morals and the most old-fashioned notions, would never accept such an one as Cassandra Darcy into her house. Yet, there seemed to be a gleam of humanity in her eye, and was she not the authoress of such stirring tales as *Spectre of the North* and *Mrs. Fenman's Letter*?

And she greeted Camilla with real affection, before running her eye over Cassandra and uttering a daunting *humph* sound. "This is your maid?" she said to Cassandra, when Petifer bobbed a curtsy.

"Not precisely, you see . . ."

"Do not stand at the doorstep, come in." Miss Griffin held the door open wide, and they entered, Camilla bestowing a swift wink and an encouraging smile on her cousin. Miss Griffin led them through the hall to a small room, painted in a cream wash that made it light and pleasant, Cassandra thought, and which overlooked a tiny scrap of garden to the rear of the house.

"I have no maid at present," Miss Griffin said, when they were all seated, Camilla and Cassandra side by side on a sofa, Petifer perched on the edge of an upright chair, and Miss Griffin presiding in a throne-like chair with gilt arms.

"My girl left at the end of the month to get married, and I have not replaced her. That is why I opened the door to you myself. Now, Miss Darcy, I have heard such of your story as I need to know from Mrs. Wytton, and a sorry tale it is, too, with an uncommon twist on the usual outcome of such adventures. That is now behind you, and I can have nothing but sympathy for a young woman who has to make her way in the world. I suppose you do not feel called to be a governess? It can be a rewarding or a thankless job, I know from my own experiences, but it provides a living and a roof over one's head."

"I have the greatest respect for any woman who takes up such a position," said Cassandra at once. "I owe a great deal to my own admirable governess, Miss Wilson, but I am afraid that despite her best efforts, I am ill-equipped to teach any young person. At least, I feel I am qualified to instruct in painting and drawing, but as to languages and music and needlework, or history and geography, I have little to offer."

"Self-knowledge is a good beginning," said Miss Griffin. "So you propose to set yourself up as a drawing mistress, in a town overflowing with talented artists of every description."

Cassandra flushed. "It will not be easy, but I believe some mamas will prefer to have their daughters taught by a woman rather than some of the masters in town. And you yourself must have felt that the chances of a publisher agreeing to publish your first literary efforts were remote."

Miss Griffin smiled at that, for the first time, and it changed her whole appearance. I should like to paint her, Cassandra said inwardly, looking at the lean, intelligent face with sudden interest.

Miss Griffin's smile vanished. "Have you any examples of your work with you? Is that a portfolio under your arm? Did you imagine that you were angling for a commission, to bring it with you?"

"Stop being so fierce, Griffy," cried Camilla. "I told Cassandra to bring some paintings and drawings to show you, because you are well able to judge how much skill she has. Come on, Cassandra, for I, too, should like to see some of your recent work."

Cassandra rose and laid the portfolio on the round table under the window. She untied the ribbons and opened it, to reveal the water-colour portrait she had done of Belle, while they were together at Rosings.

It was quite unintentional, to have that picture lying on top, for Cassandra had tucked her paintings and sketches in quite randomly, not thinking about any particular order. But a portrait of a person known to the viewer always has an extra charm, and this one, which was a quite remarkable likeness, caused Camilla to exclaim out loud, and Miss Griffin to cast a look of surprise at Cassandra.

"Why, it is Belle, Belle to the life. Look, Griffy, it is an amazing likeness; Cassandra, you have caught to perfection that wilful look she has when she thinks some scheme of hers is going to be thwarted."

"And her beauty and charm besides," said Miss Griffin, holding it up to see it in a better light. "I congratulate you, Miss Darcy; if this is not an aberration, if the rest of your work is of this quality, it is quite out of the common run. I know many artists of some years standing who could not have painted such a revealing portrait of this young lady."

Camilla was turning over the other pages. "Here is Rosings, do you remember our visit there? And, Lord, it is Great-Aunt Catherine, to the life; how very terrifying! Here are children, are these your little brother and sisters? And who is this ravishing creature, with such intelligence and humour in her face, goodness, any man who saw this would fall instantly in love with her."

"That is Emily Croscombe, my greatest friend—who was my greatest friend when . . . And the next one is her mother."

"You can see the family resemblance," said Camilla.

"Both of those were studies for oils, but I didn't have time even to begin work on the painting of Belle before—"

"I should like to know more about that whole incident," said Miss Griffin, severe again. "I heard a garbled version from Belle, and I don't for a moment believe it was the truth. Belle never does tell the truth unless it suits her, I'm afraid my best efforts never persuaded her that there is a difference between true and false. She merely sees it as a difference in focus, which is quite wrong. I very much like this pencil drawing of a young man."

"A remarkably handsome young man," said Camilla.

"That is Henry Lisser, the artist," said Cassandra, taking it and laying it under her other drawings. "I did not intend to put it there."

"Is that not the young man who . . . ?"

"He is the reason I was sent away from Rosings, yes," said Cassandra. "And, no, despite anything you may have heard to the contrary, I did not have an affection for him. This is my mama, at her embroidery, and here are some drawings I made of Petifer, who has always been a most patient model."

It brought a lump to her throat, to see the familiar faces and figures from Rosings piling up on the table. She hadn't realised that Emily had put those in; had she done it from kindness, as a memento of the home she had lost?

"My dear," said Miss Griffin, after a swift look at Cassandra. "There is never any point in looking back. And with your ability, your extraordinary skill with brush and pen, I see no reason why you should not indeed establish yourself in London. People are so very ready to have their portraits done, you know, and you have a rare gift for it. Of course, there are those who will only consider a fashionable name, and are prepared to pay the fee demanded, but there are many on the lower rungs of society who would, I believe, be very happy to have their portrait painted by you."

Camilla gave Miss Griffin a swift hug. "You see, I knew you would like Cassandra, and I am delighted to have a cousin who has such a genius."

"First things first," Miss Griffin said. "Miss Darcy should see the rooms, she may find them not quite to her taste."

Cassandra didn't like to say that any room that was more than a hutch in the garden would probably be to her taste. "Miss Griffin, I go at present under the name of Kent. I do not wish to bring disgrace on those members of the family who bear my own name."

"Yes, yes," said Camilla, "but if you don't want that unpleasant Lord Usborne to know where you are, not that I think he will waste a moment thinking about you, fortunately you never fell into his clutches, then the name of Kent will have to disappear."

"I will not live under my real name."

"Then you shall choose another, like stage actresses do."

Miss Griffin took them up the narrow but graceful stairs to the top floor. Although it was the attic floor, the ceilings were of a good height, and the central room that she showed them into made Cassandra catch her breath. It was full of light, from two good-sized dormer windows, and ran nearly the length of the house.

"You need natural light for painting," said Miss Griffin. "Or so my last lodger told me. He, however, was not a painter, but a musician. He has gone to Italy for two or three years, to Rome. But I believe that in the past the room has been used as an artist's studio."

"It is in every way perfect for such a purpose," said Cassandra, looking about her in delight.

"No, it isn't," said Camilla. "Oh, yes, you may paint in here, but who will climb two flights of stairs to view your paintings, and do you want to have strangers in your house, Griffy? I had not thought of this before."

Camilla was right, yet it was hardly as though there would be a troop of clients up and down at all hours. "It might be possible to put paintings on view elsewhere," Cassandra said hesitantly.

Miss Griffin opened a door to one side of the room. "This is a tiny bedchamber, and there is another, even smaller, off the landing, which is the maid's room."

"Are you sure you do not mind, Petifer?" Cassandra asked, as they walked home. "Will not the duties be too onerous for you?"

"Onerous? Looking after you and a writing lady, who I'll be bound, once she has a pen in her hand, wouldn't notice if a dust cloud rolled through the house? What's onerous about that? I can keep that house tidy and trim with one hand tied behind my back, most girls would give an eyetooth for such a position. She isn't a grand lady, I grant you, and it isn't a smart part of town, such as you should be in, but if you don't care for that, nor do I."

"I, care? Petifer, it's the Garden of Eden as far as I'm concerned."

"That Mrs. Higgins, the cook, seems a pleasant enough body, and since her quarters are downstairs in the basement, we won't get in each other's way."

It was a very satisfactory arrangement all round, Camilla said as they parted. "Griffy does need a maid, she told me so, and this way she only has to pay part of her wages. You can still look after Miss Darcy, Petifer, and I rejoice to know that she is in good hands, and there is that room just made for you. Do you intend to finish the portrait of Belle? I think Papa and Mama would be very glad to have such a picture."

"Even when they know who painted it?"

"Don't be absurd; we are not such a set of moralisers as you seem to think. I'll tell you a great secret: My family is very given to running away with men, and although in those cases it turned out more or less happily, it makes us very much less inclined to cast stones than your self-righteous stepfather!"

"I wonder what she meant by that," said Cassandra, yawning violently as Petifer brushed her hair that night.

"Running away? I can tell you something about that. Mrs. Wytton's sister, Miss Georgina as was, Lady Mordaunt as she is now, ran away with Sir Joshua last year. Your mama was very shocked, do not you remember her falling into the vapours?"

Cassandra was so used to her mother having the vapours that she rarely took any notice of them.

"She was saying to Mr. Partington how scandalous it was, and he said as how it must be kept a strict secret, but all we servants heard about it. Then, it was a good while ago, before you were born, I think one of Mrs. Darcy's sisters—I'm talking about the present Mrs. Darcy, Mrs. Wytton's mother—ran off with a soldier. It was all hushed up and she married him, then he was carried off by a fever or died in the war or some such thing. She's on her second husband now. And there was some scandal over Mr. Darcy's younger sister, but I never knew the details of that affair."

"Goodness," said Cassandra, sliding gratefully between the lavender-scented sheets. "However do you know all this, Petifer?"

"Servants' gossip, miss. And don't look down your nose at me, for it can come in very useful, let me tell you."

Chapter Twenty-five

Camilla Wytton waved a cheerful good-bye to her husband as he stepped into the waiting chaise and called out to the coachman to go. She would miss him, they were not long married and took a great deal of pleasure in one another's company, but he had to spend a few days in Edinburgh, and she was not fond of the grey northern capital.

"It is a long journey, and when you arrive, you will be preoccupied with your affairs; I should be left on my own in a city I do not much care for. Go, and do what has to be done as quickly as you can so that you are back in London as soon as possible."

But for once she almost felt pleased to have the house to herself, for she had a plan, and since she had a suspicion it was not something he would approve of, it was just as well for him to be out of the way for the next few days.

Even before his curricle was out of sight, she was directing the servants to clear every stick of furniture out of the dining room. It could be stored for the present down in the basement, where there was plenty of room, and as for the China and glass that was kept in the cupboards, that could do with a thorough wash and polish. Down came the curtains, with directions that they be cleaned, folded, and stored away.

"Are we to have new ones, ma'am?" her housekeeper asked, pleased by all the bustle.

"We are. I shall visit some warehouses by and by, and they can send samples to match with the paint. Jenkins, careful there with that epergne, it is a very ugly piece, I agree, but it will not improve by being dented."

That was the trouble with wedding presents, when others' tastes did not always match your own. The epergne had been a gift from a relation of Wytton's, and while Camilla's instinct was to stow it away in a cupboard and forget about it, the great aunt in question was presently in London and inclined to call unannounced. On these visits, she would always open the door to the dining room in her forceful way, and expected to see her large and expensive gift displayed on the mahogany table.

Wytton was philosophical about it, he liked his great aunt, whom he characterised as a game old bird—she had even made the trip to Egypt one memorable year when he was there looking for ancient tombs—and the monstrous thing on the table didn't bother him as much as it annoyed Camilla.

It would be as well if Lady Plantyre didn't make one of her swooping visits while Wytton was away, Camilla thought, as a maid swept past, brandishing a duster. She had a feeling that her plans would not be to that redoubtable woman's taste.

And it was taking a risk that Mr. Wytton would be pleased. It was to be her birthday gift, for his birthday was on the seventh of next month. If he could accept the epergne with a good will, then he could do the same for her present. If he didn't care for what she was doing—well, she dismissed that thought. She had too much else on her mind.

There were several things she wanted to accomplish today. One was to make sure that Cassandra was safely installed in Soho Square, and whether she needed anything that Camilla might tactfully supply. Then she would broach the subject of the dining room to her prickly cousin. But before that, she was going to find out where one Henry Lisser dwelt, and call upon him.

She had questioned Mr. Wytton about him. Had he heard of the painter?

Indeed, he had; he was a German, he believed, and making quite a name for himself. She must know of him, too, for he had been commissioned to paint a picture of Rosings, he was known for his excellent renderings of houses in their settings: "He paints the most admirable landscapes. Belle must have met him, for I am sure he was down in Kent when she was rusticated there."

Before she had seen the drawing Cassandra had made of him, Camilla would have said that Belle would take no notice of an artist, but Belle would certainly have been aware of a man who was as handsome as that. Unless Cassandra herself was not being entirely truthful, and it was an idealised portrait of a more ordinary man.

One glance at Henry Lisser's noble countenance told her that Cassandra had done no such thing; if anything, she had understated Mr. Lisser's dashing looks. Camilla's interest was immediately aroused, for this artist was exactly the kind of man that Belle would fancy; how odd that she had heard not a word about him when she saw her sister on her return to London from Rosings. Belle was never one to keep her admiration for a man to herself; last year, she and her twin sister had kept the house in Aubrey Square ringing with their sighs and yearnings for one young man after another.

"Mr. Lisser, is it not?" she said, extending a hand. "I think you are acquainted with my husband. I am Mrs. Wytton."

He smiled and bowed, and said he had the honour to have met Mr. Wytton. "We see one another at the Royal Society, and on other occasions."

"You are interested in science and natural philosophy?"

He bowed again.

"Well, I have not come here to talk about scientists, although I must say that Humphry Davy's lectures are fascinating. And I have not at present come about a commission, either, although perhaps one day we may persuade you to visit us in Herefordshire."

"I have seen engravings of your house, Sillingford Abbey, is that right? It is magnificent in the best English style, I have a great admiration for such houses."

"Now, what I want to talk about is this." Camilla had with her a flat package, and she unwrapped it to display Cassandra's painting of Belle, which she had borrowed with her cousin's consent, saying that she wished to show it to Mr. Wytton.

Henry Lisser's studio was immaculate, with none of the jumble of paints and brushes and canvases that Camilla had so often seen in artists' ateliers. He placed the picture on an empty easel, and stepped back to take a better look at it.

Camilla was watching him, and her quick eyes took in the involuntary smile that came to his lips, and a softening to his eyes. Aha, it was as she had suspected; Belle had been playing off her tricks. Unforgivable, with a man like Henry Lisser, who came from an entirely different world to Belle; whatever had the wretched girl been thinking of?

But he had himself well under control, and when he turned back to Camilla, his face gave nothing away. "I could put a name to the artist, I think. It will have been painted by Miss Darcy—a relation of yours and Miss Belle's, I remember. It is a striking likeness. I was very much impressed by Miss Darcy's work while I was at Rosings. Were circumstances other than they are, she could have made a name for herself as a portraitist, I am sure of that."

"Do you think so? So do I, and that is exactly what I want to discuss with you. May we sit down? And then I will tell you just what I have in mind, for I think you would be glad to help Cassandra out of her difficulties."

Chapter Twenty-six

Lord Usborne came into Lady Usborne's chamber to find her in a state of dishabille; she had recently arisen and drunk the cup of thick chocolate with which she liked to start the day.

He looked thunderous, and he was in one of his worst moods.

"My lady, I think you have some letters that belong to me."

She blinked at him, and even at that hour of the morning, when her eyes were heavy with sleep, he noticed how lustrous and beautiful they were. Once they had held him in their thrall, now they annoyed him.

"Don't stare at me like that, you look positively moonstruck. Tell me, where are my letters?"

She pulled her flimsy gown about herself. "I know nothing of any letters. I never wrote you any, bar a note or so, so these must be letters from some other person."

"It is not important that you know who wrote them, I merely wish to find them."

She shrugged a white shoulder. "Then look elsewhere. I have no interest in any letters you may have received; as we agreed, our private lives are our own affairs."

"As it happens, these are not private letters." That was not strictly true, for they were extremely private. "They are not addressed to me."

"Then why do you have them? Is it a matter of business?"

"It is, but the letters are personal. I ask you again, have you been in my room, looking among my papers, and have you taken anything from there? They are wrapped round and round with a ribbon, and they were in a leather box. The box is there, but the letters are gone."

"I am afraid I can't help you. I never go into your room. A servant must have stolen them, or some guest you have entertained in there."

Was she lying? He never felt quite sure about his wife, she had an extraordinary capacity for self-containment, and it made it difficult to know what she was thinking, or to trace any small, revealing expression or movement in her face or eyes that might give her away.

He flung himself out of her room. Damn it, where were those letters? To have had them in his possession, pure gold, pure gunpowder, with God knew what resting on their being in the right hands, and then for them to go astray. The right hands were, of course, quite the wrong hands as far as the person who had penned the letters was concerned, but that was nothing to Lord Usborne.

He prowled about his private room, turning over papers, even getting down on his hands and knees to look on the floor under his desk. Nothing, no sign of them. And why should there be? Had the box gone as well, then it might be mislaid. The fact that the box was still there, on his desk, but quite empty, indicated that the letters had been removed. Taken by someone who knew their value, or someone acting for a different party. What a waste of his efforts, what a dashing of his hopes should they be destroyed or returned to the person who had sent them.

Valuable as they were, these letters had not cost Lord Usborne a penny. When he had found that the duplicitous George Warren had the letters, whipped out from under his own agent's nose, he had cursed the man. Usborne had long known him for an untrustworthy, subtle man, but even he had been surprised that Warren had got wind of these particular letters; he would have sworn that no one but the writer and recipient and his own man in the employ of the writer had any idea that they existed.

What did Warren plan to do with the letters? Presumably sell them to the highest bidder. Which would be the Prince Regent, unless Usborne came up with a better offer. He had no wish to do that, for he would be out of pocket. He had no intention of selling them to the prince; he dealt in favours and power and influence, not in hard cash. No. Had he the letters, he would, at an appropriate time, probably when the prince had retreated to Brighton for his summer revels, present them to Prinny. The gratitude of a monarch, however unpopular, was worth more than any mere money.

As it was, fate smiled on him. He had found Warren one evening at Brooks, where the play was deep, too deep for Warren's pockets. George Warren came to his senses at half past three on a drizzly morning to discover that he owed Usborne above eleven thousand guineas, at a time when he would be hard put to lay his hands on a hundred. Warren had begun the evening with a winning streak that made him reckless; by midnight, his luck had turned, and there he was, faced with enormous gaming debts that, unlike the considerable sums he owed his tailor and his wine merchant, must be paid.

That was when Usborne had broached the subject of the letters. Usborne made his offer. All would depend on one last turn of the cards, with eleven thousand guineas the wager, against the letters. If Warren won, the debt would be expunged. If Usborne won, then he would take the letters instead of the money.

Warren had to accept. He drew, a knave of spade, and sat back, not knowing whether he felt fear or hope, but knowing that only eight out of the fifty-two cards could beat his knave.

Usborne drew the king of diamonds.

"Very appropriate, don't you think?" he said, with a soft laugh, tearing up Warren's vowels, and putting out his hands for the letters.

Warren, his face darkened with drink and fury, put his hand into the inside pocket of his waistcoat and drew out the beribboned bundle of letters. He threw them down on the green baize, amid the cards.

"Damn you to hell, Usborne," he said, getting up from the table with a slight stagger. "I hope they may ruin you."

Usborne took no notice of a drunken man's curse, and he had no expectation of the letters bringing him anything other than profit, of various kinds.

Now the letters had vanished, before he had had a chance to put them to good use. Who had been in this room? Who had had the opportunity to take them? And who would have known to remove the letters, rather than take objects of more apparent value that lay about on his desk and shelves?

He would have to question the servants. Or, better, he would have his man, Ratchet, question the servants. Direct questions from their master would meet with sullen silence. Skilful questioning by a man as sly as Ratchet would be a good deal more likely to elicit whether anyone in his employ had taken the letters. And God help any servant who had.

He rang the bell, and Ratchet slid into the room. He gave Ratchet his instructions, which the servant received with his usual impassivity. "And there is this note come for you, my lord. From Carlton House."

Just what I didn't need, Usborne said to himself, as he scanned the note. A summons to the princely presence.

Chapter Twenty-seven

"There is someone to see you," Petifer said, in tones of the strongest disapproval. "That painter, from Rosings, the foreign person, Mr. Lisser."

Cassandra looked up from the water-colour she was working on, her brush suspended in mid-air.

"Mr. Lisser! Here?"

"Yes, and asking for you as Mrs. Burgh, moreover."

"How very odd. Ask him to come up, please, Petifer."

"Are you sure?"

"Of course I am."

"Well, I shall stay with you all the time he's here."

"You will not, Petifer. I am in no danger from Mr. Lisser, I assure you."

"It isn't proper."

Cassandra put down her brush and gave Petifer a very direct look. "You and I are going to fall out if you try to treat me as a child, or a green girl, Petifer. I am now in quite a different situation, and I must shift to look after myself. No serious artist has a chaperone hanging about her studio lest callers step over the line—which I assure you, would never be the case with Mr. Lisser. Now, you are keeping him waiting, which is impolite."

A few minutes later, Henry Lisser came into the room. Cassandra put out her hand, and, after a moment when she felt he was going to raise it to his lips, he gave it a hearty shake.

"I never shall get used to these English habits," he said cheerfully. "You are working? Then it is wrong of me to disturb you, but this call is of a professional nature."

Cassandra was surprised to find how pleased she was to see him. She had liked him at Rosings, feeling that he was a kindred spirit, and now his open manners and genuine pleasure at meeting her again made her smile.

"A professional matter?"

"Yes, my dear Mrs. Burgh, for I gather this is now your professional name."

The smile faded. "May I ask how you know that?"

He held up his hands. "No, do not look at me in quite that way. When you do so, you resemble the portrait I saw at Rosings of your terrifying grandmother. There is nothing mysterious about it. One Mrs. Wytton, who is Miss Belle's sister, so I learn, called upon me. She told me that, for reasons which need not concern me, you are obliged to make your way in London as an artist. You had previously gone under another alias, but have now assumed the new name of Mrs. Burgh."

It sounded somehow deceitful, put like that. "There are people in London who knew me as Mrs. Kent who do not wish me well. I should be obliged if you never mention to any living soul that I am Miss Darcy, nor that I have gone by any other name than Burgh."

Mr. Lisser bowed. "I am the soul of discretion, believe me." He paused, and said with a little smile, "I have some idea of what it is like to be obliged to go by another name than one's own."

Cassandra was about to ask why, but saw by the look on his face that he regretted having said so much, so she merely thanked him for his understanding.

"Mrs. Wytton felt, and she is in the right of it, that it is very difficult to do any such thing without friends in the same line who are already established. I hope I may count myself your friend?"

Cassandra was torn between anger and gratitude. Camilla was a wretch to do this; it bordered on interference, yet she knew it was done in a spirit of practicality, not from any misguided sense of patronage.

"She brought me this," Henry Lisser went on. He put down the flat package he had under his arm, and took off the protective card.

"Good heavens, my water-colour of Belle. I had no idea she had taken it. Just wait until I see her."

"She has done you a great kindness, as it happens," he said gravely, looking down at the wilful face which Cassandra had captured so well. "I admired your painting when I was at Rosings, but at that time there was no question of your having to earn your living as an artist. Now it becomes a matter of urgency and importance that you can do so, and I assure you, it is not at all an easy thing to do. You are very young and inexperienced, and although you have had the inestimable good fortune to have been taught for many years by a master such as my good friend Herr Winter, you have not studied in London, and you have none of the contacts that aspiring artists acquire as they learn."

These were words to make her despondent, especially since she knew them to be true.

"But what am I to do? I hope to find some hours of teaching, I am sure I can instruct children and young ladies in the rudiments of drawing and painting. And, as for the rest, I must study and practise and learn as best I may."

"Do not be so quick to give up hope. You have talent, real talent. I think Mrs. Wytton has told you how keen many people in London are to have their portraits done. In particular, looking at this picture of Miss Belle, I think there are fathers and mothers who would like the world to see their marriageable daughters in the best possible light; you have caught not only character here, but the radiance and freshness of youth, which will be present even when your subject, unlike Miss Belle, is a young lady with no particular degree of beauty. As you know, I am not a portraitist myself, but I believe I may be able to put commissions your way. To begin with, however, you must have a calling card, if you understand me.

A water-colour such as this is fine in its way, but you need to paint in oils."

Cassandra nodded. "I know, and the worst of it is that I had started on the canvas of Belle's portrait while I was at Rosings. It is still there, I suppose." That is, if Mr. Partington hadn't taken a knife to it, or tossed it out on to the midden in the farmyard.

"Can you send for it?"

"I don't think so. There are reasons . . ."

"May we sit down?" Mr. Lisser said. "Thank you, we are more comfortable like this. Now, let your servant, who glowers at me in a most uncomfortable way, bring us coffee and we shall put our heads together to see what we can achieve."

Petifer had, of course, been listening outside the door, so she was in the room in a flash when Cassandra called out to her. But instead of going off directly to see to the coffee, she lingered.

"What is it, Petifer?" Cassandra said. Really, she was being tiresome today.

"My brother-in-law, Robert, is in the fruit and veg line, as you know. Once a week or so, he gets extra stuff sent up from Kent, it comes up by the carrier, who's from our village. Those paintings of yours, the oil paintings, they're all stacked up in the eaves of your attic, yes, they are, for I put them there myself, not being sure what might or might not happen to them, and knowing you'd want them kept safe."

"But Mr. Partington . . ."

"Mr. P. doesn't know they exist, for he never knew what you did up in that attic, did he? Seeing as how he said water-colours and sketches were ladylike, and oil painting wasn't, you never told him any different, and your mama never knew that you spent most of your pin money on paints. And if you ask me, a lot that Herr Winter got for you, he paid for out of his own pocket, but that's neither here nor there."

This struck Cassandra with some force. Now that she had seen for herself the price of those little bladders of oil, she realised that the sums she had duly paid to her teacher could never have covered the materials she used. Dear, kind Herr Winter. One day, she would repay him.

Henry Lisser seemed to read her thoughts. He smiled, at her and then at Petifer, and even grumpy Petifer had to give him a reluctant smile in return. "You will repay him by becoming a successful artist," he said. "So, these paintings are safe and sound, and this carrier who carries vegetables may also carry a canvas or two, I think. How can they be got from—the eaves, did you say?"

"Josh will do that for me," said Petifer. "He owes me a favour or two, and he's sharp-witted, or at least not so slow as most of them there. And he can read and write, so you give me a list, Miss Cassandra—writ clear, mind—of what you want, and I'll see what I can do."

"An invaluable servant," said Mr. Lisser, as Petifer whisked herself triumphantly out of the room. He paused. "There is something I should like to ask you, if you permit. Nothing to do with painting, rather it concerns Miss Belle."

Cassandra grew watchful. This could be slippery ground.

"Miss Belle?"

"There is a mystery here. One morning, a boy came over to Herr Winter's house with a message that I was not to go to Rosings that day. It did not trouble me, for it was a damp, grey day, and I had drawings and sketches with me that I could work on in the studio there. The next day the message was the same, and so it continued for several days more. Then I decided enough was enough, and sent a message on my own behalf, to say that my time was limited, and that if I could not come to Rosings, to complete the picture, then I must return to London."

Cassandra knew all too well what had been happening in those intervening days, as letters flew to and from Bath, and she and Belle were packed off to London.

"Then, suddenly, I could resume work, and I returned to Rosings to find that Miss Belle and you had departed, gone away, no one would say where. Also that Mr. and Mrs. Partington were grown very cool towards me." He hesitated. "I feared that I was indiscreet, that I allowed the warmth of my feelings for Miss Belle—"

"Belle was not sent away on your account," Cassandra said.

"That is what she said, in a note I received via a servant." He took a deep breath. "She said you had been in some way compromised, and that it had been decided that she also was to leave Rosings, to go with you. She made me understand that I had been asked not to come to the house because the family were anxious that word of your— 'disgraceful conduct,' she called it, forgive me, should not be spread abroad."

For a moment Cassandra was filled with fury, and then her sense of humour got the better of her, and she burst out laughing. How like Belle, how *very* like Belle! What a minx she was, just let her wait until she saw her again. But that sobered her, for what chance was there that she would see Belle again?

Henry Lisser was regarding her gravely. "Miss Belle was up to mischief? Perhaps you had better tell me the whole story."

Cassandra did not at all want to do that. It belonged to a past that might be recent in terms of days and weeks, yet which was part of an another life entirely.

"There was a misunderstanding, on account of which, I went away to Bath and Belle back to London. What brought me to my present circumstances was to do with Bath, it had nothing to do with my departure from Rosings or the reasons for it, I assure you of that."

"However, had you not gone to Bath, then . . ."

"Life is full of perhapses, I find. I got into a scrape, more than a scrape, which has led to my no longer being welcome at Rosings, and forced me to make a living for myself. That is all."

"Forgive me if I seem intrusive, but you are a member of a great family, your relatives are people of consequence and influence. I would have thought . . ."

"They can't help me, even if they wanted to." That was hardly being fair to Camilla. "Although Mrs. Wytton has decided to stay friends with me, I am not sure why." This with a wry look.

"Mrs. Wytton appears to me to be a woman who has a mind and a will of her own, which I very much admire." He paused, then smiled again. "Miss Belle, too, has some strength of character, but in her case, she has yet to find a proper channel for her energies."

Cassandra could see all too clearly that Henry Lisser was still smitten with Belle. It would never do. Kisses in the shrubbery were bad enough, but to have beguiled this admirable man and fine artist, knowing, as she must do, that the social inequality between them made it an impossible liaison, was more than mere flirtatious naughtiness.

Had Belle cared at all for Henry Lisser? At the time, yes, impressed by his handsome looks and pleasing manners. By now, she had doubtless forgotten all about him, and had moved on to some other flirt—it was to be hoped one as heartless as she was.

Henry Lisser was looking at the picture of Belle again. "If you can capture in oils the same qualities as you have here, it will be a most excellent portrait."

Cassandra's mind was running ahead. "If it is to be a calling card, as you say, then potential clients would have to see it, and I do not think that the family would care to have her portrait exhibited in a public place."

"An artist's studio is not precisely a public place. A word or two in the right place, and a visitor or two, and word of your skill will get around to fond papas and mamas, who are careful how much they want to spend. I think you can make enough to keep yourself even though you are at a disadvantage, being a woman."

Cassandra sighed. "Perhaps I should cut my hair, and pretend to be a man."

Henry Lisser frowned; Cassandra liked him very much, but he was essentially a serious man, and did not always respond to her jokes.

"Take Mrs. Page," he went on. "She is a successful portraitist, and there are several others who paint miniatures and work in different fields. There is also a family of silversmiths, with an extremely talented daughter following in her father's footsteps, I shall arrange for you to meet her. Meanwhile, my advice to you is simple: work and more work. You are not too late to attend those lectures that are open to all; in particular, let me advise you to go to Mr. Turner's lectures on perspective. They are held in Somerset Place, on Monday evenings. You will need an Academician to give a ticket; I will arrange that for you, if you will permit me to do so."

They drank the coffee which Petifer brought, and talked for a while about painting and painters and their opinions of the works on display at this year's exhibition at the Royal Academy, and how Mr. Turner frightened his fellow artists by his enthusiasm for scientific progress.

"I agree with him on this," Henry Lisser said. "Science gives us new revelations about colour and light, which are at the heart of all painting, and indeed, technology yearly adds new colours to our palettes."

"Mr. Rudge's assistant was telling me about a new yellow," said Cassandra.

"Is that Mr. Fingal? He is a very able colourist, he will surpass his master in due course, and no doubt set up his own business."

Which brought a shadow to Cassandra's face, as she remembered the debt she had incurred at Mr. Rudge's establishment. Her need for money was immediate, the time scale over which she might expect to attract clients much longer.

Mr. Lisser gave her the name and directions of other colourists and a first-class brush maker.

"At the beginning, when you are setting up a studio, there are a lot of expenses. I cannot help in any pecuniary way, but I have an easel to spare, which I will send round to you, and also some canvases, no"—he held up a warning hand—"do not refuse assistance from another artist. We are all in the same game, after all, and"—with a rueful look, which Cassandra didn't quite understand—"I know something of what it is to be exiled from one's home."

Chapter Twenty-eight

"It is a matter of considerable delicacy," Lord Usborne said. He was looking straight ahead and into the distance, not even glancing at Horatio Darcy, to whom he was speaking. "It is, in short, a matter of state, and directly concerns the Prince Regent, and possibly the future of the monarchy."

Horatio's eyes narrowed. What exactly was Lord Usborne up to? Their acquaintance was slight, the animosity between them almost palpable, yet here was his lordship, seeking him out at his club, taking him aside, and lowering his voice to make an appointment, then insisting, when they met, on leaving Horatio Darcy's chambers and walking up and down the gravel path by the river—bare of other walkers on a blustery day that promised rain.

"I dare say it is no mystery to you how matters stand between His Royal Highness and his estranged wife, Princess Caroline."

Horatio became more wary. It was no secret, state or otherwise, that the prince and his bride had cordially disliked one another ever since their wedding night. Princess Caroline of Brunswick, a cousin of the Prince of Wales, as he then was, had crossed the Channel to become a royal bride more than twenty years before. The marriage was an arranged one, with no pretence of any affection existing between the couple. At that time, the prince's amorous affairs were as entangled as ever. He was still very much in love with Mrs. Fitzherbert, whom he had secretly married ten years before, and at the same time, he was carrying on an affair with Lady Jersey.

The marriage to Mrs. Fitzherbert, in a Catholic ceremony, was not legal, as the heir to the throne could not marry without the consent of the King, his father, and of Parliament, and could not, under any circumstances, marry a Catholic, which Mrs. Fitzherbert was. She had borne him a troop of children, the Fitzroys, of whom he was very fond.

He was not fond, however, of his wife, whom he found physically repulsive, and after the first week of their marriage, when she conceived Princess Charlotte, he never slept with her again, so rumour said.

She took her pleasures elsewhere, rumour also said, and they lived apart. The hopes of the nation and of her doting father rested on Charlotte, and it was a personal and national tragedy when she died in childbirth in 1817, leaving a stillborn son and a grieving husband.

With Princess Charlotte no longer alive to inherit the throne in due course, the race was on among the royal brothers, and for the Prince Regent himself, to marry and beget a legal heir. The royal brothers, with whom the Prince Regent was not on good terms, were free to find themselves brides if they could; he, still married to the Princess Caroline, was not.

"He wants a divorce, as you must know," said Lord Usborne, "but the princess resists any attempt to make her agree to this and will not consent to any arrangement by which the prince would be left free to marry again. She has said she will contest any divorce to her utmost, and, as you know, the prince is not exactly popular."

Horatio Darcy, himself no admirer of the florid and decadent prince, was well aware of his unpopularity.

"There came into my hands, I will not say how, some letters, some compromising letters. The prince has now learnt of their existence and wants me to present them to him, as soon as may be."

Horatio Darcy waited, growing impatient. It was cold, and he had work to do. Still, he was curious as to where this might be leading.

"Unfortunately, these letters, which, as I say, came into my hands, were taken out of them."

"Oh?"

"By a person or persons unknown."

"This is no doubt very regrettable, my lord, but what has it to do with me?"

"My wife speaks highly of your abilities," said Lord Usborne, with a distinctly sly smile. "In many fields. You are, I know, a rising lawyer, with a sharp mind, and, being a younger son, are keen to make your mark on the world and thus enhance both reputation and income."

Horatio Darcy remained silent. He heard the sting in the words "sharp mind." It was not a compliment to suggest that a gentleman, even one keen for advancement, possessed a sharp mind; that was rather an attribute of the lower kind of lawyer, the men who were not too nice in their selection of clients, nor as to the cases they undertook.

"I want you to trace and recover these letters for me, and quickly, for His Royal Highness is growing impatient. I will pay you well, and should you succeed, as I am sure you will, then the gratitude of a prince is not to be sneezed at."

Now Horatio's interest truly was aroused. "Is this a legal matter, my lord? For it does not seem to be so to me. I believe there are agents who make it their business to carry out enquiries and investigations of the type that you mention."

"This is far too important, and, as I have already said, far too delicate an affair to be entrusted to that order of person. Discretion is a necessary; absolute discretion. Plus the ability to mingle in a social world higher than that frequented by the persons of whom you speak. I do not know where the letters may be, but I doubt if a common thief would have taken them."

"I see. Perhaps you can give me some more details."

"Will you accept the commission, or not?"

Horatio Darcy hesitated only for a moment. This was too great an opportunity to pass by, loath as he was to do anything for a man he mistrusted as much as he did Usborne. He despised Prinny, and would have said, if asked, that the prince's matrimonial affairs were a perpetual scandal, but then he had no strong feelings as to the rights or wrongs of Princess Caroline's situation. These were deep waters he was swimming in, but he had a streak of recklessness, and nothing ventured, nothing gained, applied as much to a successful lawyer as to anyone else.

"I will, my lord, but I shall need to know every detail as to the content and history of the letters, who else would be interested in them, and for what reasons. Did they disappear in your house?"

"They did. They were in my study."

"Then I shall need to question your servants, which is an unsavoury business."

"You may leave that to Ratchet, my man, who has already started to make his own enquiries. It is of the first importance that we arouse no suspicion, that is the other difficulty you will face. I do not want it generally known that these letters exist, or that they were ever in my keeping."

"I understand."

"I hope to God you do," said Usborne, in a sudden outburst of ire. "For it will be the worse for you if you do not. And I expect speedy action on your part, there is not a moment to lose."

Impassive, and determined not to react to the imperious tone of Usborne's voice, Horatio Darcy bowed, said he must return to his chambers, and requested Lord Usborne to ask Mr. Ratchet to wait upon him as soon as possible.

Then he turned on his heel and walked away. His mind was in turmoil; he wanted to get back to his desk, and take time to sift through in his mind all that Lord Usborne had said.

Chapter Twenty-nine

Cassandra was destined to visit Mr. Rudge again sooner that she could have imagined, for not half an hour after Henry Lisser had left, Camilla was at her door, exclaiming at how workmanlike the studio looked.

"It makes me wish I had even a modicum of talent in that direction." As she spoke, she drew out, not without a struggle, a fat notebook from her reticule. "I wish you to look at this, it is Mr. Wytton's sketchbook from his Italian travels. I dare say you are familiar with the exciting excavations presently being carried out in the ruins of Pompeii, the Roman city that was buried in ash from an eruption of Vesuvius?"

Pompeii! That was a name that brought scenes from her childhood rushing back into Cassandra's mind. Sitting on her father's lap, while he told her the story of the great eruption in AD 79, and the city that was so utterly buried, only to be uncovered as recently as the last century.

"My father planned to travel to Italy, to see the excavations for himself," she said, speaking more to herself than to Camilla. "Only he died."

She took the notebook, and began to study it. "Are these all Mr. Wytton's drawings? They are very accurate."

"He drew the ruins, but the figures and the landscapes from the paintings were done for him by a local Italian; the one within the panel is called an emblema, so he told me. The red streaks down the side are his attempts to match the colour prevalent in some of the finest of the wall paintings. Pompeian red, it is called. Do you recognise it?"

"It is not difficult," Cassandra said, taking the notebook over to the window. "It is cinnabar vermilion, a sulphide of mercury. Why, do you want this colour for some reason?"

"I have a commission for you," said Camilla. "You mentioned that you were painting a fresco for your landlady in St. James's Square, the one who turned out to be so much more and less than a mere landlady."

"Yes, I began work on designs for her morning parlour. That is why I have to pay Rudge for the paints."

"Very well. Then we shall get the paints back from Mrs. whatever her name is, for if she expects you to pay the bill, then she cannot keep the paints. I shall then purchase them, by paying over the money you owe him, and you will use the colours to paint a fresco at my house. Only you will have to work with great speed, for Mr. Wytton will be home within ten days, and I wish it all to be ready for him when he is back. It is my birthday present to him: a Roman fresco in our dining room. Do not you think it an excellent idea?"

Cassandra's head was reeling. "Camilla, you are impossible. You are full of schemes to get me out of my difficulties, but I can't believe that Mr. Wytton wants any such thing in his dining room, or anywhere else."

"He does, although he does not yet know it. He has been prosing on about redecorating the room, it is very dark and gloomy at present, and he says he can't enjoy his food in such lugubrious surroundings. I thought of Egyptian, for he is also very interested in Egyptian antiquities, and it is a fashionable style, but it is not quite to my taste, so much seems to belong in tombs and temples, and ours is, after all, a domestic interior; I do not care to have a crocodile or a hippopotamus grinning at me from across the room. Will you do it? Please say that you will."

Camilla's enthusiasm was infectious, and, looking at the graceful figures, Cassandra could see just how they might be adapted. "With flowing robes," she said firmly. "I can't destroy such shreds of reputation that remain to me by painting women in the nude in your dining room."

"I suppose not, although I dare say Mr. Wytton would like it. No, women in the classical style, and that wonderful red in the background, and some of the birds and flowers such as are drawn here, could you do that?"

"I could, I think," said Cassandra, her hand reaching for a pen. She flicked open her notebook at a fresh page, and with a few swift, sure lines produced a figure that might have stepped off the wall of a Roman villa.

"Or possibly one of those Greek vases that Mr. Wytton has so many of. Some of them are quite beautiful, although there are others which may definitely not be displayed where visitors or servants might see them. The Greeks were not altogether the thing, and I don't think the Romans were any better as far as their morals went."

Cassandra was drawing a closer view of a head done in the style sketched in Wytton's notebook, and Camilla, after a puzzled look of recognition, burst out into delighted laughter. "You have drawn me, how very funny."

"I shall make you one of the Graces," Cassandra said. "Or possibly Flora herself."

"You will do it? I am so pleased. But now, we must go to this Mr. Rudge, at once, there is not a moment to be lost."

"I do not think," said Cassandra, as she closed the front door behind them, "that Mrs. Nettleton will give up the paints without she sees the money for her rent. Besides, she may have thrown the paints out."

"She may, but more likely she plans to pass them on to some other artist whom she will get to do the work. And as to the rent, it is a trifling sum, surely."

Trifling to Camilla, perhaps, but not so trifling to Cassandra. "More than I can presently pay."

"Then I will pay it, it can be taken as a part of the fee for the wall painting you are going to do for me."

Cassandra stopped abruptly. "I cannot possibly take money for that."

"Oh, pooh, do not hold your nose so high in the air. Come down out of the clouds, Cousin. You will not make yourself any kind of a living if you plan to work for nothing. The labourer is worthy of his hire, it says so in the Bible, let me tell you. No, let me hear no more nonsense about that. And, as soon as it is done, and Mr. Wytton has seen it, then I will invite some particular friends of mine, Pagoda Portal and Henrietta Rowan, to dine. He is famously rich, he made an immense fortune in India, he is a delightful man, and it occurs to me that he would be a first-rate patron for you."

"I begin to feel overwhelmed by what you are doing for me. Especially when I suspect that neither of your parents would approve of your having anything to do with me."

"Such stuff! That is the advantage of being a married woman, for one comes under the authority of a husband, and not a parent, and Mr. Wytton is the most obliging man in that way, he would never dictate whom I might and might not see. It is not his way, and besides, he would not dare." She bit her lip, clearly cross with herself.

"It is all right," Cassandra said. "Mention of husbands, even when I am so conspicuously lacking one, does not upset me."

Chapter Thirty

Ratchet stood before him, sleek and with a slight smile on his face that was almost, Horatio Darcy thought, a smirk.

He didn't care for the look of the man at all, he would never employ someone like this as his personal servant, and he thought with a moment's satisfaction about his own grizzle-haired and grizzle-faced Marston, honest, reliable, and utterly trustworthy, although sometimes too inclined to speak his mind with the frankness he felt he'd earned after a lifetime of service to the family; he had started as a page boy in Darcy's grandfather's house a great many years ago, and had never left them.

This Ratchet was altogether a different kind of servant, a Londoner from his crown to his boot tips, wily, wise in the ways of the nobility. Trustworthy?

Darcy wouldn't pass judgement on that. He probably was trustworthy as far as it went, which was with regard to Lord Usborne, who would make a ferocious master, Darcy imagined, and one who would expect, demand, and get the trust he needed, and who would dismiss any servant who did not serve him in exactly the way he wanted.

Did Ratchet know about Lady Usborne's spy? Horatio Darcy was prepared to bet that he did, in which case, it was no doubt a useful piece of information that he would keep to himself until it became of use to him. This impression was confirmed as he went through the household staff with Ratchet. The man knew the most intimate details of all their lives, what the weakness of each one was, how long they had been in the Usbornes' employment and a great deal more beside.

Darcy had the feeling that all of this was a waste of time. "Ratchet, you think you know who has taken the contents of the box from his lordship's room, is that not so?"

"I have my suspicions, sir."

"Why have not you told his lordship?"

"His lordship has under his protection, or had, until recently I should say, a young lady by the name of Harriet Foxley."

"Go on."

"She is a demi-rep, sir, a bird of paradise as the gentlemen have it, and she has been living in a house with all found at his lordship's expense for nearly two years. Quite settled, you'd have said, until she ups and offs," he added in a venomous tone. "Which put his lordship into quite a state."

"That has nothing to do with why you're here."

"No, and I beg your pardon, sir. Anyhow, this hussy, when she was still on terms with his lordship, sometimes came to the house. When her ladyship was absent, away in the country or visiting friends. It does occur to me that on these occasions, late at night generally, with the staff mostly asleep, she had the run of the house, and more than once I came across her where she had no reason to be, snooping."

"Snooping?"

"Looking at her ladyship's papers in her writing desk, I caught her doing that once."

"What explanation did she give?"

"None, she just gave me a saucy answer when I asked her, and said I was not to speak to her in such a way. I desisted, since it is true that his lordship's particulars, at least while they keep their looks and their figures, are allowed a great deal of freedom."

"Was she looking for anything special, do you think?"

Ratchet hesitated. "I couldn't say, sir. And another time, she was going through the pockets of his lordship's coat, which he'd removed and left lying across the back of a chair."

"And she had no reason for doing that, either?"

"She did say that his lordship had put one of her earrings that had come off in his pocket earlier that evening. That was when she was looking in his coat, as I said."

"Was it there?"

Ratchet gave a genteel sniff. "There was an earring."

"And while she was at her ladyship's desk, she might have been looking for a pen, to write a note, or some such thing?"

"She might, sir. She was a bold piece, if I may say so, for another time, when I found her casting her eyes about some papers on the desk in his library, and I said she should not be there, and his lordship should hear of it, she mocked me, and said to go ahead and tell him, and she'd be ready to die laughing when he snapped my head off and told me to get back to the iron and seeing to his ruffles."

Darcy thought for a moment. What secret papers, what papers of anything other than personal importance, might Lord Usborne's mistress expect him to have at home, were she to be in the pay of someone? Usborne played no part in politics as far as Darcy knew; it weren't as if he worked at the Foreign Office or the Treasury, where he might have access to state papers.

No, clandestinely acquired private papers were more like it, and his instinct told him that Usborne's demi-mondaine was unlikely to be looking for anything in particular, merely fishing for something that looked to be of value.

"I doubt if it was anything more than curiosity," he said.

"That is true. Only"—and a look of animation crossed Ratchet's face for the first time in this interview—"that was when all was well between her and his lordship. The last time she came, which was shortly before she walked out on him, left his protection, his house, everything, just like that—then she seemed to me to have something on her mind."

"What kind of something?"

"I couldn't say. It was just an impression I got. And she was in his lordship's study, she chose to wait for him there, while he went upstairs to change; some oaf had spilled wine on his coat."

"Did it not occur to his lordship when he noticed his papers were missing that Miss Foxley had been in that room?"

Ratchet coughed, making an unpleasant rasping sound, which irritated Darcy.

"Come on, man, answer me."

"His lordship was not precisely in a state where he would be fully aware of his surroundings, nor of exactly where his piece might be."

"Disguised, was he? Why the devil didn't you say this to him when he first asked you about the papers? I dare say he wasn't inebriated then."

Ratchet's face was wooden again. "It's not my place to talk about his lordship's guests, of whatever station. He asked me about the servants and that's quite another thing, and perfectly in order."

"And making accusations about his mistress . . ."

"Excuse me, ex-mistress."

"What difference does it make? That's a line you don't care to cross, very right and proper, I feel sure. Now, perhaps you could be good enough to furnish me with Miss Foxley's address."

"Like I said, sir, she isn't there. She upped and offed."

"Yes, I heard you. However, I shall see that a thorough search is made of the premises where she was previously living, and that any servants employed there are also questioned. Or have they been turned off?"

"No, I believe a new friend of his lordship's is moving in shortly."

Darcy's face darkened. He knew who that was. He hoped to God she wasn't already there; well, even if she were, there was no need for him to meet her. His lordship's pocket was a deep one, he could pay for a couple of sharp-eyed men to look around the place and talk to the servants. They could also obtain Harriet Foxley's present address for him; he needed to have a talk with Miss Foxley.

Which proved more difficult than he had expected, although it had been easy enough to trace her to the lodgings where she had gone after leaving Lord Usborne's house and protection. He went himself to talk to Mrs. Hodgson, who kept the lodgings, for he felt almost sure that Harriet Foxley was behind the disappearance of the papers. It was a bright, sunny day, as he rode up to 53 Lisson Grove. This was not a part of town that he was at all familiar with, and he looked around with interest, impressed by the pleasant, tree-lined street and the air of neat, middle-class worth and respectability.

Not so respectable as all that, he soon found, as a tiny maid opened the door of number fifty-three, and his nostrils were assailed by a strong smell that he couldn't for a moment identify.

"Linseed oil," said the little maid, seeing his expression. "Ground floor front is a painter. We've got a poet, as well."

She offered this information with some pride, but Darcy wasn't interested in poets or painters. "Is your mistress at home?"

A loud voice came down from the top of the stairs. "That depends who wants her, and in my day, a gentleman removed his hat when he came into someone's house."

Darcy raised his eyebrows, but took off his hat. "You are . . . ?"

"If you don't know my name, why are you asking for me?"

"It's regarding a woman who rented a room here. I believe . . ."

"If you mean Miss Foxley, I've got nothing to say to you. Good day."

Darcy wasn't able to make out the woman's features, or anything about her except that she was uncommonly tall. He put his hand into his pocket and drew out a note, which he crinkled suggestively between his fingers. "It might be worth your while just to have a few words with me?"

"And who is this 'me'? Don't you have a name?"

"My name is Horatio Darcy. I'm a lawyer."

"Ah, she's got the law on her now, has she? Well, you don't surprise me, you don't surprise me in the least. I should never have taken her in; you'd think I was too old a hand to be bamboozled by a pretty face and a well-spoken manner. I should have known she was up to no good. Come on up, and we'll talk in my sitting room. If there's business to discuss, there's no need for every Tom, Dick, and Harry to hear what's being said."

Chapter Thirty-one

Horatio Darcy glanced up as his clerk showed Mr. Cribbe into the room. Henty looked as though someone had thrust a lemon beneath his nostrils; he didn't care for the likes of Cribbe, one of that subtle, insinuating breed of men who passed unnoticed amidst the low life of London, and with equal skill among the merchants and tradespeople of the town, gleaning information, looking for people who would rather not be found, picking up snippets of information for anyone who paid them a reasonable fee.

Horatio Darcy, unlike his clerk, got on well with Cribbe. He was an honest man, or as honest as one in his line of business could be expected to be. And he had a dark sense of humour, regarding his prey with a world-weary cynicism that was refreshing to Horatio, used to fustier professional associates.

"The landlady, one Mrs. Hodgson, is a cagey soul," Horatio told Cribbe. "I don't think she has told me all she knows, but I have a feeling that what she isn't telling me may not be relevant to the whereabouts of this Harriet Foxley. I do have Miss Foxley's former address, which is nineteen King Street."

Cribbe gave a low whistle. "Bit of a come-down, Lisson Grove after King Street."

"That is why you must go carefully with any enquiries at the King Street address. There may be another young lady living there now.

Miss Foxley was in Lord Usborne's keeping and discretion is essential."

"You don't want his lordship to know anyone has been making enquiries."

"The servants in King Street were questioned in order to obtain information about Miss Foxley's whereabouts, but that was all. Now we need to find out more, and any information you can glean from that establishment as to when and why Miss Foxley parted company from Lord Usborne would be useful."

Horatio didn't tell Cribbe what the letters were, and Cribbe didn't ask.

Letters, especially those tied with a ribbon, were part of his stock-in-trade. "Ladies will write them, and they nearly always regret it. The best thing the top ten thousand could do is to make sure none of their daughters ever learn to read or write, and then we'd have none of this nonsense."

"And you'd be short of clients."

"Very true, Mr. Darcy."

Cribbe got up, hitched his snuff-coloured coat into slightly better order, and received the roll of money that Darcy handed him with an impassive face.

"No expense spared on this one, then, I take it," he said, looking down at the roll of soft.

"No."

"And you want all that I can dig out, and you want it yesterday."

"I do."

Even to mention the address in King Street brought an aggrieved feeling to Darcy's breast. For some reason, he didn't care to think of Cassandra installed there, didn't care for it all.

Why was he aggrieved? he asked himself, as he reached for a quill pen and flipped open the lid of his inkstand. What was it to him, if she had chosen to throw away the last vestiges of reputation she possessed? And, speaking as a humane man, it was doubtless better that she should have a roof over her head than be starving in the streets. But she had been offered a roof; two roofs, and had spurned them both, in favour of a life—or a year or two of her life—with Lord Usborne.

It was bad taste on her part, moreover. Doubtless Usborne might be considered a handsome man, and he was certainly wealthy, but even so. . . . No, this was a waste of time. His concern was Harriet Foxley; Cassandra had briefly entered his life, on a professional basis, and had then left it. There was no reason why he should ever see her again. In fact, he told himself, as he settled down to draft a letter about the case of *Noakes v. Stewart,* due to be heard in a week's time in front of that shocking old rip of a judge, Lord Lusgrove, he never wanted to see her again.

Before he went into court in front of Lord Lusgrove, Mr. Cribbe came sidling into the office, and laid a sheet of paper on Darcy's desk.

"Your bird's flown the coop," he said succinctly.

Darcy took up the paper and read through it rapidly. Then he swore, briefly and fluently. "America, by God. Why America?"

"Mostly, they go to get away from trouble, and to make a new life. You'll see that she left his lordship's protection a good few weeks back. She was married to one Mr. Richard Morris on the twenty-ninth. He's a respectable man, well thought of in his trade, which is engraving, but two days after they was wed, the bailiffs got him and he was in the sponging house, a writ against him drawn up by Lord Usborne."

"Ah," said Horatio. "Not very pleasant, not if there were no good reason for it."

"There wasn't. A trumped-up charge, if ever I saw one. But a man like Morris hasn't a chance if he comes up against such as Lord Usborne in a bad mood."

"He wasn't in debt?"

"He had his creditors, same as any man in a trade is likely to, but nothing he couldn't and didn't intend to pay."

"So it was a malicious move on Usborne's part."

"It seems likely. Howsoever that may be, his young lady, wife I should say, who seems a redoubtable sort of woman, she got him out of there, don't ask me how, for I didn't think you'd want the details, and then they were off as quick as could be. No doubt with the letters tucked up in her box, for I'm near sure as I can be that she had the letters."

"Why would she take them? I wonder if she realised what they were."

"I doubt it," said Cribbe. "My guess is that she took them before she'd broke with his lordship, and suspected that he was carrying on with another woman. Maybe she contemplated a spot of blackmail; maybe, having some experience of his lordship's nasty temper, she took them to have some hold over him if he turned unpleasant."

"But she never used them," Darcy said, half to himself.

"In the circs," said Cribbe, shifting his weight from one stout leg to the other, "I dare say she wanted nothing more to do with his lordship. She just wanted to scarper, and scarper she has done, all the way across the Atlantic Ocean." He paused. "Will you want me to send a man after her? It'd come expensive, but if the letters are important . . ."

"They are," said Horatio. "Not in themselves," he added hastily. "But to my client they are."

Cribbe nodded. "Mr. and Mrs. Morris have sailed on the old *Lord George,* and she ain't no flyer. If I put a man aboard the next packet, which is due to sail this evening, wind and weather permitting, he can be waiting on the dockside when Harriet Morris trips ashore. Will that suit?"

"It will have to," said Darcy.

"One thing you can tell your client," Cribbe added as he went out. "At least if she got hold of those letters unlawful, she won't be showing them to no one and so they won't be doing whoever wrote them no harm."

True enough, thought Darcy as he reached for the robe he would need in court. But in this case, his client wanted the letters so that they could be read. Anyhow, he would seek out Lord Usborne this evening, and tell him that the letters had gone abroad, and it would be some weeks before he had any further news of them.

Lord Usborne was not pleased with the news that Horatio brought him; Horatio chose not to name names nor to say which part of the world their present possessor might have taken them to. Lord Usborne had already tried to wreak his revenge on Harriet Morris, née Foxley, and Horatio saw no reason to make any trouble for her; even on the other side of the Atlantic, Lord Usborne would have friends and the ability to make mischief. No, he did not think they were on their way back to the person who had written them; there was no question of that.

"At least, you can set your mind at rest that the letters have not been lost or sold to the highest bidder," Darcy pointed out. "And also"—lowering his voice—"the Prince Regent will have other things to occupy his mind over the summer; he will be going down to Brighton, I suppose, as usual?"

"Yes."

"Then, by the time he returns to London, after the summer, I shall have news for you."

Lord Usborne had to be satisfied with that.

Too bad if he doesn't like it, Darcy thought, as he left Brooks, where he never felt at home; he was not any kind of a Whig. And if Prinny was worried about the succession, taking a repairing lease this summer and shedding some of his blubber might make his chances of getting an heir more likely, should he in fact marry again.

Chapter Thirty-two

The dining room in Harte Street was on the ground floor, to the rear of the house. While Camilla had her hand on the door handle of the dining room, Cassandra paused in the hall, her attention caught by a striking portrait of a woman, not in the first flush of youth, but in the height of a mature beauty.

"This is a very fine portrait, who is the woman?"

Camilla came back and stood with Cassandra in front of the picture.

"That is Lady Hermione Wytton, my mama-in-law. She was strikingly lovely as a girl, and this portrait was painted when Mr. Wytton was a little boy, he remembers her just so, he says. And even now, she is a very fine-looking woman for her age. Some people are afraid of her, for she has a caustic tongue, but I go along with her very well, and Mr. Wytton thinks the world of her. That is," she corrected herself, "he thinks the world of her when they are not under the same roof, for when they are together too long, they argue, which is very amusing, for her wits are as quick as his, which he does not always like. Mostly, she lives in Italy. This portrait was painted by an Italian, a painter called Strozzoli. There are other, more formal portraits of her at the Abbey; she was painted as a bride by Gainsborough, although Mr. Wytton says it is not one of his best works. Mr. Wytton wanted to have this one here, in our London house, where he can see it often."

They passed into the dining room. The walls were painted in the Pompeian red that Camilla had shown Cassandra, with two panels outlined on either side of a handsome marble fireplace.

"It is a good colour," said Cassandra, looking around her, "but perhaps rather sombre, unrelieved as it is here."

"Exactly. It was always our intention to have some frescoes in those two panels on either side of the fireplace, but we can never agree on what should be the subject. So I have now taken matters into my own hands, and he can have classical figures, such as you showed me, based on those in his own sketchbook. What do you think? I have cleared the room as you can see, so you will have plenty of time to work. No, don't look down your nose like that at me; how you remind me of Papa when you do that. It is not charity, in fact, you are doing me the favour, as you can see."

Camilla's enthusiasm carried the day, and in fact, Cassandra's fingers were itching to get to some paper and start sketching. The figures presented no difficulty, and as for the faces, well, such women were generally of a type, but Cassandra had another idea. As they went back into the hall, she spent some more minutes looking intently at the portrait of Lady Hermione, before joining Camilla upstairs.

"I shall pay for all the paints and materials you need," Camilla said. "No, do not argue with me. I shall come with you, really, there is very little for me to do now that Mr. Wytton is away, and a colourist's shop is the very thing to amuse me. I have never been to one, you see. Where is his establishment situated? Can we walk, or shall I order the carriage?"

Mr. Rudge welcomed the ladies with bows and smiles, while Mr. Fingal hovered in the background. He was all obliging attention as Cassandra discussed her needs, for the paint she would use on the panel, although oil, was not quite the same as was suitable for her canvases.

"And there is a matter of paints supplied for Mrs. Nettleton, of St. James's Square," Camilla said. "Since Mrs. Nettleton has no further use for the paints, please have them collected, and then you may deliver them to Soho Square on my account."

Cassandra was astonished by this high-handed way of dealing with her former landlady, but Mr. Rudge seemed to see nothing unusual about it, and said that he would send Mr. Fingal round to collect the paints.

"And brushes, also, I believe," said Camilla.

"It is all perfectly fascinating," she said to Cassandra, as they left. "Although the smell of the paints is very strong, I hope that Griffy is not averse to the smell of linseed oil."

Fortunately, Miss Griffin was not. "In fact," she said to Cassandra, "I do not have a very developed sense of smell. My eyes are as keen as anyone's, and my hearing is acute, but I do not have much sense of smell. And what I can smell of your paints and so forth, does not offend me at all."

Petifer, of course, was used to the smells, and settled comfortably into something like her old routine, sharing her household duties with the hours she spent assisting Cassandra in the studio. She received the delivery from Mr. Rudge's, which was brought round by his assistant, Mr. Fingal, rather than the boy. "I was coming this way," he said, watching Petifer checking over the order. "Looks like you know something about paints."

"I've learned what I need to know," Petifer said repressively. Then, because Mr. Fingal was a pleasant enough man, she unbuttoned enough to ask him to help her move the easel, and to call out the items listed on the bill.

"It's all correct, I made the order up myself, and there are also the paints retrieved from Mrs. Nettleton's house, not that she was eager to let them go. But I said, 'You may keep them if you pay for them,' and she handed them over without further ado."

Further conversation elicited the fact that he hailed from the same part of the world as Petifer's brother-in-law, and they parted on the friendliest of terms when he eventually recollected that he had duties elsewhere.

Cassandra found, as so often in the past, that work was the best balm for bruised spirits. Now she discovered it was also a healer, or at least a distractor, for a bruised heart, and, indeed, for a bruised self-esteem, for her narrow escape from the clutches of Mrs. Nettleton and Lord Usborne had left her feeling she was not so well able to look after herself as she had thought; how would she have managed without the timely assistance from Petifer and from Camilla?

Well, she would learn from her mistakes, and be a great deal warier in future.

So she set to drawing the designs for Camilla's panels, for that, as her cousin pointed out, was a matter of urgency, if the work were to be completed before Mr. Wytton returned from Scotland.

She took the dancing lines of her figures from Wytton's sketches and from drawings she made of figures on the vases in the British Museum, but the faces were not idealised women from antiquity but living images. Then she took time away from the studio and the portrait of Belle to go to Harte Street, where she painted away happily, often perched on the top step of a ladder, much to the disapproval of the Wyttons' stately butler.

Chapter Thirty-three

Mr. Wytton arrived back from Edinburgh late in the evening, tired after accomplishing the return journey in the shortest possible time. He had been travelling for more than fourteen hours since leaving the inn where he had stayed the previous night, and it was a weary traveller whom the butler admitted to the house in Harte Street.

Although it was late, Camilla was there seconds after she heard his voice, exclaiming at the lateness of the hour; at how quickly he had returned; how very, very happy she was to see him.

He was not too tired to sweep Camilla into his arms the second they were alone, kissing her soundly and whispering into her ear that this was why he had cracked on so, not wanting to spend another night apart from her.

She kissed him back with equal passion, before reluctantly disengaging herself and insisting that he shift his clothes, such a state as they were in, and while he did that, she would make sure a comfortable supper was laid out for him in the parlour.

Mr. Wytton was not the man to be feeling any strain from such an arduous journey, nor from the undoubted pleasures of the night that followed his reunion with his wife, so he was up at his usual hour the next morning, calling out to Camilla as to where she had put some papers he had by him and declaring that he was hungry enough to eat a horse. So he was in a thoroughly good mood when Camilla ushered him, after preparing him for a surprise, into the dining room.

He stopped at the threshold, took in the novelty in an instant, and strode over to have a closer look at the panels. Then he burst out laughing. "Well, my love, I had thought that the decoration for this room was going to be a matter of agreement between us, and I see that you have made the decision yourself."

"You are not vexed?"

"I? Never. It is charming, quite charming, and I am vastly pleased to have pictures of you and my mama, a young mama, I notice, quite in all her beauty, in the shape of these elegant nymphs. How came you to do this? Who is the artist? He has the details perfectly correct, I am astonished."

"You should not be, my dearest, for the figures were taken from your very own notebook, which I took the liberty of showing to the artist. As to the faces, that was . . . the painter's notion; with my features taken from life, and Lady Hermione's from the portrait outside."

"She will be amused to see herself in such a guise. But how came this to be done so quickly? You must have had it arranged before I left, to have the work done so quickly in my absence and spring it on me as a surprise. Although I do not know how this may be, as my journey to Edinburgh was not planned, as you know; it was a spur-of-the-moment decision on my part to go to Scotland."

"The scheme appealed to the artist in question, and since it is intended as a birthday tribute to you, I insisted it be completed as swiftly as possible."

"Well, my dear"—putting his arm around her waist and drawing her to him—"it is a lovely surprise, and how much I shall look forward to dining in here this evening."

He went out shortly after that, leaving Camilla well pleased with the success of her scheme, and she despatched a note to Cassandra saying how much Mr. Wytton had liked her work.

But this was premature, for it was a frowning husband who joined her in the dining room later that day. They dined at a fashionably late hour, and Mr. Wytton had only returned from his club in time to change his clothes for dinner, so she had not seen him since that morning.

She knew at once that something was amiss. But before she could ask him, in her usual direct way, what had happened to make him out of sorts, he glanced behind him at the panels. "It occurred to me, just as I was going into the museum, where I was to see Haroldson, that the artist whom you employed to paint these figures is none other than your cousin Cassandra Darcy. Is that not so?"

"How did you jump to such a conclusion?"

"I am as well able to put two and two together as any man, I believe. I knew that you had the intention of helping Miss Darcy if you could, whatever my or your family's objections might be."

"Very well, I will admit that you are right. Don't look askance, you said yourself how much you liked them, do not say you are going to express some antiquated prejudice against a woman artist!"

"I care little for what sex a painter may be, if he or she handles brushes and paint in a correct and pleasing manner. That has nothing to do with what is wrong here. It is not her skill that I question, but her morals, and although you are of age, and may choose your friends—I am no ogre of a husband—I cannot feel but that you should not have anything to do with this unfortunate member of your family. And I am convinced that if your mother or father had any idea of what you were about, they would be as loud in their condemnation as I am."

"Mr. Wytton!"

"No," he said, holding up a hand as she attempted to break in. "Let me have my say. I am sorry for her. I have not met her, and I am sure that in essence she is a very agreeable girl. However, she took a false step, which has put her outside the pale, shutting the door for the rest of her life on that circle to which she could expect to belong by reason of her birth and upbringing."

"You are talking fustian."

"From what you said, her main fault is pride, which can in some ways be admirable; and I agree that she is probably not of a wicked disposition, and I can applaud her determination to find herself respectable employment in order to support herself."

"Only you are going to say that for a female, painting is not a respectable way to earn her living, because that is a province of the male half of humanity?"

"You take my words and twist them, you always do so. I can't understand how your cousin consented to take on this commission; you must have made it impossible for her to refuse. You should not have done any such thing, you should not be so quick to interfere, you have to learn to let others make their mistakes and take the consequences, without rushing in. You are the same with your sisters, and it is a sign of your kind heart, but sometimes, as now, it causes nothing but embarrassment. I do not think that for the moment you would be wise to have anything more to do with your unfortunate cousin."

Now Camilla could speak, and, white with anger, she replied with impetuous, scornful words. Camilla was not going to be dictated to by Mr. Wytton, no, nor by anybody else, her judgement was as sound as his, sounder, if she did not pass sweeping judgements on an inaccurate understanding of the facts.

Mr. Wytton was furious. "Facts!" he cried. "What say you to the fact that this Cassandra, this girl who took a wrong step, but who was determined not to let that lapse mar her life for good, has placed herself under the protection of Lord Usborne, is in fact his mistress? And that she lied to Horatio Darcy about being under the care of that Mrs. Norris whom you stigmatised as being such a dreadful woman the other night; better for Cassandra to be in her care than to join the impures, to come upon the town and end up in Lord Usborne's bed, until such time as he tires of her, and she is passed on to some other fellow of lesser standing and wealth, and so on until she sinks, a ruined woman, into decent or unhappy obscurity."

"You sound like a character from one of Griffy's novels," Camilla flashed back. "Where had you this interesting news concerning Lord Usborne?"

"I met Horatio Darcy in the club, and he told me."

"Why did he tell you, pray?"

"He is concerned that Miss Darcy brings dishonour on the family name. Since I am married to you, and he knows you are aware of her sad history, he felt that I, and you, should be informed of this further disastrous step which she has taken. Since he handles her financial affairs, such as they are, and is also acting for her family, I think we may assume that he knows what he is talking about."

"We may assume no such thing, for he is talking through his hat. Cassandra is not gracing either Lord Usborne's bed or the house where he keeps his fancy pieces—thank you, I know all about men such as his lordship."

She rose from the table and left the room, high spots of colour on her cheeks, while Mr. Wytton sat feeling that the ground had been cut from under his feet.

Of course, she would never admit that she was in the wrong, that was the trouble with women; once they had an idea fixed in their heads, there was no shifting it.

He was considerably surprised, having imagined that Camilla had gone to lick her wounds in her own chamber, when the door was flung open not ten minutes later, and there was his wife, wearing a most fetching bonnet, saying that she had ordered the carriage to be brought round; he must put on his hat, if he did not want to keep the horses waiting.

He opened his mouth to protest, to demand to know what this was about and to ask why he had to have a drama enacted in his own house; but the steely look in Camilla's eye made him feel that it might be better to do as she wished.

"Where are we going?" he asked, since, once they were in the carriage, the coachman had set the horses in motion directly, without waiting for further orders.

"You will see."

Wherever he had expected to go, it was not to Miss Griffin's small house in Soho Square.

"Camilla," he exclaimed, as she marched up to the front door. "What the devil do you think you're doing? I suppose you want your old governess to convince me that my attitude to Cassandra's laxity is too harsh; well, she may save her breath."

Camilla ignored him, which annoyed him still further, and she proceeded to set about a brisk rapping with the knocker. It opened after only a short wait, and a maidservant, with what he considered a shrewish expression, stared out at them. Camilla greeted her with a friendly "Good evening, Petifer. I am glad to see you here. Are the ladies at home?"

"Miss Griffin is not yet back, she went out to the play, but if you care to go upstairs, you will find—"

"Thank you," Camilla said, cutting Petifer's words short, and swept towards the narrow staircase without a backward look at Mr. Wytton.

What was she up to? he wondered, as he followed her up the stairs, past the first landing and on up to the top floor. There she paused before a green-painted door, listening for a moment, before giving it a couple of light taps and turning the handle.

Wytton could see a young woman, who bore a striking resemblance to his wife, seated at a table, her head bent over some work she was doing, a sheet of paper lit by a many-branched candle. She looked up, and smiled as she saw Camilla.

"Camilla, whatever are you doing here?" she said, rising, and coming over.

"Mr. Wytton," said Camilla, not looking at him; she was clearly still in a state of considerable dudgeon. "Allow me to present my cousin, Cassandra, I know how desirous you are of meeting her."

Cassandra dropped a slight curtsy and held out her hand. He found himself being appraised by a pair of beautiful grey eyes, eyes that a man might drown in, he thought irrelevantly. Camilla was talking.

"Now, Cassandra, I think Mr. Wytton would like to be assured that you have not got Lord Usborne tucked away behind that easel of yours, or perhaps stowed in the cupboard, while you paint."

Cassandra gave Mr. Wytton a startled glance. "I beg your pardon?" she said. "Lord Usborne? Why should he be here? I only hope to God that he has no idea of my whereabouts, what are you saying?"

"It seems," Camilla began, "no, there is no seems about it, Mr. Wytton was convinced that you had fallen into the hands of Lord Usborne, that he was your protector, and that you were living with him as his mistress."

"Camilla!" Mr. Wytton exclaimed. "It is really too bad of you!"

Chapter Thirty-four

Although Horatio Darcy was fond of a good novel, and read a good many of them when time permitted, he was not an habitué of Hookham's circulating library.

Lady Usborne was, for as well as subscribing to any three-volume novel coming new on to the market from a well-reputed author, she had a greater appetite for novels than that, and so, like many others of her circle, she was a frequent visitor to the library. This afternoon, she had persuaded Horatio Darcy to accompany her, before going on for a drive in the park.

Horatio Darcy should have been in his chambers, as both of them knew. He was having to rise early to attend to the papers piled on his desk by his assiduous clerk, and to take them home for late-night sessions on urgent cases. It was beginning to annoy him, not that he minded hard work, but a warning voice in his head reminded him that he was a man with a name to make for himself, and the only name he was making at the moment was that of Lady Usborne's favourite.

She brushed aside all his protestations that he had work to do, summoning him to her house or out on an expedition to the shops, and to the parties, dances, balls, soirees, routs, and drums that made up the intense social whirl of the season. Herself a gadfly, flitting from party to party, she liked to have her handsome young lawyer in attendance, and warned by her mother in a sharp letter from the country that she was making a fool of herself, and if her intention was to make Lord Usborne more attentive to her, this was not the way to do it, she became even more demanding of her lover's time.

He found her increasingly brittle moods tiring, and found himself longing for the end of the season and, unthinkable only a few weeks before, welcoming the prospect of the coming separation when she would accompany her husband down to Brighton for the months of high summer.

She took it for granted that he, too, would be in Brighton, and he hadn't yet brought himself to tell her that he would not. He could afford neither the time nor the outlay required to rent lodgings in that fashionable resort; moreover, he couldn't think of a less appealing way to spend the summer. No, he would catch up on work, enjoy having some time to himself, to visit his club, visit some friends in the country, get back into his own skin, as it were. He would promise to drive down at the weekends, but he knew quite well that he would not be undertaking the journey more than once or twice during the summer.

Lady Usborne was greeting friends at the library, inspecting the new arrivals, and keeping a keen lookout for a smart new hat or signs that any female of her acquaintance was not looking quite her best; a pregnancy—foolish woman, to risk her figure for a mewling infant; a look of melancholy—perhaps a lover had jilted her, or a husband been unkind; a gown or hat that had been seen too often—had debtors grown too many to handle?

She thrived on scandal; it bored Horatio Darcy, and he whiled away the time by browsing along the shelves. At the far end of an interesting selection of books on travel, he looked up to find himself face-to-face with Mrs. Wytton.

She announced herself delighted to see him, but something in her voice made him uneasy, and he glanced over to where Lady Usborne stood surrounded by a group of cronies, not looking in the least as though she were ready to leave.

"I have a bone to pick with you, Cousin," was her ominous opening.

His face assumed a haughty look.

"It is not the least use your glaring at me in that way," she said, with a smile. "For I am well used to Papa's showing his disapproval in exactly that fashion, and so you do not frighten me at all."

"It was not my intention to put you out of countenance," he said stiffly.

"Then it is as well that you have not done so. I was given an interesting piece of information by Mr. Wytton recently, which he had from you. I am so glad of the opportunity of putting you right about the matter, for you were quite mistaken in what you told him."

"What matter was this?" he asked warily.

"Why, you had a conversation with him about our cousin Cassandra, do not you remember? Yes, I see by your face that you do."

"I hardly think—"

"Now you are going to say that he was wrong to repeat what you said. He did so in order to warn me not to be taken in by Cassandra; in fact not to see her or have anything to do with her."

"As any husband would in the circumstances. I understand that your family feeling may have led you to think Miss Darcy to be other than she is, but—"

"This is a very public place to name names. Since you are her cousin, I'm sure she would have no objection to you using her Christian name. So Mr. Wytton was to warn me off Cassandra, but not to say why, is that it? You are not married, are you, Mr. Darcy?"

"You know that I am not."

"You have little idea of how to treat a wife, so it is as well that you are single"—with a swift, knowing look in the direction of Lady Usborne—"even if not entirely unattached. I do not take instructions unquestioningly from Mr. Wytton, nor would he expect me to, and especially not when we are talking about a member of my family."

"As to that, I bow to your superior knowledge," said Horatio Darcy, somewhat coldly.

"Yes, well, and my superior knowledge extends further than that, for I know a great deal more about Cassandra than you do, and I am very glad to have this chance to put you right."

What the devil was she on about?

"You are under a misapprehension with regard to her circumstances. She is not in anybody's keeping, I will not mention any particular person, by name, but you will know to whom I refer, and I am sure you will be glad to hear it. How you so misunderstood the situation, I do not know."

Not in keeping? How was this possible? How could Camilla Wytton have been so hoodwinked?

"My authority was good."

"That is as may be, but it was also wrong."

"If you imagine that Miss—that Cassandra is in Cheltenham, under the care of the good Mrs. Norris, then you are mistaken."

"From what I hear, there is nothing good about Mrs. Norris, nothing whatsoever. And I know that Cassandra is in London. She is lodging with an excellent woman, whom I have known ever since I was a small girl, and is setting about earning her living in a way that fills me with admiration."

He strove for a tone of polite incredulity. Cassandra had said, in that assertive way she had, something of the sort when she came to his chambers; of course he had taken no notice of her words, then. "Earning a living? And how, pray, may a person in her circumstances do any such thing?"

"There are other ways that a woman may earn a living, besides selling her body, and in this case probably her soul, Mr. Darcy."

"How?"

"That is her affair, and since you take such a very jaundiced view of her ability to settle herself respectably in London, I am not going to say another word about it."

"I hardly think that *respectable* is a word that may justly be applied to Cassandra."

"You sound just as I imagine her stepfather does. That is one of the reasons why I do not propose to tell you her direction nor how she is making her living, for I think it advisable that Mr. Partington, who sounds a thoroughly disagreeable sort of man, should not have news of his stepdaughter. Although I do feel some pity for her mama; she is a dismal kind of person, by all I hear, but I give her the benefit of the doubt, and assume that despite everything she has some tender feelings for Cassandra."

"Has she found employment as a governess? No, that would be impossible, enquiries would be made . . ."

"You may guess as much as you like, I'm not going to say another word. But, when next you see her, because no doubt in the fullness of time you will meet again, then you will owe her an apology. Meanwhile, I am sure it will give you the greatest satisfaction to know that whatever the Usborne amours with any member of the Darcy family may be, they do not involve Cassandra."

How dare she, he thought, as her barb struck home. His mouth tightened, but before he could say another word, Camilla bestowed a brilliant smile upon him, and moved away.

An apology, indeed; he owed Cassandra nothing. He did not care a jot about Cassandra or what she was doing, although he supposed it was as well if she were not Usborne's mistress. It was unlike Lady Usborne to have things wrong there, she seemed to keep a very close eye on her husband's doings. It struck him for the first time how odd that was, for an indifferent wife to be so interested in her husband's affairs.

Camilla, going towards the desk, with three fat volumes in her hand, had paused to greet some friends. Pagoda Portal, and Henrietta Rowan, his constant companion. There was an old scandal, if you liked, but when you were as rich as Pagoda, you could do much as you pleased, and Henrietta was a widow, the situation was quite different. Some words of their conversation reached his attentive ears; he should not be listening to other people's conversation, but Camilla was talking about her sister Belle. Now back in London, and he caught some words about a portrait, a Mr. Lisser, and a Mrs. Burgh.

It meant little to him, but the names lodged in his mind, and as he sat in the carriage beside Lady Usborne, it came to him. Hadn't

Mr. Partington mentioned a Mr. Lisser? Hadn't there been some trouble with Cassandra and Mr. Lisser, who had gone to Rosings to do a painting of the house and family? Had Cassandra been entangled with an artist, of all people, before she became enamoured of her half-pay lieutenant? Indignation swept over him again, what a lax upbringing she must have had, to make her so depraved.

Chapter Thirty-five

Cassandra had been more shaken than she had cared to admit to herself by the readiness with which even so eminently sensible a man as Mr. Wytton had been prepared to believe the worst of her. As her mama and governess and everyone else had said, one false step can lead to consequences that one could have no idea of. However, if there was little she could do to restore her reputation as a woman, there was plenty to do to establish her reputation as a painter.

The canvases and sketches and some of the rest of her painting paraphernalia had duly arrived by the carrier. Cassandra hoped that Josh would not be discovered, or suffer any ill consequences for carrying out this clandestine raid on her attic, an action which she knew might lead to his instant dismissal if it were discovered by Mr. Partington.

Petifer had no such fears. "He is a clever fellow, and will choose his moment well; at this season of the year, you know, Mr. P. is out in the fields all day long. Moreover, there is some building work in progress, part of the stable wall was found to be insecure, and so men and wagons are going to and fro all the time, it could not be better for our purpose."

"You must promise to let me know, though, if Josh is in any trouble upon my account."

She could see from Petifer's face that she would do no such thing, so she must just add this to the growing list of things on her conscience, and hope that he came out of it unscathed.

Meanwhile, here was the half-finished portrait of Belle to be attended to, and the rest of her preliminary sketches. Looking these over brought back more clearly than she wanted the happy, carefree days just before she had been forced to leave Rosings, when she was learning so much from Henry Lisser, could communicate with Emily every fine day, and even be amused by Belle's petulant, flirtatious ways. She put the half-finished portrait of Belle on the easel, prowling round it like Miss Griffin's cat, Petifer complained, and consulting the numerous sketches and studies that she had made of Belle.

"I wish she were here to sit for me, but it can't be helped, and I shall manage as best I can."

Cassandra set to work with energy, wearing a smock that Petifer had contrived for her to protect her gown, her hair caught up and out of the way. She had to be dragged away from her studio for meals, but Miss Griffin saw nothing unusual in this.

"I am exactly the same when I am deep in a story; it assumes more importance than anything around me, and the characters and places are more real than any flesh-and-blood people I might meet, or the streets or parks of London where I take my exercise."

Cassandra, with this kind of painting fit upon her, had to be bullied by Petifer into going out to take her own exercise; she did not confess to her maid that she had another reason apart from work that made her disinclined to venture forth, which was that she might be recognised, or, worst of all, chance to meet Lord Usborne.

With such intensity to her labours, Cassandra finished the portrait in less time than even she would have believed possible. She only wished that the original were there, in front of her, for she knew that she would in that case make some alterations to the painting. But she knew that not only was Belle out of London, at home in Pemberley, but also that, despite Mr. Wytton's handsome acknowledgement that she was not quite yet come upon the town, her Darcy cousins might not be best pleased for her to have any contact with Belle. Camilla was out of Mr. and Mrs. Darcy's care; Belle, an unmarried daughter, was not.

Miss Griffin, who had followed the progress of the portrait with wry interest, pronounced it a speaking likeness, and said that it was more than likely that Belle's parents might wish to purchase it.

She didn't add that Cassandra had done more than capture Belle's features and bloom; that she had endowed the picture with a universality that spoke to Miss Griffin of the fact that Cassandra was possessed of more than mere technique. It was a portrait of Belle, but it was also a portrait of all young women at a particular time of life. Belle was no longer a girl, but on the very brink of womanhood and adult life, with all its complexities and pleasures and heartbreaks.

"Within a year she will be married, and that particular freshness, that sense of petals unfurling, will be gone," Miss Griffin observed. "For her parents, it would be a delight to have such a painting of her as she is now." She strongly advised against any further work on the portrait: "There comes a time when any artist has to lay down his or her brush or pen, and say, 'Enough,'" she told Cassandra. "Let Petifer arrange for it to be taken round to Mr. Lisser's studio; since he is going to be so good as to let it be on display there, it can dry and be varnished there as well as here."

Cassandra went with her painting, anxious for its safety, and was relieved to see it safely installed on a stand in Henry Lisser's studio, which was in Berners Street, only a few streets away from Soho Square. He had taken it over, he told Cassandra, from a fellow countryman, who had returned to his native land for a year or so. It was a spacious ground-floor apartment, with a studio that ran from the front to the back of the house, a much bigger room than Cassandra's, and perfect for an up-and-coming artist to work and to display his works.

Cassandra stood back from her painting, and with a polite "May I?" Henry Lisser came forward to have a better look.

Cassandra could not but notice the warmth in his eyes as they rested on Belle's likeness, even more pronounced than when he had seen her sketches.

"It is remarkable," he said at last. "I congratulate you, and although my clients come to me looking for a different style of painting, as you know, I think this will attract a good deal of attention and I am very sure that you may hope for commissions to follow from this work, Miss Darcy—"

She corrected him, and he apologised. "Of course, Mrs. Burgh. Meanwhile, what are you working on now?"

A portrait of Miss Griffin was the answer. She had sat silently drawing the authoress as she sat at her desk, deep in her intricate tales, and thought that it would make an interesting picture and was a way of expressing her gratitude to her. "And a self-portrait, now that Petifer has put a full-length mirror in the studio. In the style of that portrait which Madame Vigée-Le Brun painted of herself."

Henry Lisser was right. The portrait was noticed, word spread, and among those who came to his studio were Captain Allington and his young wife, who had come to enquire about Mr. Lisser coming to paint the house in Surrey where they now lived and Allington kept his stables. The house had been a wedding present from Sophie's father, a rich London merchant. The painting was to be a present from Sophie. But all thoughts of houses and landscapes and elegant stable yards vanished from Sophie's head the second she clapped eyes on the portrait.

"Good heavens," she cried. "It is Belle, it is my cousin Belle, to the life! Good heavens," she repeated, a new gleam in her eye, "I had no idea you were also a portraitist, we were not told that you painted portraits. Belle is just this very day come back to London, she will be so pleased to see it."

Henry Lisser, taken aback at further proof of the ramifications of Belle's family, hastened to disabuse Mrs. Allington of this idea. "It is painted by an artist but newly set up in London."

"When did Belle sit for it? I wonder," said Sophie. "Given that she is never allowed to be in London for more than two minutes together, lest she get into trouble. Although, now I look at it, the artist has flattered her, I am sure her nose is longer than it appears, and her colouring not quite so pretty, nor her complexion so glowing. But then, that is what an artist is for, to show off his subject to the best advantage."

This encounter brought another member of the family to Lisser's studio, the very next day, and this was someone he was delighted to see; his heart leapt when Belle came through the door, all impetuosity and energy and blushes, as he came forward to greet her, and then astonishment as she saw the picture.

"Well, it is quite true! When Sophie told me that there was a picture of me here, I thought it was all a hum, and I should find a painting of a nymph, who happened to have a mouth like mine or some such thing, but it is not so, it is Cassandra's painting that she began at Rosings! But how came it here? And it is finished; it was not at all like this last time I saw it. Do you know where Cassandra is? I heard she was sent away to the country, but my cousin Lady Fanny does not like me to question her about Cassandra, or rather her husband, my cousin Mr. Fitzwilliam, does not. I heard Cassandra ran away with a half-pay officer," she went on artlessly, "which is a very foolish thing to do, but"—with a languishing look at Mr. Lisser—"I suppose if she were deep in love with him, she must be forgiven."

"Here is your cousin, even as you speak," said Henry Lisser, not knowing whether to be glad or disappointed at Cassandra's appearance in the doorway, and somewhat startled by Belle's artless confidences.

Belle didn't hesitate, but rushed forward to embrace and then chide Cassandra, for never writing to her, for vanishing as she had managed to do. "For you were in Bath, and then, I heard, in Cheltenham, but here you are in London. Where do you stay?"

She was the same Belle, fearless and indiscreet, and, Cassandra feared, more than ready to resume her flirtation with Mr. Lisser, judging by her frequent, provocative glances in his direction.

"I am in London to earn my living, Belle. No, do not exclaim or interrogate me, it is a long story and a tedious one. However, I am mighty glad to see you, and in such looks." Not as glad as Henry Lisser, though, by the expression in his eyes. Lord, what a fix she was now in, it had never passed through her mind for an instant that Belle might turn up in Henry Lisser's studio.

"Are you alone?"

"No, my maid is here," said Belle.

"Does she wear a cloak of invisibility?" Cassandra asked.

"Oh, as to that, I told her she might do an errand for me while I came in here, I don't need a maid to come into Mr. Lisser's studio, I believe, and besides, you are here, what could be more proper?" She bestowed a ravishing smile upon Henry Lisser. "Do not you like my portrait? Do not you think it is wondrous like me? Do you like to have it here, where you work?"

"It is here," said Henry Lisser repressively, "so that it may in due course be varnished."

Cassandra was amused to see that Belle was not at all daunted by this reply.

"Oh, stuff," she said buoyantly. Then what her cousin had said earlier seemed to strike home and she turned her huge violet eyes on Cassandra. "You said that you are to make a living as an artist? How is this possible? You are a woman, and a Darcy!"

"In London, I go under the name of Mrs. Burgh, and it will be better, for many reasons, Belle, if you do not ever refer to me as Miss Darcy, or your cousin, or even admit to knowing me at all."

Which silenced Belle, and Henry Lisser took the opportunity to strengthen what Cassandra had said.

"This is serious, Miss Belle. It is no longer a question of girlish play and pranks. I think you have already done your cousin a grave injustice and it must stop, you must think before you speak, and behave with some discretion." He smiled, to lessen the severity of his words. "I know that you can do this, for you have the use of your reason, even when you choose that it should appear otherwise."

That struck Cassandra as being a very perceptive remark, for she had come to suspect that Belle was not nearly as light-headed or light-hearted as she chose to appear.

Now Belle was serious. She looked from Mr. Lisser to Cassandra and then back to Henry again, and her eyes dropped before his steady gaze. Then she addressed Cassandra. "I never thought there would be such a fuss, you know, and you did want to get away from Rosings. But I can be the soul of discretion; I was while Sir Joshua was courting Georgina, and no one but they and I knew anything about it."

"Well then, you are to be a good girl, and just as careful in what you say and do now," Henry Lisser told her. "You must do as your cousin wishes, if she considers it is better for you not to be seen with her, or to acknowledge you as an acquaintance or relative, merely as the sitter of the portrait, then you must oblige her in this."

Belle dimpled at him. "It is all a secret; I hate secrets, except when I know about them, and I dare say I will find it all out presently, but I promise to bite my tongue, and do just as Cassandra wants. Are you going to sell the portrait, Cassandra? For I think Mama and Papa would be very pleased to have it."

"For the moment," intervened Henry Lisser, "it is not for sale."

Should she warn Camilla about Belle and Mr. Lisser? Cassandra wondered, as she walked the short distance back to Soho Square.

Petifer took one look at her face, and asked what had happened to make her look so pensive. When Cassandra told her, she looked disapproving, although she said that it wasn't no surprise that Miss Belle had turned up, like the bad penny she was, relative or no relative, or that Cassandra was troubled in her mind about her. "Best leave them to themselves," Petifer advised. "You don't want to go running with tales to Mrs. Wytton."

"Running with tales, oh, no!" Cassandra protested.

"Sisters have a way of closing ranks, and given how Miss Belle isn't one to keep her interest in any young man to herself, I expect Mrs. Wytton will get wind of her liking for Mr. Lisser soon enough."

"It won't do," said Cassandra. "Not a Miss Belle Darcy and a Mr. Lisser, however good a painter he is. I know nothing of his antecedents, although he did mention that his father was a farmer."

"Mr. Partington might be called a farmer."

"Yes, but Mr. Partington is a gentleman, and I fear that Mr. Lisser's father is not."

"There is little you can do about it, and you've enough worries on your own account," Petifer said. "Put it out of your mind, for the present; Miss Belle's fancies are apt not to be long-lasting, as you know."

Cassandra did confide in Miss Griffin, who knew Belle through and through. Her advice was the same, to leave well alone; Belle's volatile fancy would doubtless shift on to some other more appropriate young man; the worst course would be to make anything of her admiration for Mr. Lisser, or to suggest that, as a match, it would not do. "Trust me, Belle has no intention of throwing herself away on a penniless painter, however handsome he may be. And the less she is opposed in anything she does, and the less fuss that is made about it, the sooner she will move on to some new quarry. In the end, one of her admirers will fall in love with her, in a more serious way than hitherto, and as long as he is well-looking and can dance well, she will accept him."

"You are a cynic, Miss Griffin."

"We governesses see our charges grow up, and we know them better than they know themselves. Belle would never do as the wife for such a man as Mr. Wytton, for instance, while he and Camilla are admirably suited."

Cassandra's brief encounter with Mr. Wytton had not prepossessed her in his favour, but she said she would take Miss Griffin's word for it, "and Camilla does seem to be exceedingly happy in her marriage."

Chapter Thirty-six

To her surprise, as May passed into June, Cassandra found that she was beginning to enjoy her new life. The memory of her time with James was fading, and no longer haunted her with that aching sense of loss. She admitted to herself that she was glad that he was off on the high seas. She wished him well, but there was a sense of relief in knowing that she would not meet him by chance; what was past was past, and it was better that no chance encounter could kindle old feelings. Probably he had already forgotten her; hadn't Lord Nelson said that every man was a bachelor once past Gibraltar? James would no doubt find solace in the arms of a sultry Spanish girl.

She didn't want to find solace in any man's arms. She felt that James was an inoculation against love, and furthermore, she didn't need solace of any kind, she was working hard all day long. Once absorbed in painting and drawing, all the daily cares and worries fell away, and nothing existed or mattered but the forms and images growing under her hand. And, thanks to Henry Lisser, she was meeting new people and making new acquaintances among the community of artists and writers and musicians, and finding that the life of artistic London suited her well, very well indeed. She was invited to join Henry Lisser and several of his friends who met and dined in a private room in a coffee-house, off the Strand, where she was accepted in a way that she would never have thought possible.

She had attended the remaining lectures given by Turner, and every one of these was discussed and thrashed out in the evening sessions. Henry introduced his friends, the family of silversmiths, where, to her surprise and delight, two of the daughters were following in the family tradition, and producing work of a quality that made her stare. She did a design for a silver cup, based on the figures she had painted for Mr. Wytton, and the finished vessel was greatly admired and sold quickly, much to Cassandra's pleasure and gratification.

Miss Griffin shared some of her new acquaintances, particularly those in the writing line, and now that she had such an efficient household manager in Petifer, she ventured on some dinner parties of her own, where Cassandra found herself sitting next to John Murray, the publisher, Byron's publisher in fact; and a small, intense man, a poet, one John Keats, just making his name.

There were some hostile voices, of course there were. Given her youth, talent, and beauty, tongues were going to wag, as in the parallel world of polite society, and Cassandra knew that sharp remarks were passed behind her back by some of the men who were most agreeable to her face. One or two were open in their dislike of any woman having the impertinence to muscle in on the masculine world of painting, but Henry Lisser was quick to point out to them that two women had been among the founding members of the Royal Academy in the last century, and that in France it was quite taken for granted that women could paint.

"How come you to be so generous about our sex?" Cassandra asked him.

"I have a younger sister who is an extremely talented artist, who am I to say that women cannot be painters or any kind of artist? It is absurd. And as for writing, the presses would fall silent if women such as Miss Griffin did not set their pens to paper as they do."

She had an uneasy moment or two, when her Darcy looks threatened to reveal her identity; at one pleasant dinner party, she met a Mr. Silvestrini, a musician of some distinction, who eyed her thoughtfully and said she put him much in mind of a pupil of his, a girl with a wonderful voice, the former Miss Alethea Darcy.

She was quick to respond that others had mentioned her likeness to some members of that family, they came from Derbyshire, did they not, and some of her family also came from that county, perhaps there was a remote connection that she was unaware of, likenesses were a strange thing, did not he think so? And she adroitly turned the conversation to portrait painting, and in fact ended up painting his beautiful wife, although she insisted that Mrs. Silvestrini come to her studio, rather than her go to the Silvestrinis' house in Bloomsbury; she didn't want to risk running into Alethea.

Belle's portrait had done its work, and she had two or three commissions in hand, apart from the one of Mrs. Silvestrini, which was done for only a small fee as Cassandra found her looks so inspiring that she would have painted her for nothing, had not Henry Lisser intervened.

"Charge less, but charge. Otherwise you will not be taken seriously, and you do your fellow artists no favours if you undercut the market!"

Camilla and Mr. Wytton were away at this time; caring little for the social round of the season, they had gone to Paris, to visit Camilla's sister Georgina, Belle's twin, taking Belle with them. She hadn't wanted to go, Camilla had told Cassandra when she came to take her leave of her; Camilla suspected a man in the case.

Cassandra thought that more than likely. She hadn't seen her cousin since she had come to Henry Lisser's studio to see her portrait, and he never mentioned her name. She sincerely hoped that Belle's fancy had now alighted on a more suitable object for her affections.

The weather grew hotter, and London emptied of all those who could escape the heat and smells for a spell by the sea or in the country. Cassandra missed the glory of summer days at Rosings, with a fleeting pang of loss, but she wasn't affected by the warmth, and found that if she propped her windows open, her studio was more or less tolerable. In the afternoons, she would often take her sketchbook, and a novel portable water-colour set that she had bought from Mr. Rudge, out to Green Park, where she would sit in the shade and capture the people sitting and walking there.

It was a calm life, and she felt with pride that she was achieving at least a sense of tranquillity, when this new-found peace was shattered in the place where she had come to feel safest, in the first-floor room of the coffee-house.

They were a reduced party that evening, since various of the regulars were away, and Henry Lisser told her, when she arrived, hot and happy after a successful day's work, that he was expecting an acquaintance that he would be glad for her to meet, a John Hopkirk, a writer. "He is a clever, droll fellow, I think you will like him. He is only recently come back to London; he has been travelling abroad for some months. And he is bringing a friend, I do not know anything about him."

Chapter Thirty-seven

Horatio Darcy was finding the weather hot, but his spirits were unaccountably raised by the sense of freedom that the summer months had brought him, on account of his separation from Lady Usborne. There had been a difficult scene, when she realised that he meant what he said, and that he was not proposing to come to Brighton.

"In that case, I hardly think you need trouble yourself to call upon me when we return," she said, her eyes narrowing. "It is clear that you use work as an excuse to avoid my company."

"I have neglected the law shamefully these last busy weeks, and now I must catch up."

"I never heard of a gentleman being so pressured with work that he abandoned the ordinary civilities of the world into which he was born."

"I was born into a world where younger sons must make their own way; it is not a matter of civility or incivility."

She shrugged. "I believe I am not slow-witted, I am sure you could come to Brighton if you would."

He half hoped that she would find herself a new interest while at the seaside. A few weeks ago, such a thought would have been a fear, would have sent a stab of jealousy through him; now he found he did not care at all whether she did or not.

He stood on the road and watched Lady Usborne's carriage bowling away, spurts of dust rising behind its wheels; it hadn't rained for more than two weeks, and the London streets were as dusty as they were usually dirty. He gave himself a mental shake. For the next weeks, he would put all thoughts of the fair sex from his head. He would devote himself virtuously to his work, dine at his club, and look up such of his cronies as were still in town.

Yet none of this really pleased him. Something was nagging at him. On a whim, he decided to look up an old friend from school and college days, who had been abroad, in Italy, but who had, he had learned, just returned to London. They had not seen much of one another these last few years, despite the close friendship that had sprung up between them; they had taken different paths and each was making his way in the world, Horatio in the law, John as a man of letters.

John opened the front door of a neat house in Paddington and greeted his erstwhile college friend with enthusiasm. "You are looking sleek and prosperous, the law suits you."

"Nonsense, I am worn down by my labours, and envy men like you, who live in a much more interesting world than mine, which is full of dusty law tomes and equally fusty and dusty judges."

The house was full of life and colour, and Horatio Darcy realised that he was comparing it, favourably, with the large and handsome house where he had spent so much time these last months, the Usborne house in Berkeley Square. That was formal, elegant, and fashionable. John's house was none of these things, but it was welcoming, and, Horatio felt, was a happy home.

Part of the reason for this soon appeared. A small woman with a trim figure and a firm chin came out to greet the visitor, wiping her hand on a cloth and saying that she was so sorry, she couldn't shake his hand, for her own hands were covered in oil.

"Oil?"

"This is my wife, Louisa," John said, affection and pride flowing out of him. "She is a painter."

Horatio was taken aback, stunned into silence, in fact, on two counts. First, he had no idea that John was married. And then, could this composed young woman, with her well-bred air and manners, be a painter? What kind of a painter?

He had to say something, for they were both looking at him expectantly. He chose the easier option first.

"I am overwhelmed, and so very honoured to make your acquaintance, Mrs. Hopkirk. The thing is, I had no idea, that is to say . . . I saw no announcement."

"Oh, there was none," said Mrs. Hopkirk gaily. "I am of age, and I have known John forever, we grew up in the same village. And so, when we decided to marry, we simply did so."

"Without undue ceremony," added John. "Much the best way. Our wedding was attended only by my dearest Louisa, and myself, with two witnesses we called in from the street. One turned out to be a musician, so as soon as the ceremony was over, out came his oboe, and he danced us out of the church to a merry jig. He has become a good friend since then. The other witness wasn't quite so amiable. . . ."

"He was positively grumpy," said Louisa with a smile. "He told us that people didn't ought to go getting married, it led to nothing but trouble."

"However, he cheered up when we gave him a guinea for his time," finished John. "And, unlike Jessop, the musician, he will not be coming round later. Horatio, I do take this very kindly, it is so good to see you. Now, first, you must come and see Louisa's paintings, for I can tell by your face that you are thinking, 'A woman painter, that is like Dr. Johnson's woman preaching,' but Louisa is no dog on its hind legs, I assure you."

Louisa's paintings were a revelation to Horatio. She specialised in flower paintings, which he had never given much thought to, but as he took in the exquisite detailing and rich, vibrant colours, he felt a rare sense of balance and harmony come over him, and found himself revising his views.

"What do you do with them all?" he asked, as they returned to the tiny front parlour—the larger rear room being entirely given over to Louisa's work.

"Why, she sells them, and very glad we are of the income, I can tell you. For writing is a hard way to make a living, if you aren't Walter Scott, and even he, I hear, has money troubles. Anyhow, we are fortunate, for Louisa can sell all she paints, and it's a steady, comfortable income for us."

"But as a married woman, surely—"

"Oh, there is a prejudice about that," said Louisa cheerfully, "because it is assumed that upon marriage any woman ceases to have an identity, and must hang up her brushes or whatever—although I notice that no one criticises a woman for writing novels when she is Mrs. this or that. However, I work under my own name, the one that I had before I was married; after all, it is not a question purchasers ask, they do not say, 'I very much like this picture and wish to buy it, but are you a married woman?' And they sell through some shops and dealers also, who know and trust my work under that name, so we go on very well."

"You will dine with us, Horatio?" John said.

"Please do," Louisa seconded with a smile. "It will be pot-luck, for I have been working hard all day, but we shall contrive a tolerable meal for you. It would please John so much; he has often spoken about you, and your times at Westminster and Oxford."

It was an invitation Horatio couldn't refuse, and as the evening went on, he found himself feeling more relaxed and at ease than he had for a long while. Various friends of John and Louisa's dropped in, including the musician from their wedding, who was a tall man with long, thin hands and a dry wit; he held a position as a court musician, and had several amusing anecdotes to tell about his experiences.

"Although, much as I deplore Prinny—I think I can speak my mind in this company without fear of being hauled off to gaol—our Prince Regent is a musician, he does have a genuine feeling for music and a very good understanding of it."

The talk flowed from politics to books and paintings and science and foreign lands, and Horatio Darcy felt that the evening had passed in a flash when he finally found himself outside the house, bidding farewell to his hosts before setting off back to his rooms.

The renewal of the friendship with John was not confined to that single evening. He dined there again, being careful on these occasions to take an offering of fruit, a packet of tea, or anything else he could think of to augment what he suspected was a frugal level of house-keeping.

The couple made no secret of the fact that they lived off what they earned. "If we don't work, we don't eat," said Louisa, shooing the men out of the house to dine elsewhere on an evening when she had a picture that had to be finished, and delivered the next morning. "Off you go, I shall do very well for myself with whatever is in the larder that I may eat while I work."

"I know what we shall do," said John, as he and Horatio stood outside the house. "Are you at all acquainted with a painter called Henry Lisser? Louisa greatly admires his work. He tells me that two or three nights a week, he dines with other artists and friends at a coffee-house, in a private room, I believe, and that I am welcome to join them. He will not mind my bringing a friend, I know he will not, for I said that I might look in with you."

Chapter Thirty-eight

As Cassandra lay in her tiny room that night, her window open to a starry summer sky, and the sounds of the city drifting in from outside, including the melancholy hooting of an owl sitting in a nearby tree, she found it hard to sleep.

It had been a dreadful shock to see Mr. Darcy come into the room. His friend, John Hopkirk, she liked at once; not a tall man, and one who would grow stout with age, he had such a cheerful countenance and such an air of enjoying life and expecting to enjoy his company, that you couldn't but be charmed by him.

He had sat beside her, quickly discovered that she was an artist, exclaimed with delight, and at once said that she must meet his wife, perhaps she knew her work? No, well as a portraitist she might not, but he'd wager that she would be pleased with her productions, though in such a very different field. "You women artists must stick together," he said, "for you are all too rare a breed."

Cassandra knew that Horatio Darcy's eyes were on her, although he didn't seem inclined to speak to her, merely acknowledging her presence with a slight bow. Why had he come? Was he spying on her, had he been set to find her by Mr. Partington, perhaps at her mother's urging? Why did he look so severe when his eyes rested on her, whereas his face was perfectly good-humoured when he was talking to the others, and a smile and even a laugh could be seen and heard?

She was grateful when Henry Lisser came to sit on her other side, for a horrid moment she had thought that Mr. Darcy was moving in her direction. Could she simply rise and leave? These dinners were informal, people came and went, but it would look odd if she left after she had sat down at the table.

So she stayed, and kept her head and eyes averted from Mr. Darcy's end of the table, telling herself that it was mere coincidence that had brought him here. She ventured a question about him to Mr. Hopkirk, who replied at once that they had met again after not seeing much of one another for several years, and Mr. Darcy, already a great favourite with Mrs. Hopkirk, often called at their house in Paddington to share a chop and talk about books and such like, "For I am a writer, Mrs. Burgh."

She at once begged him to tell her what he wrote, and in return, he asked her about her painting, did she come from a family of artists, where had she trained, where had she her studio?

She answered these questions readily and civilly, keeping her voice low in the hope that Mr. Darcy might not hear what she was saying, but she suspected that his attention was on her rather than his immediate companions.

"This Mr. Darcy," Henry Lisser said in her ear. "I have heard of him. Is he not some connection of yours?"

"He is, but pray do not mention it, and please, on no account give him my direction. He is a lawyer, and acts for Mr. Partington."

Henry Lisser pursed his lips, and shot Mr. Darcy an appraising glance. "His face gives little away. Do you think he knew you were here, or is he here by mere chance?"

"The latter, I do hope."

For his part, Horatio Darcy was alarmed to find how pleased he was to see Cassandra, which sentiment was followed by the indignation her presence always aroused in him. She was poised and looked cool and collected. She should not; some confusion at seeing him unexpectedly would have been appropriate, and have reassured him that she was not as controlled as she seemed.

Why did she find the conversation of that man so absorbing? He was the painter, Henry Lisser, the man in the shrubbery, Mr. Partington had told him. Would women find him handsome? They might, there was a Byronic touch to him, although his hair was thick and naturally wavy, Darcy doubted if he pinned it into curls every night as the poet was reputed to do; and to do him justice, he didn't look the kind of fellow to care overmuch about his appearance. He was wearing a waistcoat under a dark, striped coat; both, to Darcy's eye, of foreign cut.

He himself wore his habitual black coat with a cherry, damascened waistcoat with buttons that had been a present from Lady Usborne, soon after he had first been welcomed into her bed.

He had an obscure feeling that he would rather not have been wearing those particular buttons, but he dismissed the thought even as it flitted into his mind. Damn it, Cassandra was rising from the table, making her excuses, she was going to slip away.

And a good thing, too. However, it might be useful to have her direction, Mr. Partington might well be in touch again, seeking information.

"You are leaving, Mrs. Burgh, is it not?" he said, getting up as well. "It is surely not safe for you in these streets at this time of night. Perhaps you will allow me to escort you to your home?"

"I shall see Mrs. Burgh to her front door," said Henry Lisser. "It is on my way. Yes"—raising a hand in farewell—"I am sorry to leave so early, but I have a picture varnishing, which needs another coat, this hot weather makes it all very difficult, since it dries too quickly."

Cassandra might have kept her direction from Horatio for this evening, but she could not deceive herself as to it remaining long a secret from him; if he wanted to find her direction—and why should he?—then he now knew her present name, he could find out where she was living in a trice.

She comforted herself with the thought that he had no need to find out where she was. It had been an unfortunate encounter, but it was over, he had, in fact, seen her quite at home in her new life, and the fact that he would disapprove of it, and of the freedom and independence she was earning for herself, was nothing to her.

Wretched man, he should stay in his own sphere of lawyers and clubs and Lady Usborne's boudoir. That was where he belonged.

Horatio Darcy would have agreed with her, had this point been raised only a little while before, but he was finding, to his astonishment, that the company he kept when with John Hopkirk, and with others of that circle, for his acquaintance among the writers and poets of London was increasing almost daily, was a great deal more agreeable than that of his other life. It would bring him no material benefit, here were no potential clients, no great men of influence, yet he rarely returned home from an evening with any of them feeling that his time had been anything other than well spent.

He didn't meet Cassandra again; he was not to know that she hadn't ventured out to the coffee-house again since that evening, telling Henry Lisser frankly that much as she enjoyed herself there, she thought it better not to see Mr. Darcy again.

Chapter Thirty-nine

Horatio was right in his supposition that Lady Usborne would be casting about for a replacement for him, for it suited her to show herself and her friends that she still, at five-and-thirty, had the power to attract a virile young man.

However, she had more on her mind than a cicisbeo, for she was concerned about Lord Usborne. He was fretting about something, and she meant to get to the bottom of it.

They had taken a large, round-fronted house in the best part of Brighton, but it was nothing in size compared to their London house, and so they were thrown together more than they were accustomed to.

She suspected that Lord Usborne did not dislike this, for he breakfasted with her, and even took her out driving and accompanied her to picnics. Very unfashionable, to be sure, although it was becoming, she had noticed, as one ever on the alert to catch the latest fads and whims, much more the thing for husbands and wives to be seen together.

Her good friend Amelia Wannop had noticed it, too, with some dismay. "Lord, five minutes a week is more than I want to spend with Marmaduke, and yet here are married couples billing and cooing together as though they were newly-weds, and had not been together for ten years and more, with children in the nursery! I blame the

Evangelicals, they are breathing a new morality into the air, and it will not benefit women, you may be sure of that."

"It will pass, these movements do."

"Don't you be so sure. Men grow more domestic, and that is the last place left to women to rule as they please. Once a man takes over authority in the home, then women have nothing but duty and obedience and all those dull things to sustain them. I am glad I am not a young woman embarking on marriage, it is a state always full of pitfalls, but they will not have the fun in life that we have had, I tell you that."

Lady Usborne did not care for this talk of young women. "You sound as though we are in our dotage."

"Two- or three-and-thirty is not eighteen or nineteen, that is all, however one might wish it otherwise. At least one can face facts."

It was easier for Amelia to tolerate being in her thirties than it was for Lady Usborne. For she had three children, while the nurseries at Usborne House were empty.

Lady Usborne changed the subject, talking about the reception to be held at the Pavilion that evening, what was Amelia wearing? Her green-and-white crape, or the new gown that she had ordered from Paris?

"There is no point in wearing a new gown on such an occasion, for the world and his wife will be there, and it will be such a crush that you will not be able to see anything but hats and feathers. And it will be stifling hot, with all the windows tight shut, for you know how Prinny is about draughts."

"It will take more than a draught to carry him off, with his bulk, it would need a whirlwind," said Lady Usborne.

"I am not so sure. He is not in good health, you know, how can he be when he lives as he does? What a joke it would be if the old king outlives him, and so he never came to the throne at all. And that reminds me, I wanted to ask you, as we are such old friends, and you share everything with me, why is Prinny so displeased with Usborne?"

Lady Usborne was not born yesterday, and though all her nerves were tingling at this remark, she was far too canny to exchange confidences of this sort with Amelia, who, old friend or no, had fingers in too many political pies to be entirely trustworthy. So she turned it off lightly, saying that Usborne had won rather too many guineas off His Royal Highness at the gaming table, which, as they both knew, was more than likely to put the prince in a pet, and cause him to frown at someone who two days later would once more be admitted to his circle of cronies.

It would suit Lady Usborne well enough if her husband could be persuaded to spend less time in the royal circle. Instinct told her that trouble could be coming in that direction, but any move away from the court would have to be done subtly and in a way not to give offence; the last thing they needed was to incur the wrath of that notably unforgiving man.

No, Lady Usborne had more on her mind than worrying about Horatio. It had been a pleasant interlude, and it was over. More pressing business awaited her, and that evening, home after the reception, and sitting with the sashes thrown up to admit a welcome sea breeze after the heat and smells of the Pavilion, she and Lord Usborne took a companionable glass of wine together, and she began her campaign to wheedle out of him just what he was up to.

Chapter Forty

Horatio Darcy walked home from the coffee-house that evening, paying little attention to the still beauty of a moonlit night, lost as he was in thought.

His first reaction upon seeing Cassandra had been irritation and annoyance, for he felt that her presence would mar what promised to be an agreeable evening out in the company of Hopkirk and like-minded people.

It was the realisation that she belonged in that company that made him examine his feelings towards her with a new honesty. John Hopkirk had taken to her at once, that was clear, and was keen to introduce her to Louisa. John didn't care if Cassandra was a Darcy or a Mrs. whatever it was; to him she was an agreeable woman, making her way in the world, in the very same world that he and his wife moved in.

And, more unsettling to Horatio, Cassandra's beauty caught at his heart. The turn of her neck, those wonderful grey eyes, her thoughtful expression yielding, when she thought he wasn't looking at her, to a delightful smile, a spurt of laughter. He could tell that she was ill at ease with him there at the table, but even with that restraint, she was, he realised, utterly captivating.

Moreover, he had to admit to a grudging respect for what she was doing. It took courage, huge courage, to stand up to a Partington, to bear the exclusion from her family, and to set about making her living—in a way that he still disapproved of, but surely one to be preferred to the other possibilities for one possessing her charms. He owed it to her, he decided, to offer friendship, nothing more. She was his kin, after all.

He found out where Cassandra was residing with little difficulty, now that he knew the name she was going under, and a few enquiries brought him the information he was seeking.

He called upon her two days later, and took her entirely by surprise, not waiting for Petifer to announce him, but following his nose—how could she work on such a hot day amid all those oil paints?—so that he arrived unheralded at the top of the house in Soho Square and walked in through the door, which had been left standing open to allow a through breeze.

She was standing before her easel, her smock wrapped round her, a palette held in one hand, and her brush in the other, looking at the canvas with such concentration that she didn't notice his arrival.

He stepped back, gave a sharp rap on the door, and a little cough.

"What is it, Petifer?" she said, without looking around.

"It is not Petifer. I am sorry if I disturb you."

She stood frozen, then lowered her hand with the brush and turned slowly round. "You," she said in disbelief. "What are you doing here?"

"I have come to invite you out for a drive," he said promptly. "I have no carriage of my own, but I have the use of a friend's while he is out of town. His horses need exercise, and so I propose a drive out to Richmond, to breathe the air."

She stared at him as though he were mad.

"Has my stepfather . . . has Mr. Partington sent you?"

"I have sent my bill to your stepfather; he is no longer a client of mine. I dealt with him in that single matter, he only asked me to act for him because it was a family affair, and that is, I am glad to say, the end of our acquaintance. He is not a man I can like."

Horatio Darcy couldn't take his eyes from her face. It was lightly tanned, no unusual consequence of being out in this weather, and this made her grey eyes even more beautiful. And, which for some reason made his heart constrict, she had a smudge of paint across her cheek.

They looked at one another for a long while, and a slight blush came to her cheeks. Then she lowered her eyes and shook her head. "I am busy, as you see," gesturing with her brush towards her painting.

"You will work the better for some exercise," he said.

"That you will, and it will give me a chance to get this room straight, which I haven't been able to do this se'enight," said Petifer from the door, where she had been standing, watching the two of them. "You go out for a drive with your cousin, Miss Cassandra. It will be an open carriage, I suppose, sir?" she said to Darcy, giving him an appraising look. "Which, with your being family, makes it all right."

Horatio offered his arm to Cassandra. "Come, we mustn't keep the horses waiting."

Cassandra couldn't help but feel a lift to her spirits as she climbed into the carriage. It was a phaeton, well sprung, with a spirited team in harness, and it brought back many happy memories of her earlier life, driving to dances and dinners at neighbouring houses, summer expeditions and picnics . . . At first rather stiff with her companion, and wary—what was he up to?—she found her hostility gradually lessening. Theirs was, after all, an old acquaintance, if a slight one.

They discussed horses, Cassandra rather wistfully admitting that she very much missed her riding: "I was used to ride nearly every day."

They drove at a steady pace through the streets of London, and then out into the country until they turned through the gates of Richmond Great Park. The carriage drove along a well-kept road between herds of grazing deer clustered beneath the trees for shade, their dapple flanks speckled further by the sunlight streaming through the branches.

It was the first time Cassandra had been out into the country since coming to London, and she relished the air, the rich colours of the trees, and the pleasant sensation of driving at speed in so well sprung a carriage.

She also enjoyed her company, although she wasn't going to admit it to herself yet. Horatio talked to her as to an equal; what had happened to the disdain with which he had first made her acquaintance?

By common consent, a number of topics were not raised. Cassandra would talk about horseflesh in general, but not about her own beloved horse now languishing, so she imagined, in the stables at Rosings. They did not talk about her painting, nor about how she had come to live with Miss Griffin. The subject of the Usbornes was also not mentioned, and Horatio was cagey about his law work. It was beginning to bore him, and it would most certainly bore Cassandra.

They had in common family connections, and she was intrigued to learn more about her father's family than her mother had ever thought fit to tell her; since her marriage to Mr. Partington, she had almost forgotten that she had ever been a Darcy.

And, with her daughter now gone, Cassandra reflected, there would be nothing left to her of that marriage, it would be as though it had never happened. Perhaps, one day, when time had healed old sores, it might be possible for Cassandra to ask if she might have the portrait of her father, painted when he was a young man. It was not a distinguished work of art, but it reminded her of him in a way that the miniature of him, which was hers, never did, it being a stiff picture of a young man in a blue coat who could be almost anyone of his age and class.

"You are very silent," Horatio said, and she realised with a start that she had been lost in her memories. "Woolgathering," she said. "What fine, fat sheep, they are Wyntons, are they not?"

"If you say so. As a Kentishwoman, I dare say you know about sheep. I can tell one from a goat, but that is about all. I grew up amid fields of corn, it is not a part of England renowned for its sheep, where I come from."

These were, Cassandra felt, when she was delivered back to Soho Square, among the happiest hours she had spent since coming to London. These, and the hours at her easel when her painting was going well. It suddenly occurred to her that she was, despite everything, more fortunate than many of her more respectable sisters, who might share the happiness of an agreeable companion, but would never know the satisfaction that work brought her.

"Nor do most men," said Miss Griffin, who was in a tart mood that evening. "And it is all very well, when the pen flows, or the brush in your case, but then there are the dark days when imagination deserts one, and it is an effort to put anything down on paper."

"Yes, indeed, and that little you have achieved stares at you at the end of the day, and you know the next morning you will have to scrape it down and start again."

Miss Griffin asked to see the sketches she had made at Richmond, for Darcy had stopped the carriage for them to take a stroll and for Cassandra to take out her notebook while the groom saw to the horses. She laughed over a picture of a comical-looking sheep, with a clump of grass hanging from its mouth.

"That bears a strong resemblance to one or two people of my acquaintance," she said. She admired the little group of mother, nurse, and little boys that Cassandra had caught in a moment of conflict, with the children battling for possession of a ball, and then she came to a sketch that Cassandra had made of Darcy. She had taken his likeness in a few swift lines, but it was the man to the life, and his energy and intelligence and masculinity leapt off the page.

Miss Griffin pursed her lips and made no comment, other than giving Cassandra a thoughtful look as she turned the sheets to show a drawing of the groom, a small, bow-legged man, holding the horses' heads.

*　　　*　　　*

Horatio called again, the following week, and this time drove her out to Box Hill, to admire the famous views. It was not such an enjoyable outing, for there was a tension between them. Cassandra was silent, she found she was once more uncomfortable being with him, and yet, when on parting he said that he was going out of town and would not therefore be able to take her driving again for a while, she felt an unreasonable sense of disappointment.

Chapter Forty-one

Horatio Darcy left town for Dorset in a temper. He was often in a temper these days, he realised as he sat back, then leant forward to adjust the glasses; chaises were wretched things, draughty and cold in winter and hot and stuffy in summer.

He had no desire to go down to Dorset. It was a long and troublesome journey, and then, when he arrived, out of sorts and cramped, he would be ushered straight into the presence of his aunt Mrs. Shawardine, who would grill him as though he were a leftover French agent.

He stretched out his legs and tried to settle more comfortably into the corner. And it was a devilish expense, all the way down there, by post. However, his aunt gave him an allowance, and she felt she had a right to dictate how he spent at least part of it, by coming at the double to see her when summoned. And it had been, what, more than two years since he'd last had to make the journey?

Why couldn't she live in Bath, like other people's widowed aunts did? At least that was accessible. But Mrs. Shawardine wasn't like other people's aunts, and then the thought of Bath reminded him of Cassandra, and that made him even angrier. God, what a fool he was making of himself, what a mix-up everything was.

And in no time at all, Lady Usborne would be back in town; she and Lord Usborne had gone north for the shooting, but Lady

Usborne was not a country person, she would be back in London as soon as she could escape from the moors.

What a pity that his aunt wasn't less of a country person. That was why she wasn't living a seemly life in Bath, of course. No, she was at Yarlton, managing the large estates which belonged to her stepson, Frederick Shawardine, her husband having meekly breathed his last many years before. While the stepson, another of Darcy's numerous cousins, lived a life of riot and rumpus in London, rarely taking part in any debates in the House, where he held the seat for Yarlton.

Frederick preferred to frequent the more notorious kind of houses of ill repute and get thoroughly disguised six days out of the seven. By the seventh, he wasn't to be found in any church, merely sleeping off the excess of the week, and gathering his strength to begin the next week in exactly the same way.

Horatio's aunt rarely mentioned her stepson to him. He hadn't married, nor was he ever likely to, and Horatio knew that, if Frederick predeceased his stepmother, which seemed probable, his extensive estates would pass to Mrs. Shawardine, and thence, so she had told him, to Horatio's elder brother. As if he didn't have enough already, thought Horatio, in a burst of resentment.

But he didn't really have ill feelings about it. He liked his brother, a hardworking, domestic man, with a brood of children to educate and provide for. And it was the way things were, younger brothers had to fend for themselves, otherwise all that carefully accumulated wealth and land, most of all the land, would be split up and distributed into parcels too small to be of any use when it came to votes and power and making sure the country was run as it ought to be.

He took out one of the books he had brought with him, a novel; the other was a collection of John's writings, but he felt he wouldn't do them justice shaking and rumbling along in this coach. Who said that the roads were so wonderfully smooth these days, that it was like gliding along? Clearly no one who had ever made this journey. The road to Brighton, maybe; the road to deepest Dorsetshire, not so.

He couldn't concentrate on the novel. The characters seemed

wooden, the plot improbable, the dialogue stilted. He knew that when he came back to it, in a better frame of mind, he would enjoy it, and find it an absorbing read.

He fidgeted into another position, crossed his legs at the ankle, uncrossed them, hunched his shoulders, tugged at his neckcloth. He had never felt so restless; whatever was the matter with him?

His aunt, damn her, noticed it straight away.

"What's got into you, Horatio? You've never been a peaceable man, but at present you're downright jumpy."

They were seated, the two of them, in the vast dining room. Fortunately, his place had been set on her right, and not down at the other end of the gleaming mahogany table, which was several yards away. A footman in full livery came and went with dishes, or stood waiting impassively at the end of the room, ready to dart forward and retrieve Mrs. Shawardine's napkin, which slid to the floor several times at each meal.

It was a strange habit, using these napkins, Horatio thought. A continental habit; his aunt had spent many years on the Continent, while her husband was alive, chiefly to get away from him, Horatio surmised, and had acquired some very un-English ways.

His aunt filled the pauses between dishes by bringing him up-to-date on the details of every family member known to her, which was a great many, and she seemed to have an intelligence network that any general would envy, being aware of the minutiae of their lives to an astonishing degree.

Horatio nerved himself for when she would move on to him; meanwhile, he half listened, responding with an occasional "Really?" or "That's very harsh" or "I would never have believed him capable of that."

This stage of the proceedings would generally last until he was left in state, nursing a glass of excellent port, which he didn't want, while he gazed either at the footmen, still lined up, or stared at the numerous family portraits hung somewhat haphazardly about the damasked walls. He'd rather look at one of Cassandra's portraits any day. He closed his eyes, reminded himself that he had sworn he was not going to think about Cassandra, and at once found an image of her in his mind, as clear as though she were standing in front of him in all her gaiety and beauty, with that smile she sometimes had on her face.

This wouldn't do. He took too large a gulp of wine and stood up. Footmen rushed forward to assist him, just as though I were some gouty old fellow, he said to himself, waving them away.

His aunt had clearly been enjoying a glass of port of her own, and she waited hardly a minute while he sat himself in one of the broad-seated, throne-like chairs, which her father-in-law, a huge man, had favoured, before she began to talk again. These chairs had always made Horatio feel at a disadvantage, especially since his aunt chose to sit her small, lean self in an upright chair, so that, although she was not a tall woman, she could look down at him as he sat beside the mercifully empty fireplace. She was a chilly soul, and was all too inclined to have a roaring fire on even the warmest nights.

"There is a problem with the chimney," she informed him, catching the look he had given to the empty hearth. "And it is remarkably warm, with this fine spell of weather. The builders and the sweep will have done their work, I hope, before the weather breaks."

As if she didn't have half a dozen other large rooms, each with monumental fireplaces, to which she could withdraw after dinner.

"I have some news for you, Horatio, of a confidential nature. Concerning the family."

"Oh?"

"It concerns you also, or will do so, if you have any sense, which is why I've summoned you here."

"Because I have sense?" he said, quizzing her, feeling more mellow after the wine and the modest amount of port he had drunk.

"This is no time for frivolity. You have always had a frivolous streak; it needs to be kept under tight control."

Judging that no reply was expected to this remark, he held his tongue.

"Frederick is giving up his seat in the House and going abroad," she announced, in her blunt way.

That did bring Horatio out of his mellow mood. "What? Giving up his seat?"

"Indefinitely," she continued.

"Abroad?"

"For the good of his health," she said.

Horatio was of the opinion that his cousin Frederick was unaware of just how much his mother knew about his life in London.

"Boys, still?" he said. It was a risk to make such a remark, but his aunt was a woman brought up in the last century, when people were less mealy-mouthed about such matters.

"You shouldn't say so, not in front of the servants, but yes."

Horatio looked around him. "I see no servants."

"No, there are none, I sent them all out. But they're probably listening at the doors."

Since the doors in question were at the far side of the room, and were large, deep, wide, heavy wooden doors, Horatio doubted if even a servant with the ears of an elephant could follow their conversation.

"Yes, it's the old trouble, but he has gone too far. There are houses in London, which cater for his tastes, I understand."

Molly houses, Horatio said to himself.

"At one of these, there has been some trouble, stories passed to the newspapers, and reports of certain incidents. Well, it will be impossible for the authorities to ignore them. Oh, they'll be hushed up, of course, but various gentlemen will do well to locate themselves outside London for a very long while, and indeed, they would be advised to leave the country. As Frederick will."

"I thought he was at Brighton."

"He was. He will shortly be in France, and will be taking up residence in Italy, where I own a house. He will not be returning to England. He has agreed to this, I have power of attorney, and," she spoke with a little effort, "he is not well. I do not think he will survive for long, because what ails him is not the sort of—There is little doctors can do when it has reached this advanced stage."

"Ah," said Horatio.

"I have never liked Frederick," his aunt said in remote tones.

"But he is my stepson, and my late husband's flesh and blood. There is no chance now of his marrying and providing me with grandchildren."

She does have courage, Horatio said inwardly.

"You, Horatio, are more of a son to me than Frederick has ever been. You were a lively little boy, but as kind as they come; you're clever, but you don't use your wits and tongue to put down your fellow men, and you've set about making your way in the world, as a younger son, with determination and energy. You have ability, you are a very handsome man—no, don't shake your head, good looks are an advantage, for a man as well as a women, if coupled with charm, which you also have. And charm is an asset in a political career. You make no secret of the fact that a political career is what you want."

"In the fullness of time, yes," Horatio said. "But I have to make my mark first."

"Well, you won't do it crawling in and out of Lady Usborne's bed," said his aunt, with one of the sudden thrusts for which she was famous. "That has to stop, Horatio. It's an adulterous relationship, which is always wrong. She's ten years older than you, which makes both of you look foolish, and you can't afford to look foolish. And her husband is a dangerous man. She's using you to play off against him, and if you can't see that, then you are a fool."

Horatio, stunned by the force of her attack, opened his mouth to protest, but she swept on. "I don't say that she won't have enjoyed the liaison. As I said, you are a handsome man, a fine scalp to add to her belt, but it won't do. Conducted with discretion, you might have got away with it. Now that it is so generally known, it is quite another thing, and Lord Usborne won't like it. And, if I may give you an excellent piece of advice, be careful with Lord Usborne. I knew his father well, and this son is just like him."

"He is not the most agreeable of men," Horatio began, but his aunt cut him short.

"I've said what I've got to say on that subject, although it does have a bearing on what else I want to speak about. Which is, regarding Frederick's seat in Parliament."

Horatio could not believe his ears. Of all the reasons that had passed through his mind for his being summoned to Dorset, this one had never occurred to him, it could not, even in his wildest dreams. She was offering him the seat, the chance to become an MP.

"You will have to spend a little time down here, but there are not above four thousand votes, and they will vote for you if I tell them to and will continue to do so until some meddling politician takes himself at his word and brings in reforms. Don't you have anything to do with radicals of that kind, Horatio, they will do nothing but harm."

Horatio, who knew that his political views were very different from his aunt's, kept silent, hugging himself with an inward joy. Parliament! Years before he could have hoped to even contest a seat, here was one dropped into his lap. Not a county seat, of course, but a seat was a seat, and he would make far better use of it than eighty percent of those presently members of the House.

"That is why you must keep away from Lady Usborne. What with Frederick, and the new morality that is starting to take hold, you have to be seen to be whiter than white; the newspapers will be ready to pounce on you; do not give them the chance."

Lady Usborne? If only his aunt knew; since she had been in Brighton, he had come to realise that he didn't care for her at all. He had been flattered, she was a most attractive woman, and his desire had got the better of his sense, as was the common lot of men. But it would cost him no pain to part from her. In fact, he had already done so, to all intents and purposes, and he felt pretty sure that she would have found herself a fine new young lover while she was at the seaside, that place of trysts and flirtations.

"It's time you married," his aunt was saying. "I may not have grandchildren of my own, but I should like to see your children growing up." She held up a hand. "You are going to say, you cannot yet afford to marry, which is true, but while you are not married, you will find yourself falling into the snares of such as Lady Usborne, and it will not do. Therefore, at such time as you choose a suitable bride, I shall give you Caldwell House."

This time, Horatio was truly astounded, and he could do nothing but stare at his aunt.

"There is the house and a neat little estate. It will not make you rich, but, properly managed, it will bring you in some three thousand a year, and provide a home for your family in due course."

Suitable bride, there was the fly in the ointment. Horatio had a very good idea what his aunt would consider suitable, and he didn't think it would match with his, at all.

"You need to marry a young lady of intelligence and character, and of good family, well brought up, naturally. Her fortune need not be large, a man always wants to put more into a marriage than his wife brings, it makes for a much more equal relationship. Find her, and bring her to me, and then I shall settle the deeds of Caldwell House upon you."

Chapter Forty-two

While Horatio Darcy's agent was sailing back across the Atlantic, bearing the news that, wherever the letters were, he was certain that they were not in the possession of Mrs. Harriet Morris, Lady Usborne, back in London for the autumn round, had been pursuing her own enquiries.

Her informer, Usborne's groom, hadn't said anything to Lady Usborne about the interrogation by Ratchet as to the whereabouts of some missing letters, for the simple reason that she had not asked him. He reported to her on his lordship's movements and that was all, nothing had ever been mentioned about letters, which were, as he'd pointed out to Ratchet, nothing to do with anyone who worked in the stables; if he was going to come round pestering servants with a pack of fool questions, then he was looking in the wrong direction. He, Peters, had never set foot in his lordship's study, nor didn't ever expect to. For why? Because he was an outdoor servant, that was why. Ratchet could take himself and his long nose elsewhere, let him go snooping round the maids and let him get on with his work.

And it was one of these maids, who had thought nothing of it at the time, who happened to ask Lady Usborne, as she reverently put away a gown new come from the dressmakers, if those letters his lordship had mislaid had ever turned up. "For that Ratchet was asking ever so many questions about them, a while back."

Letters to Lady Usborne meant love letters, and for her husband to keep letters bound in a ribbon in his study boded ill; it sounded much more serious than any of his dealings with the demi-mondes. Further discreet enquiries convinced her that the slut Harriet Foxley had been the most likely person to have removed them. Had she written them? No, why should she? She wasn't in love with Lord Usborne, and any missives penned to him by his pretty pigeons, as she scornfully called them, would, she felt sure, have been swiftly consigned to the flames of his study fire.

So why had she taken them? To have a hold over him? To blackmail him? To sell them to some weasel hack who dealt in passing scandalous items to the newspapers?

Yet, as far as she knew, none of these things had happened. Lord Usborne's frowns were to do with Prinny, she was sure, and she was quite right about that, even though she wasn't to know that the prince was pressing Usborne to know when he might have sight of the letters, which in the royal mind were going to solve all his problems regarding his divorce and remarriage.

She rang for her maid, and gave instructions for Peters to bring her carriage round immediately. Then, well away from listening ears, she told him what she wanted him to do. First, he was to find out where this Harriet went to when she had left his lordship.

"No trouble about that, my lady, for I know where she went."

"Do you? Then you are to go there directly, and see if you can find out where she is, and if by any chance any of the servants there, if there are servants, I know nothing about that part of town—it is in town, I suppose—have seen or heard of a packet of letters. A maid waiting upon her might have noticed them."

"It's quite a respectable area, my lady, although not one you'd ever venture near. There'll be servants kept, right enough."

And her enquiries, which cost her a guinea as compared to the considerable sums laid out by Horatio Darcy on his lordship's behalf, were far more successful than those carried out by Mr. Darcy. Peters, whose pleasant ways served him well, came back with the news that

Harriet Foxley had left that address several weeks before, to sail to America.

Good riddance, Lady Usborne said to herself. Would that all her husband's fancies might take themselves off to America.

And that, before leaving, Harriet had instructed the boy who ran errands for everyone in that street to take a little casket to an address in Covent Garden, where it was to be placed in the hands of one Mrs. Kent, or, failing that, her maid, Petifer.

"Petifer," Lady Usborne repeated. "Very well, Peters, I leave it to you to find out if they are still at that address, or, if not, try to obtain their present address."

Chapter Forty-three

Cassandra had, through Henry Lisser's good efforts, received a commission to paint an attractive young opera singer.

"She has not yet made her name, but she has an exquisite voice, and an equally lovely face, and will, I am sure, go far in her profession. You are just the person to paint her portrait; I know that you will capture her to perfection. Then we shall arrange to have an engraving made, for she is to play Polly in a revival of *The Beggar's Opera,* and I predict she will be the rage of London this autumn, people will flock to buy the engravings."

Cassandra was always taken aback by how practical a man Henry Lisser was; not in the least the airy-fairy, head-in-the-clouds artist of popular imagining, but an astute man of business as well as a very fine painter.

"We have to have the money to do the work we want to do, as well as to keep a roof over our heads and food on the table," he told her. "Fat commissions are good, but not always easy to come by, and each new painting takes its time. So we need to find every way possible to earn extra income from our work, and engravings should be the stock-in-trade of every artist whose work lends itself to the medium."

Miss Kennedy was delighted with her portrait, and sent round the offer of a box for a performance of *Dido and Aeneas,* in which she was singing.

"Will you accompany me?" Cassandra asked Henry Lisser, who was, she knew, fond of music. "And perhaps the Hopkirks would like to make up our number."

"I have to write a note to John Hopkirk," said Lisser. "Shall I add a message about the opera?"

He sat down at his desk, a rolltop one with pigeonholes containing neatly stacked letters, and drew out a sheet of notepaper. As he reached for a pen, his sleeve dislodged a letter that had been tucked beneath the blotter. He quickly pushed it back again, but not before Cassandra had caught sight of the handwriting, and had recognised it.

Belle writing to Henry Lisser! She went cold at the thought. How could Belle be so rash, and how had Henry Lisser, who must know that correspondence between any single man and young lady was out of the question unless there were an engagement, allowed himself to be drawn into anything so unwise?

Upon his return from Dorset, one of Horatio's first acts was to pay a call on his cousin Camilla to deliver some seeds that Mrs. Shawardine had promised her, and to carry greetings and general goodwill to Camilla, who was her goddaughter.

"No sign of her breeding yet, I suppose?" had been Mrs. Shawardine's parting words to Horatio.

"As to that, ma'am, I would hardly know."

"In the end, it is a thing no one can hide, as many a young lady has found to her cost. However, I am in regular correspondence with her father and mother, and they would have told me if it were the case." She paused. "I like Camilla, she has a head on her shoulders. She married an all-over-the-place man, now here, now there, now in Greece, now in Egypt, but I dare say he will settle down now he is married."

Horatio Darcy doubted it, but he thought it wiser not to say so, and took his leave with real affection that hid the turmoil in his heart.

Cassandra had all Camilla's brains and more than her beauty, and she was undoubtedly a young lady of character, and from as good a family as his or Mrs. Shawardine's.

But her reputation! If Mrs. Shawardine had not already heard of it, and she had not mentioned Cassandra's family except in a glancing reference to "poor Thaddeus, why ever he married Anne de Bourgh, I shall never understand"; she seemed not to have much interest in that branch of the family or in Cassandra.

Yet her running away with Eyre must be generally known, at least within the family, and it would undoubtedly come to Mrs. Shawardine's ears, sooner or later. A young woman who ran off with a man, especially a young lady who had let down the sacred name of Darcy, would not meet Mrs. Shawardine's exacting standards for a bride.

In fact, were there to be any chance that Cassandra might return his affections, of which he was not at all sure, then marriage to her would mean an end to the hopes that had been raised during his visit to Dorset; farewell neat estate, farewell the seat in the House, farewell a most promising fillip to his career.

Worse, Cassandra might become aware of it; if she had the least hint that he had made a sacrifice in order to . . . But his thoughts were running away with themselves. Was he such an arrogant man as to assume Cassandra would welcome his suit, that she would now or at any time wish to marry him? It was true that she had treated him with a great kindness in their most recent meetings, and there had been friendliness in her attitude on those drives, but what did this mean? Perhaps just that she felt more secure, had reconciled herself to a life outside the Rosings pale, and, once she knew he was acting in a personal capacity and not as a lawyer, the mistrust she had felt about him had been put aside.

Mrs. Wytton was at home.

Horatio Darcy was shown upstairs to the light-filled sitting room, its pale walls offset by the rich Turkey carpets on the floor.

"A notion I picked up from Henrietta Rowan," she said. "Have you visited her apartments? My parents, who have spent some time in Constantinople, assure me that she has caught the oriental style to perfection, while suiting it to the English climate and way of life. You have been down in Dorset, I hear, tell me how you got on."

Horatio was reticent at first, until it became clear that Camilla had had a letter from her godmother and knew all about Mrs. Shawardine's plans for him. "Everyone is so pleased, it is a great chance for you to advance yourself."

"I am most grateful to her, it was entirely unexpected."

"It wasn't unexpected, however, that Frederick would make the country too hot for himself, and have to go abroad on a repairing lease. Not that there is much hope of repair, one gathers. So, with this excellent news from Mrs. Shawardine, as regards your prospects, if not Frederick's, why do you look so long in the mouth?"

She rang the bell, and ordered coffee. "I know what it is," she continued. "It is the matter of the wife. Mrs. Shawardine wishes you to marry well; she is a hearty advocate of marriage for everyone. She is always telling me that the sooner Belle is married, the better. You would not like to marry Belle, would you?"

Horatio looked at her in some alarm, and then saw that she was joking.

"I fear," said Camilla, "that my sister is in some kind of a scrape, which in her case nearly always has to do with romantic feelings for a man, and generally one who is too old or too young, or too poor, or too something. I simply hope that it is not a question of a man who is too married."

Horatio was thoroughly taken aback, and his cousin laughed at him. "You are not a realist, I find. You do not like to call a spade a spade."

"But your own sister, you can hardly . . ."

"You have no sisters, Mr. Darcy," said Camilla, as though this clinched the argument. "No, Belle would not do at all for you. Perhaps you wish to remain a bachelor, enjoying the delights of the single life."

If she wanted to be blunt, then he would be, too.

"If you refer to Lady Usborne, I have not seen her since her return to London, nor shall I."

"A tiff?"

Really, Camilla was impossible.

"No, I shall not tease you, for you are being very frank, which I like. So you have a young lady in your eye, and you fear that she will not meet with Mrs. Shawardine's favour?"

Camilla was a great deal too sharp, how did Wytton keep up with her? How could he broach the subject?

Camilla was eyeing him thoughtfully.

"The young lady who has captured your heart, for I see that there is such an one, it would not by any chance be Cassandra, would it?"

He almost jumped out of his seat. Damn it, how had she known?

"Oh, I saw it coming. You were so cross with her, and then so angry about the Lord Usborne business, out of all reason angry. There had to be more to it than the good name of the family and all that kind of thing. So, have you told her?"

"Told her what?"

"That you are in love with her?"

This was a preposterous conversation. It had its humorous side, but he was wishing that he had not come.

"I have no idea of what Cassandra's sentiments are, towards me or anyone else. I have no reason to suppose . . ."

"Are you afraid that she is still in love with James Eyre? It seems a callous heart that will not grieve for a lost love, but I believe it was as much wild infatuation, and a desire to escape from some very unpleasant circumstances, that had as much to do with it as any great depth of attachment. There was another man, in the background, was there not?"

"The painter, Henry Lisser," said Horatio grimly.

Camilla seemed surprised. "I did not know about that. What I heard was that Mr. Partington and his sister had plans to marry her off to a local squire, for whom it was clear that Cassandra would be very unlikely to have any feelings, he sounds a dull dog. He was Eyre's friend, that is how she met James Eyre."

"How do you know all this?"

"From Cassandra herself, and from a word here and another

there, one picks up information, you know, if one is listening out for it, and Cassandra interests me greatly, I have an admiration for her, and besides, I like her, and would very much like to see her comfortably settled. Were you to marry her, would you try to put a stop to her painting?"

This was a question Horatio Darcy had not asked himself. A painter for a wife? That would be considered eccentric, indeed. "I think that to separate Cassandra from her palette and oil paints and canvases and brushes would be to trample on her soul," he said, with an honesty that surprised him. "I would never choose to attach myself to a woman who had such a streak in her nature, but Cassandra has, and it is part and parcel of her being. Besides, why should not a woman paint? You do not have to wear breeches to wield a paint brush."

"Oh, bravo," said Camilla, clapping her hands. "You have come on a lot, Cousin; almost, I feel you may be worthy of Cassandra."

"That is all very well, but what if she will not have me?"

"And what if she does have you, and the price you pay is a dowerless wife and an angry aunt? Resentment, at the damage to your prospects, is not a good foundation for a happy marriage."

"It seems a hopeless business."

"That is hardly fighting talk, Cousin. Have you any reason to suppose that Cassandra might welcome an offer from you?"

He told her about his excursions with Cassandra, and the lessening of her initial hostility. "It is hardly much to go on."

"You must tell her how you feel."

"She will back away, refuse to see me, perhaps even leave London, she has some idea of a trip to Italy, she would like to go to Rome."

"Rome is the very place for you to honeymoon; Mr. Wytton has a great many friends in Rome, and will give you an introduction to as many as you want."

"Talk of honeymoons is premature."

"You are right. You need to go away and brood on whether your ambition or your heart is to determine your immediate future. Only remember, that advancement may come in various forms, and if not now, then later. Everyone says how able you are, and so you are bound to succeed in due course. Whereas, once you turn your back on Cassandra, she will be lost to you for good."

"There speaks a woman, and from the heart."

Camilla nodded her head vigorously, and poured him more coffee. "We will talk no more about it, except that I will undertake to see if I can fathom the secrets of Cassandra's heart, and see if you have any place in that unruly organ. If you do not, if she regards you with dislike, or worse, with indifference, then your decision is made for you."

This didn't bring much comfort to him.

"In return, will you do something for me?"

He looked at her warily; something told him that a courteous "I am yours to command" might not be wise in dealing with his cousin.

"You need not look like that, it is nothing so very much. It is only that Mr. Wytton was to accompany Belle and me to the opera tonight, at the Theatre Royal. Belle is but recently returned to London, and she is moping; it is a scheme to raise her spirits. However, Mr. Wytton has been called away on business, there is some dispute about a boundary at the Abbey, so he will not be back in time for the performance and his seat is going begging. But it is of no consequence if you are otherwise engaged, for Pagoda Portal and Henrietta will be there also, so if you feel . . ."

He rose to go, bending over her hand with real affection. "I should be honoured."

Chapter Forty-four

The Theatre Royal in Haymarket, while not as large or opulent as the Opera House, also in the Haymarket, had the advantages that a smaller venue can bring, and the audience, whether sitting in the pit, in one of the galleries, or in the three tiers of boxes, had all a fine view of the stage and the singers, and also of other members of the audience.

Camilla's party arrived in good time, and Belle took her seat in the front of their box and looked about her with more animation than she had shown since she came back from her visit to Pemberley, where, according to her mama, she had suffered a distressing tendency to melancholy. That was why her parents had agreed that she might spend a few weeks in London with her sister and Mr. Wytton to cheer her up.

Her liveliness infected the others, and they were all in a good humour and prepared to enjoy the opera; even Horatio, who had been suffering from an oppression of his spirits, cheered up as the members of the orchestra began to take their places. Jessop the oboist was there, and Horatio waved at him.

"You know someone playing in the orchestra?" Belle asked, as though he were claiming acquaintance with some creature of a rare species.

"I do indeed, and he is a very good kind of a fellow."

Camilla exchanged glances with Henrietta.

"You have been keeping unusual company, Mr. Darcy," Henrietta said, turning her head to address him. "I hear from Mr. Hopkirk that you have become quite at home in literary society. Now I see that your circle is wider than mere letters, but includes the other arts."

"Hopkirk is amazing good company, and an old friend," said Horatio.

"You must come to one of my afternoons," said Henrietta. "You will meet many interesting people there, including those who are already friends, I am sure, and will enjoy excellent conversation, not to mention tea of my own mixing. We welcome all sorts, from politicians to poets, I think you would feel at home among us."

Belle was leaning over the velvet edge of the box, surveying the people in the pit and scanning the boxes opposite for anyone she knew.

Horatio saw her stiffen, then whip her opera glasses up to her eyes. What was she looking at, or rather, whom was she looking at so intently?

He didn't need opera glasses; he could see them with his own eyes, quite clearly. Sitting side by side, heads together, apparently sharing a joke, the very picture of intimacy, were Cassandra and Henry Lisser. He felt the breath drawn out of him, as though he had received a blow to the chest.

Belle sat back in her seat, her face white.

Camilla took one look, and jumped up. "She's going to faint," she said. "We need to get her into the air."

In the confusion that followed, Horatio had no time to reflect on what he, and Belle, had seen; not when Belle was outside the theatre, attracting a good deal of attention as Henrietta waved her vinaigrette under her nose, kindly lent by a stout woman just arriving for the performance.

"Come over faint, has she, poor love?" she said sympathetically. "It's this heat."

Some colour was returning to Belle's cheeks, and she opened her eyes, pressing them with the back of her hand and looking around in a dazed fashion. Then awareness flooded back into her and she looked in horror at the little crowd of people who had gathered, hoping that maybe the young lady was going to have a fit, or, better still, fall down raving and have to be carried off to the madhouse, or perhaps just expire, with her hands clasped to her breast.

The arrival of Camilla's carriage put an end to these vain hopes, and in a trice, Belle was seated, Camilla beside her, and Horatio got in after them, after assuring Pagoda and Henrietta that Belle would be well in a moment or two, it was only a faint.

Camilla took Belle's hands, and began to rub them. "What is it, Belle? Whom did you see, that upset you so greatly?"

Belle shut her eyes and gave a soft moan.

"I can tell you whom she saw," said Horatio grimly. "Her cousin Cassandra, on the very easiest of terms with that painter, Henry Lisser."

Belle cried out at that. "Oh, she is a vixen, a sly minx, all that time pretending, oh, what am I to do?"

"I think," said Camilla, with a warning glance at the coachman, whose ears were pinned back to take in every detail of this interesting conversation, "that we will discuss this when we are at home."

Once inside the sitting room, Camilla poured a glass of wine for Belle, told her to sit down, dismissed the hovering servant, and looked her sister up and down. "Now, Belle, you will please tell me what this is all about."

Belle wasn't going to give in to any display of authority without a fight, but Camilla was inexorable, and was ably seconded by her cousin Horatio.

"It is no business of yours, after all," Belle flashed out at him.

"It is," he said. "I shan't go into the reasons why, but I assure you I am not moving from here until I, like Camilla, know what this is all about. If you will not confide in us, then there is nothing to be done"—with a glance at Camilla—"other than to send an express to your papa, and ask him to come to London at once to see if he can get to the bottom of all this."

That made Belle sit up straight, abandoning her languishing airs, and give Darcy a direct, angry look.

"You are hateful," she informed him.

"My withers are unwrung," he said politely. "Now, tell us why the sight of Henry Lisser so upset you."

"It is not the sight of Henry, how could that upset me? It is to see him with that scheming Cassandra, she has had her eye on him from the start, I knew it was so; I knew she wasn't to be trusted! He told me Cassandra means nothing to him, except as an artist, and a good friend, but how can a man as handsome as Henry be mere friends with any woman? Moreover, someone who knows Henry told me that he and Cassandra were always together, in the daytime, pretending to go on about painting and colours and so on, and in the evening, she dines with him, in coffee-houses and such places."

"Surely what Cassandra does, is her affair," said Camilla reasonably.

"Not when she does it with Henry Lisser, what right has she to steal him away like that? And she will cast him aside, just as she did that man she ran away with. Only Henry is twice as handsome as he could ever have been, and she will stay with him, and I am so very unhappy."

Belle was working herself into a fit of regular hysterics. Camilla exchanged exasperated looks with Horatio, and said that bed was the only answer, bed and a composer to make Belle sleep. She rang for the maid, and, telling Horatio that she would be back shortly, went off with her sister.

Left alone, he prowled about the sitting room, in the most fretful mood, not knowing what to believe, but convinced that Belle had the heart of the matter, that Cassandra had, all this time, been more than a mere friend to Henry Lisser.

Then, more rationally, he considered Belle's outburst of venom against Cassandra. "She is jealous of Cassandra," he said bleakly to Camilla when she came back into the sitting room. "We may suppose . . ."

"That she has reason to be? That she has a foolish fancy for Mr. Lisser, I think, is more than likely, but for the rest of it, it is nonsense, we may suppose no such thing. What a pair you are, each indulging in flights of fancy because of two people sitting in a box together. Were they flirting? Did you notice? No, for before any of us could judge for ourselves, there was Belle fainting away, an old trick, and one we hoped she had grown out of. I am not at all bothered on your behalf, why should not Cassandra go to the theatre with Henry Lisser, or Henry whomever she likes? That is a freedom she has, given the life she has chosen, and you may like it, or you may not, but that is the way it is. Now, if you have mercy in you, pour me a glass of wine, for I am sorely in need of refreshment."

He did so, glad of even such a little task to help calm his jangling nerves.

"No," Camilla said, looking grave now. "It is Belle we have to worry about. What is this Henry Lisser to her?"

"And what is she to him? I assume they met at Rosings."

"He was there, certainly, and there was an incident in the shrubbery, I mean to have the truth out of Belle, for I fear she has done her cousin an injustice, and indeed may have made a good deal of mischief, with her thoughtless, heedless ways."

"Would you wish me to visit Mr. Lisser, and ask him to explain why Belle should behave like this?"

"No, for you would very likely call him out or do something equally dramatic and senseless, and then there will be the devil to pay." She saw the look on his face, and added, "As my dearest Mr. Wytton would say. I do wish he were here, for he is the greatest use in these kind of situations, he dealt wonderfully with Alethea when she was in one of her scrapes."

Horatio eyed her with a certain respect in his face. "I begin to think, Cousin, that you and your four sisters were not perhaps the easiest of young ladies to bring up."

"We all like to have things our own way, but it is in how we go about getting it that the difference between us lies." She hesitated, then said, "It has not always been easy for Belle, since her twin, Georgina, married and went to live in Paris. She misses her more than she will admit."

"Missing her sister doesn't excuse her flirting, if nothing more, with a painter. Mr. Lisser is a fine artist, clearly with a prodigious future ahead of him in his profession. But he is no match for the daughter of Mr. Darcy of Pemberley, and she must know that as well as he does. I do not think him a fortune hunter, but perhaps, being a foreigner, he is unaware of the gulf that exists between him and Belle."

"Oh, it is impossible, and it is wrong of her to lead him on, as I feel she must have done."

"I would say that Mr. Lisser is not a fool, nor one who could easily be led by the nose."

"I hope for his sake that he is not in love with Belle, but merely flattered by being the momentary object of her affections. She should have been allowed to marry Roper, and then none of this would have happened."

"What, Josiah Roper's son? He can hardly be out of school."

"He has just come down from Oxford, but you are right, he is very young. That was the reason for not permitting an engagement, and of course the young man went off to nurse his broken heart and promptly fell in love with the youngest Milford girl. They are to be married in the spring."

Darcy did not feel that Belle's love life was nearly as important as his own, it was all so youthful and impetuous, and the agony of today would be the "Who, him?" of tomorrow. He could not throw off his own feelings so easily.

"It will be best if I call upon Mr. Lisser tomorrow," said Camilla. "I can bring a feminine touch to what may be a disagreeable conversation, he will not mind so much if he is warned off by me. Were my father to hear of it, and come to London—well, I think Mr. Lisser would find that a meeting he would rather not have."

Chapter Forty-five

Lady Usborne had hoped to catch her husband before he went out of the house, but he had been called most unusually early, and by the time she was up and dressed and seated in the breakfast parlour, he was long gone.

"Something to do with a hunter he wants to try," Ratchet informed her.

Lady Usborne knew what that meant. When Lord Usborne was trying out and talking about horses with his similarly minded cronies, he would be away for hours, for horseflesh was his greatest passion. He had all the attributes of a rich nobleman: an inclination to game and drink too much, a fondness for women, and a great liking of having the world and everyone in it at his bidding, but if there was one thing that mattered more to him than any of these things, it was horses.

Lady Usborne crunched a piece of toast and considered when it would be best to waylay Usborne and present him with her information. In the late afternoon, when he would be home to dress for the evening. After that, he would be off again. The Usbornes rarely dined at home, except when they were entertaining. He would come home in the early hours of the morning, most likely far too disguised to have his wits about him.

How like a man not to be there when you wanted him; nine days out of ten, he would rise yawning from his bed a good hour after she was up and dressed, what a nuisance that today the lure of a promising horse had been stronger than his need for sleep.

So she would have to possess her soul in patience for a few more hours. She would go to Florette's, she decided, and buy a hat. Then, in the evening, she would set her news before Lord Usborne, as a tasty dish for him to savour—and to act upon. And she would satisfy her own curiosity about the letters. Who had written them? To whom? And why were they so important to her husband?

Camilla was up early. She put her head round the door of Belle's room, to see her sister, looking so young and vulnerable as she slept, that it brought tears to her eyes. Then she noticed that one hand was clutching something that looked very like a torn letter; and her tenderness vanished upon the instant. She closed the door quietly, and stood outside it for a moment, frowning. A letter. That was not a good sign, not good at all.

She went to have her breakfast, and ate a fresh roll and honey without tasting it. Then she rang the bell for Belle's maid. She gave her instructions not to disturb Miss Belle, and to make sure that she stayed indoors until she herself were back.

"Miss Belle won't be awake for a while yet," the maid said. "For all she took the powder you gave her, she was sobbing her heart out at two in the morning, I could hear her; I thought it was the kitchen cat got upstairs and went to shoo it away, but, no, it was Miss Belle that was making a howling noise, not the cat at all."

It was a fine morning, and Camilla decided to walk to Henry Lisser's studio, she felt that some brisk exercise would do her good, and on the way back there were one or two shops she could visit.

Henry Lisser was not there. His assistant was apologetic and polite, but, no, Mr. Lisser had been up and off out early. He had no idea where he had gone, nor yet when he would be back. He had merely said that he would not be working at the studio today.

"Perhaps he has gone out on a commission," said Camilla.

The assistant shook his head. "There's nothing in the book, and he didn't take no sketchbook or notebook with him, barring the small one he always carries with him. I think he's gone to meet someone, though, for he was very particular about the time, anxious not to be late, he said."

Horatio had passed a restless, disturbed night; not able to sleep for several hours after he had gone to bed, he had finally fallen into a troubled sleep, haunted by dreams of Cassandra in Lisser's arms, in Usborne's arms, in anyone's arms but his.

He arrived late at his chambers, snapped at his clerk, did some desultory work, and then decided his mind wasn't on the law. He told the clerk mendaciously that he was going out to see a client, whisking himself out of the door before Henty could ask him for details to write down in the day book.

Face facts, he told himself. Find out what the truth is, anything was better than this harrowing uncertainty. If Cassandra was in love with Henry Lisser, then he must know it, and he could go quietly away to drown himself in the Thames, or set off on a hopeless expedition to some distant and dangerous part of the world. Or, and here his musings became even more fanciful, he could challenge Lisser, and run him through with his sword.

Damn it, the man probably didn't know one end of a sword from another. What was he? A painter, the son of a nobody, undoubtedly of low origin, despite his good manners. They were part of his stock-in-trade, of course. If you earned a living painting the residences of the gentry and the nobility, you would do well to make sure there was nothing about your appearance or manners that might grate on them.

Well, Mr. Lisser grated on him, Horatio Darcy, all right. Everything about him grated, from his good looks to his pleasant ways; the man was a poseur, why had he ever left his native land and come to England? Why, if he had to set off on his travels, could not he have gone to France or Italy, or, better still, South America?

The mere thought of South America, reminding him of James

Eyre, as it did, put him in a worse mood, and he looked very threatening as he plied the knocker on the door of 44 Soho Square.

Mrs. Burgh was not at home. Her maid was not at home. Miss Griffin was not at home. Nobody was at home except him—a wiry boy with a mop of red hair—and his auntie, who was cook. He would enquire, if the gentleman would just like to wait in the hall.

"There's a peevish-looking gent upstairs, wants to know where that Mrs. Burgh is, and when she'll be back," he told his aunt.

Hard at work with a raised pie, his aunt had no time for anything else. "Call upstairs for that Petifer."

The boy shook his head. "She's out. Went out soon after Mrs. Burgh left. And Miss Griffin's gone out, too, a message came earlier from Mrs. Wytton, and she went off straightaway."

The cook put a lump of dough into the bottom of a pie dish, and gave it a thump with her hefty fist. "Mrs. Burgh and Petifer didn't go out together? Miss Griffin don't like Mrs. B. to go out on her own."

"She didn't. That Mr. Lisser came calling for her, in a hackney cab."

"Tell the gentleman that, then, and get out from under my feet, do!"

Camilla had done her shopping, one or two small items, that was all; she had no desire to linger, even in the face of shops full of enticing wares. She was thinking about Belle and Lisser, and Horatio, and wondering how such a tangle of misunderstanding and misdirected affections might be sorted out.

Belle was still asleep when Camilla returned to her house. Camilla put off her hat, and fidgeted up and down her sitting room for a few minutes before going over to her desk and taking out a sheet of notepaper. She scribbled a note and rang the bell. "Take this round to Miss Griffin. If she will come, please bring her back in a hackney cab, here is a shilling for the fare."

Miss Griffin, not at all pleased at being taken away from her latest book, took one look at Camilla's face, and put aside her irritation. Camilla was troubled; let her see how she might help.

"Sit down," she told her erstwhile charge. "I can't think while you're pacing up and down, it makes me twitchy. Sit there, on that sofa, and tell me what this is all about."

"As to Cassandra being in love with Henry Lisser," she said, when Camilla had finished, "that is all a hum. She doesn't care for him, at least not in that way. She went to the opera with him last night, and enjoyed the performance. She said nothing to me about seeing Belle there, so we must suppose that neither she nor Mr. Lisser saw her in the box, nor her fainting away. I hope that there were others in the theatre who didn't notice it either, what a way to carry on."

"It happened just as the orchestra struck up," said Camilla. "Which is fortunate."

"You are sure Mr. Lisser is at the bottom of all this? You could not be mistaken, that it was someone else Belle saw at the theatre?"

"No, for she was venting her spleen against Cassandra in the wildest way last night."

"It is clear that Belle has been carrying on an intrigue with the unfortunate Mr. Lisser. It will not do, of course it will not do. She must go back to Pemberley."

Camilla bit her lip. "Yes, but so much trouble as she has been in already! And this the worst of all, for at least her other fancies were men of her own order. I do not think that Papa will be so forgiving or understanding about a German painter."

"Really, it would be better if Mr. Lisser and Cassandra were to make a match of it," said Miss Griffin tetchily. "In her case, with her reputation already in shreds, it would not be nearly so much of a misalliance, and would make an honest woman of her."

"Oh, do not say that," cried Camilla. "For Mr. Darcy is in love with her."

"Is he so? I thought as much. That won't do, either, not for an ambitious young lawyer. People forget a scandal soon enough, as new ones come along, but if you are in the law, and rise perhaps to sit on the bench, it will always be held against you, a wife with a past."

"As to that, Horatio's ambitions are more in the political line."

"Politicians all lead scandalous lives, most of them are as corrupt as can be, so I dare say it would not matter so much. In any case, what concerns us here is Belle, and how she may come out of this scrape with her own reputation unscathed."

"She has before," Camilla pointed out.

"Her fancy has not previously alighted on such a man as Mr. Lisser," said Miss Griffin grimly. "And she has worked herself up into believing that there is more to this than to her other infatuations. It is just because he is an unsuitable match as to birth and standing; she feels that to be in love with a man of humble origin is a true romance."

"Perhaps she reads too many novels," said Camilla, with a wicked glance at Miss Griffin. Then she sighed and grew more sombre. "I can see nothing for it but for her to be sent away from London again. In which case, Papa and Mama will have some questions to ask, and it will all be very disagreeable."

Cassandra and Henry Lisser spent an interesting morning at Mr. Angerstein's residence, looking at his notable collection of Italian old masters. Henry Lisser had seen the paintings before, and acted as guide to Cassandra as they went around the big gallery on the first floor of the large, seventeenth-century house, itself a masterpiece, as Henry pointed out.

Much refreshed and inspired by what they had seen, they stopped for a quick mouthful to eat, and then repaired to Mr. Rudge's establishment, where Mr. Fingal, Rudge's assistant, had promised to show them some new colours from France.

Rather to Cassandra's surprise, Petifer was there, sleeves rolled up, grinding a dull-coloured stone in a pestle and mortar into a grey powder.

"Seeing as how you were off for the morning, I came to enquire after that paint you were wanting, and offered to give Mr. Fingal a hand," she said, when she looked up and saw her mistress standing there.

She had a slight flush on her cheeks, and Cassandra glanced from her to Mr. Fingal, who was weighing out a little pile of brilliant blue lapis lazuli on a small set of scales, and not looking at her or Petifer.

Petifer could do worse, she thought, than marry a man as expert in his trade as Mr. Fingal clearly was, and likely to have his own business soon enough. A hard-working and capable wife would be a huge asset, and Petifer would be well able to keep books as well as help with the grinding and mixing, and she'd be good with customers, too.

She would be glad for her, if it turned out to be as she suspected, but the prospect of being without Petifer gave her a feeling of desolation that quite took away the happiness of the morning.

Then she shook her head, to clear it of any such mournful thoughts, and made herself concentrate on Mr. Fingal's account of why this blue was so far superior in every way to any other.

"It's all science, now," he told them. "The old ways, such as Mr. Rudge likes, were all very well in their time, but now we need different colours and different paints. There was a colourist in from Leipzig the other day, and it was amazing what they're doing in that country."

"It is true," Henry Lisser said. "There is a great deal going on, I only wish . . ."

"Do you never go back," Cassandra asked him, suddenly curious. "To see your family?"

"It's impossible," Lisser said.

He spoke with finality, and Cassandra wondered, not for the first time, what his story was. Had he broken with his family, had he left Germany under a cloud? Herr Winter would know, but wouldn't tell her, even if she asked him when he next came to London. No, it would have to remain a mystery.

Horatio worked off a good deal of his rage and sense of powerlessness in a brisk few rounds with the foils at Angelo's. He enjoyed imagining that he was running Lisser through the heart, and also Lord Usborne, and several judges, not that most of them would be able to stand on their legs long enough to wield a sword. He finished with a fine flourish that would have ripped the guts out of any fellow lawyer who came from a family brimful of influence and parliamentary seats and advancement for all the younger sons of the house.

The fencing master congratulated him on the improvement in his sword work, although, he added, passion was no substitute for technique.

Horatio went back to his rooms to change, although he had not the least idea what he was to do with his evening. He could dine at home and read a philosophical work, by one of the Stoics, perhaps, telling him that to endure the passing day was all mankind could hope for. That was unlikely to improve his mood. He could dine at his club, where he would be bound to meet a few friends, who would exclaim about how little they had seen of him, where had he been all this while?

The answer was, in better company, in a worse part of town, but that was somewhere he most certainly was not going, this evening, or ever again. He had been seduced by that other world of the writer and the artist. Lisser's world, and he had learned his lesson.

Setting out with no particular direction in mind, he found his steps leading him to Camilla's house. It would be only courteous to call and enquire after his cousin Belle. In fact, he should have done so this morning.

He knocked, was admitted, and found Camilla in her sitting room, playing cards with that gaunt woman from Soho Square, Cassandra's landlady, what was her name? Miss Griffin. A writer of popular novels. He didn't like the sardonic gleam in her eye as she returned his greeting, she reminded him all too much of his own governess, who had had the power to quell him with a mere glance when he was a small boy.

"It is kind of you to call," said Camilla. "Belle has kept to her room, she is feeling low."

"Hysterical," said Miss Griffin. She addressed Mr. Darcy. "Do you know anything about her friendship with Mr. Lisser?"

"He has never mentioned Belle to me. He is a man who keeps his own counsel. And we are only slightly acquainted."

"Would that Belle had learned that trick," said Camilla, with a tiny sigh. "It is a case of crying wolf, perhaps. She has exclaimed and wept and exulted over so many young men that we have all concluded that she feels nothing for any of them. Should she now have formed a real attachment to Mr. Lisser, which heaven forbid, she finds that none of us take it seriously."

Miss Griffin decided that it was time for her to go home. "At least this evening I may be able to write a chapter," she said.

Camilla was ready to call a hackney cab, Miss Griffin preferred to walk, and Mr. Darcy offered to accompany her. "It is not out of my way."

"Where are you going?"

"To see a friend," he lied.

He found her more conversable than he expected, and enjoyed her caustic comments about leading politicians.

"You take an unusual interest in politics for a woman."

"For a woman in my position, you mean. No one thinks it odd for the great political hostesses to have such an interest. I find politicians lively material for my pen; they display their all-too-human faults in such an obliging manner."

Horatio's eyes went involuntarily to the windows on the top floor, but it was too early for any lamp to be lit, and they gleamed instead with the reflected light of the setting sun.

Miss Griffin had come out without her latch key, so she knocked on the door. There was no reply, so she knocked again, with more vigour this time, until the door opened a crack, and one very blue eye looked out at her.

"Tom, what are you about?" she said. "Open the door and let me in this instant!"

The redheaded boy flung the door open. "I'm glad it's you, ma'am, for I'm here on my own, and there's a dreadful old rumpus going on upstairs!"

Chapter Forty-six

When Cassandra came back to the house in Soho Square, carrying with great care samples of the new paints which Mr. Fingal had given her, she found no one at home except Tom.

"Cook's gone round to Mrs. Thruxton's for a game of cribbage, and Miss Griffin's been out all day," he informed her. "And a gent called this morning, asking for you, the tall gent with the deep voice."

"Mr. Darcy?"

"Think so."

"Thank you, Tom."

So he was back in town. Perhaps he had called to take her out driving again, he had mentioned that he thought she would be entranced by the gardens at Kew. However, he had chosen a wrong day, since nothing would have made her miss the opportunity to see Mr. Angerstein's paintings. Mr. Angerstein had opened his doors to Mr. Lisser, whose work he admired, but in general, members of the public were not admitted to the collection.

Tom retreated to the kitchen, to tease the cat and make sure the stove was burning as it should, ready for when his aunt came home. He helped himself to a slice of apple tart he found in the larder and sat down at the table to throw dice, left hand against right.

Cassandra went up to her rooms. She was wearing one of her best morning gowns, so she changed into a shabbier one, and put on her smock. She wanted to go through her sketchbook and work on the quick drawings she had made of some of the paintings from the morning. And she could try Mr. Fingal's new colours.

Absorbed in her work, she only half heard the knocker going. Then Tom's voice reached her, piping up that he'd see if Mrs. Burgh was receiving visitors, and she heard some indistinct answering words from a male voice. She put down her palette and brush, unaccountably pleased; Mr. Darcy had called again. It must be him, who else would follow Tom up the stairs, without waiting for her to say that she was at home?

Tom's voice raised in protest, a curse flung at him—no, it couldn't be Mr. Darcy—the door was thrust open, and there stood Lord Usborne.

Tom hovered behind his lordship, looking alarmed, and then the door was slammed in his face.

"We meet again, Mrs. Kent," Lord Usborne said, his voice silky and full of menace. "Or, no, Mrs. Burgh is your present alias? Perhaps we will stay with the truth, and call you Miss Darcy."

Miss Darcy! How had he found out her name? Wild ideas flitted through her head, the clearest of which was that Mr. Darcy had confided her story to Lady Usborne; pillow talk, she thought indignantly.

"I cannot say I am glad to see you. I am working, as you see, and—"

"Working," he said, in a jeering voice. "What ridiculous nonsense, to set yourself up as a painter. A woman can have no worth as a painter, she can be nothing but a curiosity, a freak of nature."

He went over to the canvas that was propped on the easel. It was a portrait of Eliza Stich, the pretty daughter of a prosperous merchant, who was having her picture taken to give as a wedding present to her fiancé.

Lord Usborne looked at it with contempt, and then he took up her palette and brush, stood in an exaggerated pose before the canvas, and digging the brush into the pile of Indian black, slashed the brush against the canvas.

Cassandra, realising what he was about, leapt forward, but was too late to prevent him from obliterating Eliza's pretty features in smears of black paint.

"How dare you!" she cried. "Out of here, go this instant, you have taken leave of your senses, you are mad."

He put down the palette. "I have improved it, I think. Being a man, my merest daubs would be better than anything you can attempt. Now, Miss Darcy"—and with these words, he took her arm, wrenching it most cruelly, and forced her backwards into a chair. He stepped back and looked down at her. "Now, Miss Darcy, we have a few things to discuss."

"We do not." Cassandra was alarmed, indeed, frightened, but she knew that she must not let him goad her. She must not get so angry that she couldn't use her wits; strength would not allow her to get away from him, but cunning might. If once she could get to the door, she might flee down the stairs and out on to the street, where she could call for help.

So she smoothed her skirts, willing her hands not to tremble, and looked him straight in the eye. "We have nothing to say to one another," she said levelly.

"By God, I'd forgotten just what a beauty you are," Lord Usborne exclaimed, his eyes narrowing. "What a little fool you were, to run off from Mrs. Nettleton's house, when you could have had London at your feet."

"Only a part of London, I believe. Women who have accepted a carte blanche hardly move in more than a small section of a particular stratum of society."

"Women who have lost their virtue in such a conspicuous way as you did are excluded from any other stratum of society, as you put it. You sound like a preacher, and you have all the hypocrisy of that breed. Picked it up from your stepfather, no doubt. Yes, I know all about your family. I've even been a visitor at Rosings, the guest of your late grandmother, what would she have had to say about your sluttish behaviour? I wonder."

Cassandra would not respond to these taunts. She must not cry out, *I am no slut;* she must remain calm and composed.

"I asked you to leave, my lord."

"My lord," he mimicked. "I shall leave when I'm ready to, and that isn't yet, I assure you. You have something of mine that I want, and when you have handed it over to me, then I believe I shall take something else I want, which you have hitherto refused me. You will rue the day when you turned away from my offer of protection, Miss Darcy. Our liaison might have lasted a fair while; as it is, it will be brief, and while enjoyable for me, less so for you. You need to be taught a lesson."

Cassandra felt a shiver of cold fear run through her. It was perfectly clear what Lord Usborne meant. To rape her would be a crime, a hanging offence, but for him to be convicted of a rape was not only unlikely, it was almost impossible. His word against hers? No magistrate would listen to a word she said. No witnesses, and her reputation, or lack of it, dragged through the mud.

"I do not think I have anything of yours."

"Oh, I think you do. A certain small box, sent to you by Harriet Foxley. A box containing letters. Ah, I see you know exactly what I am talking about. I thought that would be the case."

If only she had looked at those letters. Were they his personal letters, written to or by him? If not, why would he be so anxious to have them restored to him? And why had Harriet stolen them, and been so keen for Cassandra to have them and keep them safe? What was it she had said? "For they are all I have of value." The truth was, that Cassandra had left it to Petifer to put the box of letters in a safe place, and thought no more about them.

"I do not know where any box of letters is," she said, with perfect truth.

"Then let us see what we may do to jog your memory. Perhaps we shall start with those pretty hands of yours. I don't think trying to paint with crippled fingers will make your painting any worse than it already is, but you may not see it like that."

He was mad, he was clearly deranged. She was shut in an attic room with a man who would, apparently, go to any lengths to get what he wanted. This was a scene out of one of Miss Griffin's books, this could not be possible in the modern world.

"You think I would not do it?" he said. "No, you are quite right. I am no savage, but I had you frightened there, did I not? No, your hands are safe; there are subtler and more rewarding ways of inflicting pain. Anguish of the mind is harder to bear, as it never passes in the way that physical pain does. I fancy, Miss Darcy, that you have all your family's pride and spirit, and that to humiliate you is to hit you where it hurts the most. But, before we discuss this matter any further, let us get on closer terms. I should like a kiss, for old times' sake."

Cassandra panicked, screamed with all the power of her lungs, and launched herself forward, hurtling into Lord Usborne with her head lowered, and, more by good luck than good judgement, sent him staggering backwards, wrong-footed and winded. She lifted the chair, holding its legs up in front of her, and advanced on the furious, panting nobleman.

The door opened. "Can I be of any assistance?" said Mr. Darcy, whose voice showed no signs of his having leapt up the stairs in a few swift bounds. "Or is this a private fracas?"

Chapter Forty-seven

Cassandra had never been so pleased to see anyone in her life; it would not have mattered who had come through that door, be it Tom, or the aged person who sold flowers on the corner. As it was, the sense of relief was mingled with joy at the commanding physical presence of Mr. Darcy. And neither the boy nor the flower seller could have ejected Lord Usborne so efficiently, although Miss Griffin's calm statement that Tom had gone for the watch, and that boy's shrill, panting assertion that the Charley was just coming up the street, did much to persuade his lordship to beat a hasty retreat.

"You are not welcome at my house, Lord Usborne" were Miss Griffin's parting words. "And if you ever try to set foot in here again, you will be sorry for it."

Upstairs, Cassandra found herself unable to look at Mr. Darcy. She sank back into the chair, swiftly set on its legs again by Horatio, and for a moment she felt overcome. But she was no Belle, to cause more fuss by passing out.

And then Petifer was standing over her, a glass of water in her hand, scolding, "Take my eyes off you for one minute, Miss Cassandra, and you're in trouble again. Miss Griffin is fetching up some brandy."

Cassandra was glad of the glass of water, mostly because it gave her time to recollect herself.

Horatio glanced at Petifer, and she moved away, leaving him looking down at Cassandra, with an odd smile on his face. She looked up at him, saw the warmth in his eyes, and found that her mouth was dry, despite the water, and that her heart was thumping in a very ungoverned way.

"I have to thank you for coming to my rescue," she said finally.

"I? You were dealing with Usborne most effectively on your own."

"He would have recovered his breath, and then it would have been the worse for me," she said honestly.

"I do not wish to distress you, but why was Usborne here? It seemed more than a social call."

"Revenge, I think," said Cassandra, feeling her bruised wrist. "Oh, and the letters! Petifer, pray tell me where you hid Harriet's letters, for I feel we need to find a safer place for them than this house."

"Letters?" said Horatio, suddenly alert. "Harriet? What letters are these?"

"Letters that were, I suspect, taken from Lord Usborne. They were passed on to me by . . . by a friend, who was going abroad."

"If you mean Harriet Morris, I know all about that," said Horatio impatiently. "But why did she give them to you?"

"I had done her a small favour. She said they were of value. I do not know exactly what she meant, it was no more than a scrawled note that came with them."

"Did you read them?"

"No. I was not much interested, and they seemed private."

"Petifer, fetch them," he said. "At once."

Petifer appeared startled by this request, and looked at her mistress for confirmation.

Cassandra nodded. "I think we will find that Mr. Darcy knows more about the letters than we do," she said.

Miss Griffin came into the room, a glass of brandy in her hand, and stopped short at the sight of Petifer on her hands and knees, grubbing up a floorboard. She put the glass down with something of a bang.

"Well! Are you looking for rats? Is there rot under my boards?"

"It is a hiding place," Cassandra explained. "I had no idea that Petifer had been prising up floorboards."

"It was loose," Petifer said, sitting back on her heels and giving the floorboard a shove so that it fell back into place. Her face was red from her exertions, and she got to her feet, brushing the dust from her skirt, and holding out the casket to Cassandra.

Cassandra took it, opened it, and drew out the beribboned bundle of letters. She looked at them doubtfully. "Is it right for us to read them?"

"Bad habit," observed Miss Griffin. "Reading private correspondence."

"I am fairly sure I know what they are, and who they are from," said Horatio. "If you will trust me, Cassandra, I will just cast my eye over one to see if I am correct. If so, it is better that you do not read them."

"Very mysterious," said Miss Griffin.

"Mr. Darcy is a lawyer," Cassandra said, with a laugh in her voice. "It is in his nature to be cautious."

He smiled at her. "I shall not forgive you for that remark. May I have them?"

"Please do."

There was silence for a few moments while he read a letter, which was penned, Cassandra could see, in a foreign-looking hand.

"Is it written in English?"

"It is, although the writer's native tongue is not our language."

"Are you going to enlighten us?"

He hesitated. "Yes, but what I have to say must on no account go further than this room. You will understand why when I tell you that these letters were written by Princess Caroline."

Miss Griffin raised her eyebrows. "And they are not, I assume, addressed to the Prince Regent?"

"They are not."

"However did Harriet come by them? Did Lord Usborne give them to her?" asked Cassandra.

"No, I imagine she took them, perhaps he said something, when in his cups, or she overheard him speaking about them. They were won at cards by Lord Usborne from George Warren—ah, I see you know the man, Miss Griffin. His lordship obtained them on the Prince Regent's behalf."

"The Prince Regent?" said Cassandra, not understanding.

"Now that the Princess Charlotte is dead, God rest her soul, the next heirs to the throne, after the prince, are his rascally brothers. So Prinny would like to be free to marry again, and get himself another heir."

"Good heavens, you mean he would use the letters to obtain a divorce from his wife?"

"Exactly so."

"Would these letters be sufficient?" asked Miss Griffin.

"I believe they might."

"What are we to do?" said Cassandra. Her mind had been working furiously. "Lord Usborne didn't need the money, surely. Would he have tried to sell them to the prince?"

"I think not. I think he would like to have Prinny, who will probably soon be king, in his debt."

Miss Griffin snorted. "Any man who thinks a king will repay favours done him when he was a prince has no more sense than the cat in the kitchen. Less!"

"Does Usborne need greater influence at court?" Cassandra asked.

"It is always useful, if you are an ambitious man. There are positions and appointments, which may not carry any great remuneration, but which bestow a good deal of power upon their holder. I imagine Usborne is a man who craves power."

"What shall I do with them?" said Cassandra, looking at the letters as though they might bite her. "I should not have them, and I assuredly do not want to give them back to Lord Usborne, even though he thinks he has a right to them."

"He does," Horatio Darcy said. "He employed me to find them for him."

"Employed you!" Cassandra was aghast. Had she fended off Lord Usborne simply to hand the letters to him via his agent? Was that why Mr. Darcy was looking so pleased?

"Employed me. However, I have been unable to help him on this matter, so he will refuse to pay me for my efforts on his behalf. I wonder how he discovered that you had the letters, I do not see how he could have found that out."

"I hear that Lady Usborne is an extremely shrewd woman," said Miss Griffin. "Of course, you would know better than I whether that is the truth."

Horatio gave her a rueful look. "You strike below the belt, ma'am. Perhaps she did trace the letters to Harriet, I . . . have reason to believe that she kept tabs on her husband's mistresses. But, no, they must not go back into Usborne's possession."

"Never, ever, get involved with the private affairs of royal persons," said Miss Griffin. "A former employer of mine, my first employer, in fact, who was a courtier, used to say that, and I think he was perfectly correct."

"He was," said Horatio.

Cassandra had no doubt about where the letters should go. "We have but two choices. One is to toss them into the fireplace, and beat the ash to dust with the poker. The other is to restore the letters to the person who wrote them."

"If you will permit me to take them, I think I may arrange for them to be returned to the princess, in complete anonymity."

Cassandra didn't hesitate. "Take them, indeed." There was no smile on her face as she added, in a voice that was suddenly stiff, "Perhaps you can also inform her ladyship as to where the letters have gone."

"I have not seen Lady Usborne for some weeks," he said deliberately. "Nor do I expect to see her in the near future, or, indeed, at all."

"I am very glad to hear that," said Miss Griffin. "Petifer, come with me, we must see to some refreshment for Miss Cassandra."

Petifer had almost to be dragged from the room by Miss Griffin, with many a dark look at Mr. Darcy.

"She doesn't trust you," Cassandra said, laughing at him.

"Never mind," he said, moving towards her, and holding out his hands. "Provided you do, I shall be content with that."

And Cassandra walked into his arms, and sank into his embrace, her lips seeking his as he ran his hands through her hair and held her tilted up to his face, kissing her with a passion that made her dizzy, and then looking into her eyes as though he would devour her.

"Cassandra, my dear heart, I have to tell you that I am deep in love with you."

Cassandra's own heart was overflowing with the ecstasy of finding herself loved, and it was from the heart that she told him his feelings were returned. "I do not believe you can love me as much as I do you," she said, blushing and laughing for the sheer joy she felt.

"Never, in all my life, have I been so happy," he told her, drawing her still closer to him.

Their embraces were not allowed to last long. Miss Griffin rapped at the door after a few minutes only of mutual rapture. "You must be off, Mr. Darcy," she said. "You have business to attend to, and Cassandra has had an exhausting day. You may call tomorrow at noon."

Cassandra woke the next morning to a sensation of great peace and happiness. It took her only a second to remember the events of the previous evening, and to realise why she felt like this. Horatio Darcy in love with her! And to think they owed their present understanding to Lord Usborne, for it was when she saw Horatio fly to her defence that she realised what she had been hiding from herself, that she had fallen head over heels in love with him.

She lay back on her pillows, luxuriating in the thought that a few hours would bring Mr. Darcy to the doorstep and refusing to let herself think for a moment of the problems that their attachment must bring to a man so necessarily concerned with his reputation and position in the world. Her sense of elation was interrupted by Petifer bustling into the room, a gown over her arm, saying that she must get up, this very minute, for there was a note come round from Mrs. Wytton: She was wanted directly at Mrs. Wytton's house.

"I can't go anywhere," said Cassandra. "Mr. Darcy is calling here at noon, Miss Griffin told him to come."

"Mr. Darcy will have to see you at Mrs. Wytton's. Miss Belle is not well, the doctor is called, and from what Miss Griffin says, Mrs. Wytton is in despair, and has some idea that you can help to make Miss Belle more comfortable."

"If there is anything I can do, I suppose . . ." Cassandra's sentence was lost in a yawn. "How tiresome that girl is, and in love with Henry Lisser, how can anyone do anything about that?"

"You say that very blithely, 'in love with Mr. Lisser,' as though it were the most normal thing in the world! A nice state of affairs for one in Miss Belle's position. I know she flirted with him something dreadful when he was at Rosings, but she cannot be in love with a painter of low birth and no family! Mr. Darcy will not permit it."

"You are right, but the heart doesn't always do what it's told. And Mr. Lisser is an attractive man."

"Don't you go saying that in front of Mr. Darcy, mind," warned Petifer, taking away the remains of the chocolate which Cassandra had drunk almost without noticing. "He's none too easy in his mind with regard to you and Mr. Lisser."

"Jealous, you mean."

"I do, and it'll do neither of you any good for him to remain so. Show him he has nothing to worry about in that direction, that's my advice."

"He's a fool if he thinks any such thing. He has seen us together, do we look like a couple in love?"

"No, I dare say not, but when a man is as deeply in love as Mr. Darcy is with you, it blinds him to reason and sense. Now, shift yourself, for Miss Griffin is waiting to call up a hackney cab."

While Cassandra was on her way to the Wyttons' house, Horatio Darcy, shunning his chambers, was walking in Green Park, striding along at a formidable pace, as though to work the fidgets out of his limbs. Dear God, it made him so happy, to be in love and to have his affections returned; the feelings he had had for Lady Usborne, or for any other previous objects of his attentions, were nothing to this, there was no comparison.

And yet, beneath the exhilaration was concern. The cold voice of reason could be argued with; it could not be ignored.

His aunt would not approve of his marrying Cassandra. Broadminded she might be, but that would be going too far. Cassandra, in Mrs. Shawardine's eyes, was a ruined woman. Young men with aspirations for success and high office could not, in a censorious world, marry such an one as Cassandra and hope to keep their place on the ladder; not unless they had huge wealth and the status conferred by being a scion of a great house. Cassandra herself might have been protected from the evil consequences of her elopement if she had been possessed of a large fortune and a great name—but that was not the case.

So, were he to have the inestimable joy of becoming Cassandra's husband, which indeed he wished to be, then it was farewell to a seat in the House, good-bye advancement, adieu to all the ambitious plans which his aunt's generosity had made possible.

There was no squaring the circle. The choice was stark: the woman he loved, or his career. And if he gave up his career, was there the possibility that he would resent the woman for whom he had sacrificed it? Or, if he made the worldly choice, would he ever sleep peacefully again, knowing that he had lost Cassandra, who seemed indeed to already be part of him?

But was she really so? She had given herself freely enough to James Eyre, curse him, and what of her feelings for Henry Lisser? Was she, in fact, the glorious, loving woman she seemed, or was she, in truth, fickle and false? Had she not fallen into his arms in rather an abandoned way? Was it love or scheming? She said she loved him, but . . . The thoughts tossed to and fro in his head. He knew the answer, but could not quite bring himself to accept it. The clock struck; heavens, he was due in Soho Square in a quarter of an hour, he must hurry.

Cassandra found Camilla in nothing like a state of despair, for that was not in her cousin's temperament, but she was worried about her sister.

"Bother Mr. Lisser. He is a charming man, no doubt, and certainly a handsome one, but he has caused us all nothing but trouble, as I have told Mr. Wytton, who is just back from Herefordshire."

Mr. Wytton entered the room at that moment, pat upon his cue, yawning wildly. "Your servant, Miss Darcy," he said to Cassandra. "You Darcy women live dramatic lives, I have to say. And Mr. Lisser is a good deal too free with his kisses, by all accounts, you in the shrubbery, Belle somewhere else."

Camilla shot her husband an exasperated look. "You have it all wrong. Cassandra did not kiss Mr. Lisser in the shrubbery; she is not in the habit of kissing anyone in the shrubbery. That was Belle, who is all too prone to kiss young men wherever they are."

"You are harsh on your sister."

"I wish you would take this matter seriously," said Camilla.

"Let Belle run away with her painter, for goodness' sake, and then at least we will be done with her and with him."

"Mr. Wytton!" exclaimed Camilla, sounding really annoyed now.

"What, my love?" And then, with an apologetic glance at Cassandra: "I am sorry; I am not to mention people running away. However, your family do it all the time, I expect hourly to hear that Alethea has run off with some unsuitable young man, leaving her groom practically at the altar."

"I wish she would, but that is neither here nor there. We must somehow soothe Belle and restore her to a calmer frame of mind. Cassandra, it occurs to me that were you to convince her that there is nothing at all of a romantic nature existing between you and Mr. Lisser, then at least the jealous part of her emotion can be removed."

"Will she believe me?" said Cassandra. "If she has worked herself into a state, I doubt that anything I say will carry any conviction with her."

"I suppose Camilla is right?" said Mr. Wytton, eyeing Cassandra. "For, if you were to marry Lisser . . ."

"Cassandra does not wish to marry Mr. Lisser," Camilla said with great firmness. "You must know that Mr. Darcy is in love with Cassandra; and I hear him on the stairs now, not a word about Cassandra and Mr. Lisser, if you please."

Cassandra was struck by the very easy terms that Camilla and Mr. Wytton were on, their mutual attachment shining through their frequent disagreements and allowing both of them to speak their minds without in the least lessening the affection they had for one another.

Horatio came into the room, and Cassandra's heart leapt to see him. He had eyes for no one but her, but he shook Camilla's hand and bowed to Mr. Wytton, before crossing to Cassandra, taking her hand, and pressing it to his lips. "I had word from Miss Griffin that you were here and not at Soho Square. I trust, Cousin, that I do not intrude?"

"Not at all," said Mr. Wytton, answering for his wife. "It is a family matter, after all. We were talking about Mr. Lisser," said Wytton, looking intently from Horatio to Cassandra, and exchanging a smile of intelligence with his wife. "Belle is infatuated with him, it seems, and it will not do."

Horatio frowned at the mention of Mr. Lisser. "That man! He causes nothing but trouble."

Cassandra was about to come to Mr. Lisser's defence, but a warning look from Camilla made her hold her tongue. Mr. Lisser was, in any case, more than capable of speaking up for himself, should the occasion arise.

Belle chose that moment to make her entrance. She was wearing a light muslin dress that floated about her, emphasizing her ethereally fair looks. Her violet eyes were big and full of tears; she greeted the visitors with a trembling lip and cast herself down on the sofa.

"Ophelia, to the life," said Mr. Wytton. "Belle, you are a loss to the stage."

That brought her out of her wilting pose, and she sat bolt upright, her mouth now pouting as she glared at her brother-in-law. "You do not know what it is to suffer," she exclaimed in tragic accents. Then she cast a look of hatred in Cassandra's direction. "You! I wish you had not come, you are no friend to me!"

"What fustian," said Mr. Wytton impatiently. A furious look from Camilla silenced him; Cassandra knew that she must keep control of herself; were she to look at Mr. Darcy, she was sure they would both burst out laughing, and Belle would be genuinely hurt.

She went forward, and knelt down beside Belle, who tossed her head away, biting her lip and gazing steadfastly out of the window.

"Listen to me, Belle. Everything I ever said to you about Henry Lisser is true. He is a friend and a colleague and that is all. I have never been in the least in love with him, and I never shall be."

"How can you tell such fibs! I saw you at the theatre, yes, and so did you, Mr. Darcy, and you were mighty distressed by it as well. Would he have been so angry," she said, appealing to Camilla, "if he had not seen with his own eyes how close their heads were, how intimately they sat and spoke."

"You saw us at the opera," cried Cassandra, "and that is the reason for all this? I never heard anything so absurd."

"You were in the box, alone with him, you spoke and looked at no one but him."

"Nonsense. We were accompanied by Mr. and Mrs. Hopkirk— no, stay, they were late, they arrived just as the orchestra was striking up the overture."

"Which is precisely when you fainted," said Camilla. "Was that not so, Mr. Darcy?"

"Yes. That is, I did not exactly notice . . ."

"No, for you were as shocked as I was by the way that Cassandra and Henry Lisser were carrying on," Belle said, with another sob.

Cassandra's patience snapped. "Carrying on, indeed! Don't you dare say such things about me." She rose swiftly to her feet, and turned, eyes blazing, towards Horatio. "And you thought the same? Shame on you!"

Her bubble of happiness had burst. The joy with which she had greeted the fresh day had blown away in a cloud of misunderstanding and jealousy. Was his opinion of her really so low? What had last night meant, after all? Had he kissed her just because he thought he might take advantage of her, that she was clearly willing to kiss any man who came within her orbit? What proof had she that he had any real affection for her at all?

"Upon my word," she flung at him. "I am not sure there is anything to choose between you and Lord Usborne, in your beliefs as to what kind of a person I am."

Mr. Wytton had folded his arms, and was watching the scene with an air of evident enjoyment. "Please continue," he said, when Cassandra fell silent, and stood there, her breast rising and falling, and her eyes sparkling with rage and tears. "You look magnificent, and this is as good as a play."

Horatio, who had gone quite pale under the onslaught of her attack, was about to speak, even though Camilla was shaking her head at him, but he was forestalled by the door opening and the butler announcing, "Mr. Henry Lisser. I said as how you weren't at home, madam, but he said he could hear you were, and Mrs. Burgh, too, and he wouldn't be denied. He is an extremely forceful gentleman, I may say, but if you like, I will summon Charles, and we shall see him out."

"No, no, it is quite all right," Camilla said.

The butler gave Mr. Lisser a darkling look as he admitted him into the room, and withdrew.

Cassandra had never seen Mr. Lisser look more striking or dashing. And the effect on Belle was magical; she was transformed into an eager, glowing girl, her radiant eyes smiling at the painter as he held the centre of the room, glancing round with an arrogant look at the circle of Belle's transfixed relations.

"I think I should address myself to Miss Belle's father," Lisser said. "However, I understand he is at present in Derbyshire. So perhaps I can speak to you, Mr. and Mrs. Wytton, about this?"

"About what?" said Mr. Wytton evenly.

"I wish to ask for permission to pay my addresses to Miss Belle, and to ask for her hand in marriage."

Belle gave a whoop of delight and cast herself into her lover's arms. Mr. Wytton sighed, and Mr. Darcy shook his head.

"You will of course want to know something of my station in life, and my prospects, and my ability to support a wife."

"Stop there," said Mr. Wytton. "This is all very fine, but it is out of the question. I know that I speak for Mr. Darcy. I am sure you are a most excellent painter and all that, but there is such a difference . . . In short, it is not a match that anyone in the family will sanction."

"May I be permitted to finish?" said Mr. Lisser, with an hauteur that Cassandra had never seen in him before. A suspicion was beginning to form in her mind, and, by the swift look that Mr. Darcy gave the painter, in his as well.

"I go in England under the professional name of Henry Lisser. My name is, in fact, Heinrich von Lissa, and I am a younger son of Prince von Lissa, of Brunswick—"

Belle gave a little scream, and looked for a moment as though she were about to faint again.

Mr. Wytton's eyebrows rose. "Indeed? May I ask why you choose to pass yourself off under another name, and why you are in England, working as a painter?"

"I am an artist, this is my profession, and it will remain so. My father is a nobleman of ancient lineage, with a very great interest in the arts, and he is himself a fine painter. I would have pursued my career in my native land were it not that as a student, I became active in politics, revolutionary politics." He paused. "I do not know to what extent you may be aware of the situation at present in my country? On account of my activities, my presence was unwelcome, despite my father's influence at court, and I had to absent myself; in short, to flee the country, in order not to be imprisoned, or possibly worse."

Belle clung to him even more intently.

"As to fortune, I have some money of my own, and I am earning a good living from my brush, and I will be happy to lay out my exact financial position to Mr. Darcy's man of business. As to birth, we are in the *Almanach de Gotha,* and can trace our ancestors back to Charlemagne's day; that cannot be a bar to my marrying Belle."

Here he looked down at his fair companion with such doting affection that Cassandra was moved to the heart.

"You are fortunate, Belle, to have inspired such feelings in a man like Mr. Lisser," she exclaimed.

All the tension had drained from Mr. Darcy, who was surreptitiously trying to slide his hand around her waist, but she moved away from him. He had misjudged her, and she could not forgive him.

Camilla, smiling with relief and pleasure, was apologising to Mr. Lisser. "Why did you not say earlier?"

He gave her a rueful smile. "Do you know, it is something like in the fairy tales? It was heartening to see that Belle loved me for myself, despite my lowly rank. But now I am no longer a frog, but a prince, and all it needs is for me to kiss the princess!"

"Later will do," said Wytton. "Well, this is a red-letter day, the last of you five Miss Darcys has found herself a husband, and I hope, Henry, if I may call you so, that you will enjoy the happiness that marriage to Camilla has brought me. My love, ring the bell, and tell Rivers to bring up a bottle of champagne, so that we may drink a toast."

Cassandra told herself that she was truly happy for Belle, and she strived not to show what a bitter cup she herself had drunk from. "You will have to brush up your German, Belle," she said, with an effort at levity. "Miss Griffin told me that languages were the only study that you had any inclination for."

Horatio was looking at her with a worried expression, ashamed that his mistrust had so dimmed the radiance there had been about her when he came into the room only a short time before. How could he ever have doubted her, or his own feelings for her?

He watched Cassandra, making a valiant effort to enter into the general rejoicing as she congratulated Mr. Lisser; then he felt a gentle touch on his arm. Camilla was beside him, and addressing him in a low voice.

"Have you asked Cassandra to marry you?" she said bluntly.

He coloured. "Why, no, because last night—oh, you have not heard about last night? You have, a note from Miss Griffin? Then I do not need to tell you about it, but I had not the time or the opportunity, then, for that dragon of a woman drove me from the house. And besides . . ."

"Cold feet?"

"Certainly not," he said, haughty and ill at ease.

Camilla gave him a little push. "Go on, then. Do it."

"Do what?"

"Propose."

"In front of all these people?"

"Witnesses," said Camilla. "You will be unable to back out of it."

"I do not wish to back out of it," he said resentfully.

"Then do it."

He looked at Cassandra's bleak face, and took a deep breath. "Cassandra," taking two long strides that brought him to her. He sank on one knee. "My dearest, Cassandra, I love you. Will you accept my heart and my hand?"

There was a moment's complete silence, and then Cassandra, her eyes alight with joy, put out her hands to haul him up and, in true Belle style, flung herself into his arms.

"Oh, better than the play," said Wytton, applauding. And as the door opened, he cried out, "Rivers, two bottles of champagne, if you please."

Rivers wasn't bringing in the champagne, but another visitor, in the shape of Mrs. Shawardine. She stood on the threshold and surveyed the scene through her *face-à-main,* a weapon she had deployed to devastating effect for most of her life.

"Well! What may I ask is the meaning of this? Who is this young man entwined with Belle? I never saw such a thing, in the morning, and in public! And Horatio, why are you holding on to that young lady in such an inappropriate and affectionate way? Who is she, do I know her? She has a great look of the Darcys about her."

After a moment of pure astonishment, Camilla leapt into action, coming forward to greet Mrs. Shawardine, to lead her to a seat, to order Rivers to bring refreshment.

"If that is champagne, you may pour me a glass, Mr. Wytton," she said. "Belle, who is this man?"

Horatio ushered Henry forward. "May I have the honour to present Mr. von Lissa, a German presently residing in London? He is the son of Prince von Lissa, who—"

"You're one of Wolfgang's boys, are you? Yes, you take after him. I knew your dear father very well, years ago, when I was in your country for my health. You will convey my compliments and salutations to him when you write. Am I to take it that Belle has come to her senses and has chosen you for her husband, instead of all those fledglings she has been mooning over?"

Two patches of scarlet burned on Belle's cheeks, but even she knew better than to take on Mrs. Shawardine.

"And you do indeed know Cassandra," Horatio said, and Cassandra dropped a curtsy. "Who has done me the honour to accept my hand in marriage."

"You're Cassandra, are you? Your stepfather wrote to me, telling me what a hussy you had grown up to be. You don't look like a hussy to me. No, do not bristle up, Horatio. I know all about Cassandra's unfortunate past, and if you've chosen her for a wife, so be it, for I shan't bless the union."

Horatio, in his turn, bit back a retort. "I am sorry to hear that, Aunt, but I intend to marry Cassandra just the same."

"In which case, you had better get that appalling man to part with her share of her grandmother's money. No, I shall do so, he will listen to me. When are you to be married?" she said abruptly to Cassandra.

Cassandra was at a loss. She had felt that familiar chill sensation at Mrs. Shawardine's harsh words; what did "bless their union" mean? But if she were to get some of her fortune, would not that make life much easier for Horatio, as well as for her?

"I shall marry Cassandra with or without a dowry. If she does have any of the fortune to which she is entitled, that it will be settled on her, and on our children. I am well able to support a wife, I believe."

"Hoity-toity," said Mrs. Shawardine. "And don't you look so high-and-mighty, miss, neither. I can see you're a Darcy through and through, it's a pity you didn't remember some of that pride when you ran off with that rapscallion Eyre. Mind you," she went on unexpectedly, "I can't say I altogether blame you, for I came near to running off with his father, long ago. It wouldn't have done, however, and it was a very wrong step for you to take." She turned back to Horatio. "If you marry Cassandra, you do realise that she will never be accepted in the drawing rooms or ballrooms of the top ten thousand? No vouchers for Almacks for her daughters, if Sally Jersey still rules the roost, of that you may be sure."

"I do not give a fig for Lady Jersey, nor for any other of those witches. We have our own circle of friends, where we shall do very well."

"That's as may be, but your friends won't get you a seat in Parliament, I'll be bound."

"No," said Mr. Wytton, who had been eyeing Mrs. Shawardine with awe. "His merits will, though, I am sure of that."

"When I want your opinion, Mr. Wytton, I will ask for it. You are not a Darcy, please keep out of this. At least Belle is going to make a match that won't bring shame on the family. Does her father know of this engagement?"

"There can be no engagement until I have spoken to Mr. Darcy," said Henry. "I shall post down to Derbyshire directly."

Mrs. Shawardine was looking at Cassandra again. "When do you propose to marry, if marry you must? I trust you will do it with discretion, the fewer people who are there the better."

"Tomorrow," said Horatio recklessly. "By special licence."

Cassandra stared at him. "Do I have no say in this?" She could not imagine that even tomorrow was soon enough. "Can we not marry today?"

"Too late, it must be before twelve o'clock, but I must be off, I shall have to find a bishop."

Camilla was laughing at him. "Where do you propose to do that? They do not lie about in the street, waiting for impatient bridegrooms, you know."

"You're a fool, Camilla," said Mrs. Shawardine abruptly. "Who is that clergyman who is cousin or some such to your mama, the man who will inherit Longbourne when your grandfather dies?"

"Good Lord," said Camilla. "I had forgotten that he has been elevated or translated or whatever it is that happens when you exchange one set of gaiters for a more purple pair. Mr. Collins is presently in London, for I had a note from the tedious man, announcing that he intends to call. He is staying at his club, you may go round there and dig him out, Horatio, for if he should happen not to be about, I dare say there are a dozen others there who will do as well, quite half the bench of bishops are there on any given day, I believe."

"It is fortunate," said Mrs. Shawardine, now at her most magisterial, "that there is a good excuse for such a very discreet wedding, apart"—with a sharp look at Cassandra—"from the one of not wanting to draw attention to anything Cassandra does."

Wretched woman, thought Cassandra, who still wanted to know why Camilla and Horatio had exchanged those meaningful glances when Mrs. Shawardine had been so outspoken about her dislike of their marriage.

"Why is that?" said Mr. Wytton.

"Because it will be considered only proper, coming so close to a death in the family."

"Who has died, for God's sake?" cried Camilla.

"That is why I am in town, which none of you cared to enquire about. As you know, I am seldom in London these days. However, I received the sad news that my stepson, Frederick, was wounded in some vulgar brawl in a gaming hell, three nights ago. I came to see what I could do, to be greeted with news of his death."

"Poor Frederick," said Camilla.

"Nothing of the kind," said Mrs. Shawardine, who did not, it was true, look at all like a grieving stepmother. "I think it better for all concerned that his life should be terminated with a sword. I do not think he would have cared for a life abroad. No, no false protestations of grief, if you please, Camilla. He was an unpromising boy, who grew into an indolent and vicious man, his misdoings helped to bring his father to an early grave, and the world is a better place without him. There. You may write to your brother, Horatio, and tell him the news. Mr. Wytton, you may ring for my carriage, all these family entanglements are very tiring for a woman of my years."

"Phew," said Mr. Wytton, when he and Horatio came back from seeing her into the carriage. "Her years, indeed, she could see us all under the table first. What a truly terrifying woman, Camilla, my love, you must promise me you never become like that. I shall have it put in writing, and you shall sign it. Horatio, are you off?"

"Yes, on my bishop hunt." He swept Cassandra up. "Never look so doleful, sweetheart, it will all work out."

"What did she mean, she would not bless our union? She was talking about more than the usual good wishes, Horatio, was not she?"

Horatio sighed. "There was some idea of her putting me up for Frederick's seat. That is all."

"And she will not do so, because you have not chosen a suitable wife."

Camilla intervened. "Stop it, both of you. Cassandra, Horatio is old enough, and man enough, to decide for himself whom he will marry and upon what terms. Do him the courtesy of saying no more about this, but merely paying attention when he sends word as to which church and at what hour you are to be married. Mr. Wytton shall give you away, and we shall attend as witnesses and to see that the knot is properly tied. Letty did say that Mr. Barcombe was coming to town around now; I wonder if he by any fortunate chance is in London. For if so, he may marry you, and then it truly is all in the family."

"I should honeymoon in Italy, if I were you," Wytton said almost casually. Cassandra knew why he was saying that; a quiet wedding, followed by a period abroad, might mean that the scandal of her former elopement, which was still not generally known, might be forgotten sooner that way.

"Except that Lord Usborne will spread it abroad," she said to Camilla.

"I have an idea as to that," said Camilla. "Leave it to me. I remember my father saying what very bad terms the late Lord Usborne and Mrs. Shawardine were on, I think we may have help from an unexpected quarter there."

Before he went, Horatio took Lisser aside. "There is a matter, quite unconnected with Belle or Cassandra, that you might help me with. I suppose that your father is very well in at court, that he might know how to get, shall we say, a package, safely to a certain English princess without any of those English agents who watch her every step getting wind of it?"

Mr. Lisser looked interested. "It is exactly the kind of task at which my father excels. Dine with me, and you can tell me what you wish done."

It was a very happy group that assembled at eleven o'clock the next morning at St. Clement's Church. There had been a momentary panic, unbeknownst to Cassandra, when the bishop had asked Horatio if his intended bride had her father's permission to marry him. However, Horatio was not a lawyer for nothing, and he found no difficulty in pulling the wool over the bishop's eyes, by pointing out that Mr. Partington was not Cassandra's father, and that Mr. Darcy was head of the family.

Which had the advantage of being true, and Bishop Collins was not inclined to question anything purporting to come from Mr. Darcy, of whom he was afraid.

Her cousins attended the bride to the altar, with Miss Griffin and Petifer watching from the front pew. Mr. Wytton gave Cassandra away, Mr. Lisser was best man, and Mr. and Mrs. Hopkirk arrived in time to kiss the bride and join the little party for the wedding breakfast at the Wyttons' house, and to wave the joyful couple off on the first stage of their journey to Rome.

Epilogue

Cassandra sat on the broad stone window ledge of the high-ceilinged room, looking out over the sunlit roofs of the Eternal City. She could hear bells, Rome was full of bells, and in the distance she could just see the pillars of the Forum. Her sketchbook lay open on her lap, but she closed her eyes and let the sun warm her face and her body, clad in the most diaphanous of shifts.

Horatio sat up in the bed, a huge and stately affair, with cupids and beasts carved and gilded all up and down the posts. They were staying in the Palazzo Strozzi, which was owned by old friends of Mr. Wytton's, a charming and eccentric pair, with a swarm of clever, lively sons and daughters, all of them enchanted to have the English newly-weds to stay.

Horatio held out his arms. "Come back to bed, sweetheart, before the maid brings in some more nourishing food."

Cassandra slipped into the bed beside him, laughing at him. "They say you have to keep up your strength, to do your duty as a husband."

"You are an abandoned hussy," he said. "And it's time you learned to be a dutiful wife."

They were interrupted by a knock on the door and the arrival of a beaming maid, with a tray piled high with fruit and rolls and various other delicacies. "Also, there is a letter, from England," she said, with pride.

"Who is it from?" asked Cassandra, attempting to eat a plum with one hand while she caressed Horatio's neck with the other.

"If you do that, I can't concentrate. It is from my aunt, Mrs. Shawardine."

"Oh," said Cassandra, suddenly not feeling so full of joie de vivre after all. "What does she say?"

Horatio let out a whoop of delight, and gave Cassandra a hearty hug, almost upsetting her bowl of plums. "I thought it would be so. The party sent down a man they wanted to have the seat, and they sent Alcock, what folly!"

"Why so?"

"Alcock's father is another one of the succession of people with whom Mrs. Shawardine has an ancient feud. So, she writes, since from what she hears the scandal associated with your elopement is not generally known, and she has made sure Usborne will never speak of it, she wishes me to return to England and be elected to Parliament!"

"However did she silence Lord Usborne?"

"Aha, she says something about that. Good heavens, it was Usborne who ran Frederick through with his sword! My word. In return for my aunt hushing up the whole affair, he is to keep silent, and forget he has ever met you. He is in disgrace with the Prince Regent, she adds, which puts her more in charity with the man—that will be on account of the letters, dear heart—and has retired to the country, with Lady Usborne, who is, rumour has it, increasing!" Horatio put down the letter. "It is humiliating to admit it, but I don't believe Lady U. ever cared tuppence for anyone except Usborne himself. I wish them well, and I shall be very glad indeed if Usborne takes to the land, and I never have to see him again."

"I suppose the child is his?" said Cassandra, with a sly glance at Darcy.

It was a moment before he took that in, and then he removed her plums and reached out for her.

"Because I am blessed with a kind nature, I shall ignore that remark, and merely say that I hope our daughter inherits your beauty and your smile and your lovely eyes, but not your artful tongue."

"Nor our son your arrogant ways."

"No chance of that with you for his mama, but one thing we may be sure of, they will all have the true Darcy spirit; how can they possibly escape it?"

Much Ado About You

Eloisa James

Never marry for love, it's the worst reason of all…

Finding herself under the unlikely guardianship of the kind but shambolic Duke of Holbrook, Tess Essex is suddenly faced with her duty: marry well and marry quickly. Once that's taken care of she can arrange matches for her three younger sisters: Annabel, Imogen and Josephine.

But just when everything looks like it might be in order Tess's own fiancé gets cold feet and one of her sisters elopes with a reckless young lord…

And is Tess really as sensible and proper as she thinks she is? Lucius Felton is a rogue whose own mother considers him irredeemable but he is delicious and obscenely wealthy…Surely she can't really be contemplating marriage to one of London's most infamous rakes?

Absurd as it seems Tess fears she may have fallen utterly and completely in love…

'So full of dashing cads in breeches that it's got me seriously hot under the collar. Bravo for Eloisa!'　　FIONA WALKER

'Great fun! I couldn't put it down. Move over Georgette Heyer!'　　DAISY WAUGH

'Hurrah! Romance is back in fashion. No grisly body count, no lurking serial killer. The only four-letter word is love. Choc-full of romantic heroes that would give Darcy a run for his money. Sheer joy from beginning to end.'　　CAROLE MATTHEWS

ISBN-13: 978-0-00-722948-2

Come Away with Me
Sara MacDonald

A chance meeting between two old friends leads to an obsessive love which unearths long-hidden secrets and causes a bitter rift between families.

Jenny and Ruth were best friends at school until Ruth abruptly moved away from their Cornish village and they lost all contact. Fourteen years later, a chance meeting on a train throws both their lives into turmoil. As they begin to fill in the gaps from the years that have passed, their old friendship sparks back into life.

One glimpse of Ruth's son Adam sends Jenny into a spiral of love, grief and obsession. Adam is the image of Jenny's husband, Tom, killed suddenly and tragically six months earlier. As Jenny discovers the truth about Adam, a powerful bond springs up between them that will have unforeseen consequences for both families.

Come Away with Me is a moving and provoking portrayal of how two women challenge each other's identity in what becomes an unbearable life swap.

Praise for Sara MacDonald and her novels

'A beautifully written tale'   *Belfast Telegraph*

'Thoughtful and compelling storytelling'   *Choice*

ISBN-13: 978-0-00-720157-0

The Villa in Italy

Elizabeth Edmondson

Four strangers are summoned to the Villa Dante, a beautiful but now abandoned house above the Ligurian coast. Each has been named in the will of the intriguing Beatrice Malaspina; not one of them knows who she is. Delia, an opera singer; George, an atom scientist from Cambridge; Marjorie, a detective novelist and Lucius, a Boston banker, come to Italy, only to find out that the mystery deepens.

Spring flowers into the joy of an Italian summer, and the Villa Dante, with its frescoes, and once-magnificent gardens, comes back to life. As water flows again through the cascades and fountains, the four visit the mediaeval tower close to the house, and find themselves face to face with their troubled pasts in a way they never could have foreseen.

The villa works its magic and slowly they are changed, as the sorrows of their wartime experiences grow into the possibility of hope. Now they can receive their unexpected inheritance and, as devastating secrets are finally revealed, the even greater gift of a new life.

Praise for Elizabeth Edmondson

'I loved it'   *Woman*

'A very interesting book, not only because it gives a flavour of life – it's a way of imbibing history'   *Oxford Times*

ISBN-13: 978-0-00-722377-0

The Winter Rose

Jennifer Donnelly

An epic tale of secret love and hidden passions.

It's 1900 and the dangerous streets of East London are no place for a well-bred woman. But India Selwyn Jones is headstrong: she has trained as one of a new breed, a woman doctor, and is determined to practise where the need is greatest.

It is in the grim streets where India meets - and saves the life of - London's most notorious gangster: Sid Malone. Hard, violent, devastatingly attractive, Malone is the opposite of India's cool, aristocratic fiancé. Though Malone represents all she despises, India finds herself unwillingly drawn ever closer to him, enticed by his charm, intrigued by his hidden, mysterious past.

The Winter Rose brings the beginning of the twentieth century vividly to life, drawing the reader into its wretched underworld, its privileged society and the shadowland between the two, where the strict rules of the time blur into secret passions.

'There's a hint of mystery, lots of interesting characters and locales such as India, Africa and California, with turn-of-the-century London at the centre of an engaging book. Recommended.'
BARBARA TAYLOR BRADFORD

'So vividly imagined that it's like time-travelling back to 1900'
Eve

'Melodramatic set pieces keep this romp rattling along, with drugs, prostitution and robbery adding colour to a world defined by poverty and corruption.'　*Daily Mail*

ISBN-13: 978- 0-00-719132-1